Dan Jenkins's
Billy Clyde Puckett
is back.
And this time, he *runs* the damn team . . . .

W9-BWJ-809

PRAISE FOR
RUDE BEHAVIOR

"One of the funniest writers America has produced
. . . No social mores are safe from
Mr. Jenkins' skewer.
He gleefully punctures political correctness, big-time
sports, fans of big-time sports, the media, 'gubmint'
bureaucrats, bigots, Yankees, native Texas bubbas
and the film industry."
—*The Dallas Morning News*

"His funniest work yet . . . Jenkins scores again. . . .
Rude Behavior, a book loosely about football,
is a monument to courage because it dares
to tackle political correctness."
—*Rocky Mountain News*

"I laughed out loud every two minutes while reading
Rude Behavior. Who could ask more of
a book than that."
—Bud Shrake, co-author of *Harvey Penick's Little Red
Book: Lessons and Teachings from a Lifetime in Golf*

"*Rude Behavior* is like the Bible except funnier
and about football. What I mean is everything in
Rude Behavior is true. Believe in the word
of Dan Jenkins or you'll
probably spend eternity watching Olympic
ice-dancing videos."
—P. J. O'Rourke

"*Rude Behavior* is definitely Dan Jenkins' rudest
book—and also his funniest."
—Mary Carillo, network sportscaster

Please turn the page for more extraordinary acclaim . . . .

BOOKS BY DAN JENKINS

Novels

Rude Behavior
You Gotta Play Hurt
Fast Copy
Life Its Ownself
Baja Oklahoma
Limo *(with Bud Shrake)*
Dead Solid Perfect
Semi-Tough

Nonfiction

Fairways and Greens
Bubba Talks
You Call It Sports but I Say
    It's a Jungle Out There
Football
    (with Walter Iooss, Jr.)
Saturday's America
The Dogged Victims of
    Inexorable Fate
The Best 18 Golf Holes
    in America

Rude Behavior

Dan Jenkins

Island
BOOKS

ISLAND BOOKS
Published by
Dell Publishing
a division of
Random House, Inc.
1540 Broadway
New York, New York 10036

ISBN: 0-440-23560-X

Reprinted by arrangement with Doubleday

Printed in the United States of America

Published simultaneously in Canada

September 1999

10 9 8 7 6 5 4 3 2 1

OPM

*Again for June Burrage Jenkins,
with your basic boundless love.*

*And for Herman Gollob, old friend
and brilliant editor, or maybe it's the
other way around, with your basic
thanks and appreciation for the
manuscript surgery.*

*And finally for all those good pals
who contributed a line or two to this
escapade, most often unknowingly.*

*I'm Texas born, Texas bred, and when
I die I want to be Texas dead.*

—BIG ED BOOKMAN

If you don't believe I love you, honey, just ask my wife.

—FROM A SONG BY GARY P. NUNN

WINNERS HAVE A BAD CASE OF THE WANTS.

—A SIGN ON T. J. LAMBERT'S WALL

Rude
Behavior

Part One

He's Not Here

1

It was with his usual alertness that T. J. Lambert noticed the shapely adorable when she came in the bar with her two best friends, which some people used to call tits. My astute wife would have given her an endearing name right away—Too Tight and Too Cheap. T.J., on the other hand, made some kind of noise that could pass for a whimper and said, "Damn, Billy Clyde, that little sumbitch down there is so good-looking, I believe I'd crawl through two sewers and walk across a mile of razor blades just to touch the hammer of the guy who's nailing her."

Maybe you think that's a crude way to begin. But I can tell you that in all of my saintly, uncrude life, I've never seen anything totally crude, except for some of those photo-op delicacies Chef Timothy or Chef Bernard likes to put on your plate—at $50 an organic baby carrot.

Dine out often, you get to see your share of those carved-up deals. I've seen a melon swan, no bullshit. A tomato looking like a rose. I've even seen a mashed potato ocean, this big splat making little waves all around my meat.

Actually, I guess I *have* seen a few other crude things. A fumble on first down is as close to crude as you want to be. And a good many of those end-zone celebrations can be fairly crude, particularly when they dance all the way to Mozambique and back.

Then there are those tricks the fun-loving zebras like to play on you. Call holding whenever it strikes their fancy. Ground can't cause a fumble. Hands in the face. Pushing off. Defensive holding. Call "inadvertent" something or other. That kind of crude shit.

Life was simpler when me and Shake Tiller and T.J. played. The quarterback didn't wear an evening gown and a string of pearls. Pass interference was when you broke a guy's ribs. Today it's excessive frowning. Shake got so many ribs cracked on crossing patterns, he'd have a right to be a full-time painkiller dope fiend today.

We were sitting at the bar on a late April afternoon in T.J.'s new favorite hideout. A cozy tavern called He's Not Here.

I'd taken a flight out of La Guardia, landed at D/FW around two in the afternoon, and rented my Cadillac-Buick. A Cadillac-Buick was what my Uncle Kenneth used to call any car that cost more than the one he could afford to drive.

For me a Cadillac-Buick was something big enough to climb in and out of without getting a clubfoot or a withered arm.

Giving me directions to He's Not Here, T.J. had said, "Go out Camp Bowie past that freeway fork where you have to get killed, but not as far out as where women go to buy things." Which meant Neiman's. I'd eventually found the joint in an old shopping strip, snuggled in there with Ewell Dewell, chiropractor, Idella's Fashions, and Little Slim's Barber Shop.

The weather was an in-betweener. I was wearing my standard-issue khakis, brown loafers, white button-down shirt, and the dark blue windbreaker that advertised *Mondo Bimbo*, one of Shake Tiller's more deeply philosophical films.

I was also wearing my plaid golf cap, not as a disguise but to keep the Texas wind from making my thinning brown hair look like the last, tattered flag above the Alamo.

As I might have expected, He's Not Here was one of those establishments where you were likely to find a few more whipdog salesmen than you would polo players. Splotchy gray industrial carpet with tales to tell. A few tables from the oilcloth family. Dark booths along two walls. A filling station clock. A cigarette machine, a small parquet floor in a corner for the Freds and Gingers, and an L-shaped bar with swivel stools and Naugahyde padding for the elbows of customers who needed to think it over awhile longer before they went home to the cuss fight.

A jukebox and Fritos joint. Dining and dancing.

The tunes on the jukebox indicated that music began with Hank Williams and ended with Patsy Cline, but today's anthem, being played constantly, was Gary P. Nunn singing, "If You Don't Believe I Love You, Honey, Just Ask My Wife."

Much of what you needed to know about the ambience of He's Not Here could be found in the black lettering on the white sweatshirt worn by the convivial lady behind the bar. I didn't normally take the time to contemplate the messages on T-shirts and sweatshirts, but this one asked to be studied more closely. In black lettering, the message smartly said:

**GO FUCK YOURSELF,
IN CASE I FORGOT
TO MENTION IT
EARLIER**

I asked the bartender what her name was. She said she'd like for it to be Michelle Pfeiffer, but she'd had to settle for Kelly Sue Woodley.

Her snug jeans suggested good legs. She had creamy skin, a sharp little nose, shrewd eyes of swimming-pool blue, and America hair. Amber waves of grain.

Good-looking stove. Lady somewhere in her forties. One who'd seen two husbands run off with go-go dancers, a mobile home burn down, and a Honda Civic wash away in a flood. But all that was purely a guess on my part. It had to do with the so-what expression on her face.

After T.J. made that romantic remark about the shapely adorable, I rattled the ice in my Junior and water and said I was glad to know he still read Keats and Shelley. Thought I was being funny.

"Shirt-lifters." The coach smirked.

"Shirt-lifters?"

"Look under an old boy's shirttail, see if he's got a mule dick."

"Shirt-lifters," I said again. "Keats and Shelley?"

"All them poets."

Not all of them, I said. I was pretty sure I remembered from college that old Percy Shelley tried to drop the hammer on every woman in Europe except the madonnas in the picture frames.

"Vast majority will lift your shirt," he said. "And you better not call 'em fags anymore, Billy Clyde. A bunch of *sensitive* sumbitches might run a parade through your livin' room."

I said I didn't need to be told that. I'd been to Broadway shows. I read newspapers. I watched television. I'd listened to acceptance speeches on Oscar night. I was aware the PC brigade even wanted to rewrite the Bible. One of these days I'd look up and God wouldn't be Our

Father. God would be Our Ellen or Our Gavin, hallowed be thy sexual orientation.

"We get our share of PC crap around school," T.J. said. "Seems like every professor on campus can find something he wants to fuck with."

"I never did trust a man who carried sonnets in his pocket."

"Save the Hispanials. Salute the gender women. Support your local shirt-lifters. Teach more Africranium literature. I told our chancellor the other day his professors better not bring any of that do-good bullshit around my football players."

"It's good to have a chancellor you can talk to."

"He's a realist, you know that. Likes to win, get him another wing on the library. Get him one of those buildings where the beards and smocks jack around with test tubes . . . collect insects."

"I suppose *shirt-lifter* is better than *fag*," I said casually. "Sounds almost jovial."

"Shirt-lifters . . . greyhounds . . . Fifis . . ."

"*Greyhounds?*"

"They like their bus stations."

"I should have studied the poets closer."

"All I remember is some of the junk they tried to get you to read. If they were good poets, it rhymed. A bad poet didn't make any sense at all, except to other bad poets. I did notice the shirt-lifters wrote more about daffodils than they did pussy."

"Not easy to rhyme pussy," I said. "I guess Shakespeare found that out soon enough."

"I didn't have much luck with Shakespeare."

"Made people talk backwards is what I remember."

"Forsooth," T.J. said, his lip curled up on his pink face.

"Do what?"

"Forsooth. Old Hamlet and them. Forsooth this.

Forsooth that. Damned if they didn't what-ho and forsooth everything that came along. 'What-ho, Hamlet,
old buddy? Why don't you hand me a Budweiser before
you throw a forsooth at that other fellow over there in a
skirt?' Now, shit, Billy Clyde, can you imagine people
talking like that in real life?"

"Not sober," I said honestly.

It appeared to be time for more whiskey. I needed
another highball, a young scotch and hydrant water. The
coach needed another vodka cranberry, his health drink.

"Fix us up," he said, sliding off the stool, pointing at
our glasses. "Wilbur has to go turn in a term theme."

I watched T.J. take the scenic route to the men's
room, which was by way of Too Tight and Too Cheap.
He stopped to say something to her. She rewarded his
comment with a hearty laugh.

Of course she did. She'd already laughed heartily at
something Ralph said to her. Ralph, the tired carpet
salesman. She'd already laughed heartily at something
Wayne said to her. Wayne, the tired vinyl siding salesman. Your shapely adorable generally laughed heartily at
anything a friendly fellow said to her—if he had no visi-
ble sweat stains.

"You tried that honey-baked Hamlet?" a voice said to
me from three stools away.

"I'm sorry . . . ?"

"I heard you all talkin' about ham. I got a honey-
baked ham for Christmas. It was real good."

Another tired salesman. Said his name was Rollin. He
worked for Porch Casual and was happy to say he could
get me a good deal on an eight-piece set of patio furniture, including a recliner with arms. Only $319, and they
shipped nationwide, all the way up to New York and
Indiana.

I thanked him for his interest in ham, or Hamlet, and

my New York terrace, and refocused on Too Tight and Too Cheap.

You couldn't help looking at her like you would a wild animal on the Discovery channel. Her with a margarita in front of her, a cigarette in her hand, and a look in her eyes that said she was only there to ruin your life.

She reminded me of those tricksters you'd see in Beverly Hills and Vegas. Drop-dead light hooks who'd hauled their racks out of their little hometowns to go scoop a rich guy somewhere, no matter if he was bald as a hubcap and wider than a Ford pickup.

A type of lady known to Shake Tiller, serious book author and filmmaker, as your rack-loaded wool driver.

As a matter of fact, Shake's latest book was with me on this trip. It was called *The Average Man's History of the World.* His publisher had just sent me an advance copy, and I was looking forward to having it solve a good many of life's riddles for me.

Shake had been moved to write his book because of a review he'd read about another writer. I'd never heard of the writer in question, and I doubted that Shake had either because he called him Umlaut Doublehyphen. In any case, the reviewer had said that Umlaut Doublehyphen's work was "vital" because it "strived to trace the murky shiftiness of meaning."

"Meaning's been murky and shifty way too long," Shake had said. "It's time somebody got to the bottom of it." So Shake started on *The Average Man's History of the World.*

Too Tight and Too Cheap was a rack-loaded wool driver, all right. As Shake Tiller might have pointed out, she was a modern-day version of the steel-bellied airhead, the smokin' kind of babe who could dive into a vat of whiskey and rescue a man's hard-on.

Anyhow, there I was, settling in for a long evening.

First day on the road, no urgent appointments, pocketful of whipout. Enjoying my Juniors and Marlboros, and already being entertained by the way Too Tight and Too Cheap pretended it was hilarious when T.J. asked her what kind of sexual harassment she liked best.

2

Looked as if I might have to throw a rock at Kelly Sue to get us another drink. At the moment she was being held captive by the program on the TV that rested up on a ledge in a corner of the bar.

I studied the TV screen. Long enough to see further evidence that the collapse of civilization was on schedule. Two fat women were snarling and shaking their fists at two sullen teenage girls. One of the girls wore a low-cut, hip-high minidress with tattoos on her thighs. Her jagged hair was purple and orange, and paper clips were plunged into her nose and eyebrows. The other girl was barefooted in jogging shorts and halter top, her short hair was red and black, her fingernails were long and black, and her tongue had been pierced and a large piece of green and gold jewelry was stuck in it.

Wondering how bad that would make your tongue hurt, I watched as the two teenage girls hiked their cheeks, pretended to fart, then nonchalantly gave their mothers the finger. This caused the camera to shift to a stricken host, a man whose silver hair closely resembled an Oakland Raiders helmet.

Then a commercial came on. I was reasonably sure it

was a commercial for tourism or why would two shirt-lifters in tank tops and little swimming briefs be admiring the sunset on a deserted beach in Jamaica?

Kelly Sue must have read my mind. Fresh drinks arrived.

"That program you're watching," I said, nodding up at the TV. "It's all part of the collapse of civilization, brought about by your liberal Democrats and your socialist college professors, although some people like to blame sex, drugs, and rock and roll."

"Is that what it is?" she said. "I thought it was two little sluts who ought to have their butts beat."

While she lit a cigarette of her own, a Merit Ultra Light, my wife's brand, I nodded toward the shapely adorable at the bar and said, "Who's the homewrecker down there, just came in with the Guns of Navarone?"

"Somebody's daughter," Kelly Sue said, not bothering to look.

"I mean seriously."

"Oh, seriously?" she said. "You must mean Tracy."

"Tracy have a last name?"

"Tracy don't need a last name."

I couldn't argue with that. I'd watched Tracy slink to the jukebox and back, winning the hair-tossing contest, giving everybody a good look at touchdown cleavage, otherwise known as the plunging, short-sleeve silk blouse she was wearing, letting all of us admire the killer legs that her tight black miniskirt and high heels displayed conveniently.

In my world, killer legs came under the heading of gorgeous when other women spoke of them and holy-goddamn-shit when men did.

Myself, I figured Tracy's body had stirred the hearts of every psycho-warpcase-lesbo in her aerobics class.

I said, "She's probably waiting for a guy who looks

like a movie star. Fluffy hair parted in the middle. Get many movie stars in here?"

"She *is* particular," Kelly Sue said, "but I think it has more to do with first-class air travel."

"I like first-class air travel."

"You do?" she said. "Small world, isn't it?"

Kelly Sue poured herself a mug of coffee and returned to her talk show, looking confident that the collapse of civilization had been delayed until tomorrow, at least.

When T.J. came back from taking care of Wilbur, I asked him what he'd found out about Too Tight and Too Cheap.

He said, "I asked her what she was doin' in here. I told her what I figured was, she might have retired and moved to Colorado after she won the Super Bowl again."

"She understood that was a compliment, I assume."

"Seemed to. She batted her eyes."

"Does she know who you are?"

"Yeah. She says she roots for the Purple."

"What about me?"

"No."

"What do you mean, *no?*"

"I mean I said I'm with Billy Clyde Puckett and she said who's that?"

"Youth deal." I sighed.

"Yep."

"It was a better world before youth got hold of it. Youth should have stuck with drugs and sorry music and been happy with it. But no. Youth had to not know who anybody is."

"We saw the best of it, Billy Clyde."

I agreed with a nod.

"For one thing," the coach said, "you never had to

worry that every time you stuck your dick in something, it might be Cambodia."

"No radio activity. Those were the days."

"Your shirt-lifters brought that shit across the street."

"I wonder if it was one shirt-lifter by himself or if it took two or three of 'em to carry it?" I didn't expect an answer.

We sat quietly for a moment. The coach ate Fritos.

I said, "It was a better world before a lot of things. The baseball cap worn backwards. Rap. The bowl alliance. Your whole-grain police hadn't passed a law against any food that tastes good. Sausage and eggs weren't a felony. A cheeseburger didn't get you shot at."

"I've been arrested for food in my own home," T.J. said.

"Your own home? Forty-two sixteen Bellaire South?"

"Donna Lou's gone nuts about her weight," he moaned. "Everything in our house has fat-free, low-fat, no-flab stamped on it. I only get real food two days a week. A person starving to death would go in our kitchen and keep right on walking. I said the wrong thing the other day, got my ass eat out. I said she wasn't ever gonna be Jane Fonda anyhow, but I didn't care, so what the fuck? You ever come across any low-fat mayonnaise, Billy Clyde?"

"Why?"

"Have you?"

"I don't think so."

"You'd know it if you had."

"I would?"

"You better believe it. I wish some scientist would get to the bottom of it. We can instant replay a touchdown in slow motion but we can't invent a low-fat mayonnaise that don't taste like monkey puke. I'm tellin' you, man. That stuff don't just ruin tuna fish, it can poison a whole fucking city."

"I'll be on the lookout for it."

"God *damn*, it's awful."

T.J. made the kind of face he used to make when he'd tear into the opposing team's backfield to open a can of quarterback.

"Have the animal rights people come to Fort Worth yet?" I said. "Talk about mean. You might want one for middle linebacker."

"What do they do?"

"What do they do? I'll tell you what they do. They burn down neighborhoods, set fire to innocent bystanders. They not only don't want you to eat veal, they'll put a bomb in your car if you don't kiss a calf on the mouth and send the fucker to Harvard."

"I don't know what the world's comin' to." T.J. yawned. "Can't have sex. Can't eat food. Next thing you know, it'll be a crime to tackle the sumbitch with the football."

I said, "I'll tell you what the world's already come to. They've worked it out where it's okay for fags to fuck each other in the ass, but it's against the law to smoke a cigarette in the same room."

Kelly Sue overheard me, looked around with a grin, and said, "That ought to be up on the wall."

"Anything in good taste," I said, thinking she'd probably like to have the bumper sticker I'd seen on a camper as I drove in from the airport. It said: SODOMY IS NOT A CIVIL RIGHT.

I mentioned it to Kelly Sue. Yeah, it was one of her favorites, too, she said. She'd already seen it on several good Christian automobiles. If I wanted one for myself, she added, I could pick one up at any of those full-detail car-wash joints—they all had gift shops.

As usual, nobody had bothered to ask me why I was back in town. The tired salesmen didn't ask. Wayne and Ralph knew me from football and TV, but they were like most people in the old hometown. They thought of me as never having left.

Most people who were born or raised in Fort Worth never moved away, and never even wanted to. They assumed you hadn't either, and even if you had, they were sure it was only because of circumstances beyond your control, and you'd be back as soon as you got through dealing with "all them Jesse-type Jacksons" up in New York, or "all them gay-type queers" out there in California.

I'd go back two or three times a year for one reason or another. Might go back to Fort Worth or Dallas to make a speech for money, or play in a golf tournament for fun and charity, or take part in a seminar on sports or television—for not enough money. This was my life after being a great American and wonderful human being with a football in my arms or a TV mike in front of my mouth. I hadn't lived in Fort Worth for twenty years. But that never seemed to register on most of my acquaintances, even people who went as far back with me as McLean Junior High.

Junior high. That's what the seventh, eighth, and ninth grades used to be called before society was vastly improved by some genius who stopped eating tofu long enough to think of "middle school."

The way most of these well-meaning people greeted me was the same way Wayne and Ralph did in He's Not Here. Wayne had nodded and said, "Hey, Beely, how yew doin'?" And Ralph had nodded and said, "Hey, Beely, yew awight?"

I'd responded with my usual, "I guess I don't hurt all over."

"I hear *that*," Wayne had replied.

"Tell me *I* don't," Ralph had said. Ralph had then spoken to the world, or maybe it was a wall, when he mumbled, "I know I said something right one time, but I think it was before I was married."

Anyhow, I was back in town for a dead-serious reason this time. I needed to talk to T.J. about something more important than Hamlet or any of the other worldly subjects we'd been discussing. This was the trip where I first brought it up to him about coaching our expansion team.

3

I should point out that I only referred to it as *our* expansion team when I was in a mood to talk big.

The majority owner of the West Texas Tornadoes was going to be my father-in-law, of course. Big Ed Bookman. And there was no guarantee at the moment that we were even going to get in the league. Three other cities were in competition with us—Honolulu, London, and Mexico City—and the NFL had made it clear that only two new franchises would be selected. Our competition was exotic, to say the least. Two were in foreign countries, and some said the other one ought to be. What did all that Hawaiian hookey-lau wikki-wocky have to do with the rest of the United States anyhow?

I don't normally act excited about things. If the world was splitting apart around me, my tendency would be to light one more Marlboro and hum something by Irving Berlin. But I did get excited, inside, anyhow, when Big Ed said he was thinking about going after an expansion team.

It was about two years ago when I was having dinner with Big Ed and Big Barb at River Crest Country Club that he mentioned it. It was after I'd been in Dallas making a speech to a small group of CEO's—my current life in crime. Tell sports stories, do Q & A, scoop fifteen grand.

Groups I'd speak to liked to hear me say things like "Football's not an 'I' game, football is a 'we' game." Sound like fucking Knute Rockne. Then do the Q & A.

"Who's the greatest ball carrier you ever saw, Billy Clyde?"

"You mean besides me and Gale Sayers?"

Wait for the laugh.

The bite of pork chop was halfway to my face that night when Big Ed said, "Texas can use another pro football team—I want us to go after it. Out there in West Texas is the best spot. I'm reading about London and Mexico City and Honolulu wanting a team . . . what's wrong with the United States?"

Making a little joke, I said, "I guess Texas can use a third pro team—to go along with the Dallas Cowboys and the Dallas Cowboys' egos."

"A pro team is a good long-term investment. It'll always be worth more than you paid for it. But you're gonna have to run it. My money, your expertise. What do you say?"

Acting cool, I said I'd like it better than playing in pro-ams and sucking up to captains of industry.

We immediately applied for the team and made a couple of presentations to the expansion committee, doing shit I arranged. Showing a video, handing out survey results, talking about the wonders of deep West Texas as a fertile geographic region. There's no time frame on such things. You get in line and wait for the owners to expand.

So that was the birth of the Tornadoes.

The plan was for me to be the general manager and president, own a piece of the team, but I wouldn't even own as many shares of the stock as my wife. This was something Big Ed insisted on, being the level-headed bidnessman that he was.

Big Ed had always pronounced the word *bidness*, as in, "If people would just get a job and mind their own god-damn bidness, there wouldn't be any trouble in the world, except for two or three of your ethnic groups, and they wouldn't cause so much trouble if vigilantes were what they used to be, and I'm a bewildered son of a bitch if your ethnic troublemakers don't seem to be getting a hell of a lot of help from your head-sick liberals."

Shake Tiller could recite that speech almost as good as Big Ed, although my wife wasn't bad at imitating her own daddy.

The day my financial interest in the team came up, I mentioned to Big Ed that the bidness arrangement was fine with me because Barbara Jane and I were one of the happiest couples *People* magazine had ever discovered.

Big Ed said this was because his daughter and I hardly ever saw each other, a fact that made his ass hurt if he thought about it too much.

I said we often lived apart because Barb was always going off to make a movie, and I no longer enjoyed being on film locations, quite frankly, because there was very little for me to do but sit in a folding chair and nod off, burning my hand with a cigarette.

Big Ed said he hadn't stayed awake through an entire movie since Spencer Tracy died.

I said he hadn't missed much, other than thirty thousand unsuspecting people having their blood splattered on walls, ceilings, windows, and highways.

Barbara Jane made sport of the situation when it came to her attention that she'd own more stock in the franchise than me.

"I get to design the uniforms," she said on one of those rare occasions when we were both home in our Manhattan apartment. We were having breakfast with

Human Dog, our light-blond male Yorkie, who went everywhere with Barb and didn't rule our lives any more than Hitler ruled Germany.

"Amusing idea," I said, enjoying my eggs over light and Owens sausage, which I had shipped up from Texas regularly.

"I think I just might do that." She looked serious about it.

"No way."

"Well, as I understand it," she said, "this cowgirl owns more of the team than you do."

I said firmly, "I'm doing the uniforms. We're not wearing teal."

She looked across the table at me, her face in a pout.

"I'll tell Daddy," she said.

Then she laughed out loud at her remark, her threat, largely because I didn't laugh soon enough. When Barb laughed huskily, Human Dog—Hume, for short—would smile. Hume would also sing if you said words like *caviar*.

Laughing at her own jokes was something Barb had been doing since Paschal High. She said it let people in on the fact that she was trying to be funny. She claimed she had to do this because most people were too unhappy in their jobs and miserable in their homes to have a sense of humor.

I was with her on that. As I'd observed it, most people in the world didn't have a sense of humor for the simple reason that they weren't Americans. It was hard to have a sense of humor, I often said, if you were always hopping around in a jungle trying to keep shit from biting off your feet, or squatting in a desert and waiting for a leaf to grow out of your sandal so you could eat dinner.

I told my wife that morning that she was so smart about so many other things, she didn't need to be smart about football uniforms.

* * *

It was well known to the league that our expansion team would be located sort of halfway between Amarillo and Lubbock. We'd been lobbying strongly with the NFL owners, pointing out that Texas was second only to California in population now. This had happened because thousands of people in the midwest and northeast had discovered that Texas didn't have rust. So they loaded up the U-Hauls and moved to Texas to fondle high-tech shit, discover real barbecue, and get stuck on freeways for four and five hours at a time.

Big Ed had bought up all the land he could get his hands on between Amarillo and Lubbock, and a lot of land in the surrounding vicinity. It might look like worthless dirt today, but not in the grand scheme of things.

"Your smart bidnessman thinks ahead of the bumpkins" was the way Big Ed explained it to me.

Our modern stadium would hold 75,000. No dome or retractable roof. And not a hole in the head like the Cowboys had. It would be exposed to sandstorms, rainstorms, blizzards, and, well, tornadoes. Weather should have as much to do with football as anything else, Big Ed said.

We were still trying to decide exactly where to build the stadium. It would be in the vicinity of Gully Creek, Texas, but that was a secret.

Big Ed would lease off some of the land to developers, who would use it for light industrial parks, shopping malls, upscale homesites. The area would certainly become a "prime destination," to use real estate lingo, after our pro team gave it major league status.

T.J. said, "You got a lot of if-come going on here, Billy Clyde, if you don't mind me saying so. How you know the NFL owners are gonna vote you into the league?"

"All the signs look good with the expansion commit-tee," I said.

"Owners been known to lie."

"Only to players and the press, usually, or coaches they're getting ready to fire. Beware of the public vote of confidence."

T.J. snickered. "What you gonna call your new town, Lubbarillo?"

I smiled at him.

"Amarillock?" he said.

For now, I said, I was calling it Big Food. Code word.

"Big Food?" he said. "I've been to Big Food, Texas. I was out there trying to get me a tight end one time."

"You haven't been to Big Food," I said. "I made it up, Big Food."

"You made up Big Food? You sure?"

I said, "Yeah, I'm sure. Big Ed and I were out there looking at land one day. We went to breakfast at this diner in Tulia. The biscuits and gravy looked like carry-on luggage. I told him we ought to call our town Big Food, Texas, in honor of the cuisine of the region."

I said we had plenty of choices for a stadium site. Hereford, Earth, and Dimmitt to the west. Floydada, Matador, Silverton to the east. We were leaning toward Gully Creek in Floyd County. Might be where the sta-dium would wind up, but no use getting people excited before we had a team. For public consumption, I was referring to it as Big Food.

"Start your own town," T.J. said. "Call it No Roof, Texas."

"No Roof?"

"You know . . . tornadoes and shit."

I said the name of the town shouldn't make much difference. Not if the New York Giants and Jets could play in New Jersey, and the Washington Redskins in Landover, Maryland, to say nothing of Dallas playing in

Irving, Texas, and Detroit playing in Pontiac. Michigan. It seemed to me the Tornadoes could be from Tulia, Tahoka, Dookie—anywhere west of Dallas.

"I wouldn't want to be from Dookie," T.J. said.

"Neither would I, but what's your reason?"

He said, "I had me a running back from Dookie. Twone Sanders. *T-w-o-n-e*, it was spelled. Closest his mama could come to Tyrone, which is what she called him. My coaches called him Twone. Or tried to."

"Not an easy job for anybody, I suppose."

"He was a shifty little thing in high school," T.J. said. "Fast. Do this, do that. But the minute we got him, he couldn't piss down his own leg. Funny how that'll happen sometimes. You get fooled by the level of competition. Twone was a good kid, though. I kept him on the squad for five years, full ride. He got his degree. He's a high school coach now in Nacogdoches. Of course that kind of *good news* never gets on your fucking sports pages."

"Hardly ever," I said.

I didn't elaborate on it, but it was no mystery to me why good news had a hard time getting in newspapers.

On a personal level, I didn't think I'd bother to read a story under a headline that said: TWONE GRADUATES. But I'd be less than honest if I didn't confess that I might buy the newspaper and eagerly read the story if the headline said: TWONE WAVES HIS DICK AT TRI DELTS.

Kelly Sue came over about then to say Tommy Earl called. Tommy Earl said to tell us something important had come up and he wouldn't be able to meet us at He's Not Here, but he'd catch up with us for dinner later on at Bust Out Jonah.

I hadn't heard of Bust Out Jonah—it was new. But I was assured by Kelly Sue and T.J. that it already ranked up there with Railhead and Angelo's. This was high praise. It meant Bust Out Jonah was among the few truly great barbecue joints in greater North America, all of which happened to be located in Fort Worth, Texas.

I always listened patiently when people bragged about barbecue places they liked in other parts of the country. In all of my travels I'd never passed up a barbecue joint somebody strongly recommended, even outside the south. Most of it was different, and some of it was okay, but outside of Railhead and Angelo's in Fort Worth, I'd never wanted to elope with any of it.

"Ribs?" I inquired of Kelly Sue and T.J.

"Oh, yeah," Kelly Sue raved. "Ribs, brisket, chopped . . . ultra-lean, no strangers. Pintos, slaw, potato salad. Eight ninety-five, all you can eat."

I'd been tricked before. People told you a barbecue place was good but when you went there you found eyeballs in the chopped sandwich and boiled deli meat passing itself off as sliced brisket. A barbecue joint didn't deserve legendary status unless the meat literally fell off the bone, unless you wanted to wear the sliced brisket for a blazer, unless the meat was smoked so good you didn't even require any sauce.

"Is it seriously good?" I asked both of them.

"Is it *good?*" T.J. said, looking bewildered by the question. "Does a tornado like a trailer camp?"

4

There was a time in my life when I thought I'd never come across another human-type-being on this particular planet as big or strong or mean or hungry as T. J. Lambert. He'd been all-conference in football and food at the University of Tennessee before he became all-pro in football and food with the New York Giants.

When we were teammates and pals in New York, T.J. was a cherub-faced six-three, 247, and it was part of his legend that he once ate a dozen foot-long deli sandwiches and six dozen hard-boiled eggs while drinking whiskey one night in a no-name saloon on Third Avenue. The deli sandwiches, which T.J. insisted on calling lunch meat sandwiches, came from the no-name deli next door to the no-name saloon. Those of us who witnessed the feat accused him of showing off, to which he'd said, "Fuck, I'm hungry, is that awright with everybody?"

The coach was a smaller man today. All these years after he'd dough-popped his last pro-bowl quarterback. Age, fumbles, and making sure his scholar-athletes pissed in a bottle for the trainer every week had shortened him an inch or two. His weight was down to 225.

He now walked three miles a day. Never jogged. Joggers died quicker than shrimp, he claimed.

T.J. was a big player for our era, but that was before this day and time, when your average lineman comes in at six-five and 310 with biceps bigger than a nephew of the Goodyear blimp.

Before steroids, in other words.

We were sitting alone at one of the redwood picnic tables in Bust Out Jonah, ahead of the evening crush. We'd been through the buffet line, where a bony little man with a gin-red face in a soiled Texas Rangers baseball cap had heaped various wonders on our trays: ribs, sliced brisket, beans, potato salad, the works.

I'd paid the sullen woman in the hair curlers at the register. She had condescended to look up from her romance novel—no sex below the waist—long enough to take the money. Near as I could tell, the title of her bodice-ripper was, *The Commodore's Other Two Mistresses.*

Now T.J. and I were talking football as we lapped up the barbecue, and the coach was saying you couldn't compete today in college or the pros unless your offensive line looked like a row of RV's and your tight end was a hippopotamus on roller blades.

He said, "What you hope to do is find some people who can move better than others, and some who can hold better than others, but you start with size. If you don't have size, you're just talking to yourself, and not making much sense either."

I said, "Looks to me like the linemen are too big to be as smart as they used to be."

"Game ain't changed any, Billy Clyde, not really," he said, gnawing a rib into chrome. "Your genius coaches like to say it has. Idiot broadcasters and writers fall for their doo-doo, pass it on to the idiot fans. The more complicated you can make it sound, the smarter you think you'll look. You can't be totally dumb and play offense, but defense? Fuck. Just wait for the snap and hit somebody."

I was doing an adequate job on the ribs and brisket myself. While I was at it, I was thinking that no phony chef with his root-crusted, pureed compote of range-fed woodpecker had ever come up with a taste treat to match good Texas barbecue. Not if what you wanted to do was put cuisine down your neck.

T.J. said, "I love to hear them genius coaches talk about their 'soft zone-man' coverage, their 'slow-bump-rotation-fade-flex-seam-zip' defense. I mean, shit, half the time, you can't get kids to do what you tell 'em to do. Not today. No livin' way."

"Not even with cars and money?"

"I'll tell you the truth, Billy Clyde. You wouldn't want to gift-wrap none of their IQ's."

T.J. put some coleslaw between two slices of lean, tender, mesquite-smoked brisket, making himself a two-bite sandwich. It looked so scrumptious, I had to fix one for myself.

He said, "On defense, they're gonna play the ball or the quarterback. Your big-time coach says, 'We were in the right rotation, they just made a great throw and a great catch.' That's what he says when he's trying to explain the touchdown pass that got his butt beat. In college, that's how he explains it to the chancellor and the heavy-duty boosters. In the pros, that's how he explains it to the idiot sportswriters and his idiot owner."

I said you could make the case that most idiot sportswriters were bigger idiots than most idiot owners because the idiot sportswriters had forgotten to get born rich like most of the idiot owners.

"But we're not talking about Jim Tom Pinch," I said.

"Naw, he ain't no idiot," T.J. agreed. "Might be borderline now and then, some of the shit he writes."

Jim Tom was our pal. I had known him since he wrote

for the *Fort Worth Light & Shopper*. He had helped immortalize Shake Tiller and me when we'd fought for the TCU purple. He had been a good enough sportswriter to type himself into a staff job on *The Sports Magazine*—*SM*, they call it—up in Big Town Every Street's a Boulevard Apple Gotham. That's where T.J. got to know him, when we were with the Giants.

"He's the only sportswriter you can still trust," I said.

What I meant was, Jim Tom Pinch was the only sportswriter I knew of today that you could get drunk with, laid with, tell a secret to, or share the truth with, and not see it in a headline at the checkout counter on your way out of the supermarket. Jim Tom was a throwback to the old days, a guy who protected his sources. He always said this kept him better informed, made him a better journalist in the long run. I could see how it would. I could also see how it would keep him from getting killed.

"Jim Tom knows he don't need not to cast the first stone," the coach said.

I said, "You're right, he don't . . . doesn't."

"It was a sad day when sportswriters decided they all wanted to be Woodford and Bernbaum."

"Yes, it was."

"Fucks up sports, is all it does."

"Tries to."

"Your media ought to be happy enough fucking with politicians."

"That's right. Do something useful. Except you can't hurt a politician anymore—not enough to draw blood."

"You can't?"

"No, it's impossible. All the politician has to do is go on TV, smile at the world, and say he doesn't understand the question. Then look sincere and talk about how much he cares about people."

"Sumbitches can *talk*, I know that."

"They care about you. They care about me. The baby boomers eat it up like yogurt."

"We're baby boomers, ain't we?"

"Yeah, but we feel bad about it. Besides that, we were in the first wave—the best kind."

That was about as much as I ever discussed politics now. I said to T.J. it tickled me to remember that I ever thought it was fun to discuss politics. The old college days. Everybody sitting around bitching about shit, complaining about the Establishment, not letting anybody with a different point of view finish a sentence—unless it was time to roll another joint, grab a beer, fix a drink, or go get ice cream.

Then you got a little older and it sunk in they were mostly all hypocrites, the politicians. Maybe you could find a "statesman" somewhere—if he'd been shot at in a war.

On any level—local, state, national—the wise thing to do was vote for the candidate that looked the least dangerous, if you voted at all.

T.J. said, "My daddy never voted for a man who was short. Looked to me like Roosevelt might have been short, but I found out he was in a wheelchair most of the time."

"All I plan to do is sit back and watch it on cable."

"Watch what?"

"The collapse of civilization."

"I guess I'll watch it, too, if it don't conflict with a game."

An empty platter was available to toss our bones on. We sat in silence for a moment, except for the sound of succulent ribs being devoured.

"Kids today," T.J. finally said, taking the conversation back to football, shaking his head, as if there was no hope of finding a serum for this plague he was forced to deal with.

He went on, "They think they can make up for any mistake with their speed and agility. Everybody thinks he's a Neon Deion. Mostly what they want to do is go for the interception, build up their stats. Their teammates? Tradition? Old rivalries? School spirit? Piss on all that. If they've got a daddy at all, he's worthless, and Mama don't talk to nobody but Jesus. No wonder they've got Charles Manson for an agent. All they care about is how many zeroes on the paycheck. And I don't just mean your Africranium Americans either, Billy Clyde, so don't call me some kind of racist motherfucker."

"What's the answer for a coach today?" I asked. "Other than prayer?"

"More ribs, as I see it."

We carried our trays back to the bony little man with the gin-red face behind the serving counter. "We'd be obliged for more grub," T.J. said.

The bony little man was slicing and chopping hunks of brisket and slapping the meat on buns in a rhythm he had perfected long ago. He shoved two slabs of ribs at us.

"Some of that brisket, too," I said.

"I see y'all ain't no hungrier today than a hungry machine," the bony little man remarked.

When we returned to the table I asked T.J. if the bony little man with the gin-red face was Jonah.

"That's Roy," T.J. said. "Ody Bradshaw is the owner. Ody's one of your talk-big shitass dwarfs. Probably on the back nine at Mira Vista right now, two or three thousand down. Loves to gamble on the golf course."

"Knows more about golf than Jack Nicklaus, right?"

"That's Ody."

"But he couldn't hit water if he fell out of a boat?"

"That's him again. I've had quarterbacks with the same affliction."

"Who's Jonah?"

"Ody says Jonah's the god of gambling."

"Ties in," I said.

"The name of the place might not make sense to anybody but Ody," the coach said, "but it don't scare anybody off. If we'd waited till after six to come here, the line would be out the door, down the street, all the way around the lumberyard. Ody's made a lot of money, mostly in the food business. When I first met him he owned a steak joint out on Hulen. He copied it after the Outback. Called it Kill 'Em and Eat 'Em. It was real successful but he hauled off and sold it one day. Tommy Earl says Ody sold it because he ran out of waitresses he could fuck. But then he opened an Italian restaurant in Dallas. Pasta Capone. I haven't been there but I hear it's done so good, he's franchising it. Ody and Tommy Earl are partners in some things. They own He's Not Here together, although Tommy Earl don't want too many people to know he's in on it. He says it's necessary for a man to have a place to drink where his wife can't find him."

The thought crossed my mind that Batman and Robin couldn't find He's Not Here—unless Little Slim was their barber.

"Tommy Earl's something else," T.J. said. "Did you know he keeps a secret pad for his sideline wool?"

"I'm delighted he can afford it."

"He says his New Year's resolution is to fuck more this year."

"Some people paint."

"His secret pad's in the Forest Park Apartments. Up on the seventh floor. Great view. You can see the downtown skyline from the bedroom, TCU stadium from the living room."

"Are you kidding me?" I said, genuinely surprised. "Are you talking about the *old* Forest Park Apartments? That building I thought was a skyscraper when I was a kid? The one on Forest Park Boulevard?"

T.J. said yep.

"That's the neighborhood where he and Sheila live!" I didn't ordinarily raise my voice like that. "Don't they still live on Pembroke?"

T.J. grunted another yep.

"But that's where he lays up with his honeys?" My voice was still a level higher than normal. "Two blocks from his *own house?* Two blocks from his *wife?*"

"It's a convenience deal," T.J. said. "He says convenience is becoming more and more important to him."

"I guess it *has*," I said, shaking my head.

The coach couldn't help chuckling about something else. "He's got Sheila conned into thinking he walks twelve miles a day for his health. Around the neighborhood. Six miles in the morning, six miles in the evening. Of course he's not walking at all. He's over there with his sideline wool. I reckon he's getting *some* exercise."

I glanced at some softball players as they came in covered with grass stains and sweat. Men and women both. Six of them wore the blue and yellow of Don Kendall's Quality Carpets. Three of them wore the proud red and white of Al's Blinds & Shutters.

As they passed by our table, a chunky girl said to a teammate, "You wasn't as poor as me. We was so poor, if a boat ride at the lake was ten cents, all I could do was stand on the dock and holler, 'Ain't that cheap!'"

Still thinking about geography, I said to T.J., "You know what? Tommy Earl even grew up in that neighborhood, same as I did. We never knew each other when we were little. I was older. Tommy Earl's folks moved here from Corsicana when he was—I don't know, nine, ten. I lived on Warner Road with my uncle. Tommy Earl lived on Ward Parkway."

"That's the other thing," T.J. said. "He likes the nostalgia of it. He says it helps."

"Helps what?"

"His hard-ons."

"Nostalgia helps his hard-ons?"

"He says when he has trouble getting it up, it's usually because of whiskey, and the old neighborhood makes him think about Paschal High and Rosalie Ward. That takes care of it."

Another pause for cuisine intake.

Then T.J. said, "I kind of understand what he means. But in my case it was Glenda Draper. Except I made the mistake of going back for a reunion at William Bedford Forrest High. It was a feed-sack deal."

"That bad, huh?"

"I remembered Glenda in a bikini layin' around the swimming pool. There she was in an awning."

"High school reunions can be troublesome," I said. "How big is Tommy Earl's secret apartment?"

"Three bedrooms. Big enough for social gatherings."

"He entertains?"

"Once a month. Sometimes more often. Him and Ody Bradshaw hold a meeting of what they call the Gourmet Dinner Club. I've attended a few."

"Somehow I don't think you're talking about food."

"Naw, I'm basically talking about shapelies. Your light hooks, your amateur sport-fuckers, your restless wives." T.J. broke into a grin. "You can order from the menu or go through the buffet."

"The usual supply of Pams and Kims, I take it."

"I *have* met a couple of Pams up there. How'd you know?"

"Aw, just a stab in the dark."

"There's a Pam that gets drunk and cries. She's with

Delta. The other Pam gets drunk and belligerent. She's with American. Ody hands out gift certificates, to Neiman Marcus and fancy boutiques and shit. They're worth a thousand dollars, sometimes more. I've heard him say the amount varies. It depends on a shapely's good-naturedness and enthusiasm."

"I hope Tommy Earl keeps an abundant supply of condoms on hand," I said. But then I had a second thought. "Maybe he doesn't need to. Most of the Pams bring their own these days, or so I hear."

"Tommy Earl don't use condoms. He says condoms are for queers."

When I stopped laughing, I said, "Doesn't he know about all those diseases yet? It's been in most of the papers."

T.J. said, "He knows about 'em but he says he's put so much alcohol and nicotine and chemicals in his body over the years, no disease in the world would stand a chance going up against all that shit."

5

Tommy Earl had followed me by four years as your stud-lovable running back at Paschal High and TCU. But fans in the city who kept up with such things recognized that there were considerable differences in our crowd-pleasing careers.

Among other things, Tommy Earl hadn't made All-America or all-conference or even all-city, the Horned Frog teams he played on hadn't won any conference championships, hadn't gone to any bowl games, and he hadn't been a first-round draft choice.

He dismissed those differences as God's witless oversight. Tommy Earl liked to say it was the same reason God often ignored all the earthquakes and tidal waves that jacked around with people who lived in grass huts and houses on stilts. Might not be fair, but God was God—what could you do?

Tommy Earl had been drafted by Tampa Bay, somewhere around the sixth round, but he barely lasted two seasons in the NFL. Mediocre would be a kind description of his pro career. He stayed injured, or pretended to be injured, most of the time. The Bucs finally released

him because of what would be known today as an attitude problem.

Tommy Earl reflected on his NFL experience somewhat differently.

"Assholes want you to look at film all the time," he
liked to say. "None of it ever has a plot. Tampa . . . St.
Pete. Great place if you're eighty years old. Fuckin' team
ought to have a tube of denture grip for a logo."

He had returned to Fort Worth and married the
Easter card, his old steady, Sheila Roberts, the art history major and former Cotton Bowl princess. They'd
had two rotten kids, who may well have turned rotten
because of the names Sheila strapped on them—Bryson
Thomas and Sheila Teresa Aubyn—and Tommy Earl
had been unhappily married ever since. Meanwhile, being unhappy had never entered Sheila's mind, especially
after she clawed her way into the Junior League.

Careerwise, Tommy Earl had tried to get rich—and
failed—in numerous ventures.

None of us could forget Tommy Earl's Totally Nude
Furniture, or Tommy Earl's Pawn, Gun & Tacos. Other
attempts included:

Green Side Up, his short-lived landscaping business.

T.E.'s Pre-Driven Sedans, his used-car lot.

Not for Everybody, his sadly named men's clothing
store.

Papaw's Camper City, his effort to cash in on the
AARP trade.

But none of those were my favorites.

My first personal favorite was Bruner's School-Color
Caskets.

What Tommy Earl hadn't counted on was that most
people didn't much give a shit about what color casket
they'd be buried in, except for the occasional graduate of
Texas A&M. Tommy Earl wound up selling nothing but

maroon caskets, and not enough of those to stay in the business very long.

My second personal favorite was Yeryee's Chicken Delight. Another standout. This was a fast-food operation aimed at the city's black citizens. Tommy Earl remembered the word from his youth. Remembered his granddads, uncles, and cousins insisting that when you hollered out "Yeryee!"—that very word—any black person within earshot would come running.

Tommy Earl swore he saw it proved over and over as a little kid. An uncle, granddad, or cousin would holler, "Yeryee!" and here would come a black person, almost out of nowhere, saying, "Yass'im, you axin' for me?"

Needless to say, it didn't take long for Tommy Earl to make the harsh discovery that the magic word didn't encourage black people, white people, or any other kind of people, to come running as fast or as often as the words Kentucky Fried Chicken or Popeye's.

The main thing Tommy Earl got from the fast-food business was the memory of something a customer patiently hand-carved into the wall of the men's room at Yeryee's Chicken Delight. It said:

> **TAKES TOO DAMN LONG**
> **TO GET FRIES IN THIS**
> **FUCKIN PLACE**

One way or another, Tommy Earl had managed to hack out a decent living for himself and his family through the years, but he was the first to admit that he kept coming short on BMW's and country club memberships.

Then it happened. Two years ago.

Tommy Earl was having lunch alone at Herb's Cafe one day. Reading the paper. Eating the good end of a chicken fried steak, the end that didn't make you think you were chewing a mouthful of rubber bands. Suddenly, he got this brainstorm. The kind of brainstorm, he said later, that the computer nerd must have got when he figured out a way to slingshot "them goofy astronauts" up to the moon and back.

"What's this country all about?" he asked Vera Lagrone, one of the tenured waitresses at Herb's. A slow-moving woman in her fifties whose slicked-down hair reminded most customers of black shoe polish.

Vera said, "I don't know about the rest of the United States, but it ain't about tips in this shitheap."

"Fear," Tommy Earl answered himself matter-of-factly.

"Fear of what?" said Vera. "Having to eat cat food in my old age?"

"Fear of all them gangs."

"What gangs?"

"Them gangs that make you afraid to walk down the sidewalk of a family neighborhood at night. Gangs that make you afraid to drive home at night. Afraid to park your car in a mall. They're on TV every evening, in the paper every day. It's in the paper today. Man out walking his dog in Ridglea, good neighborhood, but he gets his ass killed for no reason other than a bunch of subhuman teenage snotballs decide to do it."

"Nothing a public hangin' won't cure," Vera proposed nonchalantly.

After lunch, Tommy Earl dashed off to see a buddy of his, a city detective named W. H. ("Waffle House") Grimes, a man who wore a size too-small suits and had a stomach overhang that would have beckoned a group of rock climbers.

The detective, who'd once played tackle for Baylor, provided Tommy Earl with some statistics that made Tommy Earl's heart leap.

To start with, Tommy Earl learned, there were known

to be ten thousand armed teenage gang members in Fort Worth. "Fantastic," Tommy Earl had said, perhaps a bit too excitedly. Then he'd heard that there were over twenty thousand armed teenage gang members in Austin, over thirty thousand in Dallas, and over forty thousand in Houston.

But there was more. Drive-by shootings were on the rise. Just in the past six months, exactly 1,237 drive-by shootings at vehicles and private homes had been reported in the Metroplex alone, Metroplex being a term originated by a disc jockey to describe Fort Worth, Dallas, Arlington, and all of the surrounding and interconnecting K marts and Home Depots.

"Great!" Tommy Earl yelled out.

"We definitely got us a epidemic here," Detective W. H. ("Waffle House") Grimes said. "I'll tell you something else, Tommy Earl. I never in my life expected to be afraid of a damn teenager, but you look in them kids' faces today, there ain't no soul there."

That clinched it for Tommy Earl.

He went racing off to see another buddy, G. T. ("Grease Trap") Reid. Grease Trap Reid had played middle guard for Texas A&M and was now a loan officer at South Side People's Bank. It was through this friendship that Tommy Earl borrowed the money to start up Gang Resistant Systems, Inc.

Some people thought it was courageous of Tommy Earl to borrow the money even before he went to the Texas A&M campus and hired Professor Ron Hipple, an engineering genius, to invent the product he had in mind.

So it was that Gang Resistant Systems, Inc., started to manufacture the sheets of thick fiberglass-based material—a form of bulletproof glass—that could be used to protect the doors and windows of motorists and homeowners who'd become paranoid about a group of people the *Light & Shopper* had begun to call "soulless, mindless, gutter-crawling, scum-sucking, scab-carrying, teenage terrorists."

Orders for the product started pouring in. Tommy Earl Bruner suddenly owned three BMW's, had joined four country clubs, and was saying to anybody who was interested, "I'm doin' so good, I might as well have invented the fuckin' microchip."

Tommy Earl was the other reason I was in town on this weekend. He was a firm believer that we'd be awarded an NFL expansion team, and he wanted to purchase some of the best acreage in the general vicinity of what I was calling Big Food, Texas.

He had big plans for a real estate development wrapped around a championship golf course.

"Like all that shit they do over in Florida and Carolina," he'd said to me the first time we discussed it on the phone. "You've seen what they do over there. Upholster a swamp, move some dirt around, jack up some condos and patio homes—win, win, win."

"You mean like everybody goes away happy?" I'd said.

"Hell, yeah. Bank's happy, homeowner's happy, developer's happy. Am I lyin' to anybody?"

At Bust Out Jonah, I was about to go into some details with T.J. about our competition for an expansion team when gin-red Roy waved a brisket sandwich at me. His way of motioning me to the phone.

It was Tommy Earl.

Things had delayed him longer than he'd expected, he said, but he was at He's Not Here now, so why didn't we come on back over there?

I said, "I'm on, what, a scavenger hunt? I'm twelve years old again?"

"Sorry, Claude. It was unavoidable."

Claude. He had been calling me Billy *Claude* for

years. Even longer than Elroy Blunt, the country music star who'd almost died of several heart attacks from betting so much on us when I played for the Giants—and finally did die, along with three members of his band, when he did a bit too much coke one night, got behind the wheel of the bus, and bet the drummer he could steer it with his mind while he juggled four golf balls. The bus had veered off a bridge and dropped into the Intracoastal Canal near Palatka, Florida. The drummer survived and later said, "Elroy drowned tryin' to make a bet the bus would float."

Anyhow, Tommy Earl had been calling me Claude ever since a young writer with no sense of history had gotten my name wrong in the *Fort Worth Light & Shopper*. It had happened on an occasion when I was in town to receive some kind of an alumni award from TCU. One of those plaques they gave you that made good firewood after you peeled off the metal part that said the university appreciated your loyalty and devotion, meaning your annual financial contribution.

"Billy Claude Puckett, Old Twenty-two, we'll never forget him," Tommy Earl said on the phone.

Another of his long-running jokes. My jersey number was 23. Maybe not as familiar as Old 77 or Old 98, immortals Tommy Earl referred to as "Bronko" Grange and "Doak" Harmon.

"What was unavoidable about it?" I asked.

He cleared his throat, mumbled something.

I said, "I don't suppose it had anything to do with the Forest Park Apartments."

"That T.J. knows how to keep a secret, don't he?"

"You weren't in the sack? Tell me you weren't."

"This hard-on showed up, Claude. It was a big-time bulb, a fucking blue veiner, man. I didn't ask for it, I wasn't thinkin' about it, but there it was, and like we've always said, it's unlucky not to take advantage of such things."

"Like *who's* always said?"

"Everybody. Lucky people. I did the right thing, didn't I, Claude? A man wouldn't be fair to himself, would he? If he went around ignoring opportunities like that?"

"You're asking for my approval?"

"Well, you know how much I've always admired you."

I laughed and told him T.J. and I would come on back over to He's Not Here after we got on the outside of some more ribs.

6

"It's good to see those again."

T.J. was saying hello to Tracy.

She was, as any fool should have known, with Tommy Earl Bruner.

The happy couple was sitting in He's Not Here at one of the tables from the oilcloth family. Tommy Earl formally introduced me to Tracy as his "fiancée-to-be." She giggled, and still didn't have a last name.

Behind the bar, Kelly Sue put drinks for T.J. and me on the counter. I went over to fetch them.

"You might have given me a hint," I said, meaning Kelly Sue might have tipped me off earlier that Tracy was one of Tommy Earl's collectibles.

She said, "You've been on TV. I thought you were intelligent."

"That," I said, "is one of America's great misconceptions."

"Is that why you quit announcing the games? Everybody's dumb?"

Kelly Sue wasn't the first person to ask me why I'd quit CBS two years ago. My standard answer was that I got tired of hearing Larry Hoage, America's most-loved play-by-play man, saying, "If you ask me, Billy Clyde, I'd say this quarterback's negatives aren't too positive."

Or maybe I got tired of standing next to him in the booth and hearing him say, "I don't know about you, Billy Clyde, but this kid seems to be weak in the strong areas."

Or maybe I became weary of having to go to dinner with Larry and the director and producer and talking about nothing but ratings and shares all evening, like America's future in the twenty-first century was riding on it.

What really happened was, I wanted to speak the truth in a telecast—the truth about the stupid or crooked zebras, or the morons for coaches, or the selfish and spoiled athletes—but TV won't let you do that. You become a highly paid shill, and one day I just decided I couldn't do it any longer.

The network tried half-heartedly to keep me. With more money, but not with any freedom to say what I wanted to say on the air. All they really wanted was my name value, anyhow. They'd have been just as happy with a Miss America who could smile but couldn't talk.

Anyhow, I walked. I might have been the biggest moron of all to let pride knock me out of all that easy money—broadcasting is like stealing, frankly—but the other thing was, I was bored fucking to death.

At that very moment I was in the clutches of what you call your basic midlife crisis, wondering what the hell I was going to do for a career—other than make speeches, and do corporate "outings," and eventually wind up dead on a golf course or behind a podium.

Which was why, in my solitude, I was praying for the West Texas Tornadoes to become a reality. I'd have a real job.

But now to Kelly Sue, I said, "I didn't announce the games. I commented on the games . . . drew funny

lines on your screen with an electric pencil. A Teles-
trator, they call it."

"I thought you were good at it."

"Thank you."

"You didn't talk all the time."

"Thank you. I tried not to. Television turned me into
a smoker, though. I'll give TV credit for that. I never
smoked a cigarette when I fancied myself an athlete, but
there's nothing to do in TV but sit around in meetings,
and you watch a lot of boring games. I lit up one day.
Now I'm a militant addict."

"Well, you were good on the air. You didn't act like a
god-awful volcano had erupted somewhere and the lava
was headed for my living room just because Dipshit
completed a pass."

"It was back-breaking work." I smiled. "Time to find
a job in the shade."

I joined my pals at the table, where T.J. was admiring
Tracy while trying not to look like the honey was running down his leg.

Tracy had changed costumes. She now appeared to be
ready for a cocktail party in Vegas. She was wrapped like
a mummy in a cream-colored minifrock. No stockings,
spiked heels.

The minifrock only covered her from midway down
her best friends to just below her ass. It barely restrained
her treasures and looked fully capable of cutting off her
breathing if she gained a single ounce of weight from the
glass of white wine she was now having.

I feared that if she made any sudden moves, the
minifrock might split apart and go squirreling around
the room, frapping innocent people upside the head. I
might add that her hair had been rearranged differently
and looked a little damp.

Which encouraged me to assume her costume change
had occurred after she'd spent a pleasurable two hours

on her back, with her legs spread for Tommy Earl's face, occasionally murmuring, "Oh, yeah, baby, do it . . . go there . . . bring it."

Tommy Earl was rich-guy casual in a navy-blue cashmere crewneck over a denim shirt with a standup collar. Corduroys, tassle loafers. His fluffy brown hair was parted in the middle. I wanted to ask if he was trying to look like Harrison Ford's long-lost twin brother, but then I would have had to explain to Tracy that, no, I wasn't sure whether Harrison Ford *had* a long-lost twin brother—right, Harrison Ford, the actor—and, well, fuck it. Life was full of missed opportunities.

Even the dumbest cornerback could have read the look on Tommy Earl's face as he slid his arm around Tracy's shoulders and squeezed on her. A man proud of his possession. It was the look that said, "Tell me I haven't gone out and won me a Super Bowl with this one."

"How's Sheila?" I asked playfully.

"I told you he was funny," Tommy Earl said to Tracy. "Didn't I tell you he was a witty motherfucker?"

Tommy Earl lit a cigarette and said he wasn't sure he'd ever get married again if his marriage to Sheila ever broke up.

"Marriage is tough duty," he said with a grin. "Instead of gettin' married again, I think I'll just find a woman I hate and buy her a house."

T.J.'s laughter shook the table.

When the coach calmed down, he cleared his throat and asked Tracy why he hadn't seen her in He's Not Here before.

She reminded him that he'd seen her earlier today.

"I sure did," T.J. said. "Lord God, I did."

Tracy said, "When I have any free time, I go to clubs downtown or out on the north side, if there's any good music happening. I don't go to places like this just to *drink*, although I don't have anything against drinking. I didn't even know this place *existed* till I met Tommy Earl."

"It doesn't exist," I said. "None of us are here."

Tracy looked at me curiously.

T.J. asked what kept her from having any free time.

"My job," she said, letting Tommy Earl light her cigarette.

"What do you do?"

"I'm a fashion model."

"Oh? Where 'bouts?"

"Right now I'm at Members Only Lingerie."

Normally, when guys hear this kind of news they trade fraternal glances, and it's with those fraternal glances that they often impart such information to each other as:

1. This lady could fuck you till your heart blows out of your chest and sticks to the ceiling.

2. This lady could swallow Arnold Schwarzenegger's leg.

3. This lady either lives with a coke dealer or a guy in a rock band who hasn't washed his hair since 1978.

I was pleased the coach and I maintained our nonchalance.

"It's a nice place," Tracy said. "We have a good clientele. It has a lot more class than Naughty Girls Lingerie. I worked at Naughty's for six months. Out on I-35? Like if you're going to Waco?"

T.J. nodded.

"I mean Austin," Tracy corrected herself. "I don't think you ever go to Waco unless you live there."

"And can't do anything about it," Tommy Earl interjected.

"I used to go to Waco for the seafood," I said riotously.

Tracy stared at me again.

Then she said Members Only was in a much better location than Naughty's. Members Only was downtown near Sundance Square, close to a lot of restaurants and movies. Working downtown, she didn't have to put up with the T & T crowd like she did out on I-35, and she was very thankful for that, no shit.

"What's the T & T crowd?" T.J. asked.

"Tattoos and trailers."

The coach's laughter knocked over a drink.

Tommy Earl said, "Sugar, you shouldn't make sport of them people. That's the backbone of America you're talking about."

"You could fool me," Tracy said. "A lot of shithooks is all I ever saw."

A little later on, I excused myself for a moment. I walked over to the quiet end of the bar, gesturing to Kelly Sue for a phone.

It occurred to me that I ought to call the hotel downtown and let somebody know I was in the city, and I'd be there before the night was over.

I didn't want an incompetent desk clerk to give my suite away to a Peruvian novelist in town for the Friends of the Library's Unbought Books & Unknown Authors dinner, or give it away to a young wrangler in town for the Southwestern Ranch Management Seminar.

Kelly Sue placed the phone on the counter, said to dial nine for outside, and it was okay with her if I wanted to call Pakistan or Egypt or wherever my wife was making a movie now.

"Switzerland," I said, "but I just want to call the hotel, tell 'em I'll be late."

"Switzerland? Really?"

"She'll be there a few weeks. I've been over there once. I'm going back again. I don't usually go anywhere I can't speak the language, except New Orleans."

Kelly Sue gave me a look.

"That was a joke," I said.

"Just wanted to make sure."

The bartender sipped from her mug of coffee.

"Now, Kelly Sue," I said, "did you know old Tracy over there is a lingerie model?"

Going off to help a customer who yelled at her, Kelly Sue looked back over her shoulder. "For Tommy Earl or the general population?"

I got the hotel on the phone but the minute I heard the voice on the other end of the line I knew I was in trouble. I was in as much trouble as America itself.

It was a young woman's voice. The voice of the New Age. The voice of an individual that modern education—no reading, no writing, no arithmetic, no discipline—has unleashed on the world. The voice of the person whose first question at a job interview is "What is my career path?" The voice of the child that modern education has set loose on society to discover that, much to its horror and our inconvenience, it might someday have to deal with people who—holy shit—might require it to *do something*.

"Excuse me . . . ?" the voice said.

"Puckett," I said. "I have a reservation for Suite 362, my usual. I won't be arriving till later tonight, but go ahead and check me in. You have my Amex on file."

Long pause.

"I don't find a reservation for a Duckett, sir."

Always a tester. Were you bigger than this? Were you known for your patience, your charity, your kindness toward people? Or did you want to reach into the phone and drag the poor child out so you could choke her to death?

"It's Puckett," I said. "*P-u-c-k-e-t-t*. Fort Worth's own."

"Fort Worth's what?"

"Could I have your name, dear?"

"I'm Janet Lawrence, sir, the assistant manager."

"Is the manager there?"

"He's at dinner right now."

"Can you switch me to the concierge?"

"She called in sick."

"Janet, can you see the bell stand from where you are?"

"Sir?"

"The bell stand. Can you see anybody over there? Maybe a blond guy, smiles a lot for no apparent reason. Looks like he's spent some time on a surfboard. See him anywhere?"

"You mean Sean?"

"That's him. He knows me."

"Sean is on duty, sir, but he's not around right now."

"Of course not. He's probably in the garage trying to help a guest find his Lexus that's been lost for two days."

"I'm sorry?"

"Janet, let me explain something to you. I don't know how long you've been in your job at the Sundance Palace, but I've been staying at your hotel in the same suite—362—for more than ten years. I've spent maybe, oh, eighty or ninety million dollars in that hotel, and that doesn't include room service or the bar or the gift shop, so whether or not you can find my name on your computer, I assure you I *do* have a reservation. Just do me a favor and—"

"Here it is!"

"Good."

"Billy Clem Puckett. You're arriving tomorrow."

"It's Billy *Clyde* Puckett and I'm here now."

"You're in Fort Worth?"

"Yes, I am."

I think that sentence may have had a weary sound to it.

"Oh, I see. You're asking if you can have the room a day early?"

"Not the room, dear. The suite. The suite I always have when I stay with you. Or something similar. And I'm not a day early. I'm right on schedule. When Frank comes back from dinner he'll explain it to you."

"Who's Frank?"

"Frank Simmons. You don't know the name of your manager, your own boss?"

"I know Sergio."

"Who's Sergio?"

"He's the manager."

"What happened to Frank?"

"If he was the previous manager, I believe I heard somebody say he went to the Ritz-Carlton somewhere in Florida."

"Maybe I'll stay there tonight."

"I beg your pardon?"

"Nothing. Just hold me a room. Broom closet. Anything."

"Sir, I've punched it up. Three sixty-two *is* available."

"Fine."

"I should warn you that you will be on a smoking floor."

"I certainly hope so."

"I'm sorry?"

"Nothing. See you in a while."

I hung up, exhausted. I stared down at the floor. When I looked up, Kelly Sue was putting a fresh drink in front of me.

"It used to be easier," I said.

"Travel?"

"Life."

7

It was two hours later, or maybe three. Only Junior and Drew knew for sure, or Justerini and Dewars, as they are more formally known, and I found myself in a completely different type of establishment, but another one Tommy Earl had a financial interest in.

We'd all slid out of He's Not Here and into our respective cars and gone into steering-wheel combat with some of the bumpy streets that had enabled more than one pavement contractor to join a country club, and we'd wound up on University Drive down in Forest Park.

The place was called Tuxedo Junction.

If you took one of those big Barnes & Deli bookstores and let old Doc Goebbels remove all the books and burn them, then put in a stage and a dance floor, you'd have Tuxedo Junction.

Red and Crystal were up on a small stage making big-band sounds. Red on the piano, Crystal on the vocals. But you could hear trumpets, trombones, clarinets, saxophones, drums. They came out of an assortment of large black boxes, as if Harry James, Tommy Dorsey, and

Woody Herman had been trapped in there since 1946
and were trying to blast their way out.

I thought I might be in an old newsreel the minute I
walked in. Crystal was singing "It seems to me I've heard
that song before," and there was activity all over the
dance floor.

Gray-haired codgers in plaid sport coats and Grecian-
formula geezers in pink, green, and yellow sport coats
were dancing with sway-back dames with piled-up hair.
The women wore tight slit skirts, frilly blouses, and an-
kle-strap shoes.

All of the couples were grooving and spinning and
twirling, obviously feeling the music, doing these dances
that Fort Worth historians would fondly remember as
the Poly Drag, the Dallas Push, the Riverside Shag, the
Dirty Boogie, the Jersey Bounce, and a popular old step
whose name would be a big hit today with your table-
pounding liberals, the Nigger Shuffle.

We were in a "wrinkle bar."

Tommy Earl coined the name. He had wisely observed the over-sixty trend setting in on society. He'd
seen his first establishment of this nature in Houston, a
place called In the Mood. He'd seen another one in Dallas, a place called Summit Ridge Drive.

That was enough. He'd rounded up Ody Bradshaw
for a financial partner—Ody's money, Tommy Earl's
"creativity"—and they'd opened Tuxedo Junction, and it
was a rousing success.

"Wrinkle bars are money machines," Tommy Earl
confessed to me. "I know it ain't a nice way to describe
most of my customers. Folks in their sunset years. But
they can't hear too good, anyhow."

His timing was perfect, he boasted. People were living longer. Exercising. Eating their bran. Bypasses, hip
transplants, gallbladders out. Running the checkup-
clinic marathon—fuck it, Medicare paid, right? Kids fi-

nally on their own, self-supporting. New wives replacing the fat ones. New husbands replacing the dead ones. It all played a part.

"It's the Senior Tour," I remarked.

T.J. by now had called home to tell Donna Lou he was with me, that I had forced him to drink more whiskey than he should have, and that he had forgotten what a bad influence I'd always been on him.

I spoke to Donna Lou while she was on the phone. I told her she was one of the few totally sane and completely objective people I'd ever known, and I was sure she'd understand about our car trouble.

I think I might have heard a giggle before she hung up.

Kelly Sue had joined us to help out with the cigarette smoking. She had closed He's Not Here early. She had the authority to do that. She closed it because the clientele had dwindled down to two out-of-work golf cart salesmen discussing a stock tip on the Nasdaq.

She was sitting next to me. Our round table was in a corner of the club, as far removed from Red and Crystal's amps as we could get to avoid having to read lips.

Kelly Sue said she hoped I didn't mind if she made it look like we were together. It would keep the Grecian Formulas from hitting on her.

"But you don't have any physical obligations tonight," she said, patting me on the arm.

"Good," I said, "because I've got this pinched nerve in my neck . . . and this ruptured disc . . . and a hip that's been—"

Her poke with an elbow indicated I'd made my point.

It must have been Junior—certainly not me—that got around to asking Kelly Sue about her basic history.

She was from Alabama, it turned out, which wasn't the only reason she knew something about football. Her mama, Sue, and daddy, Kel, had both gone to school at the University of Alabama. In fact, her daddy had played on Alabama's Rose Bowl team of 1945, the one with Harry Gilmer, the boy-wonder quarterback. Her folks were Crimson clear through, she said, capable of lapsing into a chorus of "Go, Alabama," the fight song, at almost any given moment. They'd lived long enough to revel in some of Bear Bryant's national championships.

Kelly Sue said, "I won't say my mama was a big football fan, but I heard her say once there were only two things she still wished for in life. She said she'd like to see Europe someday, and she'd like to beat those Notre Dame shitasses, just one time."

Kelly Sue had gone to school in Tuscaloosa but only for two years. She'd dropped out after getting knocked up by Jimmy Gene Page, the wide receiver with good hands and no character. Abortions weren't trendy in her day, and besides that, she'd rather have had a baby than Jimmy Gene Page.

She was proud of her daughter, Susan, who was now twenty-seven. Susan was a graduate of UT-Arlington. She was a smart and attractive girl who'd learned how to do things on a computer that were incomprehensible to anyone over the age of fifty. Susan was still single, but occasionally entertained the overnight guest. She was an assistant sales manager for a medical supply company, and lived in one of those apartment complexes north of Dallas that was about as close to downtown Dallas as the Oklahoma state line.

None of this had anything to do with how Kelly Sue got to Fort Worth. What had brought her to Fort Worth twelve years ago was another marriage. She had been tending bar in a nice club in Birmingham when she met a handsome liquor salesman named Mel Brewster. They got married and immediately moved to Fort Worth, uprooting her daughter from high school, because Mel was offered an opportunity to take over a better territory. Or so he claimed. What he'd had an opportunity to do, she learned, was find a new set of bookmakers who didn't want to put his feet in cement.

"Once again I confused sex with love," Kelly Sue said. "I thought Mel was a good person. I didn't find out till after I married him what a lying, worthless, lowlife maggot he was."

"Did his feet wind up in cement?" I asked.

"Who cares? He disappeared, is all I know, leaving me in a strange town with no money and a daughter to raise." She sighed. "Two times. Jimmy Gene Page and Mel Brewster. Twice I've gone to Downtown Dumbass City."

I asked her why it was that in all of my trips back to Fort Worth I'd never come across her in a saloon somewhere. She said the likely explanation was that she'd worked in places that were outside my boundaries.

I inquired if any of the places had featured happy hours, big-screen television sets, cheese sticks, plastic burgers, and shooter specials.

"They all did."

"Well, there you have it," I said.

Tuxedo Junction continued to be crowded well after the dinner hour, which greatly pleased Tommy Earl. He said he'd tried life without much money and it was a stone-cold bitch.

"Man, all I know is, I'm glad I don't have to rely on bullshit anymore. I'm outta that line of work. Fucking sales."

"You're still in sales," T.J. reminded him. "You sell all that bulletproof glass to protect people from the scum."

"I don't sell it," Tommy Earl said indignantly. "I *present* it. My customers beg for it, I make it available. There's a big fucking difference. If you're trying to sell something to somebody, the somebody usually don't want it in the first place, so you got to call on your bullshit. Ain't nothing complicated about it."

Kelly Sue nudged me, slyly directing my attention to a gray-haired couple eavesdropping on our conversation. Wrinkle regulars.

"People ought to have sympathy for salesmen," Tommy Earl said.

"Why?" said Kelly Sue.

"They have to eat shit, that's why," Tommy Earl said. "Salesmen eat two-thirds of all the shit produced in America."

"That's not true of a woman salesman," Kelly Sue said. "If you go in Neiman's, or some other good store like that, and if you're not a regular customer, the sales-lady makes *you* eat shit. Big moment in her life."

"That is really true in Dallas," Tracy said.

I was about to say they'd overestimated my curiosity on the subject when Tommy Earl said, "Okay, but that's a woman deal. I'm talking about the poor bastard who can't feed his family if he don't sell something. Hi, how you doin', sir? Come on in here. I'm here to help you any way I can, but let me eat some of your shit first. Boy, I love to eat shit. You probably know this about me because you can see how tired I am. Just goddamn stoop-shouldered, polyester, wore-out, flop-down, headache tired. Sometimes I eat shit in the morning. Sometimes I eat shit in the afternoon. I always eat shit on my coffee break. Yes, sir, you gimme a lot of shit, I'll eat it for you. I guess I've been eating shit for, oh, twenty-five or thirty years. My daddy ate shit before me. His daddy ate shit before him. They were in sales, of course. Hell, my wife eats shit, my kids eat shit, my whole family eats shit. What can I do for you, good buddy?"

Pleased with his routine, Tommy Earl glanced around

our table, and over at the gray-haired couple, the eaves-droppers. "Am I lyin' to anybody?" he said.

Rising to leave, the eavesdroppers could only gape at Tommy Earl as if he had developed some hideous deformity.

8

The wrinkle bar crowd had thinned out. Some of the regulars left sore and limping. Some left drunk and hobbling. Some left angry at their wives or husbands for dancing too often with the wives or husbands of other wives and husbands. And some left angry at their wives and husbands for not being able to hear better.

I caught the tail end of one conversation as the couple left.

"What'd she say?"

"What'd *who* say?"

"Bernice."

"Bernice sat where?"

"Bernice *said.*"

"Went where?"

"She *said* you get moody when you drink."

"Tuesday? I can play Tuesday."

"Oh, shut up, Jimmy—gimme the damn car keys."

Tommy Earl had been boxing Drew and soda around pretty good, and he'd lapsed into a feel-up mode where Tracy was concerned. Tracy seemed to be happy enough, smoking, staring into space. Kelly Sue had ordered a steak sandwich on toast, side of chunky hash browns, and a pot of coffee. Her midnight snack looked so good, T.J. and I had ordered the same thing for ourselves.

This was when I finally got around to talking about the owners of the other franchises that were hoping to get in the NFL.

I started with the Hawaii Volcanoes.

The team in Honolulu would be owned by the Akagis, but there was only one Akagi who mattered. That was Rushi Akagi, oldest of the three brothers, head of the family business. He'd gone to UCLA somewhere back in his past, which was where he'd acquired the nickname Tokyo Russ. He was the wisest of the three brothers, the one who spoke the most English. It wasn't all that much, but it did amount to substantially more than "Chicken, shrimp, or beef?"

It was through the guidance of Tokyo Russ that the Akagis had amassed one of the world's great fortunes. They'd started out by ripping off our electronic gadgets, which didn't make them all that different from other successful people of the yellow peril persuasion, Big Ed liked to say.

Then they'd branched out. Tokyo Russ led the family into real estate. He bought up all the property in the Hawaiian islands that wasn't already owned by other rich Japs, and bought up all the property on the North American continent that wasn't already owned by Disney, Bill Gates, the Mafia, the Baptist church, or the Bass brothers.

Tokyo Russ had increased the family fortune when he steered Akagi Industries into the artificial skin tissue market in the U.S. The smartest minds on Wall Street hadn't foreseen that there would be a huge demand for artificial skin tissue.

Tokyo Russ had explained it in an interview with a woman on CNN. "I have good idea, no need for research," he said. "Americans like to cover up scabs and freckles. Like to look nice all time. Wives like to look nice for other wives. Husbands like to look nice for girlfriends, ha, ha."

A recent venture of the Akagis, however, hadn't done so well. They'd invested heavily in Odor Killer clothing after their scientists came up with a secret chemical that could be blended into fabric and was supposed to prevent bad smells. The underarm stink in knit golf shirts, for example. It would also combat all of the varied odors one often discovered in one's underwear.

Millions of these Odor Killer garments—shirts, blouses, shorts, panties, pajamas, swimsuits—were manufactured by the Akagis and offered for sale in the U.S. They flooded all of our golf shops, boutiques, retail stores, outlet malls.

Maybe you missed their Odor Killer TV commercial, I said. It didn't run long. The one where the handsome man and beautiful woman embraced in their home and said:

Him: "What's that I smell, dear?"

Her: "Why, it's the fried chicken I'm cooking, darling."

Him: "Great! I can smell dinner. What a treat. You must be wearing your Odor Killer blouse."

Her: "I am! I took a lesson from your Odor Killer golf shirts."

Him: "Isn't it wonderful to smell something besides our yukky old armpits for a change?"

Me, I would have thought Odor Killer apparel was a can't-miss deal. I would have based it on the simple fact that Americans had been caught up in the no-smoking craze. A cigarette smoker hadn't smelled anything in years, good or bad. But there were fewer places where Americans could smoke, therefore fewer Americans were smoking, which meant more Americans were smelling things, and some of the things they were smelling for the first time were all of their rancid varieties of body odor.

Why this was healthier than smelling the aroma of a Marlboro had yet to be explained to me. Nevertheless, I was as stunned as the Akagis when Americans soundly rejected Odor Killer garments, which had cost the Akagis millions.

I'd read something in *USA Today* that may have explained it. The story suggested two things. One, Americans perhaps had grown accustomed to their sour body odors, as Europeans had centuries ago, or two, we no longer noticed our body odor because so many immigrants were pouring into the country on an hourly basis and were crowding into our buses and elevators.

Big Ed had been quite pleased when he'd heard the Akagis had dropped a few million. He said, "One of the great myths is that the Japs are smart. Don't ever forget they started a goddamn war with us they should have known they couldn't win. The first real fight they got in with us, we kicked their ass at Midway. They were real smart there. Oh, they're good at sneak attacks, but what else? They've been picked like chickens on Wall Street. They've been beat like a drum in Hollywood. They've been ironed out in California real estate. If your Jap bidnessman would bow down a little lower, he'd see he's standing in his own shit."

Big Ed's attitude may have been influenced by the fact that he'd been a young fighter pilot in World War II, a man who earned the DFC and all kinds of other decorations. Big Ed and his P-38 had knocked off more than one flock of Sessue Hayakawas.

It was known that Tokyo Russ and his brothers were having other financial troubles of a domestic nature, I continued. All three brothers had recently been through costly divorces. They'd dumped their stubby Jap wives and married women who didn't wear kimonos and skip around the yard trying to catch butterflies.

The other two Akagis, Joe and Jumbo, had selected tall, stacked blondes from Stockholm who'd modeled Odor Killer swimwear for them.

Tokyo Russ had been more adventurous. He'd married Rachel Tompkins, a London actress-model who was all too familiar to British tabloid readers. Although she was only thirty-three, Rachel had already been married to an Italian count, a Formula One driver from Argentina, a Colorado ski-area developer, a Turkish movie producer, and a Swiss arms dealer.

Big Ed wondered if Rachel's reputation and past history would hurt Tokyo Russ's chances of being taken into the NFL—would the NFL owners want a wife like her in their "family"?

Yes, I'd said. All you had to do was look at a photo of her. Then I was sure of it after I heard about the stage name Rachel had chosen for herself, hoping it would be a boost to her career in show business.

The stage name she'd chosen was Mandy Rice-Davies. The mere mention of that name, I believed, would bring a pleasant, knowing smile to every NFL owner who had a sense of history.

T.J. said, "I'll tell you what, Billy Clyde. We've got some fruits and nuts on our faculty who'd have to put cold rags on their foreheads if they heard you call 'em Japs instead of Jap-oh-nese."

I said, "Well, if Big Ed runs into any of those distinguished educators someday, he can ask them if they'd prefer 'dirty little slant-eyed, back-stabbing Nips.'"

The sole owner of the London Knights was Neville Trill.

Neville was an albino runt, only five feet tall. When he dined out or socialized in public, he liked to wear a spiked German helmet from the Great War, jodhpurs, riding boots, and a soccer jersey. A writer for the *Daily Telegraph* in London once described him as "a comical little wanker trying to imitate a hand grenade."

Neville Trill was only thirty-one, but the main thing anybody needed to know about him was that he was worth two billion dollars.

He'd made his money in what could loosely be called the music industry today. He'd started out at the age of eighteen as a songwriter for the popular British rock group, Fuck Shit Piss.

After the raging success of the group's first album, *Shit on My Chest*—music and lyrics of the title song by Neville—he became a manager and producer as well. This put him in a position to sign up other artists from both Great Britain and America in the rock, rap, and alternative music categories. He now managed such successful groups as Knob Polish, Anal Trip, Partial Birth Abortion, Whore Mongers, and Sperm Party.

With such a powerhouse client list, the rest was history for Neville, financially speaking.

He became fascinated with American football when the Dallas Cowboys and Chicago Bears played an exhibition game in London's Wembley Stadium. Thinking the game was the place to be that afternoon, he obtained a sideline credential from a friend on *Tatler* magazine, a credential he referred to as a "backstage pass."

What the sideline ticket did was give Neville a chance to be close to the sights and sounds of the sport—the bulging muscles straining to burst out of the sleek uniforms, the speed-induced slobbering and cussing that came from inside the face masks, the colorful farting and belching.

Neville was enthralled. Then and there, he vowed to own an NFL team someday. So he started letting the league know how much money he had, letting the league

know he was interested in bankrolling an expansion
team. After naming his club the London Knights, he
opened an office in Mayfair, arranged for the home
games to be played in Wembley Stadium when the time
came, and began toying around with the team logo.

My assessment of the Knights' first logo was that it
looked something like a pirate in dreadlocks waving a
cutlass at the NBC peacock, but then I'd never been a
big fan of complicated logos.

To me, the best logos had always been the simple
ones. The Old English *NY* for the New York Yankees,
the longhorn noggin on the side of the University of
Texas helmet, and the swastika had always struck me as
being perfect for the debonair crowd that ran Germany
one time.

There was an article about American football becoming popular in England in *The Sports Magazine* that was
written by my old pal Jim Tom Pinch. Neville confessed
in the story that he didn't pretend to understand the
rules of American football, although like most Brits he
found the "armor" we wore incredibly fantastic.

Jim Tom quoted him saying:

"In point of fact, I find the American rules stupen-
dously boring. For instance, if one can get one's hands
on the ball, in whatever fashion, mind you, why
shouldn't one be permitted to advance it in the appropriate direction until one is apprehended? I also find there
are far too many round-table discussions throughout the
course of a game. Huddles, I believe they are called. We
don't have this in our soccer football. We simply play
on."

T.J. spoke up, saying it wouldn't seem right to him
for an Englishman to own a team playing football.

"Foreigners ought to stick to soccer," he said. "Pile
on . . . fuck one another every time they score a goal."

"Foreign deal?" I said.

"Way it looks to me anyhow," T.J. said, stretching his arms, popping his neck. "Europeans and them. Your Latins."

"That dog-style thing could be why there's so little scoring in soccer," I said.

"Afraid of the consequences?" Kelly Sue laughed.

"That would be my reason." I looked at T.J. "Can that many "soccer moms" be wrong?"

"What a game," he said. "Can't use your hands. Short pants. Fucking riots."

This left the Mexico City Bandits.

The original majority owner of the franchise, Chico Monriquez, a dope dealer whose lifelong dream was to bring the NFL to his country, was now either dead or living in a cave in Peru. He fled Mexico City after becoming involved in a drug-smuggling scandal with two generals in the Mexican army and three agents of the CIA.

To keep the dream alive, Chico's brother, Ramon, took over the franchise and the effort to acquire an expansion team. Ramon liked to wear T-shirts with amusing slogans on them. DEATH TO POLICE was one.

Ramon soon fled the country after getting involved in a drug-smuggling scandal involving an Austin, Texas, accounting firm, a Nashville music company executive, and two former White House lawyers.

But it had all been for the best. The franchise was now in the hands of their cousin, Eduardo Baptiste Ocheria ("Bappy") Ramirez, one of the world's richest men.

Not many days went by when you couldn't find his name in the gossip columns or stories about him in the fashion magazines. He was fifty-six years old but still known as the "severely handsome global playboy."

You'd find him mentioned for his vicious polo, his

flaming tango, his expert skiing, his fearless powerboating, his skillful hot-air ballooning, his daring glider flights, and his eagle-eyed big game hunting.

Most photographs of Bappy were taken in one of his dens. Him posing with a high-powered rifle in safari togs, surrounded by antlers, hides, furs, skins, and glassy eyes.

He was known to have killed his first animal at the age of ten and was once quoted as saying he prayed every evening that God would continue to supply him with animals to kill.

Bappy's wife may have been mentioned in the columns and magazines more often than him. She was the former Naomi Lauranette Foster of Dallas, "the effortlessly gorgeous, fiercely stylish, fun-loving Texas-born socialite."

Naomi was around fifty-five years old but didn't look a day older than a startled seventy under strong lights. You could tell from most any photo of her that she held a death grip on the international face-lift record.

One of the more interesting things about Naomi Lauranette Foster was the fact that when she was in Highland Park High School in Dallas, her name had been Naomi Sienkowicz.

There was no question in the minds of certain people that if Naomi hadn't invented the name of Naomi Lauranette Foster before she entered the University of Texas, she'd never have been asked to pledge Pi Phi.

That information was courtesy of Big Barb Bookman, my mother-in-law, who kept up with such things. Vitally important things like old family names and a list of the finest neighborhoods throughout America.

It wasn't a question of snobbery on Big Barb's part. It was a simple matter of caution.

Enormous wealth and power was a tradition in Bappy's family. His great-great-grandfather, his great-grandfather, his grandfather, and his father had all been presidents of Mexico. They'd all brought something to various regions of the country—indoor plumbing, electricity, marijuana, automobiles, kitchen appliances, cocaine, canned food, and color TV.

Bappy and his sister, Olga, paid little attention to business, although like most heirs they expected to receive more money on their investments this year than they received last year, and they expected their business managers and investment people to see that this happened or confront the possibility of having their hands pounded by sledgehammers.

Bappy held the title of president of the family business, but the empire was now said to be run by Naomi with the assistance of an elusive gentleman named Carlos ("The Leaf") Garcia.

Bappy and Naomi often hopped from one of their palatial homes to another. They lived in Cuernavaca, San Miguel, Santa Fe, Positano, Marbella, Hamburg, St. Moritz, Nairobi, Mala Mala, Zurich, Paris, and London. And Naomi was even known to be on good terms with God.

I'd found that out in a magazine, thanks to my wife.

Barbara Jane had once insisted I look at a photograph of Naomi in *Rich & Famous*. It showed Naomi in a long red gown and her most recent face. She was greeting guests at a party in their twelve-bedroom chalet in St. Moritz and explaining in the caption how God had helped her pick out the furniture and other decor:

"I prayed hard and God told me to go to China and buy these beautiful woven rugs. Without God's help, I would never have known the chinks did such things."

There were two dead husbands in Naomi's past at the time she captured Bappy. If nobody else did, I'd found it curious that her two ex-husbands had been wealthy oilmen in Houston and both had drowned in the bathtubs of their River Oaks mansions.

Naomi and Bappy met in Kenya, oddly enough. It happened when he'd been on a trip to East Africa to shoot the rest of the small animals he'd failed to kill in all of his previous trips. Naomi had happened to be in Kenya at the very same time. She had gone on a candelabra safari with her date, a career Phi Delt from Austin. They'd gone with another Pi Phi from the University of Texas, who was with a Sigma Chi from Chapel Hill, a Theta from SMU who was with an SAE from Stanford, and a Chi Omega from LSU who was with a Kappa Sig from W&L.

Fate played a hand in Naomi meeting Bappy. Their safari camps hadn't been that far from each other. The meeting occurred early one evening before sundown. Bappy was admiring his reflection in a pond, a watering hole, when Naomi came along to admire her own reflection in the same pond.

Their love affair ignited instantly.

Naomi, as it happened, had been holding a glass of red wine as she stood at the edge of the pond.

"It's a Tignanello," she said to Bappy. "No additives."

He'd been overwhelmed by her impeccable taste in wine.

There was wide coverage of their wedding, which took place almost immediately. The ceremony was held in an obscure Nepal village in the foothills of the Himalayas, and conducted during a tea break of a match during the World Elephant Polo Championships.

I'd read about elephant polo in Jim Tom's magazine. A team consisted of six players and three elephants, two players sitting on each elephant. The competitors were armed with long bamboo mallets. The teams went by such names as the Sips & Dins, the Hip Flasks, and the

San Francisco Corkscrews. The sport was played only in
Nepal, one of the poorest countries in the world, because it was the only place where the people would accept jobs as dung collectors. Evidently each chukker of
elephant polo required a good many dung collectors.

"Just when you think rick folks can't get no sillier,"
T.J. said.

Bappy and Naomi were known to have promised the
NFL they'd build a stadium in Mexico City that would
hold 120,000 fans, 20,000 riot police, and 10,000 undercover police. The job of the undercover cops would be
to guard against kidnappers and pickpockets.

They were also guaranteeing the NFL they'd build a
stadium that wouldn't collapse, even during the strongest earthquakes, and couldn't be destroyed during the
most passionate riots imaginable.

I liked their team logo. The sombrero. Made sense.
But I was of the opinion that the team could have had a
better nickname than the Bandits.

Actually, I said, if they really wanted to strike fear in
the hearts of their opponents, they ought to be called the
Mexico City Tap Water.

9

The evening ended at 2:00 A.M. We spent some time in the parking lot looking for Tracy. She eventually appeared from around a dark corner, wide awake, wiping her nose.

Tommy Earl whispered to me that he was seriously in love. He intended to buy an engagement ring and pop the question. I reminded him that he was married to Sheila, the mother of his children, his wife of twenty years.

"Aw, shit," he said, looking disappointed.

Tommy Earl and I agreed to have breakfast together in the morning. Talk commerce. T.J. and I agreed to have lunch together tomorrow. I said I'd come out to his office in the coliseum.

T.J. remembered that his own car was back on the campus. Tommy Earl and Tracy volunteered to take him. Tracy said she knew of an after-hours club we could go to after they dropped T.J. off. I said it would take a pill that hadn't been invented yet to get me in an after-hours club.

Kelly Sue and I were left alone in the parking lot,

smoking another cigarette, standing by our cars. My Cadillac-Buick, her '92 Accord.

"I enjoyed tonight," she said. "I really did."

"I enjoyed having your voice of sanity along," I said. We were silent for a moment.

Then she said, "You don't want to fuck, do you?"

"No. Do you?"

"No. I'd rather be friends."

"Me too."

"Good. That's settled."

I found myself laughing.

"What?" she said.

"What we just agreed on."

"About fucking?"

"Yeah."

She said, "I just don't like complications."

"Hate complications," I said. "What's your position on guilt?"

"Hate guilt."

"What about obligations?"

"Hate obligations more."

"I wonder if we're missing out on some fucking?"

"There's always that possibility."

"I'm glad we've thrashed this out," I said. "I've had this resurgical vasectomy reversal, I should mention, and . . ."

She blew smoke at me. Women did that, for some reason.

I said, "Kelly Sue, I want to know something. Seriously. You're not glued to Fort Worth, are you? Would you move somewhere if a good opportunity came along?"

"It would depend on where it was," she said. "Like if it was on the planet Earth? Yeah, I'd move."

"That's good to know."

"Why?"

"Well, if we get this team," I said, "I'll have a lot of semi-executive-type jobs to fill. I can think of some you can handle."

"This would be out in West Texas, wouldn't it?"

Smiling faintly, I said, "I'm afraid so, but they do have cable, and quite a bit of fine dining in strip malls."

She looked at me hesitantly, then said, "You're serious about this, aren't you?"

I said, "Absolutely. I like to think I'm a pretty good judge of people. I trust my first impressions. They always seem to be the most accurate. Okay, I've only known you since this afternoon, but I already know you're intelligent. I know you have a sense of humor. I know you've raised a daughter by yourself. I know you're proud of her. You must know about hard work or you couldn't have done a good job. That's not a bad résumé."

"I'm just a bartender." Apologetic expression.

"So?"

"That's mostly all I've ever done," she said. "That doesn't bother you?"

"No," I said, frowning slightly. "That just means you're a business manager, a public relations expert, cop, philosopher, stand-up comic, and, uh, creative bookkeeper."

I could see by her look that she appreciated what I'd said and was flattered by my incredible insight into her true character and the art of bartending.

"I've changed my mind," she said. "Let's fuck."

It was the way my wife would have said it. Letting me know she was joking. Strangely enough, all afternoon and evening Kelly Sue had been reminding me of Barbara Jane in small ways.

Her wit, her perceptions, her husky laughter at the right time, at the right things. The calm, graceful, fluid way she moved around.

And yet she and Barbara Jane were from completely different backgrounds. I chalked it up to the fact that life was a funny old dog, as somebody once said.

I gave Kelly Sue a friendly hug and opened her car door for her. She gave me a friendly kiss on the cheek, and said, "If you get a chance, stop by the joint again before you leave town. I'll buy you a Frito."

I said I would if I got my health back.

I limped into my suite at the hotel with a minimum of difficulty, drank a small bottle of Evian from the mini-bar, threw away the mint on my pillow, and quickly read myself to sleep with Shake Tiller's book, *The Average Man's History of the World*.

From the book I immediately learned that Creation was probably the oldest thing in the world. Then I learned how Creation came about. There was this Presence—you know, like up there? And one day this Presence came in contact with an early form of methamphetamine, and . . .

Part Two

Downtown Dumbass City

10

Tommy Earl claimed the best way to handle a hangover was with food. Good food, preferably, which differed from comedy food—your Thanksgiving grouper, your veggie burger. Those kind of laugh riots.

First, Tommy Earl said, you hit the hangover with scrambled eggs and a double order of Owens pattie sausage. Follow that up with biscuits and cream gravy. Three biscuits, large bowl. Keep the sorry son of a bitch—the hangover—off balance with an enchilada omelette, side of corned beef hash, a waffle with maple syrup. Drink several glasses of milk—real milk, not that 1 percent piss for heart patients. Lay in as many cups of coffee as you can hold. Throw about four Advil at it for good measure. Then while it deals with all that, let it worry about the possibility of getting hit with more biscuits and gravy while you smoke half a pack of Winstons.

"Teach the motherfucker a lesson he won't forget today," Tommy Earl said through his pain. This was during the first hour of our breakfast.

Now he was about halfway through punishing the hangover with all that as we sat in a booth in Ora Mae's Bite Shop on Magnolia.

I had already treated my own hangover to a chocolate milk shake. Next came some Marlboros with coffee. Then three soft-boiled eggs stirred up in a cup with bits of crisp bacon and pinches of toast. My own remedy for hangovers and bad colds, a dish I usually prepared for myself when I was home alone and nobody was around to get sick looking at it.

But I'd gone ahead and concocted the dish at Ora Mae's anyhow, figuring I couldn't make too many of the customers ill. All I could see from our booth by the front windows were two bidness women with rotund hair, three bloodstained hospital workers, a table of laborers in bandanna headwear and construction boots, and two Shriners in business suits having the big breakfast before going off to pull other Shriners out of ditches.

I was wearing a dark blue work shirt with the tail out, a pair of khakis, a black baseball cap. The gold lettering on the cap said OFFICE BITCH. This was the title of a Shake Tiller film that certain short-sighted critics had accused of ridiculing the feminist movement.

Tommy Earl hadn't managed to shave, but he was dressed rich-guy casual again. He wore a houndstooth cashmere sport coat over a custom-made soft white cotton shirt and light blue jeans that were pressed and creased.

The immortal Ora Mae's was due south of downtown but within sight of downtown's glass towers. It was on one of the four or five main thoroughfares crossing through what was once an area of fine old homes, shady streets, manicured lawns, prominent churches, good public schools, a handful of movie theaters, and some good restaurants. All of that was generally known as the South Side, and Barbara Jane and Shake Tiller and me had all grown up in various parts of it.

But all that was a long time ago. Now Ora Mae's was squarely in the middle of what people referred to as the

Medical District. It was called this because of the three large hospitals nearby that seemed to grow larger by the day, even as you gazed at them, and were flanked on all sides by doctors' office buildings and clinics. Unfortunately, the Medical District was also surrounded by an ample portion of sad decay—sad to anybody who came from the old South Side. It was particularly sad to me because I remembered a time when little kids could play touch football in somebody's front yard without having to sidestep a rusted appliance, or watch one of their teammates get mugged or kidnapped, or see the ball explode in the air from the rapid fire of a handgun.

Small wonder Tommy Earl was getting rich in bulletproof glass, but a man wasn't supposed to complain about the decay of fine old neighborhoods in America. It was called social progress.

While Tommy Earl rested and read the sports section of the *Light & Shopper* between courses, I did two of my favorite things, smoked and drank coffee. I also kept thinking about the old hometown.

There were now a couple of other "districts" to go along with the Medical District. There was the Art District and there was the Historical District. I thought about how these "districts" used to be called the West Side and the North Side.

The Art District was just west of downtown and obviously derived its name from the fact that four very fine museums had sprouted up near Casa Mañana, the theater-in-the-round. The theater had been there awhile. It was sort of a mini-dome where you could go see road company productions of Broadway musicals you had forgotten existed.

I wondered if the people who called it the Art District ever thought about the fact that it was across the street from Farrington Field, the city's high school football

stadium, where Shake Tiller and I once brought pride
and glory to Paschal High. It was also across the street
from the Will Rogers Coliseum, where the country's
oldest indoor rodeo was held every year. Maybe not.
Maybe most people in Fort Worth just thought of football and rodeo as part of the art world.

As for the Historical District, it was still important to
scholars of John Wayne–type things. The north side was
why Fort Worth had once been nicknamed Cowtown. It
was where the old Chisholm Trail made a rest stop,
where the livestock exchange, the stockyards, and the
Swift and Armour meat-packing plants once flourished.

Growing up, a lot of us mainly knew it as a rowdy
section of town where you could get your butt kicked by
a real cowboy if you weren't careful. Over the years,
however, it had gradually been painted up, scrubbed
down, dance-halled, electric-guitared, Western-bouti-
qued, and semi-quiched into a tourist attraction. There
were still some real cowboys around, but mostly you
could go out there today and get your butt kicked by a
piece of turquoise and silver jewelry.

Then I was remembering how some neighborhoods
were still identified in the same old way—a good thing
because most people didn't know where a particular
street was unless they lived on it or drove to work on it.

Over There by Forest Park. That was still a neighborhood to a lot of people, especially me, having been
the one where I more or less grew up. Up There in Park
Hill. That's the neighborhood that gave us Barbara Jane
Bookman. Still a very good neighborhood. Hadn't "lost
its tone," which was something a real estate lady said to
Barbara Jane and me one day when we were looking for
a Manhattan apartment to buy. The phrase had caused
Barb to laugh convulsively. Out There Around TCU.
Another perfectly acceptable neighborhood, even
though T. J. Lambert lived there. Down There by Colo-

nial. This was still a fine neighborhood with a country club in the middle of it, although some people thought of it as an annual golf tournament with a neighborhood around it. It was Shake Tiller country. He'd had the good fortune of growing up in the one-story red-brick house on Stadium Drive, in that crucial spot where you could say you lived Down There by Colonial, Out There Around TCU, or Up There in Park Hill. All three were accurate.

There were other neighborhoods in town that could be pinned down in conversation. People said things like Down There in Tanglewood . . . Over There by River Crest . . . I Guess You'd Still Call It Arlington Heights . . . and the ever-popular It'll Always Be Poly to Me.

To be current was another matter. Considering how fast the suburbs were growing, spreading, sprawling, and considering how fast some of the older neighborhoods were rotting, people had learned to direct you to some of the newer areas in such descriptive terms as Halfway to Dallas for Christ's Sake, Damn Near in Weatherford, and Way the Fuck Out on Hulen.

I was still dwelling on all this when Tommy Earl put in an order for creamed chip beef on toast.

Then I could have sworn he uttered the word *quarry*.

"That'll be my lure," he said. "Championship golf course built around a quarry. Deep mother. The signature hole will be a par five that doglegs halfway around the quarry. Maybe I'll put the whole goddamn back nine around the quarry."

"A quarry?" I said.

"It's what you've got to have now," he said." All you got to do is look at the ads in the golf magazines."

"Are you talking about a *rock* quarry?"

I wanted to make sure of the word.

He said, "Rock, dolomite, gravel, linoleum—don't make a fuck. If you don't have a golf course built around a quarry, you ain't for shit. Come to Quarry Ranch Country Club and Residential Community. Garden homes on the rim, one ninety and up. Live the dream life at St. Quarry Muirfield Golf and Racquet Club. Town houses, patio homes, condos. Quarry Oaks, Quarry Palms, Quarry Village. All I want's in on it."

He thought a minute.

"Get one of them famous architects to design the Tumbleweed course around it. Hire a cheap fucker to design the Armadillo course."

"Tumbleweed?" I said with a look. "Armadillo?"

"I need thirty-six holes," Tommy Earl said. "It'll be a much better lure. Tumbleweed will be the championship course, the one on the quarry. Armadillo will be the easy course. Old fuckers' course. I don't think small. You ever known me to think small?"

"Can't say that I have, but . . . Tumbleweed and Armadillo?"

"Indigenous to the area," he said. "Think about it. We're out in West Texas. Tumbleweed? Armadillos? My plan is to call the whole community Tumbleweed Pointe. Put an *e* on the end of it."

"Put an *e* on the end of what?"

"Put an *e* on the end of *Point*."

In a serious voice, I said, "You intend to put an *e* on the end of a word in West Texas?"

"Damn right. You want to know why?"

"It might cure this fever you've given me."

"Because that *e* ups the price of a spec home by twenty thousand dollars. That's all the *e* does."

Tommy Earl shook his head sadly.

"You really don't know anything about the real estate business, do you?" he said. "Tumbleweed Pointe ain't gonna *be* for people in West Texas. Tumbleweed Pointe is for the miserable bastards in Minnesota, Ohio, Michigan—all that shit up there on the top of your map. People wore out from diggin' theirselves out of ten feet of snow every day, all winter long, every winter. People about to retire from their crummy jobs. Making big ones and little ones for twenty-five years. Whatever the fuck they did. People who can't wait to join a private club, own their own golf cart, live inside a security gate where the nigs can't get at 'em, not that nigs bother me any."

"Don't people go to California and Florida to do that?"

"Not anymore."

"You've researched it, have you?"

"I have, but I didn't need to. I been there. It's all over for California. Way too many rats in the cage out there. And Florida, Christ."

"Florida's worse? Why? Hurricanes?"

"That's part of it."

"Too many hurricanes named Nigel?"

"The biggest problem Florida's got is their hurricanes don't kill their mosquitoes. Sons of bitches not only don't die, they multiply and come back with bigger dicks than most guys I know."

"But all that's good for you, right? Good for Tumbleweed Pointe?"

"Bet your ass. Let me drop a statistic on you, Claude. One million people retire every year in the midwest alone. All I want is one percent of those upstanding citizens. A thousand home buyers a year at Tumbleweed Pointe. Scooping up my condos from one twenty-five to two-fifty. Grabbing my garden homes from two-sixty to three-forty. Hell of a lot of 'em building mansions for seven-fifty and up."

"You don't think any of those mansion owners will mind that West Texas doesn't have an ocean?"

"Why should they?" he said. "They'll have *your* National Football League heroes and *my* championship golf course. In an elegant neighborhood. Little bit of heaven's all it is. I figure I'll need about eight thousand acres to do it right. Five hundred acres for the two golf courses, plus the clubhouse, racquet club, health spa, and shopping village. The rest for residential. I'll want it in the same general vicinity of your stadium, naturally. Tell Big Ed I'm prepared to offer him two hundred dollars an acre."

I said, "You want eight thousand acres of Big Ed's land, near the stadium complex, for two hundred dollars an acre?"

"That's a good price for raw land. For no water, sewer, streets, sidewalks, or utilities. Damn good price."

"I'll mention it to him but I believe I know what he'll say."

"What's that?"

"I think he'll say I can tell Tommy Earl to go shit in his quarry."

"You know, Claude," Tommy Earl said, "your father-in-law needs to keep an open mind about things. Here I am with a great concept, but it's the same old story. I can't get the man with the muscle to go for it till I give him a blowjob."

I said I was sure Big Ed felt the property was worth at least three thousand dollars an acre. Maybe five thousand after the stadium went up.

"See?" Tommy Earl sighed. "See what I mean? There I am. Right there in Downtown Blowjob City."

As Tommy Earl spoke, the order of creamed chip beef and toast was plunked down on our table by a moody, gum-chewing teenage waitress. Her name tag read *Nelda*, and her face hinted that she hadn't left any lipstick or other makeup in any Wal-Mart or Eckerd's on one entire side of town.

Before she turned away, I politely asked her to bring us a clean ashtray and fresh cups of coffee.

"God," she muttered, looking irritated.

"Wait a minute, young lady," I snapped. "Is that going to be too much trouble for you?"

"*No*," she said defiantly.

"If it is," I said, "I'm sure we can find you some help around here."

Snatching up the ashtray and walking off, she said, "I just don't see why everybody always *wants* somethin'."

I couldn't help laughing.

Tommy Earl looked at me closely. "The thing Big Ed don't understand is how I'm the one who's gonna have to deal with all the bureaucrats. All those gubmint buttwipes you can't kill but have to get along with."

"Big Ed understands," I said. "That's why he bought up all the land. All he has to do is sell the dirt. Developers like you have to worry about the bureaucrats. To tell you the truth, I can't imagine Big Ed talking to a bureaucrat for more than two minutes without trying to rip his throat out."

"That's what I mean," Tommy Earl said. "Big Ed don't know what it's like in the trenches. He's a boardroom fighter. Money-whip your ass. He knows how to bring a CEO to his knees, make him piss blood for a week. He don't ever have to jack with the nuts and bolts. He leaves all the stress to poor bastards like me."

"T.E.," I said calmly, which was how I usually addressed him, "pardon me for bringing this up, but if there's anything you are *not* noted for, it's your stress."

He went on, "Claude, there's not a son of a bitch in the world that'll give Ed Bookman three thousand dollars an acre, or even two thousand dollars an acre for that land. But you take this proposition to him. You tell him I'll give him one thousand an acre for a parcel of eight thousand acres. In case you ain't good at arithmetic, that's eight million dollars. Now, you tell your father-in-law I'll do that. I'll pay him the thousand for the eight thousand acres—if he'll handle my financing."

With raised eyebrows, I said, "You want *him* to give *you* the money to buy *his* land?"

"It won't be a gift, Claude. It'll be a loan. Any developer who comes in there is gonna have to borrow the money somewhere. I'm just asking Big Ed to be my banker. I'll even make him a partner."

"Big Ed doesn't do partners. That's why he's Big Ed."

"I'll give him control. Fifty-one percent."

"You'd have to start with that."

"I'd want to retain artistic control, though. Like any well-planned community with security gates, there'll have to be an architectural review board. I'd want to be the head of it. I don't want some fag architect coming in there and designing houses that look like they're under construction except they're already finished."

"If it's a loan for eight million dollars, what can you possibly put up for collateral, if I may be bold enough to ask?"

"All that lice that likes to rob and kill people."

"The teenage gangs?" I laughed.

"You don't call that collateral?" He looked insulted. "My secret-formula protective glass ain't collateral?"

"You said the gangs."

"They go together. My product's valuable, but so's the scum. Your amoral scum is multiplying day by day, right out there on the street. That's pure gold, all that lice."

"Most people aren't as happy about that element of society as you are," I said. "But I guess Gang Resistant Systems could be part of your collateral."

"What do you mean *part*, Claude?"

I reminded him that I was aware of his association with Ody Bradshaw, his participation in He's Not Here, Tuxedo Junction. I said I was just curious if he owned anything else of value, in case Big Ed asked me about it.

Tommy Earl said he considered his teenage slime to be enough collateral to buy the Taj Mahal, and he'd wager that most banks would agree with him, but as for other assets, he confessed that he and Ody did own some other property.

They owned a three-story red-brick building over on Rosedale they were leasing to the Zanzibar Charismatic Evangelical Baptist Prayer Church & Late Night Supper Club.

They owned a large space in a shopping strip on Bluebonnet Circle that had failed as Bert and Ida's Discount Golf but had now found success as the Gay Hindus Temple.

And they owned a warehouse on Vickery that was presently occupied by the Harley-Davidson Buttfucking Spookhunter Avengers, or so the name of the patriotic organization read on their black leather jackets.

I said I thought I could speak for Big Ed in stating that their present real estate holdings wouldn't be of too much interest to him.

Nelda arrived back at our booth with two mugs of coffee, a clean ashtray, and almost the same thing as a smile.

She said the man behind the register—the daytime manager, Cliff—he wanted to know if I had an autographed picture I could give Ora Mae's to hang on the wall. Cliff promised he would hang it in a prominent place.

I informed Nelda that I didn't walk around with eight-by-tens of myself, but I would scare something up and mail it to the establishment.

"Who are you?" she said, looking mildly troubled.

Laughing, Tommy Earl said, "It's not who he is, it's who he was."

"I used to play football," I said to Nelda. "After that, I was on TV for a while."

"On TV, really?" she said. "Do you know Lance Culver?"

"No." I smiled.

"I bet you know Kristi Savage."

"Afraid not."

"Melody Sash?"

"Nope."

"Richie Grace?"

"Sorry. I don't know that I've even heard of Richie Grace."

"You're joking, right?"

"No."

Nelda looked disappointed, almost distrustful as she left.

I mentioned to Tommy Earl that you went through many stages in life on your way to becoming a mature person.

One of the first stages was when you realized there were current pop music stars—gigantic ones—you'd never heard of. Not too long afterward you arrived at another stage. That was when you discovered you'd never even heard of most of the top-rated TV shows, much less any of the actors who starred in them.

"How many stages are there?"

"There's at least one more. I know I'm getting close to it," I said. "It's the stage where you've never heard of several major movie stars, or any of their hit movies."

"That must make it hard to be around your wife and old Shake Tiller when they're in a show biz mode."

"I lie a lot."

Tommy Earl said, "I've seen all those movies Shake's made. Hand jobs."

His critical review came with a gesture.

"That's what Shake calls them," I said, "but they've somehow made money, so now he's in a position to try to make good movies. I hope this is a good one he's making now, seeing as how my wife's in it."

Tommy Earl said he thought a good movie could be made about a poor bastard like himself. A man who had to deal with gubmint bureaucrats.

"*Unelected Assholes* would be my title for it," he said. "You know how you read in the paper once a year about some lunatic who shoots a bunch of innocent people? Goes in a Picadilly Cafeteria and sprays everybody with an automatic weapon? I figure bureaucrats drove him to it. He walked in with his automatic weapon and said to the manager, 'Is this where they eat?' Then he opened fire—*bam, bam, bam.*"

"Interesting theory."

He said, "Let's say I want to do something simple, Claude. Like, uh, build a car wash out there in that town where your football team's gonna be. Sounds easy, don't it? All I have to do is get the plans drawn up and build it, right? That what you think?"

"I have a feeling you're going to tell me there's more to it."

Heavy on the sarcasm, Tommy Earl said, "Oh, just a tiny bit."

Tommy Earl leaned back in the booth, lit a Winston, organized his thoughts for a second, and said, "First I have to go to the building department, which is where a shithead who's never built anything makes sure I can meet all his building codes. Then I have to go to the zoning department. That's where an asshole who's never built anything wants to know all about my parking facilities, my setback, my site plan, my neighbors, and my long-term land use."

"Sounds like fun," I said.

"The fun hasn't even started," he said. "Now I go to the landscaping department to see a prick who's never built anything, let him instruct me on how to comply with all his guidelines on how to keep the neighborhood beautiful. After that, I'll go to the county engineer's office, where I'll wait in line—like you do in all the other departments—before I see a fuckface who's never built anything . . . listen to him tell me how to build a car wash that won't cause any traffic problems. You listening, Claude? I been through this.

"Then I have to go see a fire marshal who's never built anything, or ever put out a fuckin' fire. This turdhat will give me a list of twenty things I'll need to do to keep the whole block from burning down. Somewhere in the middle of all this, I'll find myself smiling at a dicknose in the health department. I'll sit there and smile while he reads me off a list of regulations I'll have to follow to keep from spreading disease among all his Siamese cats and geraniums."

"I guess you're pretty tired by now," I said, lifting my coffee mug.

"A lesser man would be," he said. "But I've been pacing myself because I know when I get all that done, I've got to get me a water plant permit from the Department of Natural Resources, a sewage plant permit, a rest room operating permit, a drainage permit from the Department of Transportation, a driveway permit, an excess-water-runoff permit, and a 'strong storm' protection permit from the Corps of Engineers. Did you hear me? I said a strong storm protection permit. That's opposed to a chickenshit storm, right?"

"You're embellishing this a little, tell the truth."

"Yeah, I wish," he said. "I haven't even come to the hard part yet. I haven't mentioned the dedicated people at the Department of Environmental Resources. They're real good at thinking up three or four hundred varieties of golden-cheeked warblers I can't fuck with."

"You're a warbler killer, that's why."

"Oh, hell, yeah. I'm a warbler killer and a red-cockaded-woodpecker murderer. The fact that nobody's seen one in a thousand years don't make a shit. Besides the golden-cheeked warbler and the red-cockaded woodpecker, they like to sit around and think up three hundred species of plants I might poison. But what they're best at is coming up with a Loch Ness Monster, or a close friend of a Loch Ness Monster. Make sure I won't bring *them* any serious harm."

"The Loch Ness Monster?" I laughed. "The Loch Ness Monster's in Scotland."

"The Loch Ness Monster's not in Scotland if an environmental shitass says he's seen him hanging around my car wash!"

"The Loch Ness Monster is mythological," I said, still laughing.

"He is, huh? Tell that to an environmentalist. You know what your environmentalist says to that? He says bring him the scientific proof in writing and be sure to have it notarized."

I said, "How the hell does anything ever get done?"

It was a serious question. I doubted Tommy Earl had been exaggerating all that much.

He answered, "If you're a warbler killer like me? You have to hire you an established building contractor. The building contractor has to put up with the same crap, but he knows the short cuts. Who to go down on, who to pay off, how many retarded cousins of bureaucrats and regulators need jobs."

The waitress appeared, placing the check on the table.

"Was anything all right?" she asked.

"Was *anything* all right?" I laughed. "Yeah, anything was fine."

I insisted on paying the check for Tommy Earl's banquet and my breakfast. I tipped Nelda generously, more than she would make from ten Shriners the rest of the day. We walked outside and stood for a moment.

"Off to see Tracy?" I said, only half-joking.

"Naw," he shook his head. "I need a day off. She's got the equipment, though, don't she?"

"I hope you're not getting in too deep," I said. "Seems to me there's a lot of that out there. Turn over a rock, six more shapelies crawl out—all of 'em with a rack. They pretend they're only interested in having some fun, a little sex, right? But give 'em enough time, don't they want the whole package—life insurance, charge cards, medical and dental, pension plan?"

"This one ain't no cuntski, Claude."

"Cuntski," I murmured, smiling. I hadn't heard the word since the last time a Pittsburgh Steeler spoke to me.

"Do me a favor, Claude. Don't present my proposal to Big Ed on the phone, okay? Wait till you get him in person."

"Okay."

"When will that be?"

Good question, I thought. The Bookman Oil & Gas building out on the west side of Fort Worth was still headquarters for Big Ed's bidness, but you might also find him in Manhattan in the huge, ornate office-apartment he kept on a top floor of the Plaza Hotel, which Barbara Jane called the *Titanic*—"Daddy's on the *Titanic* this week." Or you might find Big Ed taking a nap on his G-5 while it's zinging him off to play a new golf course or kick somebody's butt in another board-room.

"I don't know where he is right now," I said. "I think he was over in Bali the other day, buying a mountain from pygmies. I'm sure I'll see him before the owners meet in LA to vote on expansion."

Tommy Earl said, "You and me will be talking by phone and fax, Claude. I'll see you back down here after you get your football team."

"I'm awed by your confidence."

He handed me a folded-up piece of eight-by-ten paper. "You'll enjoy this. Copy of something Tracy gave me. One of those things you find on the Net, gets passed around to appreciative people. Tracy doctored it up a little."

We exchanged outdated high-fives and walked away in different directions to our cars.

I sat behind the wheel of my Cadillac-Buick, lit a Marlboro, and read the document.

TOMMY EARL'S PERFECT DAY

6:45 AM–7	Alarm. Cigarette. Piss.
7:00–7:45	Sneak blowjob from overnight girlfriend of wife.
7:46–8:15	Massive dump while enjoying newspaper story of two dozen bureaucrats burning to death in fire.
8:16–8:30	Limo arrives. Bloody Marys on hand.
8:30–9:30	Colonial Country Club breakfast. Biscuits, gravy.
9:31–11:30	Par front nine at Colonial, win $500 from assholes.
11:31–12:30	Lunch. Steak sandwich, three Bud Lites.
12:31–12:45	Blowjob from former Miss Texas contestant.
12:46–2:30	Par back nine at Colonial, win another $500 from assholes.

2:31–3:30	Limo to Eagle Mountain Lake. Sip martini, eat Miss Teen Texas during drive.
3:31–6:30	Afternoon on houseboat with six Miss Universe contestants. Girls invent sex games, share drugs, talk dirty. Nap.
6:31–7:30	Limo to expensive Fort Worth hotel. Call wife, tell her you have arrived safely in Seattle. Be home late tomorrow.
7:31–8	Shit, shower, shave.
8:00–10:30	Watch live CNN coverage of mad gunman killing 1,000 bureaucrats in Washington, D.C., office building. Celebration dinner at fancy restaurant. Smoke joint in bathroom. Chateau Laffite Rothschild. Dozen oysters. Veal chop, pasta, green salad. Dessert. Cognac. Cappuccino.
10:31–11:30	Group sex with three recent Miss America contestants of mixed racial origin.
11:31–12:00	Full-body massage. Girls quietly get dressed, call a cab, leave.
Midnight	Sleep.

I caught myself smiling. That Tracy was a card. But I wadded up the paper and threw it out the window. No man needed to be caught with a document like that in his possession.

11

There were a couple of hours to kill before I went to meet the coach, so I decided to cruise down a few memory lanes. Try to recall what used to be on this corner or that one before they put up a Whataburger. Cruising down memory lanes can be a disappointing thing to do unless you're prepared for some of the old houses and streets to look considerably smaller than you remembered them—who lived here now, a bunch of midgets?

As was my custom, I drove by some landmarks that touched my heart more than others.

My old neighborhood, for instance. At one time I could have named the people who lived in every house on our street. I could still remember the standouts. Old Lady Thompson, who chased you with a rake if you ran through her flower beds. Old Lady Coppage, who had twenty-two cats and fourteen dogs. Poor Mrs. Dudley, who was always bad sick. Crazy Miz Reynolds, who wore an aviator's cap and riding boots and had a pilot's license. Marydell Hunter, who had the first serious rack I ever admired. And Nasty Jack Patterson. If you gave Nasty Jack a quarter, he'd swallow a goldfish and make it come out of his nose, alive.

For a long moment I stopped in front of the little stucco house on Warner Road. That's where Uncle Kenneth had raised me from the age of six. Which was after Steve and Dalene Puckett went off in opposite directions one day, him to Fresno, her to Mobile. Parents of the Year, Uncle Kenneth called them.

The magnolia tree was still in the front yard. I could still see the limb I used to climb and sit on while Uncle Kenneth would have an intellectual debate with one of his wives, who were plentiful.

He had his best debates with Connie the manicurist. Connie of the tall hair and clanging jewelry and hefty rack.

"You lazy jackoff," Connie would say to my uncle during one of their intellectual debates. "This town don't have enough florists to beautify a sick load of shit like you."

Chewing on a toothpick, Uncle Kenneth would reply, "Yeah, well, I ain't sayin' I married a dog but I *do* notice you like to stick your head out the window when we go for a drive."

"Just fuck you and all them golf clubs in the trunk of your car," Connie would snarl. "And fuck ever' golf club in ever' fuckin' closet of this unflushed toilet you call a home, you fuckin' wad of phlegm."

"Connie, put a headcover on it," Uncle Kenneth would calmly say, popping open a beer and tumbling onto the couch in front of the TV.

Then Connie would be gone and here would come Dorothy, Norma, Patsy, and Melba, although I couldn't remember in what order exactly.

I thought about the day I asked Uncle Kenneth how I got the name Billy Clyde. It wasn't my daddy's name, his brother. Did I have a granddaddy named Billy Clyde? A great-granddad?

Uncle Kenneth was practicing chip shots in the yard. He said, "Naw, it was your daddy's idea."

"What gave him the idea?" I asked.

My uncle said, "Your daddy didn't give it a lot of thought, if you want the truth. I think he said something to Dalene, like, 'Why don't we call him Billy, Johnny, Joe, Bobby . . . one of those deals?' That's where the Billy came from. Steve was fairly casual about most things. Some things were more important to him than other things. Naming a kid wasn't as important to him as driving a convertible with the top down."

My mother had added the Clyde part, I learned.

Uncle Kenneth explained it like this: "She was named Dalene after her own daddy, Dale Norwood. Her mother's name was Clydene. Clydene Dixon. Dalene wanted to name you after her mother, but she couldn't name you Clydene, a woman's name. Not unless she wanted to raise a kid who'd shoot and kill her as soon as he learned how to use a gun, so she went with Clyde. It was a compromise deal."

Parked in front of the house, I wondered who lived next door now.

Clarence and Viola were history. Clarence sold furniture and was real tired all the time. Viola didn't do anything but stay home and drink gin, smoke Camels, and keep up with soap operas, and I never saw her wear anything but a pink housecoat.

They'd have us over for dinner sometimes, and Viola would always remind Clarence to say a blessing before the creamed tuna on toast, like a blessing was the thing people ought to do in front of a little kid. Clarence would nod, slump over at the table, close his eyes, we'd all join hands, and in a low voice Clarence would say, "What a time . . . what a beach . . . there's your dog. Thankee, Lord."

The most interesting feature of their house was the

bathroom. It had side-by-side commodes. They'd had it built that way, I heard. I hadn't seen a bathroom like it since—and didn't expect to. Even as a little kid, I was intrigued by some of the audio possibilities it presented if it was in full use. Uncle Kenneth once said he imagined the only time Clarence and Viola ever got excited about anything was when they both had diarrhea.

Uncle Kenneth's house wasn't all that far from dear old Paschal High. As was the case with most public schools in America, the alma mater of Barbara Jane Bookman, Shake Tiller, and my ownself had gradually begun to look like something other than what it had been. What it had been was a low-slung Art Deco brick building with pretty lawns and trees and playgrounds all around. It seemed real nice and modern in our day.

I didn't know it was Art Deco then, of course. If somebody had said anything about Art Deco when I was in high school, I'd have thought they were talking about a saxophone player.

Now the low-slung Art Deco brick building was covered over by some kind of white facade, and what appeared to be storage bins or warehouses were protruding on all sides. Today a debate raged among old grads as to whether the school looked more like an outlet mall or a correctional facility surrounded by used-car lots.

From everything I'd heard, I knew high school discipline wasn't what it used to be. For instance, if Coach E. A. ("Honk") Wooten had ever caught me or Shake Tiller or any of our teammates eating a piece of pie à la mode in Herb's Cafe, it would have been twenty hard licks on the gym-shorts ass with his long wooden paddle, plus thirty laps around the football field, plus fifty push-ups on our fingertips, plus a humiliating lecture that would make you think you'd pushed an elderly lady into the path of a city bus.

We weren't all that happy about it at the time, but we realized in later years that this was the kind of discipline that won football games. There were even those of us today who believed it actually made better citizens of us.

Jesus, pie à la mode a crime. Fit a rap lyric around that, Demonce.

One thing I wanted to do was make sure the elegant bluff-top neighborhood where Barbara Jane had grown up hadn't lost its tone yet, so I took a spin through Park Hill, hung around awhile, and flooded my mind with more memories.

From birth through high school, Barbara Jane lived in the big stone house on Winton Terrace. It was a house built out of limestone blocks and cream-colored brick. It had terraces, balconies, patios, a gorgeous lawn, huge oaks, and a great view of the downtown skyline from the front yard.

During our sophomore year of college Big Ed decided to have the whole mile and a half of Winton Terrace repaved, recurbed, and even planted with shrubs and flowers in the vacant areas of the winding road where no homes existed. Make things look better all around.

He paid for the improvements himself. Consequently he thought the name of the street ought to be changed to Bookman Circle. Big Ed felt sure the other Park Hill residents would want to show their appreciation in this way, even if they hadn't thought up the idea themselves.

Big Ed lobbied for the name change with the other homeowners, largely by saying, "Who the hell was Winton anyhow, and what did he ever do for you?" The vote was unanimous against changing the name of the street, as most of us predicted. We figured Big Ed was too rich and powerful to be all that loved and respected by his neighbors, or most anyone else outside his family and close friends.

What did surprise us was how Big Ed took the defeat. He didn't explode with anger, cuss Democrats for thirty minutes, as if a Democrat lived in Park Hill, or have somebody's bank note called in.

He just walked around with a tight-lipped expression for a few days, and finally said one night at the dinner table, "There are times when democracy has its goddamn drawbacks."

Not that Big Ed didn't have his revenge, or what he thought of as revenge. Six months later he moved. He moved the family into the even larger Tudor Revival house they now owned, the orange-brick villa that stood on six acres of lawn and gardens across the street from River Crest Country Club and had a sweeping view of the city's oldest golf course.

The house on Winton Terrace seemed like a castle to me back then, and it seemed like the perfect house for Barbara Jane's parents, Big Ed looking like John Connally's twin brother, Big Barb always looking like the Duchess of Kent talking to a Wimbledon ballboy. Most people thought they still looked like that.

As I sat in front of the old Bookman residence in Park Hill, I thought of how the place wouldn't appeal at all to the brainless little wife of some spoiled, pampered, overpaid professional athlete today.

I could hear the brainless little wife's reaction to the house. "Where's the cooking island, hello? I don't see a sauna. My God, no exercise room, no media room, no game room, no wine cellar! Where are the twin walk-in freezers? Where is the six-car garage? Only twelve thousand square feet and no marina? How *dare* the real estate agent show us this! We can't possibly live here, Bubba Jack Jimmy Joe."

But I didn't like to think about the obscene money

being thrown at sports today by the executive morons who ran network TV. All it had done was turn most professional athletes into rude assholes.

And yet here I was, hoping to acquire an expansion team so I could throw obscene amounts of money at athletes myself. That was assuming I'd know how to put together an organization and have the patience to deal with the precious darlings. The steroid studs who'd block and tackle for us, and the "skilled positions" people who'd throw and catch and run with the football for us—if it wasn't too inconvenient for them to stop talking to their lawyers and agents long enough to fucking do it.

12

You had to hand it to good old American know-how, I thought. There I stood on a bluff in Fort Worth, Texas, holding something to my ear the size of a pocket calculator, and I could clearly hear the person I was talking to in Switzerland.

The person I wanted to talk to was my wife. Tell her I loved her. Tell her I missed her. Tell her I'd see her soon. Tell her I was leaning on my car and having a cigarette across the street from where she used to live. Tell her I wouldn't be surprised to see her folks come out the door and holler at Shake and me to stop throwing the football so close to their windows.

But Barbara Jane didn't answer in her suite at the Beau-Rivage in Lausanne. I was talking to Adelle in the production office.

Shake had taken over most of the Beau-Rivage for the film company. It was the most convenient place to be, he said. Translated, this meant the hotel had given him its biggest and best suite.

In case you hadn't been to Lausanne lately, the Beau-Rivage was still on the lake, still offered all the charm you wanted in the way of marble floors, tall carved ceilings, and big oil portraits of people in thick layers of clothing, and it was still within walking distance of Chateau d'Ouchy, the best restaurant in town, not that there was a bad *pomme frite* in the whole country.

Adelle reminded me that it was six in the evening there. Barbara Jane and Shake and some others had already gone to Chateau d'Ouchy for drinks and dinner.

There is never a good time to call anybody in Europe, as you may know. When you're at breakfast, they've gone to lunch. When it's after lunch for you, they've gone to dinner. When you come home from dinner, they're asleep, and when you come home from a night on the town, they've finished breakfast and gone to work.

Adelle did have some news to report. The title of the film had been changed again.

Shake had originally sold a novel he wrote called *The Past* to a thin young man in Hollywood named Ronnie Detweiler, age thirty-two, who ran Osaka Pictures. Despite his youth, Ronnie Detweiler was known as a good deal maker in the industry, although some people were distracted by his looks. A gleaming diamond earring decorated his left ear and a large emerald earring decorated his right ear, his fingernails were painted green, and he usually wore a Phantom of the Opera mask when he walked around his office during story conferences.

That deal was made five years ago.

Shake wrote the first six drafts and three polishes of the script for *The Past*. There was a time when Jodie Foster was set to star in it with Robert Redford. This got Shake excited enough to buy a tan Jaguar and have his house in the Hollywood hills redecorated and a swimming pool installed.

Then two years passed. And it was during this period that Redford had the script rewritten seven times by his own writers. This resulted in Jodie Foster's part becom-

ing so small she quit the movie, after which Redford quit
the movie, then the director quit the movie, then Ronnie
Detweiler pulled the plug on the project, saying the
whole idea was a piece of shit.

"Piece of shit" had long ago been embraced as a favorite expression of studio executives. They used it to
describe most movies in development, most movies in
production, and any movie that didn't gross more than
$150 million the first weekend after it had been released.

Shake's reaction to the plug being pulled on his film
was not what anyone might have expected.

"This is good," he said. "I've been seriously fucked
over by Hollywood. Now I feel like I'm really a part of
this town."

Another year went by. That was the year Shake was
given the opportunity to make *Mondo Bimbo*, his low-
budget "thrillcom"—Hollywood talk—about a female
cop who worked undercover to trap sex maniacs. The
undercover female cop was played by Sandi Reynolds, a
former Miss Universe contestant from South Carolina
and frequent sleepover guest of Shake Tiller's.

Barbara Jane described *Mondo Bimbo* as an hour and
forty-seven minutes of a former beauty queen trying on
bad clothes.

But *Mondo Bimbo* was successful. It was talked about
all over town, even in a Hollywood hangout called The
Ending Sucks, a restaurant and bar catering to heartbroken writers, old character actors you might recognize
from their spark plug commercials, and aging character
actresses you might recognize from their regularity commercials. It made enough money to attract the attention
of the head of production of Mitsutani Pictures, another
thin young man named Cubby Butler.

It was Cubby Butler who gave Shake the deal to write,
produce, and direct *Office Bitch*, which made even more
money. *Office Bitch* was the movie that really established

Shake in Hollywood despite all the feminist groups that boycotted it.

So after those successes, it didn't require much of a sell for Shake to convince Cubby Butler to let him revive *The Past* as a film project. The young mogul did so gladly, saying it could be a very good "dramady."

Cubby Butler was thirty-five years old now and weighed a little over one hundred pounds if you dipped him in linguini and white clam sauce. He'd lied, cheated, and maimed his way up from the mail room to become the president of Irving Manfred & Associates, or IMA, the powerful talent agency. From there, he'd lied, cheated, and maimed his way into the job as the head of Mitsutani Pictures.

Some people were relieved that Cubby Butler only wore one earring, but I didn't think you could overlook the fact that it was long and dangled.

Cubby often referred to himself as a Valley Girl, and when he would say, "Well, *this* Valley Girl believes the fourteen-to-seventeens . . ." you wouldn't hear the rest of it because you'd be too busy keeping your distance.

But he'd given Shake these deals, which went a long way with us—helped convince us he shouldn't be exterminated yet, for the good of mankind—although it was Cubby who changed the title of the movie based on Shake's book from *The Past* to *The Pest*.

Cubby explained that he'd misread the title in the first place, believing it to be *The Pest*, otherwise he wouldn't have bought it. He'd never have bought a work titled *The Past*. Apart from everything else, it sounded *biblical*, for God's sake. Would that skew with boomer babes? Hardly.

Shake thought it over and decided *The Pest* might not be that bad of a title. It was the story of a woman named Enid deciding to change her life, run away from a husband who'd become something of a pest.

Well, that wasn't what I thought it was. I thought it was a movie about Enid, a bright English professor at some small college in Texas, a woman married to Boyd, the college football coach, a guy who was slowly grinding her down by saying things like, "College ain't nothin' but high school with cigarettes and coffee." Enid was my wife's role.

But after everybody was settled in Lausanne and the cameras were rolling, Cubby showed up to announce that he'd thought it over carefully and *The Pest* was a terrible title. It sounded like a Hitchcock thing. And wasn't Hitchcock dead, hello? The film simply had to appeal to women or he might as well throw the money in the old flusheroo. So he was changing the title to something that had come to him while he was driving over to meet David for masa-crusted fried oysters at Alex & Rodney's in Malibu the other night.

The title that had come to him was *Melancholy at Dusk.*

This happened on my first trip over there. I was in Shake's suite in the Beau-Rivage when Cubby announced the title change. He incorporated it with a lecture on making movies and knowing a good title when he saw one.

"You could not use a title like *Casablanca* today," he said. "What is it, a Mexican beer? *Patton?* That's a title? I mean, who *is* he? *Tell* me something, I'm *waiting.* Movies are not real life. Things must, like, *happen* in movies. Nothing ever happens in real life. Somebody bakes a cake, swell. Somebody can't find a parking space. Bor—ing! Okay, cancer, maybe—occasionaly. Just to throw in something, quote, *big.* What I'm saying is, movies are different. Trust me on these things, people."

Shake didn't look too upset and Barb and I knew why. He wanted to make this movie so badly, he didn't care if they called it *Kathie Lee Gifford's Christmas Vacation with the Easter Bunny and Lawrence Welk.*

Then Cubby said, "Of course, we'll have to pay off the title in dialogue. Enid, you could say, 'I always get melancholy at dusk.' That could work in the dinner scene."

Hearing this, Barbara Jane Bookman, the actress, looked as homicidal as Bette Davis ever had. Hume buried his head.

She said, "I can't say 'I always get melancholy at dusk.' I couldn't say 'I always get melancholy at dusk' if I *got* melancholy at dusk."

"Perhaps you can say it with a spin of some sort," Cubby said.

"Oh, okay," Barb said. "Let's try this. 'I'll be a motherfucker if I don't fucking get melancholy at dusk every fucking day, especially in this fucking movie.' Does that work for anybody?"

Cubby sipped from his glass of Perrier before saying, "My title's not a hit. I'm getting this."

He was kind of singing his words.

"It's coming to me here in this room. Is something testy going on here? Are we testo, kiddies?"

He was feeling something in the air, his arms upraised, rolling something invisible around in his fingers.

"I have a serious question," my wife said to him. "Do you have an alternative lifestyle as a human being?"

"Oh, that's *funny.*" Cubby smiled. "That is *very* funny. You *must* say that to someone in the film."

"Why don't you do that, Enid?" I said, addressing my wife by her role name. My only contribution to the confab. Made her laugh.

Now I was hearing on the cell from Adelle in the production office that the title of the movie had been changed again. The new title was *Melancholy Baby.*

No, she wasn't joking.

13

Churning straight at me with a football under his arm was Tonsillitis Johnson. He was trying to bust out of a poster-size picture frame. In a bright purple jersey, silver pants, and dark purple helmet, Tonsillitis had just trampled two Baylor Bears, leaving them for dead. I was in T.J.'s office.

The coach was in a meeting and I was passing time, admiring some of his memorabilia. His faithful secretary, Paula Cox, brought me an ashtray and said she understood addictions—she'd wanted a cigarette every goddamn minute of her life for the past twenty years, ever since she'd quit.

Paula was a no-nonsense woman in her early fifties, a person you'd call lumpy if you didn't admire wide hips. Her square face was holding its own against three layers of makeup. She wore big round tinted eyeglasses and jangled with costume jewelry.

T.J. inherited Paula as his secretary when he took the head coaching job at TCU. He didn't want to keep her at first, but soon found out she was the only person in the athletic department who could fix a paper jam. Then as time wore on she became indispensable to him as an aide who could keep her mouth shut. To most of the studs who played for T.J., past and present, she was affectionately known as "Payday Paula."

T.J.'s office was in O'Brien-Baugh Coliseum. The coliseum hovered above the south end of Carter-Swink Stadium, the bowl that held sixty thousand for football. Inside were all of the offices of the athletic department, and it was where the Frogs annually tried to compete in basketball, usually with a lineup of leapers who could do everything but make layups and shoot free throws.

In T.J.'s purple-carpeted office, I was surrounded by an assortment of scholar-athletes who'd made us all proud, especially T.J.

On the wall next to Tonsillitis in another large frame, the incomparable Artis Toothis tripped nimbly through a field of deceived SMU Mustangs. Artis was Tonsillitis's cohort, the other halfback on T.J.'s first winning teams at TCU, the teams that ended fifteen years of agony, cussing, and furniture-kicking for the bleeding and bruised boosters of the Horned Frogs.

What made those fifteen dismal seasons even more dismal was the fact that they'd followed a blissful period of some forty years in which TCU consistently turned out championship teams, bowl teams, and All-Americans, not the least of which were Marvin ("Shake") Tiller, glue-fingered wide receiver, and B. C. Puckett, line-wrecking halfback, although I'd never been drunk enough to suggest that Shake and I had brought as much gridiron glory to the school as Slingshot Davey O'Brien, Slingin' Sam Baugh, Swanky Jim Swink, Doomsday Bob Lilly, or a batch of others who'd come under the heading of Too Numerous to Mention.

All schools had their down cycles. Even Alabama, even Notre Dame. But TCU's lasted so many seasons, they accumulated bark. Most of the blame for the period of gloom rested with the university's board of trustees.

In their infinite wisdom they kept appointing chancellors who believed theology was more important than the football program, and people of even average intelligence knew such an idea was financially irresponsible.

What made it worse, those same chancellors hired a succession of football coaches who believed reading the Bible to players was more important than giving them cars and spending money. This was more than irresponsible. It was suicidal.

Providing college players money and modes of transportation was still the time-honored method that had proved successful for every university that was interested in having winning football teams. You could take it back way past Notre Dame's Knute Rockne paying his Fighting Italians and Fighting Poles to win one for the Gipper.

As most people connected with TCU were aware, it was Big Ed Bookman who single-handedly brought the program back. Tired of seeing the Frogs lose consistently, and thereby heaping embarrassment on the city of Fort Worth, and tired of waiting for fate to step in and smarten up a chancellor, Big Ed took matters in his own hands.

Big Ed had a degree in geology from TCU and a law degree from the University of Texas, but his allegiance was with the Frogs. He'd played enough defensive end to earn two letters at TCU just after the war, after he'd come back from shooting down Japs in his P-38.

First thing Big Ed did was seize control of the board of trustees. The board mostly consisted of old ranchers and the old widows of old dead ranchers. Big Ed bought his way on to the board with the gift of a dorm, then called a meeting and suggested the board needed a lot fewer cases of Alzheimer's on it. He persuaded all of the current members to resign by saying that if they didn't, he'd buy their ranches and put their scrawny butts in nursing homes. After appointing a group of younger bidnessmen and faculty members to the board, he went out to hire what he called "the right kind of chancellor."

Big Ed's idea of the right kind of chancellor closely paralleled my own, meaning a man who enjoyed a cocktail and a winning football team and left the sermons to the preachers. Such a man was Dr. Glenn Dollarhyde.

Big Ed found Dr. Dollarhyde at Middle Georgia College in Rifletown, Georgia, where he was president. His qualifications were impressive. He was a chain-smoker with a hacking cough, his driver's license had been suspended at the time for a series of DUI's. But more important than anything, to Big Ed at least, were his achievements as head of the institution. It was no small thing that during Dr. Dollarhyde's ten years as president, the Middle Georgia Fightin' Rednecks won eight national football championships in the small-college division.

"The man's a winner," Big Ed said.

Dr. Dollarhyde benefitted from excellent timing after he arrived in Fort Worth. It was in his first month as chancellor that TCU found itself needing a new football coach. A headline in the *Light & Shopper* said it all:

COACH STUBBY BRISCO KILLED IN PLANE CRASH.

Stubby Brisco was one of those TCU coaches who led the Frogs down a trail of 1–10 seasons. He was killed in a private plane of Fat Jack Simms, a car dealer and Frog booster, while they were on a recruiting trip in Alaska. What kind of athletes they'd hoped to recruit in Alaska was something of a mystery to myself and others, but there was little mystery surrounding the two female companions who also died in the crash. Mona and Gabrielle didn't happen to be their wives.

It was true I'd helped T. J. Lambert get the head

coaching job. T.J. at the time was an assistant coach at
the University of Tennessee, his alma mater. I felt that
T.J. would bring discipline, some badly needed creativity, and a sense of realism to the program. I had faith
that he'd be the right man in the right place at the right
time. I convinced Big Ed of all that, and Big Ed instructed Chancellor Dollarhyde to hire him.

My faith in T.J. was mainly based on the belief that
T.J. would be lenient on earrings and headbands if the
fuckers could play football at all.

Payday Paula brought me a cup of coffee and asked if
I wanted any of the little sugar cookies, hard candy, or
popcorn she kept on her desk. "You *are* an ex-smoker." I
smiled. I thanked her and said I'd just make do with all
the heroes on the wall.

She said, "I call 'em the walls that ate Fort Worth."

I stared at Tonsillitis and Artis and thought about how
they'd been lured away from signing with Nebraska,
Notre Dame, UCLA, Florida State, Oklahoma, Texas,
and Colorado.

Nobody could argue they weren't worth all those
hundred-dollar bills that found their way under their pil-
lows and into their dop kits. Tonsillitis and Artis led the
Frogs to two bowl games before they skipped their senior year and moved on to more permanent employment
in the NFL, Tonsillitis going to work for Minnesota,
Artis for Green Bay.

Big Ed had been so happy with what Tonsillitis and
Artis did for TCU football, he'd presented the university
with a gift of $2 million to be used for such educational
purposes as a new press box elevator, a new weight
room, new stadium lights, and a new scoreboard.

Tonsillitis and Artis got Coach Lambert off to a good
start at TCU. It was this initial success that helped pop-

ularize one of T.J.'s strong beliefs, which he'd made into a sign for his office. I smiled as I read it.

WINNERS HAVE A BAD CASE OF THE WANTS

Clitorrus Walker and C. S. ("Convenience Store") Roberts were also up on the wall. Two more runners who liked to butt tacklers, make their hats ring. They took the Frogs to the win over Clemson in the Peach Bowl and the win over LSU in the Poulan/Weedeater Independence Bowl in Shreveport, which proved that if a post-season game dug deep enough it could find a corporate sponsor.

Big Ed was so overjoyed with those successes he donated the funds for a wing on the library.

I lingered a moment in front of the photo of Clitorrus Walker to make sure the inscription said what I thought it said. It did.

"To Conch Lambrin. Good lunch, alwades."

An extra-large poster in an oak frame occupied a prominent spot on the wall next to the TV set. It was a poster of the ferocious Tucker twins, Orangejello and Limejello, two of the game's greatest running backs.

Four years ago it was those two locomotives who led the Frogs to their best season since the Puckett-Tiller team that went 9–2, finished number five in the nation, and whipped Penn State in the Cotton Bowl.

It was the Tucker twins who led the Frogs through a season of eleven wins and no losses, and then led the comeback that tied Notre Dame in that thrilling Cotton Bowl game, 21–21, the game that wrapped up the national championship for TCU in most of the polls.

O-ron-gell-o and Lim-on-gell-o was how their names were supposed to be pronounced, according to their mama, who'd worked at Winn Dixie. And then, unfortunately, it was the same Tucker twins who were responsible for TCU receiving a stiff penalty from the NCAA, the two-year probation that included no bowl games, no TV appearances, and the loss of twelve scholarships.

The NCAA's investigators never uncovered any concrete evidence of wrongdoing on the school's part, but they said there were just too many sports cars in the parking lot of the athletic dorm—action had to be taken. T.J. stomped around for weeks in a fury, saying the NCAA consisted of assholes who practiced "selective punishment." If that wasn't so, he asked, how come none of their lapdogs ever got penalized? Notre Dame and them?

Privately, however, he laid part of the blame on O-ron-gell-o. He confided that O-ron-gell-o never should have greeted the NCAA investigator at the door of his off-campus apartment that day wearing his gold Rolex, which was the size of a grapefruit.

The NCAA penalties didn't bother most Frog fans. I said at the time it was a small price to pay for a national championship. Besides, the team's success combined with the NCAA penalties to give friends and boosters of the university two of the most popular bumper stickers in the history of the university bookstore's bumper stickers.

One of them said: OUR MAIDS WENT TO UT.

The other one said:

**I WOULD RATHER BE
ON PROBATION
THAN LOSE TO BAYLOR.**

Big Ed was so proud, so overjoyed by the Frogs winning that national championship, he gave the school $3 million, this time earmarked for expansion to the science and communications buildings.

Payday Paula came back in to catch some secondhand smoke.

"Want a Marlboro?" I offered.

"Oh, dear me, no," she said. "If I smoked one, I'd smoke three packs before dark."

She inhaled the passive smoke of my Marlboro, closed her eyes and swooned, said thanks, and left.

Two of the school's leading sophisticates dropped by to say hello while I was prowling around T.J.'s office— Rabbit Tyrance, the athletic director, and W. F. ("Wet Fart") Lorants, the sports information director.

"Billy Clyde Puckett, how in the world yew doin'?" Rabbit said, shaking my hand enthusiastically, grinning like he thought we were good friends. He wore his usual brown western-style suit and string tie.

I said fine. I asked how he was doing. He said fine. He added that if he was doin' any better he'd be under arrest.

W. F. ("Wet Fart") Lorants had put on a little weight. He wore red suspenders, double-thick glasses, and his uncombed hair was starting to show bald spots. He shook my hand and made an effort to break Rabbit's NCAA record for enthusiasm.

"Hoss, whur at oh baugh gone gee dat?" he said.

I could only guess at what that meant. It was along the lines of everything else he'd ever said to me in the ten years I'd known him, which was ever since Rabbit Tyrance skillfully managed to hire him away from Northeast Mississippi Methodist. It was along the lines of the things all other college sports information directors had ever said to me, those in the southern part of the United States, anyhow.

"How are you, hoss?" I said cheerfully. My conversations with him generally ranged from hoss on hoss to stud on stud.

"Hoss, harby caw curty bone, he jatter clob it, donkey?"

"You never know." I shrugged.

He looked satisfied with the answer.

I'd never been sure about the origin of W.F.'s nickname, and I hadn't cared to delve into the question too deeply. I assumed it had something to do with his initials and a quaint fragrance that had made a dramatic impression on someone in his past.

Most people who addressed him by his nickname in polite company—and I was among them—tended to say it quickly so it wouldn't offend anybody. "Hey, Weffert, old buddy." *Weffert* worked.

Rabbit Tyrance earned his own nickname at TCU by being the slowest halfback in the school's history. He'd played in the mid-sixties in an era when players went both ways. All he ever did on defense was look up and wave at the passes that sailed over his head, and as a ball carrier he wasn't just slow, he was energetically clumsy, frequently becoming a victim of what was known in some circles then as self-tackleization.

Rabbit had never left the campus. After graduation he joined the landscaping crew, but soon there was an opening for an assistant ticket manager, and he filled it. About a year later he became the golf coach, although he'd never played golf. Then he got the ticket manager's job after the longtime ticket manager, N. D. ("No Dice") Mabry, drowned in a peculiar accident. While on his way to work one day, N. D. ("No Dice") Mabry got tied up in traffic on University Drive and tried to avoid it by going around a bridge. Unfortunately, this required driving his Dodge through the Trinity River. It was about a week later that the Dodge and his body were found on an embankment below the fifth green of Colonial Country Club. It was a tragic reminder that N. D.

("No Dice") Mabry had never been known for his patience.

Rabbit served as ticket manager for eight years, and that's when he was curiously appointed athletic director by a demented chancellor named Dr. B. T. ("Bible Thumper") Norris.

The job had become available after TCU's longtime athletic director, Darrell Scarborough, resigned to take the AD's job at Miami University. Darrell Scarborough had tried to come back as soon as he found out the Miami University that hired him was the one in Oxford, Ohio, not the one with the palm trees, but the job had already been given to Rabbit.

"I feel real bad about Darrell," Rabbit said at the time. "I think it was a mistake any of us could have made."

T.J. had no respect for Rabbit. This was largely because Rabbit was responsible for arranging TCU's future football schedules. As T.J. saw it, his personal won-lost record as a coach would be considerably improved if it hadn't been for "the idiot athletic director."

Rabbit had kept scheduling intersectional games against the likes of Auburn, Nebraska, and Penn State, or Georgia, Ohio State, and USC.

T.J.'s teams would now and then win one of those rugged intersectional games without losing half the squad to injury, and he and I both thought this was testimony to his coaching brilliance.

With TCU's future schedules still littered with legendary powerhouses, T.J. often posed the same question to me and other friends that he posed to Rabbit Tyrance. The question was: "What the fuck ever happened to all the Tulanes and Vanderbilts?"

Rabbit's explanation for lining up the powerhouses was simple enough. "We need the revenue," he said. "Title Nine."

Athletic directors and football coaches liked to blame Title IX for everything wrong in the world.

Title IX was the federal law which mandated that any university wishing to accept federal money or federal grants, for any reason, had to provide programs for female students to compete in athletic competition comparable to those programs for male students. Title IX was a big win for the feminists.

Fine. Except your college football coach was aware that his sport produced four times the revenue of anything else the university was involved in. T.J. often dredged up the old battle cry, "Sixty thousand people never filled a stadium to watch a fucking math quiz."

Thus, T.J.'s description of Title IX went like this: "Title Nine is the backward-ass federal law that says if my football team has an intersectional game scheduled against Ohio State in Columbus, Ohio, then our girls archery team gets to fly round-trip first class to England, stay in the best hotel in London, and spend six months looking for fucking Robin Hood in Sherwood Forest."

"How's it going with Title Nine?" I asked Rabbit Tyrance.

"Oh, Lord," the AD moaned. "Gettin' worse all the time."

With defeat in his voice, Weffert said, "Bartchy gammersom burly, butcher aweddy dooner."

"That's too bad," I said, looking concerned.

They both nodded.

I said, "Well, at least the Lady Frogs are good in golf this year, I hear. Didn't I read in the *Light & Shopper* where they have a good shot to win the NCAA?"

Weffert said, "A offer goo, boo em whuppers benoan letcher daggy."

"Really?" I said.

Rabbit Tyrance and Weffert Lorants shook my hand again. The AD said they had to be running along, they just wanted to welcome me back home, and if there was anything I needed while I was here, well, if it could *be* done, it would *get* done. I thanked them and said everything was pretty much under control.

At the door, Rabbit said, "If our gals do win the NCAA, your old father-in-law might give us another dorm, whaddya think?"

I only smiled. I didn't have the heart to tell him I wouldn't count too heavily on a financial donation from Big Ed if the TCU girls won a golf title, but he might say ain't that nice.

14

The reason we went to He's Not Here for a nutritious lunch of hard-boiled eggs, Fritos, and whiskey was because Coach Lambert was in the mood to celebrate.

T.J.'s meeting with the chancellor and some of the department heads had gone well. Coach Lambert had received the assurance of everybody in the room that the junior college transfers he'd recruited would have no academic problems.

T.J. said he made his position on the subject quite clear. If they wanted the kids to win football games, don't cloud their heads with too much book shit.

Now T.J. was saying how happy he was with his recruits. It looked like each one might be a warp-your-ass stud-bubba. This was when we were driving to He's Not Here in my Cadillac-Buick.

"The future's all up to my jucos," he said.

I'd never known what football mind invented the word *juco* to abbreviate *junior college*, but I assumed it was somebody pressed for time.

T.J. explained that it wouldn't have been necessary for him to recruit any jucos if he hadn't been robbed by Notre Dame and Nebraska.

The loss of Nemesis Moon was particularly painful, he said.

Nemesis Moon was a blue-chip linebacker from Lake Gooch, Texas. He'd signed with Notre Dame over TCU at the last minute, giving travel destinations as his reason. He'd been leaning toward TCU in the first place because the Frogs were in the Western Athletic Conference now, the WAC, and he knew they would be taking exotic road trips to Honolulu and San Diego and a place he called Utah, Wyoming. But he changed his mind when it was pointed out to him by a Notre Dame recruiter that during his five years in South Bend, the Irish would be playing games in Tokyo, Singapore, Belfast, and Istanbul, not to mention Los Angeles and Miami.

"I be needin' to broaden myself for future curriculars," Nemesis had said to T.J.

Still mourning the loss, T.J. said wistfully, "Nemesis could have cured our defensive ills. Slap a poultice right on it."

Nebraska slipped away in the dead of night with Clark Bates, even though he was already driving a Lexus GS 300 he'd found parked in front of his home with purple and white ribbons tied on it.

Clark Bates was a top-rated high school running back from Big Valley, California. T.J. hated to lose him but it somewhat eased the pain that Clark Bates intended to change his name to Rashad Dyshon Tafoya Tyfoonia.

T.J. had recruited ten jucos in all, and the ones he was happiest about came from Southeastern Institute of Assemblies of God & Plumbing.

I'd heard of Southeastern Institute of Assemblies of God & Plumbing, I thought. I was sure it was the junior college in Clarabeth, Oklahoma, that was best known for teaching basketball to seven-foot-tall East African tribesmen before sending them off to major universities that were interested in making it to the Final Four.

The running backs made him smile in his sleep, T.J. said.

"Who are they?" I asked idly.

"Got me another set of twins. The Fowlers."

"Twins?" I said. "Like O-ron-gell-o and Lim-on-gell-o twins?"

"Better."

"Can't be."

"They are."

"They haven't done it yet."

"They will."

"I'll have to see it."

"They're just as big and faster than the Tuckers."

"Faster?"

"I got to tell you, Billy Clyde. They're so fast, God ain't even heard about 'em yet."

I was happy to see the coach so enthusiastic about the Fowler twins, but I did wish I hadn't been taking a drag off a cigarette when he told me their names.

Budget and Avis.

15

He's Not Here was a festival of good cheer, and Kelly Sue made room for us at the bar by asking six regulars to slide one stool to the right. The regulars who slid were Wayne and Ralph from those wonderful carpet and vinyl siding days of twenty-four hours ago, and Iris, the out-of-work bank executive, Raymond, the temporarily idle money manager, Fake Doug, the out-of-work meat salesman, and Real Doug, the out-of-work paper salesman.

There wasn't much difference between Fake Doug and Real Doug. They had indestructible sideburns, bushy mustaches, hair the color of Frosted Flakes, and stomachs that had known the splendors of fried food.

Kelly Sue had named them. One Doug had ventured into the bar a few days ahead of the other Doug, therefore the first Doug became Real Doug and the second Doug became Fake Doug.

Real Doug addressed me first. "We were just talkin' about it, Billy Clyde. Is there anything more useless than a *status-report* phone call? Asshole boss calls up, wants a *status report*. He can't wait to get the whole fuckin' answer? I mean, shit."

I smiled.

Kelly Sue smiled and edged me a Junior.

Her America hair was in a ponytail and she was wearing another sweatshirt with a message on the front, a dark red shirt with white lettering. I admit I was once again intrigued by the message on her shirt. This one said:

> **I DON'T LIKE QUESTIONS.**
> **I DON'T LIKE ANSWERS.**
> **I JUST WANT TO DANCE.**

"Where'd you get that shirt?" I asked.

"I had it made."

"Is that your sentiment?"

Grinning, she said, "I heard one of our Olympic athletes say it on TV. She was a hurdler. Her name was Twilotta . . . I want that cap."

I couldn't remember which cap I was wearing. I took it off, saw it was the one that said OFFICE BITCH across the front.

"Shake Tiller movie," I said. "Ever see it?"

"You know, I wanted to, but the lines were always too long," she said, rewarding herself with a laugh that reminded me of my wife again.

I presented her with the cap. She put it on, studied herself in the mirror behind the bar. "It's the real me," she said. "You leaving today?"

"That was my original plan, but I started having all this fun, so I guess I'll do what I usually do."

"Which is what?"

"Let fate handle it."

There was some shuffling around at the bar and Iris wound up on my right. A trim little chick, thirty-fiveish. She was wearing a snug navy-blue tailored suit and high-

neck white blouse—job-hunting togs. Nice figure. A
pretty face, crinkly brown hair.

Iris offered me her hand, saying, "We haven't been
formally introduced. I'm Iris McKinney."

"Hi," I said. "I'm—"

"I know who you are," she said.

"What do you do, Iris?" I asked.

"I drink vodka and smoke cigarettes."

"Sounds like a worthwhile occupation. Why do you
hate football?"

"Did I say I hate football?"

"You haven't asked for my autograph."

"I don't hate football. I just don't like my ex-husband."

Iris lit her own cigarette and said, "Actually, I was a
loan officer at Southwest Bank . . . before Reece Simpson decided to *downsize*."

"Reece Simpson was your boss, I take it."

"He had a dual role. He was my boss *and* a prick."

I made a sympathetic noise.

"He was just a little prick for a while, then he got that
letter."

"The letter?"

"He applied to be a big prick and they approved it."

I laughed.

Sipping her drink and gazing straight ahead, Iris said,
"So . . . I'm in the middle of a career change."

"So am I," I said. "Or I will be if we get the expansion team in the National Football League—the West
Texas Tornadoes."

"I've read about it," she said. "Where 'bouts in West
Texas?"

"The exact location hasn't been chosen. Out around
Amarillo and Lubbock. Left of Amarillo, right of Lubbock. Or the opposite."

"I saw a tree out there once. See if you can put 'em near the tree."

"We have to get the team first. There are four franchises in the race for two spots. Some days I like our chances better than other days."

"What happens if you don't get picked? Try again?"

"Right. I sit here in this bar for five years and try again."

T.J. said, "Iris, you picked out your new profession yet?"

"I have," she said. "I'm going into sexual therapy. The economics of it look appealing."

"Leave him alone, Iris." That came from Kelly Sue as she was pouring a drink for someone.

Iris said, "There are different kinds of sexual therapists. I plan to specialize in men."

"Really?" I said. "I thought women liked to talk about it more?"

"Studies show men need the most help. The largest group of men who need help are those addicted to sex with prostitutes. The number is in the millions, according to recent surveys."

"Don't you need to go to shrink school or something?" I said.

"No, just a college degree, an office, and a desire to help people."

Like any normal person, I said, "I wonder how the sexual therapist goes about curing the man addicted to prostitutes?"

"I've looked into it," Iris said. "You establish a fee, then on a weekly basis you provide unforgettable blowjobs."

Laughter all around, from T.J. as well.

Realizing I'd been had, I said, "I gather I'm supposed to buy you a drink now, is that the deal?"

I motioned to Kelly Sue to back up Iris's Stoli-rocks.

"You're supposed to ask another question," Iris said. "Since the man's been cured of hookers, how does he get cured of the blowjobs from the sexual therapist?"

"Okay," I said. "Since the man's been cured of hookers, how does he get cured of the blowjobs from the sexual therapist?"

"They get married."

More laughter exploded. Iris looked pleased.

It was a short time later when Iris selected Raymond, the temporarily idle money manager, as the person she wanted to sport-fuck that afternoon.

Raymond declined, caressing his imported beer. Iris said he just got so many offers he was bored, or didn't he like her looks? Raymond said her looks were more than adequate. Iris said *"Adequate?* "My looks are fucking *adequate?"* Raymond told Iris to chill. "We aren't the same people," he said. Iris said, "Good Christ, you think you're better than me!" She then said Raymond ought to carry around a little mirror so he could look at his superior self all day long. Then she paid her tab and left. Raymond looked around at all of us and said, "What'd I do?"

"Aw, nothin'," Fake Doug said. "It's just a woman deal."

"Yep," said T.J. "I'd say you can chalk up another one to menopause."

"God, y'all are deep," Kelly Sue said, rinsing out glasses. "You see right through everything."

16

Legend had it that if you hung around He's Not Here long enough, you'd eventually meet Ody Bradshaw.

As soon as the baldheaded runt with the big voice came in the front door, I knew it had to be him.

Him in his red visor, blue polo shirt, baggy khaki shorts. Him with his pudgy legs exposed in a pair of anklets and spikeless Footjoys. I'd never understood those dainty little anklets, why some guys insisted on wearing them with their shorts and golf shoes. I could only assume they wanted to look like shirt-lifters.

Ody marched straight to the phone near our corner of the bar, shouting at the bartender, "Kelly, fix me a Bloody-bull-Mary with three drops of Tabasco, pinch of salt, stick of celery—and it won't do me no good if I can't see through it."

He downed two Bloody-bull-Mary see-throughs while he talked bidness on the phone. T.J. and I couldn't help listening as he dropped so many names, he could have used a backup alphabet.

He dropped the name of his law firm six times. Like it upgraded his pedigree to be represented by McCripple, McCrab & McCarron. He dropped the names of a

dozen guys who came from rich families in town. Names
he obviously thought of as Fort Worth's equivalent of
Vanderbilts and Rockefellers, Mellons and Carnegies.
Made it sound like they were his good buddies, and
they'd all been sitting around the men's tavern at River
Crest together, discussing ways to improve the world.

But I knew Ody couldn't have been sitting around
River Crest. He wasn't born rich and he worked for a
living. Besides, I knew River Crest better than Ody
Bradshaw did, or ever would.

The Bookmans had been members at River Crest forever, which meant I'd spent many a summer day out
there during high school scouting out the set decoration
around the swimming pool, and signing Barbara Jane's
name for lunch. And I'd spent many a college day there,
doing the same thing, and the occasional grown-up day
there, trying to act like a grown-up. So I was well aware
that the only topics that ever got discussed around the
club were how America would be better off if everybody
in the media could be sent to prison for treason, how the
white race was in danger of becoming extinct if people
didn't stop electing Democrats, and how much everyone
had enjoyed Peter Duchin and his orchestra last Saturday night at Ted and Bonnie Crudeoil's spectacular debutante party for their lovely daughter, Fatikins.

I also knew the names Ody dropped didn't mean shit
to anybody outside the walls of River Crest, and one or
two other private clubs in town, except to a talk-big guy
like Ody Bradshaw.

When Ody Bradshaw got through on the phone he
slapped T.J. on the back in a display of warm friendship.

T.J. introduced us and Ody tried to give me a bone-
crushing, macho handshake, the kind short guys invariably offer people of normal size.

Being a veteran of introductions, I was prepared for
Ody's handshake. I gripped him high, achieving a stand-

off; thus I'd be able to play the piano again, if I ever took it up in the first place.

"How 'bout you two?" Ody grinned widely. "And they say there are no heroes left in America."

He ordered us a drink on the house, snapping his fingers at Kelly Sue.

This happened so quickly, I couldn't stop him. My basic policy was never to allow strangers to buy me drinks in a bar. Strangers didn't really want to buy you drinks, they were time bandits. They wanted fifteen minutes, thirty minutes, an hour out of your life. Talk to you till you were almost on your hands and knees, begging for mercy.

Ody bought about twenty minutes of my time, but T.J. shrewdly escaped. He excused himself to go let Wilbur turn in another term theme, and on his way back he took the precaution of stopping to visit with Wayne, Ralph, Raymond, the Dougs, and Kelly Sue.

This left me alone to hear about Ody's round of golf. He took me all eighteen holes. I heard how bad bounces, sprinkler heads, spike marks, and carelessly placed out-of-bounds posts had screwed him out of a 79, but it was good enough to win the money from Wop Spizzo, Spick Clark, and Jew Bob Goldstein.

He didn't even hear me say, "Do I look like a golf cart?"

He was busy on his primary mission of grinding me through the industrial carpet, down past the concrete foundation, on into the dirt, and halfway to China.

Now I was hearing about the twenty-four spec houses he was starting up on a parcel out around Weatherford, and how Buster Shelton was the best builder in town if you were talking about post-and-beam construction and wanted to maximize the lakefront view.

He shared the information with me about a nursing

home stock I ought to buy if I liked a little suspense in my life. "You roll the dice now and then, don't you?"

I heard about a credit card stock I ought to buy, but not until the current president had been fired and a pack of mad dogs had torn out his heart and liver.

I heard that Tommy Earl Bruner, his partner and my friend, would be a better businessman if he'd concentrate more on *execution* and less on *vision*, if I could grasp his meaning.

"You're tryin' to get that pro team, ain't you, good buddy?" he said.

"Yes, we are."

"If I was the NFL, I'd go for London and Hawaii, no offense."

"I'm glad it's not in your hands, no offense."

"Why the hell would they want to go to West Texas?"

"It's a ripe area—growing population, enthusiastic people. Texas needs another team, and West Texas is the best TV market for it. We'd be in there between Dallas and Denver, but what am I trying to sell you for? You're not on the expansion committee, are you?"

"Done all the spade work?"

"Two years of it. I've had more cocktails with NFL owners than they've had with their wives."

Ody told me about *his* wives. It took him three tries, but he'd finally found a good one. Suzy was a keeper—a big improvement over "Shopping Mall Shirley" and "MasterCard Melissa."

Okay, Suzy was a Jap, somebody he'd met on a trip to San Francisco. But her being a Jap wasn't a big drawback . . . other than when you were around people who'd look at her and you could tell they were thinking, "She can't be your wife, she's a Jap." People gave themselves away like that.

A small price to pay, he said, for what you got with a Jap wife.

Clean, real clean. Not many things cleaner than a Jap. Kept her muff as clean as her sink and baseboards. Didn't know shit to talk about either. Another bonus. And she had that built-in knack for doing beautiful yardwork. I ought to see his lawn and hedges, I wouldn't believe it.

Now, my wife, he said, old Barbara Jane Bookman. There was one of the great beauties. Obviously a great person along with it. Class on class is all it was.

Ody remembered Barbara Jane as a model in all those magazines, up there on all those billboards. He'd sure been a big fan of that TV show she'd starred in, whatever the name of it was, and he was sure he'd seen all of the movies she'd made. She was something else, you bet, and he'd often dreamed about fucking Barbara Jane Bookman.

"Excuse me?" I said.

He said, "I've seen some gash in my day, buddy, but believe me, what you got there is top of the line. Tits, ass, face, the whole package. Man, I could dive into *that* and stay a month."

He picked up on my look.

"But I don't want you to take it personally," he said.

"I'm afraid I already do," I said, trying to decide whether to beat the shit out of him myself or let T.J. squeeze his head till his eyeballs dropped out and rolled around on the floor like Titleists.

He grinned weakly. "Why? We're just guys talkin' here. See, I have this philosophy about women. Like, you know, I don't think a man ought to love a woman so much he wouldn't let a good friend fuck her."

I was forced to laugh.

Then I took out my trusty Mont Blanc and wrote the statement down on a napkin—*A man should never love a woman so much he wouldn't let a good friend fuck her.* I figured I'd come across an intellectual line for a Shake Tiller movie.

Ody said, "What you up to there?"

I said I was jotting down his philosophical gem to make sure I wouldn't forget it.

"You've had that outlook for a good while, have you?" I said.

He said, "Aw, I just kind of developed it over the years. Ought to be a law, though, huh? Men have to stick together, don't you think? Hell, we're outnumbered four to one. Nice visiting with you."

Ody gave me a friendly tap on the shoulder, hollered at Kelly Sue not to burn it down, and left.

Kelly Sue came over with a smile and said, "You don't know the best thing about Ody Bradshaw yet."

"I know everything about Ody Bradshaw."

"No, you don't. He has five cars."

"I'm impressed."

"He has an old Corvette, a two-door BMW 850, a Jaguar, a Mercedes 500 SL, and a Range Rover."

"Great. Five cars, three wives."

"His house at Mira Vista has a name . . . you know, like, Shady Grove, the Pucketts? Happy Pecan, the Woodleys?"

"What's the name of Ody's? Third Wife?"

"Five Cars."

17

It was late afternoon when I coaxed T.J. over to a booth in a quiet corner. Worked on him some more about coaching the Tornadoes in case they became your basic reality.

We'd discussed it several times in the past few months, mostly on the phone. He was intrigued, then he wasn't. There were other coaches I had in mind, but T.J. was the man I wanted. Friendship aside, he was a hell of a good football coach.

If we got the team next month, I wanted a coach next month. There'd be a slewpot full of things to get done in a year and a half—the fastest year and a half in our lives.

All I wanted was T.J.'s word on the deal.

My word to him would be good. Signatures to come later. Unlike the self-interested, self-serving, Perrier-drinking swindlers who populated today's bidness world, the word of a guy from our generation was golden.

A guy broke his word in our day, he didn't get to keep his corporate jet and shapely adorables. He lost the respect of everybody who knew him, sometimes got his kneecaps turned into butter, and sometimes wound up going indoors to play wife for Leroy.

This time, I worked on T.J. for over an hour. What I basically said was I hated to see my alma mater lose a good coach, but he'd done all he could at TCU. He'd flipflopped the program, given the Frogs a national championship, put them in bowl games. Every successful college coach knew when to leave or step down. He did it before the school and the fans grew tired of him.

"I want to do both," T.J. said.

"Both what?"

"I want to coach the Frogs one more season. Then I'll resign, coach your team—if you've got one."

This was new. Something he hadn't brought up before.

He said, "I have to see what Budget and Avis can do this fall. Might be something wonderful."

I said I doubted he was going to be a contender for number one. The best he could hope for would be to win his division in the WAC, wind up in a second-tier bowl game.

"It's time to move on, T.J.," I said. "There's a lot to do if we get the team. You're saying you want to leave everything up to me? Every decision? Till next winter? While you're fucking around trying to beat New Mexico and Wyoming?"

There wasn't that much for the NFL coach to do, T.J. argued. Most of the preseason decisions would be made by the president and general manager or the owner. Me and Big Ed.

I said, "Listen carefully to this. Seven-year contract. Twice what you're making now. Which is what? Four hundred? Four-fifty? You'll have raises and bonuses built in for winning . . . for, you know, playoffs and stuff. Plus, you make your own Nike deal, and you'll have a TV show. You'll be fat-man rich. Tommy Earl will build Donna Lou her dream house. You'll never have to put up with any of that recruiting crap again, being nice to

people you wouldn't give the time of day if they didn't
have a kid who played football. You know all this as well
as I do. In the pros, it'll just be you and what you like,
X's and *O*'s. Where's the problem?"

T.J. said, "No problem. That's real generous, Billy
Clyde, and I accept the offer—starting next January."

I slumped. "Come on, man. Gimme a break here."

He said he didn't give a hoot about the offices and
other facilities. I could handle all that. Just give him a
desk and a blackboard. He could hire a staff of top assistants in no time. He knew who he'd hire. Nobody who
wanted to be a head coach someday, that was for sure.
Guy would stab you in the back, cause unrest among
your players. T.J. would know exactly which assistants
he'd want around the country, and Big Ed's checkbook
would make them available. One of the assistants would
be a key man, he said. A guy who knew how to sneak-
lace the pregame coffee.

We'd both been introduced to speed when we went to
the pros. That pregame coffee in the locker room had
made more than one pro want to rape and plunder
whole villages.

As for the chore of picking the players from the expansion pool and the college draft, T.J. said those were
the two most overrated things in the sport, other than
game plans.

"Do you agree they've overcomplicated the hell out
of the game, Billy Clyde?"

"I know . . . I know," I said. "It's still blocking and
tackling, but your team needs a *coach*."

Evaluating the talent and stocking the team would be
the easiest part of the whole deal, he said.

Guy walked splay-footed, he didn't play for T.J.

Guy never looked you in the eye when you were talking to him, he didn't play for T.J.

Guy's agent had stockbroker hair, big briefcase, talked too fast, he didn't play for T.J.

Guy's daddy asked too many questions, he didn't play for T.J.

The winning mix in the pros was the same as the winning mix in college. Quarterback with a strong arm, size, mobility, inventiveness, guts. Preferably white. Everybody in the offensive line, tackle to tackle, over three hundred pounds. Upper-body strength, good grip for holding, know how to mask the roids. Tight end optional on the black-white thing. Size, hands, reliable blocker, never dropped the short-yardage third-down pass.

Africranium-American on your running backs. Speed, bounce-off, lateral vision. Durability as important as size. Vomit at the idea of fumbling. Get horny when they see the end zone.

White punter, reads books.

Placekicker, speaks English.

Entire defense: big and agile, quick on the perimeters, street mean, psycho motherfuckers.

I extended my hand to him with a grin. "You talked me into it. Do the Frogs one more year, then you're mine."

Looking confident, he said, "We'll win some games our first season. With parity what is today? Shit. Is the pope a bear?"

So there it was, all in a handshake. If we had a team, we had a coach.

18

Getting out of town before something inappropriate happened was my admirable goal.

I drove T.J. back to his car at the coliseum. He invited me home for dinner, saying if I showed up Donna Lou would cook something decent. I was forced to decline. The reason I declined was because I'd already made a dinner date with Kelly Sue. It was the bartender's night off and she'd asked if I wanted to try out the new gourmet restaurant in my hotel. Having no better offers at the time, and figuring she didn't get a chance to do that kind of thing too often, I'd said yes.

I cleaned up, slipped into my all-purpose black blazer, and met Kelly Sue in the hotel's gourmet room, which, incredible as it seemed, was called The Gourmet Room.

Kelly Sue arrived looking like somebody else. She wore a lightweight tweed button-up jacket over a dark red silk blouse with a collar, a slim black skirt, kind of slit up the front, and heels. Her America hair had wriggled out of the ponytail and tumbled down her shoulders. Put a briefcase in her hand and she'd have looked like the lady executive of a big company who was going to use her femininity to close a deal.

We did our share of cocktails, talked about everything but football, and finally poked around at a long dinner. I had the pork chops, hold the peanut butter sauce. She had the roast chicken, hold the pineapple sauce.

We were on coffee and cigarettes when Kelly Sue said, "I haven't told you what Iris McKinney said to a guy in the joint the other day. She was sitting at the bar. She'd been eyeing this guy who was kind of cute. Not a regular. I don't know who he was; it doesn't matter. Iris finally turned to him and asked if his wife was a generous person. The guy said, yeah, he thought so. She was probably as generous as the next person. Iris said, 'Good, then she won't mind if I borrow your dick for an hour or two.' I fell out."

"Pretty funny."

"A moment for the highlight film."

Grinning, I said, "I hesitate to say this, Kelly Sue, but there are certain members of the male population who might be prone to take that story as what you call your indicator."

"Only somebody with no moral fiber to speak of." She was returning the grin.

"Well, that eliminates me. Can I ask you something?"

"Of course."

"You know how people get a look on their face sometimes? Like they might be weighing the pros and cons— the risks and rewards—of a situation? I don't have a look like that right now, do I?"

"You want the truth?" She laughed.

Rumor had it the evening lasted quite a while longer, but I didn't know anybody who'd suggest that anything inappropriate happened.

No guy anyhow.

Part Three

Nudity.

Sex.

Adult Language.

Adult Content.

19

Air travel lost most of its charm when bonus-point passengers became one of the more disagreeable facts of life. Now there were higher fares for people who needed to travel and bargain fares for people who had no reason to go anywhere and ought to stay home. The bonus people even crammed into first class today in their thongs, jogging shorts, and tank tops, and slung their body odor at the person in 3-B, which was occasionally me.

Then air travel lost the rest of its charm when a group of militant nonsmokers kidnapped all the airline executives and threatened to stick ice picks in their children's eyes if smoking sections weren't eliminated altogether, even on overseas flights. This advanced the cause of onboard sleeping and increased the sale of paperbacks in terminal gift shops, but all it had done for smoking travelers was ruin what used to be a stress-free and pleasurable experience.

I had to admit, however, that it made the serious smoker more creative. On short flights, you always traveled with a sheet of cellophane and a roll of Scotch tape. They were to put over the smoke detector in the john in

case you needed a quick puff or two to keep the bad
weather up ahead from ripping off the wings.

Long flights required careful planning now.

For instance, I never booked an overseas flight without checking on the equipment ahead of time. Make sure
I'd be on an old 747, DC-10, or L-1011. Something
with the galley down below.

First step after the seat belt sign went off was to make
friends with the stew—the Pam or the Kim—who'd volunteered to do the cooking. That was your smoker.

She could show you the little elevator that went down
to the galley. When the movie came on, she could invite
you down there with her.

No, there wasn't much space in the galley, what with
all the chicken Kievs, wild rice, and broccoli, but there
was room for two people to stand and smoke—and
maybe do one or two other things. It had long been said
that on night flights some sex had gone on down in those
galleys, but I only had Shake Tiller's word on that.

The other thing you could do, if you were some sort
of recognizable person, was get invited up to the flight
deck, to sit around for a while with the captain. Young
people weren't aware that the captain used to be called
the pilot, and the first officer used to be called the co-
pilot, and the second officer used to be called the junior
pilot, or the flight engineer, before the new jets eliminated him altogether.

Pilots became known as captains when computers
started flying the jets, captain being a more accurate
name for the man reading the newspaper.

I liked it that the captain and crew could smoke on
the flight deck. This was a good thing. I very much
wanted my captain to be able to smoke if he cared
to. Otherwise, you might be on the flight with him the
day he said, "Oh, really? You're telling me I can't

smoke? Well, let's see how tough *this* mountain thinks it is!"

Fuck that.

My Swissair flight from New York to Zurich was operated by a Delta crew. Captain Brandon was a football fan as well as a smoker, so I was privileged to enjoy three visits to the flight deck. The cooking stew, whose name *was* Pam, curiously enough, was a male heterosexual fan, so I was able to go through half a pack of Marlboros on my four visits to the galley.

The rest of the time I dined, dozed, and let Shake's book tell me some more world history.

Dinosaurs tended to stay in a foul mood most of the time, I learned, and acted extremely rowdy when scantily clad blondes yelled insults at them, such as "Guess who's going to be *extinct* someday, Mr. Ugly?"

I also learned that the Greeks invented gods, naked boys, the shot put, and thought. Socrates came up with the first thought when he looked around at everybody and said, "The mind is in the head—and why are we all wearing bedsheets?"

I'd been told by Big Ed before I left not to get stranded on an Alp.

He reminded me that the NFL expansion committee was going to meet within six weeks, possibly even sooner, to hear final presentations from everybody, then make their decision on the two new franchises. The meeting was still scheduled for LA, but the exact date hadn't been set.

Big Ed was delighted we could go into the LA meeting and announce that we had T. J. Lambert for a coach.

After I'd gotten T.J.'s handshake on the deal, I'd called Big Ed in his New York office on the *Titanic*, otherwise known as the Plaza Hotel, to tell him the good news.

He said, "I hate to think what's liable to happen to TCU football with T.J. out of there, but bidness is bidness."

"What can I do between now and the meeting?" I asked. "Kiss some owner in the ear again?"

"I can't think of anything. We've poured enough whiskey down their necks, shown 'em enough phony surveys. They know we're financially responsible. It's all up to geography."

"I'm glad you're including me in the financially responsible part."

"The hay's in the barn. All we can do is wait. Tell my daughter I'd like to see her someday. I'll see you in LA, hotshot."

Switzerland was the easiest country in the world to move around in. A cog rail would put you on top of the tallest Alp. A train would take you through the thickest Alp. Swiss trains were smooth, quiet, clean, comfortable, and always on time. If a Swiss train was ever ten seconds late, six railroad workers were executed.

There were even superhighways all around the Alps and through the cities—up, down, over—and they were marked better than any roads you'd ever been on. Impossible to get lost.

Swiss highway signs said:

**TAKE NEXT RIGHT IF YOU WANT TO GO
TO GENEVA—STRAIGHT AHEAD 3
MILES FOR EXCELLENT RACLETTE**

Or:

**EXIT NOW FOR THE HOTEL IN BERN
WHERE YOU MADE A RESERVATION ON
THE PHONE LAST NIGHT**

And:

WARNING: LAST EXIT BEFORE TUNNEL OR SAY HELLO TO AUSTRIA, YOU PORTUGUESE FOOL

But there was nothing easier in Switzerland than getting off a plane and getting on a train. All you had to do was go down an escalator.

The train from Zurich to Lausanne took two hours. I sat in the dining car most of the way, first enjoying a traditional English breakfast—fried eggs up on top of bacon—then the *Herald Trib*, the London papers, and smokes.

It's how you ought to be able to go from Fort Worth or Dallas to Houston or Austin, but the politicians want you to get killed on highways or in airplanes.

My first night back in Lausanne I dined with Barbara Jane, Human Dog, and Shake in the director's suite, enjoying a bowl of $22 lentil soup and a $55 club sandwich. My wife had a $47 plate of chicken salad. Shake had a $72 filet mignon with a $44 plain omelette. He had felt like steak and eggs, a pregame meal, and that was as close as room service could come to it. Hume had a $34 rotisserie chicken.

I implored Shake to tip our waiter, Charles de Gaulle, generously.

Shake did, saying Cubby Butler would want it that way. It was play money anyhow, he said. Most of the production expenses on *Melancholy Baby* would be written off against the studio's current box-office hit, a remake of *Fire Maidens from Outer Space*.

Barbara Jane and Shake were pleased to hear that I'd talked T. J. Lambert into coaching our NFL team, if we ever got one, and Shake complimented me on the choice, saying T.J. would bring a lot to the dance: pride,

dignity, hard work, imagination, the ability to fart on
cue.

"He doesn't do that so much anymore," I said.

"Why, he can't do it like he used to?"

"He can still *do* anything you want," I said. "Loud,
long, assorted colors. I think he's lost interest in it."

Shake said, "He doesn't even fart at the Stop & Shop
while the fat girl's trying to ring up his beef jerky and
beer?"

"Not that I know of."

Barbara Jane said, "I know he still farts in crowds.
Don't tell me he doesn't fart in crowds. That's how he
integrates back into society when he starts to feel separate and confused."

That was about all the time either of them had for
anything I was involved in. But no big deal. I'd learned
that when movie people were in the middle of a production, they didn't pay much attention to other topics. And
the topic they wanted to discuss that night was Jack
Brothers.

He was the well-known actor who was my wife's love
interest in the movie. Enid's love interest. His character
was that of a "sensitive man." A man who had given up
his successful career as an investment banker to try to
become an artist. A man willing to put his soul on the
table and see if anybody wanted to stick a fork in it. This
was Shake's idea of the type of man a woman would find
attractive if she'd been married to a football coach for
eleven years.

Jack's role name was, conveniently, Jack. Shake had
done that to save himself some trouble. On the set, directors frequently liked to call an actor by his or her role
name.

But if Jack's role name was "Frederick," for example,
and Shake called for "Frederick" to take his mark on the
set, Jack Brothers might not know who the director was

talking about. He just might sit there in his deck chair, thumbing through an issue of *Vanity Fair*, or looking up at the ceiling, waiting for "Frederick" to show up. This way, if Shake called for "Jack" to come to the set, Jack Brothers would respond promptly.

You learned little tricks like that in the business, Shake confided.

Jack Brothers had been in town a week, but they hadn't been able to get a good take on his first scene yet because he failed to see the humor in it and was having trouble saying the lines and showing the right reactions.

I knew what they meant after I watched them try to shoot the scene for the next three days.

The scene was in a sidewalk cafe in Lausanne. Enid and Jack were having coffee in the sidewalk cafe. It was what film folk called an "exposition scene." Enid talking about the past.

The part of the scene that kept giving Jack so much trouble read like this in the script:

Enid: You know how young people in love some-times have a song? Like, "Listen, dear, they're play-ing our song?" Like, you know, Rick and Ilsa and "As Times Goes By" in *Casablanca?* That kind of thing?

Jack: (smiles knowingly) I do, of course. When I was involved with a girl named Laura in college, our song was "Crazy."

Enid: Oh, that's a great song. I love that. Especially the Patsy Cline version.

Jack: I believe one of those country fellows actually wrote it.

Enid: Willie Nelson, yes. My song with Boyd was the national anthem.

Jack grins slightly.

Enid: When we were trying to decide on a date to be married, I suggested a week in October. Boyd looked at me as if I'd injured him. "That's the World Series," he said. So I suggested a day in late November. He said, "That's Ohio State-Michigan." I asked what he thought about the week between Christmas and New Year's. He looked hurt again. "Those are the bowl games," he said. January was out, of course. That was the NFL playoffs and the Super Bowl. We were married in February. Nothing happens in February. You never hear "The Star-Spangled Banner" in February. Our song.

Jack Brothers was supposed to look amused throughout Enid's speech, then laugh appreciatively at the end. But he didn't get it.

Sitting close by in Barb's personalized deck chair, I overheard the talk my wife and Shake had with the actor about the scene.

"Jack, I really don't understand the trouble you're having with this," my wife said.

"Well, for one thing, I don't see the humor in the scene, but mostly I'm offended."

"*Offended*," Shake said. "What the hell are you offended about?"

"I don't think it's proper to make fun of our national anthem."

"For Christ's sake, nobody's making fun of the national anthem," Shake said. "The joke's about a guy who can't decide on a wedding date because it keeps conflicting with a sports event on TV."

"I understand *that*," Jack Brothers said, "I'm not stupid."

"Well, then?"

Jack said, "I still don't—"

But Barbara Jane cut him off. "They always play the
goddamn national anthem before a sports event, *Jack*."

"They do?" he said.

His look was the kind some women were left with
permanently after a bad face-lift, except Jack was a guy—
almost.

Looking at Shake, my wife spoke acidly. "Maybe he's
right. Maybe it would work better for Jack. Better for
America, even. We make the song '*Que Sera, Sera*.' What
do you think?"

"That *is* a lovely song," Jack said hopefully.

"See?" Barbara Jane said to Shake with a look.

Barb enjoyed a long and successful career as a commercial model in New York—toothpaste queen, panty
hose princess—starting right after college, then her TV
show had a successful run of seven seasons, and she'd
been making movies for the past eight years, but she
could still pass for a young woman on film.

My wife's face and figure hadn't lost a step, and no
uninvited color had crept into her streaked-butterscotch
hair. Barb had always been very grateful for her natural
beauty, and had tried to do something with it besides
have lunch.

The nights Barb and I spent in our hotel suite alone,
giving room service a workout, passed as quietly as you
might suspect they would for a woman who liked to read
movie scripts and a man who liked to have a dog in his
lap while he read crime novels or the London tabs or let
Shake Tiller tell him the Crusades failed because Richard the Lion-Hearted didn't dress properly for the warm
climate.

My wife was unique among actors. Unique in that she actually read an entire script, all 115 pages of it. Barbara Jane was never without at least ten scripts to read, always on the lookout for a part she thought would be right for her, or a film she would love to be in, or a role she would eat dirty underwear to get, as they said in show bidness. Most actors only read a script to find out how big their own part was. The plot was for others to worry about.

That first night I noticed Barb toss a script into a wastebasket only moments after she'd started reading it.

"Too many car chases?" I said.

"Three in the first ten pages."

"No good part for a leading lady?"

"One."

"Does she drive one of the cars?"

"Not after she turns into a bat."

20

Our pal Jim Tom Pinch, the trustworthy scribe, showed up in Lausanne one day by total surprise, and the first thing he did was show me his "Whitney Houstons." He said I couldn't believe how much the dental implants had improved his sex life.

Jim Tom was in his early fifties now, but he looked like the same guy I'd always known—semi-handsome in a ragged, slightly hungover, dark glasses, rumpled khaki jacket, faded jeans kind of way. His carry-on bag was slung over one shoulder and the case for his laptop was slung over the other shoulder, which left one hand free to smoke and one hand free to drink. Travel tip, he said.

He arrived while I was sitting alone in the lobby bar in the afternoon, taking a break from filmmaking, and rooting for the Swiss quartet to take a break from "Twist Around the Alpenstock," if that's what it was. I was having coffee and some of those finger sandwiches they did so well, and reading my favorite London papers, the *Daily Telegraph* and *Daily Mail*. I liked the *Telegraph* because it constantly poked fun at—brutalized, actually—our PC crowd, and I liked the *Mail* because it ran delicious stories about Parliament guys cheating on their wives and getting caught with teenage girls.

One of the mildly disturbing items I happened to see in the *Daily Mail* was about Neville Trill. He was quoted saying his London Knights were an "unequivocal certainty" to be an NFL expansion team for one simple reason: "American telly." Neville pointed out that if he were to schedule all of the Knights' home games to start at one in the afternoon, which would be 6:00 P.M. in the eastern U.S., the game would spill over into prime time and create an even larger audience for America's "so-called comedies and dramas."

The first questions I asked Jim Tom were about expansion. I wondered what his inside sources were saying? Did he know where the Tornadoes stood? Had the commissioner told him anything off the record?

The commissioner, Val Emery, was a man the owners had chosen a year ago to succeed Bob Cameron, who'd retired. Val Emery was a well-dressed middle-age fellow who'd been an executive on the men's professional tennis tour. He was chosen because he wouldn't know much about football and the owners could control him. Merely to look at Val Emery told you he might be an expert at straddling fences.

"Vapid Emptysuit?" Jim Tom said. Which was the name Jim Tom had given the commissioner, in print. "Nothing from him. Nada. Zip. London's a cinch, I think, despite the owner. How about Neville? Is he a beauty? What'd he do, jump out of somebody's stomach? He's terrorizing the spaceship. Look down, he's still hanging on. Congratulations on T.J."

"That's supposed to be a secret."

"You won't read it in my pamphlet. If I were you and Big Ed, I'd look at it like I was in a three-way fight with the slant and the beaner."

Jim Tom had tried to reserve accommodations at our

hotel, a place some of Shake's film crew were calling the Beau and others were calling the Rivage, like they often wintered or summered there, but he'd been turned down. He wondered if Shake or I could help.

Andre, my frog buddy behind the front desk, agreed to let Jim Tom have a one-bedroom suite for three days, but we were told the suite absolutely had to be vacated in three days because a "most important guest" was arriving from Southwest Asia, a very old customer.

"Towel head or stove lid?" Jim Tom asked.

Puzzled, Andre looked at me. "Unimportant," I said.

Jim Tom bragged that he was on his way to breaking his old record for travel expenses at *The Sports Magazine*, the publication that employed him as a senior writer. Friends of Jim Tom's were aware that his monstrous cash advances and expense-account reports at *SM* had long since passed into legend, but he hadn't slowed down.

He said he was utterly fatigued from trying to find me. First, there was the week he spent at the Dolder Grand. Barb and I knew the Dolder Grand. It was a luxurious hotel on a hill overlooking downtown Zurich. A layer of skin before you bought the first cappuccino. Jim Tom said he fell into a nest of contessas at the Dolder. Scooped the one with the overbite.

Then he looked for us at the Palace in Gstaad. We knew that one, too, from a spaghetti lunch. It was an even $500 if you didn't want sauce. Scored an adventurous American wife whose husband constantly talked on the phone, Jim Tom said. Took a while to get the bracelets and necklaces off.

"Hebes give head now," he said.

"You're shitting me?"

"Scout's honor."

Jim Tom was a two-time loser at marriage and was now involved with an attractive lady named Nell. Jim Tom and Nell lived together in Gotham and were still getting along fine, although they'd recently become journalistic rivals. Once his editor at *SM*, Nell had left to become editor in chief of *Babe*, the new sports magazine for women.

"She's trying to hire me," he said, "but I keep telling her I can't write that crap. 'Connecticut's Prettiest Soccer Moms,' 'How to Pack for the Walk Through Tuscany,' 'Attention Parents: Figure Skating Starts at the Fetus.' . . ."

Jim Tom and I became good friends when he was the mechanic on a book I wrote about my football exploits. Better to put it another way. It was the book I talked into a tape recorder and he made sense of when he typed it. The title was *Semi-Tough*, but Jim Tom always said it should have been called what all books by athletes should be called, *How I Learned to Alibi for My Career with the Help of an Underpaid Sportswriter*.

The reason Jim Tom turned up in Lausanne, he wanted to see me—and Shake Tiller as well—for a remember-when piece on our famous New York Giants team that won the Super Bowl. This year was the twentieth anniversary of that deed, he reminded me. I was shocked to hear that. It hadn't occurred to me. And what the fuck bidness did it have being twenty years ago, anyhow, when it had only been five or six years ago, if not yesterday?

Jim Tom said, "You lost ten years doing TV with Larry Hoage."

"We were a great team," I said. "Not a lot of talk about Tracy and Hepburn after we went on the screen. 'Looks like the Pack woke up the Cowboy offense, Billy Clyde. That's why I always say it's best to let sleeping bags lie.' "

Larry Hoage was relentless. He still was, but it was somebody else's problem now.

Jim Tom sat around with me in the lobby bar for a

while, long enough to tell me about the piece he was going to do, but first he gave the bell captain a picturesque Swiss note to take his carry-on bag and laptop up to his room. The Swiss note could have been worth $50 or $5. Jim Tom didn't know and didn't care; it was the magazine's money.

What I heard from Jim Tom was that our godlike Giants were going to be remembered and immortalized in a story by him, with a layout of old photos in sepia tone. Give it an antique look. It would run in the special pro football issue of *SM* next September.

We talked about how much the game had changed since then.

To start with, the Giants of my day played at Yankee Stadium and the dogass Jets played at Shea. Now they both played in New Jersey on a piece of land where mob guys used to dump bodies.

I'd played against the Baltimore Colts, not the Indianapolis Colts . . . against the Los Angeles Rams, not the St. Louis Rams . . . against the Cleveland Browns, not the Baltimore Ravens . . . against the St. Louis Cardinals, not the Arizona Cardinals . . . against the Houston Oilers, not the Nashville Oilers, or were they the Tennessee Hound Dogs?

"We have some loyal owners, don't we?" said Jim Tom.

Another thing, I said. It seemed like only yesterday that Seattle was known for rain, Tampa was known for wheelchairs, Jacksonville was known for sailors, and North Carolina was known for tobacco. Now they were known for Seahawks, Buccaneers, Jaguars, and Panthers.

"That's okay," he said. "Maybe one day we'll see something out in West Texas besides truck stops."

21

Half a day on a movie set was all Jim Tom could take. It would have been enough for anybody under the circumstances. What we did was sit around an interior location for three hours the next morning and watch Jack Brothers try to impersonate an actor. Then Shake broke for lunch.

Adelle in the production office had booked an entire restaurant where the cast and crew could have lunch every day of the shooting. The restaurant was made out of cobblestones and portholes. It looked so old, I figured it might have been the place where they all sat around arguing one night until somebody finally said, "Why don't we call it Switzerland?"

Jim Tom and I lunched at the long table with Barbara Jane, Shake, Jack Brothers, and some of the other dignitaries—the director of photography, costume designer, makeup artist, script supervisor.

It came up during lunch that Jack Brothers enjoyed telephone solicitations. Some actors didn't have enough hobbies or friends. A telephone solicitation to me was an opportunity to say, "How about this one? Go fuck yourself, asshole."

But when Jack said he liked them, Barb hurtled into a routine:

"Hello. Yes, this is Mr. Brothers. Well, hi, Jerry. How are you? You did say your name was Jerry? Great. Jerry with MCI. Jerry, do me a favor. Hold on just a second. I want to go get my cup of decaf, then I want to hear everything about your offer. Where are you calling from, Jerry?"

Even Jack Brothers laughed. He was uninsultable. Barb added that he also enjoyed mail addressed to Occupant.

After lunch Jim Tom chatted with some of the other people that were important to the making of the picture. People who worked "behind the camera."

The makeup artist, Sandy Boren, stared at Jim Tom's teeth and said, "Oh, my, those really are quite marvelous."

"I call them my Whitney Houstons," Jim Tom said.

"And you are so right to do that," said Sandy.

Jim Tom was provided an opportunity to use his Spanish when he stood for a moment at the coffee urn with Balderamma Pinero, the cinematographer.

"*Uno whiskey con agua con ice por favor,*" Jim Tom said to him. "That's the only phrase I learned when I was in your country."

"You've been to Westwood?" Balderamma said, and went on his way.

Shake's assistant director was a guy named Eddie Rich. He was in charge of shooting traffic, street corners, skylines. Things Shake didn't want to fool with. Turned out Eddie was a serious Golden Domer, somebody who'd gone to Notre Dame and never got over it. Eddie knew Jim Tom's byline and wanted to meet him.

"Oh, man, it's great to shake your hand," Eddie said to Jim Tom. "I still remember that story you wrote about Bruno Zipko."

"Who?" Jim Tom asked.

"It was five years ago," Eddie said. "Bruno Zipko. Our fullback who had to go to the Gulf War, got wounded, but came back and made All-America. You wrote a great story about him. He said that thing just like the Gipper. I cried, man."

Jim Tom nodded. "Right, I remember. He said he was laying wounded in a ditch . . . blood gushing out of his leg. He couldn't move. All he could do was watch his blood mix with the sand and form more mud. But he closed his eyes and thanked God for three things—he was alive, he was Catholic, and he played football for Notre Dame."

"That's it, that's it!" Eddie said. "What a guy, huh?"

"I made it up."

"What?"

"I made it up," Jim Tom repeated with a shrug. "He didn't say anything close to that, but I know what you Domers like to read, so I dolled it up a little."

Eddie Rich looked like he'd been stabbed in the chest.

"I hate to hear that, man."

"Sorry."

"What did Bruno really say?"

"I think it was something on the order of I hope we can go out there tomorrow and kick the fucking shit out of Purdue."

Now Eddie Rich looked heartbroken. "All this time," he said, "I've always had Bruno Zipko right up there with George Gipp."

"Who never said 'Win one for the Gipper,' incidentally."

"What do you mean?"

"I mean Rockne made up that bullshit, too. I did a lot of research on Gipp for a special I helped with on ESPN."

"I'm glad I missed it."

"Gipp was a great athlete, but he was a bum. A tramp. He never even graduated from high school in Laurium, Michigan. He hung around Chicago for three years after high school, shooting pool and playing poker before Rockne paid him to come to Notre Dame. Then he became a drunk. He never went to class. He was frequently seen in poker games in the Oliver Hotel. Before his last season he went to the University of Michigan to see if Fielding Yost would pay him more money than Rockne to play football. Yost wouldn't, so Gipp went back to Notre Dame. Some of the old-timers who were on the team are still alive. They told me that even on his dying bed he'd never say anything close to 'Tell the boys to win one for the Gipper.' What he probably did was ask Rockne to go find him one last drink and a cigarette. Gipp's a classic case of the legend becoming the fact."

Eddie Rich said, "It's been a real pleasure, Jim Tom. Thanks for ruining my life."

The costume designer was Mary Magdalene Davis. She was a slender, pretty woman of forty-five, forty-six, despite the wire-rim glasses. She was better looking in person than a lot of actresses. In fact, she'd tried to become an actress in her youth, but I was told the camera didn't like her. The camera didn't like everybody. A curious thing.

Jim Tom was intrigued with Mary Magdalene Davis. He desired to make her acquaintance, but first he needed information. He wanted to make sure she didn't have a female "companion."

"Wool stroker?" he asked in a whisper.

"Straight," I said.

"You sure?"

"Is Shake's word good enough?"

"Golden."

"Mary Magdalene, huh?" he said to her, thinking he'd found the right moment, stepping in to light the cigarette for her. "So . . . you only fool around with guys on a cross?"

She looked at him without expression.

"We should get to know each other," he said.

"What for?"

"We could be friends."

"Let's have lunch," Mary Magdalene said. "I'll have my people talk to your people." And turned to leave.

"Whoa," Jim Tom said.

"*Whoa?*" She whirled around. "You said *whoa* to me?"

"I want to invite you to dinner with me tonight. In my suite."

"You want me to have dinner with you in your suite tonight?"

"Yes. Very much."

"You're a total stranger. Do I look like someone who is so desperate she wants to have dinner in a hotel suite with a total stranger?"

"No, you just look like a beautiful woman I would like to spend some time with."

"Is that so?"

"Yes, it is. If you need references, Billy Clyde and Shake and Barbara Jane will be happy to tell you what a swell fellow I am."

"Married, I assume?"

"No. Not legally. I mean, no. Look, it's not a big deal. I just thought we might have a nice dinner, some laughs. I tell you about sports, you tell me about movies."

"It seems rather pointless. I don't see how we can get to know each other very well in one evening."

"Sure we can. Easy."

"Easy?"

"Yeah, I just pour a little whiskey down your throat and set fire to the drapes."

She laughed. His closer. It had worked again.

Jim Tom and Mary Magdalene Davis enjoyed a magnificent affair that lasted close to eighteen hours. He said they might have engaged in unnatural sex acts a fifth time—and might have even fallen deeply in love—if it hadn't been for her long dissertation on loneliness and hysterical crying jags.

22

Anybody but a stupid imbecile—the worst kind—or an editor at *The Sports Magazine* would have known that the only reason Jim Tom Pinch wanted to come to Switzerland was to jump contessas and eat raclette. But I was happy to have him around awhile, one reason being he'd already done most of the research for his piece on us antique Giants, and this helped me catch up on what was going on with some of my old teammates.

I was still keeping in touch with the ex-brass. Burt Danby had acted as the owner in our day, being the president of DDD&F, the advertising and public relations agency that had bought the team from the Mara family.

Burt was retired now, living in Palm Beach, competing in serious croquet tournaments, not wearing socks with his satin slippers and tuxedo. I'd been in his home on Via Vizcaya. Not huge but nice. Rich Guy Chateau.

Burt was now with a fifth wife, Cynthia Grant, the fashion designer who became famous when she created the grimy, syphilitic, death-from-overdose look that was so popular a few years back. He seemed happy.

He still liked to be called The Big Guy, still spoke of

certain women as stoves and stovettes—a habit I'd picked up—still described some of our team parties as all-skates and sperm-o-ramas, and he often confessed that he dearly missed the glory days when he could produce a hard-on without a truss and a rubber band.

Burt had no idea who owned the Giants now. Neither did I. The franchise was operated by a company that was part of a venture capital takeover of a leveraged-buyout spin-off of a merger with a multinational conglomerate, or it might have been some other kind of Wall Street shit.

I only knew that the guy who spoke for the Giants on TV and in the papers was Gray Shannon, a wethead in a three-piece suit. One of those assholes who'd mastered the art of looking serious, never revealed where he stood on any issue, large or small, and was totally unfindable by phone and unavailable for an appointment. Today's ideal CEO.

Naturally, I kept up with Shoat Cooper, the old coacher.

I'd speak to Shoat on the phone two or three times a year. Our old coach was still living in his cabin in Triple Gulch, Montana, "happy as a Mexican with a car that'll start," what with his satellite dish, his hunting dogs, and all the fish he wanted to catch.

Not *fish*. "Feesh," as he pronounced it.

A couple of years ago, T.J. and I had gone out to visit him for a weekend. It was in the late spring but before schools had closed. When you visited Montana, you had to make sure you went before schools let out. Before schools were out, there were only fifty-seven people in the whole state and no cars on the road. After schools were out, there were 140 million people in the state and a traffic jam that stretched from Yellowstone to Glacier.

Triple Gulch, we discovered, was a general store and gas pump. It was about an hour and a half drive from

Missoula, but Shoat's cabin was another fifteen miles up a hill, hard by a rushing stream, no neighbors in sight.

Shoat's best friend was a hunting dog named Marvin. The dog was named after Marvin ("Shake") Tiller because he could "go get them birds" just like Shake could go grab a pass in a third-down crunch.

Shoat was the person you had to call or go see if you wanted to know how Morgan Bujakowski was doing down in Brenham, Texas, living alone in Logan & Lillian's RV Park. Morgan was known to us as Buji or Old Army when he was the New York Giants' number-one assistant during our reign of terror. Mainly the guy in charge of our rock-ribbed defense.

It made me smile to remember how there weren't any offensive and defensive coordinators in our day. Certainly nothing resembling a special teams coach, linebacker coach, tight end coach, personnel director, salary cap administrator, any of that silliness. Shoat ran the offense, Buji ran the defense. Two nameless dunces graded film, noticed that blocking and tackling might be important, and would be around one season, gone the next, replaced by two other nameless dunces. Nothing else to it.

The reason you had to see Shoat about Morgan Bujakowski was because Buji no longer communicated with anybody who hadn't been in a uniform during World War II. When anybody tried to remind him that World War II was a long time ago now, he'd say, "Not if you was in it."

Buji started out playing ball at Texas A&M just after Jarrin' John Kimbrough was there—that's when every Aggie was in the corps—and he wound up transferring to West Point and played ball there just before Glenn Davis and Doc Blanchard. In between he went to war and served with exceptional valor. Buji hit Omaha Beach on D-Day and led a bunch of gung-ho Rangers up a cliff on a mission to wipe out some German gun placements, hollering, "You keel them scogies over there, I'll keel these over here!"

We were all aware that Buji was in poor health now and didn't have long to go. What he'd thought was arthritis had turned out to be the unmentionable incurable, so he was getting his affairs in order. But there was evidence that he hadn't lost a sense of humor.

He'd said to Shoat, "I went to see the doctor to get a pain pill for my arthritis and I come out with the damned old queen of diamonds. They gimme six months at the most. So I reckon if you know any old gals with contagious diseases who'd like to get laid, tell 'em to come see me."

Buji had added, "This dang tumor in my brain makes me do odd things, Shoat. Like I'll be jackin' off and forget why."

Buji badly wanted to be buried in Kyle Field or Michie Stadium after he passed on. He figured he'd earned it with service to his country and to the A&M and West Point gridiron programs. He didn't want a tombstone or a plaque anywhere. Just plant him underneath the football turf. Hell, it could even be down around the five-yard line for all he cared. Then anybody who remembered him could be sitting in Kyle Field or Michie Stadium during a game one fine autumn Saturday afternoon, and they would say to themselves, "Old Bujakowski's down there somewhere—goddamn if he didn't keel hisself some Germans."

Shoat was writing letters to A&M and West Point in Buji's behalf, and a few other veterans were writing letters in Buji's behalf, but not much progress had been made. The logic on the part of the institutions seemed to be that if you buried Buji in Kyle Field or Michie Stadium, then one day you'd be pressured into burying a woman down there too, and what the fuck business did a woman have being buried in Kyle Field or Michie Stadium?

Apart from the frustration of trying to get his old friend buried in a football stadium, Shoat Cooper couldn't have been happier.

Talking to his dogs. Clicking around on his dish. Eating his scrambled eggs right out of the skillet. Dumping the cans of tuna and a glob of salad dressing into the mixing bowl and mashing it up for his halftime treat. Sitting by his rushing stream, peeling a loaf of Hebrew National salami and eating it like a drumstick. It was a good life.

23

I experienced a shock to my nostalgia when I read the printout of Jim Tom's research on my old teammates. He said he wasn't sure how much of the information he was going to use when he got around to writing the piece; it would be up to the muse.

All of it was interesting stuff to me, although nobody had dumped his wife to marry a Cowboy cheerleader or a Laker girl, nobody had grown a beard and was writing poetry in San Francisco, nobody had gone to work as a recruiter for the Fellowship of Christian Athletes, nobody had resigned from the Fellowship of Christian Athletes, nobody had gone to India to sit down and stare at his feet, and only one of the group had gone to prison.

During that interlude when Jim Tom was with Mary Magdalene Davis, I spent one afternoon at a sidewalk cafe with coffee, cigarettes, Human Dog, and Jim Tom's notes.

I read about the offense first. My crowd.

THACKER HUBBARD, *tight end:* Big old quiet boy. U. of Idaho. Majored in sheep and snap-count. Claims to have never read a newspaper, magazine, or book.

Lives on small ranch outside Boise. Doesn't miss New York noise or foreigners. Can't remember what happened to Super Bowl ring. Thinks ex-wife flushed it down toilet.

I recalled his wife's name, Marilyn. She'd left him several years ago, ran off with a man who thought more highly of electricity and indoor plumbing than Thacker did.

SAM PERKINS, *right tackle:* Played at 260, most of it in biceps. College ball at Oregon State, but home LA. Rumor liked boys better than girls. Rumor fueled by Sam sketching women's clothes at team meetings.

Owns successful boutique, Santa Monica . . . boutique name: Prissy Missy . . . thinks about franchising . . . still single.

Even though he didn't act like it or talk like it, we always knew Sam was your basic shirt-lifter, but nobody cared because he could hold better than anybody in the line. Ankle, arm, belt, facemask, chinstrap, crotch. He knew all kinds of ways, and hardly ever got caught. Shoat encouraged holding, but I always thought it would have been better if he hadn't been quoted once saying, "If you ain't cheatin', you ain't tryin' to win."

PUDDIN PATTERSON, *right guard:* Hall of Fame guard, pride of Grambling . . . highly popular with team . . . Law degree when retired from football. Prominent criminal attorney in old hometown, Lafayette, Louisiana.

Spends most time keeping coon asses out of jail for sexually molesting their mothers, sisters, aunts, cousins.

Puddin opened up holes I could sleep-walk through.

Shoat said to Puddin one day he was so good he could "block himself white." Puddin said, "You know what, Shoat? It's lucky for your country ass I like to win football games."

NOBAKOV KORELOVICH, *center:* Teeth like fangs, one dead eye, terminal crewcut. Went to Notre Dame . . . known as the Pope to teammates . . . Only with Giants 3 seasons. Went to Browns, Cardinals, Dolphins . . . Picked up blitz better than any center . . . Ate sportswriter's prescription glasses one night on Rush Street after writer mentioned Irish loss to Northwestern . . . Died two years ago, Key Largo, where worked as bartender. Choked to death trying to win bet he could eat 30-pound baby tarpon off hook.

The Pope. Some guy. He did eat the silver fork that night in Clarke's, winning the $200 bet from Shake Tiller.

EUGER FRANKLIN, *left guard:* All-Pro stud from Nebraska . . . No. 1 draft choice . . . extremely quick for big man . . . but big-time trouble-maker . . . led revolts among black players . . . Assistant now with Steelers . . . seeks head job.

Who could forget the white shoe issue? Euger aroused our other black players and they demanded we switch to white shoes. Shoat tried to stand firm, saying, "Do I look like a fuckin' deputy sheriff in Selma, Alabama?" But he finally gave in. We went to white shoes.

BABY DEAN McCOOBRY, *left tackle:* Wide-eyed rookie, University Texas, in Super Bowl year. Devoted Longhorn . . . Wore burnt-orange tux and entire wedding party wore burnt orange when married wife, Carlynn.

Manages Office Depot, Austin, today. Still collects match books.

Baby Dean became immortal for trying to sing the "Eyes of Texas," which T.J. used to make him do at mealtime in training camp. Baby Dean's words to the UT alma mater usually came out:

Eyes of Bexis are upon us, all the beverage day.
Eyes of Bexis are because if, their ducks is in the
   way.
Do don't thank you can despise them, who behind
   their days.
Eyes of Bexis go behind me, till Garland goes their
   eggs.

MARVIN ("SHAKE") TILLER, *split end:* Humble man known for his modesty. He and I both agree he's greatest pass receiver in history of game. . . . Lives Hollywood . . . writes books, movies . . . amateur pharmacist.

AL ("ABORT") GOODWIN, *wide receiver:* Olympic hurdler. Won bronze at Munich, lost by nose to Russian and East German.

Teaches history today at U. of Colorado, alma mater . . . Still stays in shape, runs twenty-five miles a day . . . eats nuts off ground . . . climbs medium-size mountains . . . earns extra income working in bike shop . . . family worries about his overexercise . . . 4 angioplasties in past 2 years.

Al was a good sport. His job was to run a deep sideline route on every single down, occupy a defender. That was all Shoat asked of him. Run deep, stay out of everybody's way.

I really don't remember Al catching more than one ball in five years.

BOOGER SANDERS, *fullback:* Maniac redneck, played at Alabama . . . comes from Waveland, Mississippi, on Gulf Coast . . . Shoat Cooper's quote: "Booger's so southern, he thinks Auburn and Clemson are states."
Today owns nightclub between Gulfport and Biloxi. Loves being in midst of new gambling casinos. Name of club: Git After It . . . singers, dancers, waitresses wear G-strings only . . . highlight of evening: Booger pours honey on girls, customers pay to lick it off.

Booger was a great blocker. Shoat said he could hit people hard enough to hurt a good Catholic. He also said Booger was so tough, he could "piss wider than a sawblade." I never quite knew what that meant.

BILLY CLYDE PUCKETT, *running back:* Last great white runner . . . 4-time All-Pro . . . Career ended early by Dreamer Tatum . . . turned knee into molasses . . . unappreciated network announcer . . . said fuck it and quit . . . married to movie star Barb Bookman . . . loyal Horned Frog.

It was to Human Dog that I said, "Notorious for studying his game plans by the light of a jukebox."

HOSE MANNING, *quarterback:* Most effective QB in NFL . . . throwback to old days . . . called own plays . . . doubled as placekicker . . . knack for finding open man . . . threw nose-up ball, easy to catch . . . Led Giants to one Super Bowl win, three division titles . . .
Moved back home to Oklahoma City . . . got rich in food supply business . . . retired now . . . lives half year in Palm Springs . . . devoted golfer . . . ask how often he plays, says, "Just days."

I wanted to remember to tell Jim Tom the best-kept secret about Hose. He was the first modern pro quarterback to smoke and drink on the field during games. Our equipment manager, Teddy Bryan, built a little compartment in all of Hose's game pants to hold a tiny flask of Jack Daniel's. Teddy also constructed pouches in the front of his game jerseys for his pack of Winstons and lighter. When he felt like it, Hose would take a swig of Jack. He'd light up in the huddle, have two quick drags, and the Pope would eat the cigarette before we'd break for the line of scrimmage.

Shoat gave up on trying to send in plays the first season Hose was with the Giants. He gave up in the first quarter of our opening game with the Redskins one Sunday at Yankee Stadium. The third time a play came in from the sideline, Hose cussed, called time-out, strolled over to Shoat and said, "You called it, you go out there and run the fucker."

I took Human Dog for a stroll along the lake promenade, let him have a brief flirtation with a miniature schnauzer. The flirtation ended when the owner, a woman who looked like a full-grown schnauzer, jerked on the leash, rattled off something at me in fluent Nazi, and gruffly walked on.

Back to the sidewalk cafe, then, to read the notes on the Giants' defense.

T. J. LAMBERT, *left end:* No better defensive end, ever . . . forced teams to run opposite direction 70 percent of time . . . all-time great U. of Tennessee.
Spirit leader & captain of Giants' Super Bowl team . . . cinch for pro football Hall of Fame . . . Today: successful college coach at TCU.
More than anything else, rival captains might remember

T.J.'s competitive attitude when he'd meet them for the coin flip.

"Fuck all you tootie fruities" was what he usually said.

HENRY KNIGHT, *left tackle:* One of first truly big men . . . played at 6-7, 285 . . . Pride of Arkansas AM&N (never minded when Shoat called it Agricultural, Mechanical and Nee-grow) . . . Moved back home to Ocheecannypulia, Arkansas . . . helps wife run food stop/bait store.

Henry was big, yes, but not too agile, and not too energetic. Which was why he got his nickname, "Room," all of us constantly hearing Shoat say, "Henry, just go on out there and take up some room."

Lois, his wife, liked to say that Henry would watch intermediate algebra on cable before he'd leave the couch to go get the clicker.

RUCKER McFARLAND, *right tackle:* Smart player . . . steady performer. Made All-ACC three years at North Carolina State.

Played 5 seasons . . . took government job . . . lives Charlotte.

Rucker was more interesting than that. In my mind, he held some kind of record for the way he met his wives. He met his first wife, Holly, on a float in the Peach Bowl parade. He met his second wife, Trudy, when he was trying to pay his respects to his dead uncle and went to the wrong funeral home, and he met his present wife, Maureen, at a crash site.

Rucker had gone to work for the National Transportation Safety Association by then, and Maureen was a safety rep for her flight attendant union. They were wandering around what was left of Delta Flight 508, stepping over arms, legs, elbows, charred luggage, pieces of fuselage, and it was love at first sight.

F. TOLAN GATES, *right end:* Good athlete . . .
Stanford man . . . well-connected socially.
Advised many teammates on money matters . . .
joined prominent investment firm, San Francisco,
after pro career.
Lived in mansion Pacific Heights with beautiful
wife, Gloria . . . owned private plane, seagoing
yacht, collected antique sports cars . . . missing
nearly 7 years now.
Whereabouts unknown, was about all you could add.

PERRY LOU JACKSON, *strongside linebacker:*
Legendary hitter . . . college: Texas South-
ern . . . Some say he ranks up there with Jordan,
Butkus, Nobis.
Brother of Wire-Hair Jackson, man who killed
four Oakdale prison guards in escape attempt . . .
All-Pro with both Giants, Packers.
Today: makes good living with gun shop in Miami.
I needed to remind Jim Tom of something. That on
game days Perry Lou would tuck a towel in his belt with
the nickname he'd chosen for himself on it—"Hitt
Man." Nobody ever dared tell him it was misspelled.

SALTER BINGHAM, *middle linebacker:* Steady
player . . . not flashy . . . UCLA grad.
Team trivia expert . . . real sports fan. Always
vowed to work in sports when retired as player.
Happy now as women's soccer coach at Syracuse.
Salter got some raw deals. Sportswriters said he was our
"soft spot" as the middle linebacker, and they wrote that
when he played for UCLA, he was personally responsible for three straight Southern Cal running backs winning the Heisman.

HARRIS JONES, *weakside linebacker:* Surprise ad-
dition to team . . . basketball star at Michigan

State . . . drafted by Giants even though never
played college football.
Makes home in LA . . . standout on beach vol-
leyball team . . . owns and runs health food store.
Credited with inventing popular mystery vita-
min . . . keeps people awake for 48 consecutive
hours.

Harris never made many tackles but his leaping and
arm-waving ability would make it difficult for
quarterbacks to throw to their left, to his side, because
he'd be jumping up to obscure the passer's vision and
flapping his arms like a windmill.

**JIMMY KEITH JOY, STORY TIME
MITCHEL,** *c-backs:* They go together, much in
common . . . both All-Americans . . . Jimmy
Keith at Kansas State, Story Time at Purdue . . .
quick, savvy cornerbacks . . . Both good musi-
cians . . . formed rock group, Speed Freaks . . .
still tour, make records, but no big hits since
"Bodobber Doobie Dop" and "Boopy Tooby
Looby."
Both live on road . . . no mailing address.

It was said around the Big 10 that Story Time was so fast
in college, he once went from armed robbery to probation overnight.

VARNELL SWIST, *free safety:* San Diego State
product . . . crucial figure in Giants secondary . . . considered first NFL player to wear earring . . . 5 times Pro Bowl.
Well-known for his battle cry—"I fickin' to blitz, I
fickin' to blitz!"
Moved back home to San Diego . . . 8 children . . . manages lawn maintenance business.

I hadn't seen Varnell since I worked in TV and was in
San Diego for a game. He came up to the booth to visit.

He said his business was going well, but those sprinkler systems were a little bit of hell.

> **BOBBY STYLES,** *strong safety:* Native of New Orleans . . . former running back at LSU.
> Drafted as ball-carrier but moved to defense . . . suffered chronic fumbleitis . . . Shoat Cooper's remark: "Bobby couldn't hold on to the football if it was lodged in his colon."
> Still lives in New Orleans, works odd jobs when not in prison.

In many ways Bobby was our most colorful character. He thought of himself as a good cook, used to invite us over to his apartment for dinner, and talked like a chef in the French Quarter—"You take dat sauce, boy, and put dat sauce on dat crawfish, and I mean, ooo, boy, dat's good stuff."

There were always rumors that he bet on games, but I don't believe he ever bet against his own team—he never played like he did—even though he frequently referred to an opponent as a six-and-a-half dog, or a three-and-a-half fave, or referred to a particular game as "a lock for the Over."

Bobby retired after our Super Bowl season and moved back to New Orleans. Said he wanted to go out a winner, and besides that, he was offered a good business opportunity. A fellow needed to plan ahead, he wasn't always going to play football.

It was a year or two later that we heard about his first stint in prison on a counterfeiting charge. That was the short time he went indoors. I think he did five years the second time.

T.J. was the last of any of Bobby's teammates to see him, as far as I knew. It was the time T.J. took the Frogs to Baton Rouge for a game against LSU, and Bobby dropped by their hotel.

T.J. said he wasn't as outgoing and talkative as he'd once been, and you couldn't accuse him of being a sharp dresser anymore—he was in a T-shirt and grimy jeans—but he swore he was okay, he'd just wanted to say hidy. That was the meeting where T.J. asked him if there was anything he could do for him, and Bobby said, "Yeah, you got change for a hundred?"

RANDY JUAN LLANEZ, *special teams:* Punt and kickoff returner . . . stunned Jets with 98-yard kickoff return in Super Bowl . . . native of Montevideo, Uruguay . . . learned shifty moves as youngster growing up in soccer riots.
Quit football early to be ballroom dancer . . . competes in ballroom dance contests on international level . . . leading vigorous campaign to make ballroom dance an Olympic sport.
The last any of us heard, Randy Juan had moved from New York to Quincy, Illinois, having heard from somebody that it was a hotbed of ballroom dancing.

It was no reflection on T. J. Lambert, who played his heart out, but one of the things I remembered best from our 31–28 win in the Super Bowl was how our defense—our highly praised and much-publicized defense, I might add—gave up four touchdowns to the dogass Jets, which put us in a ditch we damn near didn't crawl out of.

That plus the doves, the four-minute convocation that eventually drew catcalls, and the jet fighters all being up there on rockets red glare.

24

Two phone calls hastened my own departure from Switzerland a week after Jim Tom Pinch left, and while I didn't like leaving my wife and dog, I didn't mind leaving Jack Brothers, a man who couldn't act his way out of a used-car commercial if he wore a cowboy hat and sat on a goat.

The first call was from Big Ed.

Big Ed instructed me to meet him in LA within the next five days. We had reservations at the Beverly Hills Hotel. So did every owner in the NFL. So did Val Emery, the smiling commissioner, who was known behind his back by names other than "Vapid Emptysuit," two of which were "Tapioca" and "Air Ball."

This was going to be it. Final presentations would be made. The expansion committee would make its recommendations. The owners would vote on the two teams to take in. The commissioner would hold a press conference and make the announcement.

Secret ballots would be cast by the thirty owners. A two-thirds vote of the majority was required for admittance. This meant we needed twenty votes from somewhere.

We knew there were four votes we'd never get. Dallas didn't want another team in Texas. Denver and Arizona were afraid we might infringe on their TV market. And the three-piece wethead who ran the Giants, Gray Shannon, would abstain, fearful word might leak out that he had taken a position on something.

It was a source of worry to me that the other three hopefuls didn't have our peculiar geographical problems in regard to TV and self-interest, which made us the underdog in that respect. But I hoped this was balanced out by the fact that England and Mexico were foreign countries, and Hawaii was the same thing as a foreign country, sitting way out there in the ocean all alone.

I asked Big Ed on the phone, "Have you heard any gossip in the bidness world about our competition?"

"Nothing to speak of," he said. "I understand the Jap's recovering from some of his financial woes. No way to know what's going on with those people down in Mexico. All I know is, that wife of Bappy's couldn't spend all his money if she had four hands. I guess the little twerp over in London is still getting rich with his noise music."

I didn't have the heart to tell Big Ed I'd read in a London paper where Neville Trill was now managing two more of the hottest groups on the music scene, Sluts for Lunch and Toe Jam.

Big Ed said, "I keep hoping the little twerp will get caught in a hotel room full of naked gypsies, but I guess that would only make him a sympathetic figure in today's deviant world. I'll tell you. It's like trying to figure out what's on Helen Keller's mind. Nobody connected with the NFL will say anything. I'd wager the damn CIA couldn't even find out what's going on with the NFL, but I guess that's nothing new for the CIA. I've had people make phone calls. I even had the president of the United States make calls for me. Two owners hung up

on him. Three others told him to mind his own goddamn bidness. Personally, I don't think people ought to
talk to the president of the United States that way, even
if he is a devout asshole."

"You should at least respect the office," I said.

"Damn right. I've known every president since Ike.
I've dealt with every one of them, including Ike. But I've
never been anything but cordial . . . respectful, even
when I've had to put up with one of those idealogues.
Nothing more dangerous than your idealogue, Billy
Clyde. You can file that right now under What Makes
Sense. But I was nice every time I was in the Oval Office
trying to talk to one of those fellows about the oil bidness. Bad as I wanted to, I never said the trouble with
this country is there's never a Lee Harvey Oswald
around when you need one."

"I think it's best you kept that to yourself," I said.

"Deliver me from your idealogues. They're a bigger
danger to this country than your liberals, although I
reckon the two go together most of the time. You know
why your idealogues are dangerous? The silly sons of
bitches think they can make shit taste like whipped
cream. How's my daughter? She won't return my calls."

"They seem to be having a lot of problems with the
movie," I said. "She's preoccupied."

"Beats me how anybody can have problems making a
movie. Don't you just get people to stand in front of a
camera and play like they're somebody else?"

"That's how you and I see it. They take the point of
view that it's a little more artistic than that. Where you
calling from, Ed?"

"We're in San Diego. La Jolla."

"Doing what?"

"Oh, Barbara wanted to visit two of her sorority sisters. I saw it as a chance to go to the Callaway plant."

"Barbara has two old girlfriends from Fort Worth who both live in La Jolla now? That's amazing."

"Yep. Old Bonnie and Corky. They finally married enough times to wind up rich and suntanned."

"Give Big Barb a hug for me. What's Callaway doing for you?"

"I'm tired of giving up distance off the tee to a bunch of turkeys the same age as me."

"I don't blame you. It would piss anybody off."

"Yesterday I worked with the Silver Cantaloupe. I tried it with a forty-two-inch titanium shaft and only eight degrees loft. It gave me twenty more yards. But I want more than that. Today I'm gonna try the Platinum Watermelon with a forty-nine-inch titanium shaft and only four-and-a-half-degrees loft. I'll see you in LA."

"I'll be there with some more of my favorite football anecdotes. Take 'em inside the huddle. Dazzle 'em with a little more footwork."

"I look at it this way, son. If they're not smart enough to pick us, they're not smart enough for us to hang out with."

25

A delicate problem arose with the other call I received, although it wouldn't have been a problem if Barbara Jane hadn't answered the phone.

I was having a perfectly good time that evening, sprawled in a cushiony chair in my baggy gray sweatsuit, savoring room service orders and my reading material.

I'd just been laughing about an article in the *Daily Mail*. A Mrs. Sarah Bonewittle, a prominent animal rights activist, had committed suicide by dashing out of a restaurant in Chelsea and throwing herself in front of a speeding delivery truck, and all because her husband had ordered the veal chop.

I was still chuckling when I overheard Barb on the phone.

"Who is this?" I heard her say in a sharp tone. Which prompted me to turn toward her and recognize the look.

It was the look that sometimes made a man think he was in a submarine movie with an alarm sounding—*wooup, wooup*—but I wasn't in a submarine movie, and what I next heard was my wife's smart-aleck voice saying, "It's Kelly Sue in Fort Worth, dear. Isn't it sweet of her to call?"

Barb handed me the phone and stood there giving me a look, arms folded, holding a cigarette.

I smiled innocently at my wife. "It's a bartender I met at one of T.J.'s hangouts in Fort Worth. Place called He's Not Here."

"That's the name of it?"

I nodded.

"They're such socialites down there."

Taking the phone, I said, "Kelly Sue, what's up?"

Kelly Sue was giggling when she said, "That better be a wife who answered or I'm gonna be hot."

"That was Barbara Jane," I said. "Your voice has changed, Kelly Sue. You sound just like a woman."

My wife didn't laugh.

I made another try. "I thought I told you never to call me here, Kelly Sue."

"Not working, is it?" the bartender said.

"No, it isn't," I replied.

In my honest opinion, I didn't think it was much fun, talking to two women at once, one on the phone, the other one exhaling smoke at me.

Kelly Sue said, "I thought you'd want to know about Tommy Earl and Ody Bradshaw."

"What about them?"

"They shot each other."

"They *what?*"

"They're not dead, they'll be okay, but they shot each other."

I looked at Barbara Jane with astonishment and said, "Tommy Earl Bruner and another guy shot each other."

Barb said, "Why, they got bored fucking Kelly Sue?"

"I heard that," Kelly Sue said. "She is *very* quick."

"Yes, she is."

"Yes, I'm what?" Barb said.

"Kelly Sue says you're very quick."

"You're in deep shit," Kelly Sue said. "I'd better hang up."

"Wait, I want to know what happened."

"Who was the other dumbfuck that got shot with Tommy Earl?" Barbara Jane asked.

"Guy named Ody Bradshaw," I said. "A real dumbfuck. Short. Loud. Nothing like Tommy Earl."

"Right. Tommy Earl's a lovable dumbfuck."

"True."

"Why don't you call me back when there are fewer interruptions?" Kelly Sue said. "I'm at the joint."

"It's okay," I said to the phone. "What was the deal? Are they hurt bad? What the hell happened?"

Barbara Jane took a chair, picked up a script.

I lit a Marlboro and sat down to get comfortable.

The story as I heard it from Kelly Sue:

Ody and Tommy Earl made a move on each other's wife. Ody had always lusted after Sheila Bruner. He'd never fucked a "nice woman" before, and certainly not a Junior Leaguer. And Tommy Earl had always been curious about Suzy Bradshaw. He'd never fucked a Jap-o-nese before, at least not a real clean one.

Turned out Ody had taken "the neglected Sheila" to lunch three or four times, ostensibly to talk about her and Tommy Earl, see if there was anything he could do to help their relationship. It was the least he could do for his business partner. What were friends for?

Tommy Earl hadn't taken Suzy to lunch, but he'd taken her up to his secret pad in the Forest Park Apartments. Told her it was where he entertained clients. Maybe one of these days she could help him arrange an "Oriental dinner party" for clients. Something exotic. Might be good for commerce.

Somewhere along the way, Ody put his hand on Sheila's knee, and Tommy Earl put his hand on Suzy's knee. This got back to their husbands, of course, and Ody and Tommy Earl each carried a gun, of course.

Kelly Sue guessed that she and T.J. were about the only two people she knew in Texas now who didn't carry guns, or keep guns in their cars.

Tommy Earl called Ody and said there was something important they needed to talk about. Ody said he'd been thinking the same thing. They agreed to meet for breakfast at Ora Mae's Bite Shop the next day.

They arrived at the same time and met out front on the sidewalk. Tommy Earl immediately said, "What's this shit about you tryin' to fuck my wife?"

This conversation was pieced together by Kelly Sue after she talked to Tommy Earl at home and visited Ody in his room at All Saints.

Ody said, "Why do you care? You don't never fuck her no more."

Tommy Earl said, "That don't mean she ain't my wife, you sorry-ass chunk of shit, and dwarf to boot."

Ody said, "Well, I didn't fuck her, did I? So what's the goddamn problem?"

Tommy Earl said, "The problem is, you *tried* to fuck her."

Ody said, "Tryin' don't get it done, where I come from. And while we're at it, what's this shit about you tryin' to fuck Suzy?"

Tommy Earl said, "I wouldn't have fucked Suzy if she didn't want me to, and she didn't act like she wanted me to, so I didn't—not that I wouldn't have eat her if the opportunity presented itself."

Ody said, "Don't nobody eat my wife but me!"

Tommy Earl said, "How do you know? She's inscrutable, ain't she?"

Ody said, "Goddamn the goddamn! You making fun of my wife 'cause she's a Jap?"

Tommy Earl said, "I'm saying she's an inscrutable

sumbitch and you don't know what the fuck she's up to half the time."

Ody said, "I don't, huh?"

Tommy Earl said, "Not if it ain't stir-fried."

Ody said, "Oh, yeah? How you know what Sheila's up to? Them what's in the Junior League don't have pussies?"

Tommy Earl said, "Some do, some don't. My wife by God does, and it ain't for fuckin' loudmouth double-knits."

Ody said, "It's for fuckin' somebody besides *you*, I'll guarantee you. All I did was give her a little pat. Tell her if she ever felt lonely, I was available to talk to."

Tommy Earl said, "That ain't tryin' to fuck her, is it?"

Ody said, "Not in my book. While we're on the subject, you been known to fuck other wives."

Tommy Earl said, "Never a good friend's wife. I might fuck the wife of an acquaintance, but there's a big difference."

Ody said, "Hell, I guess they *all* become acquaintances after you fuck their wives."

Tommy Earl said, "I'll tell you what. I'm tired of talking about this shit. You go near my wife again, you'll wish you were in Egypt with a fuckin' pyramid over your head."

Ody said, "Yeah, and you go anywhere near my Jap— my wife—again, I might just shoot your ass!"

That's when they pulled out their little nickle-plated .38 pistols. Fortunately, neither one was a very good marksman.

Ody fired four shots. He hit the sidewalk, a parking meter, a fender, and the sleeve of Tommy Earl's favorite cashmere sport coat.

Tommy Earl fired four shots. He hit the sidewalk, the sky, a mailbox, and the loafer on Ody's left foot. It looked like Ody might lose his big toe, but he said it wouldn't affect his golf swing. Might even help it.

A rather clever headline in the *Light & Shopper* read: GUNFIGHT AT THE ORA MAE CORRAL!

I might find Tommy Earl's quote in the paper amusing, Kelly Sue reported. She read it to me. Always the diplomat, Tommy Earl said, "It was just one of those unfortunate misunderstandings about a business decision. You know how it is. When two fellows get in a heated discussion and call each other everything but a white man, somebody's liable to get shot."

She added that Tommy Earl and Ody weren't going to press charges against each other. They even said they'd stay friends and business partners.

I thanked Kelly Sue for calling with the news and all the updates. She said she was sorry her phone call got me in trouble.

I said, "Oh, I'm sure the Scriptures will see me through it."

She laughed and we hung up.

26

Barbara Jane got out of her chair to question my honesty and integrity. "Deceitful prick," I believe, was how she addressed me.

"Me?" I said.

"No, the poltergeist that just flew through the room."

"What'd I do?"

"How long have you known Kicky Jean?"

"Kelly Sue."

"Kelly Jean . . . Kicky Sue."

"It's Kelly Sue. Kelly Sue Woodley."

"Your little girlfriend in Texas. How long?"

"Kelly Sue's not my little girlfriend, and she's not all that little. She's about your size."

"When were you going to get around to telling me about her?"

"Tell you what? That I met a bartender in Fort Worth? I know bartenders everywhere."

"Will any of the others be calling tonight?"

"Why do you want to start a fight with me?"

"I'm not trying to start a fight, I just want the truth."

"You don't have enough movie people to be mad at?"

"I'm just curious about how well you know Kicky

Jean. You obviously know her pretty well. She thinks she knows you well enough to call you long fucking distance in Switzerland."

"It's Kelly Sue. Kicky Jean's not a bad name for somebody, though."

"You obviously like this person."

"I do like her. So will you."

"Yeah, right."

"That's my prediction."

"It is, huh? Well, here's mine. I say a woman who calls you in Switzerland will boil your rabbit."

I had to laugh.

"When did you plan to tell me about her?"

"Tell you what?"

"That she *existed.*"

"Do I tell you about every bartender I meet? Hi, honey, I met this great bartender in Cincinnati. She was almost as great as the bartender I met in Denver, or maybe it was Miami—I get my oceans and mountains mixed up."

"I bet I know one thing about her. She's good-look-ing. If she weren't good-looking, you wouldn't have be-come such good friends she'd call you in fucking Swit-zerland."

"Is this gonna be a long one? If it is, I need a drink to go along with the cigarettes."

I went to the bar to fix myself a Junior and water.

"Anything for the movie star?" I asked.

"An honest husband would be nice."

"That is such shit."

"I'll have a vodka rocks."

"Count Smirn or Abbott?" Texan for Absolut.

"The Count will do."

I made the drink, handed it to her.

We took up our positions. Her on the sofa, me in the hard-back chair at the desk. Human Dog was at the other end of the sofa, trying to get some sleep after his veal marsala.

"How long have you known her?"

"Two days."

"How many nights?"

"I was in the joint three times. It's on Camp Bowie, not too far out. In one of those old shopping strips. T.J.'s kind of place."

"But not yours, of course."

"It's a little too intellectual for me. All that talk about opera with the carpet salesmen. I found Kelly Sue more interesting."

"I'm sure you did."

"Conversationally."

"That too."

"You know, you're giving a bad rap to somebody you're gonna be friends with someday. Kelly Sue's fun. She's a big fan of yours, too."

"I'll send her an eight-by-ten. Remind me to get her address."

"I promised her a job—if we get the team."

"You *what?*"

That was kind of loud, I thought.

"I promised her a job. We're gonna need people. She can do a lot of things."

"Anything standing up?"

"She's smart, quick. She can be an office manager, in charge of personnel, accounting, community relations. Lots of stuff."

"Fuck the general manager."

"This is one of those times when I really like the movie business. The picture's going lousy, so you take it out on me."

"I'm perfectly aware of what you think about the movie business."

"That's another bad rap. I don't hate movies. I like

movies. I just don't like to see movies being made. How many doughnuts can I eat?"

"You don't understand the process."

"I understand you and Shake like to make movies. That's good enough for me. But you're right. I don't understand all the meetings, talking about bullshit. And they call it art."

"Shake and I don't call it art. We *do* call it a craft—and I can't tell you how fascinating it is to have the process criticized by somebody who's never worked a day in his life."

"I've never worked a day in my life?"

Human Dog woke up, looked at both of us, went back to sleep.

"You played a game for a living. You did color for a living."

"I never knew you had so much respect and admiration for what I do."

"I do have respect and admiration for you—as a person—and you damn well know it. Yes, you got knocked down. Yes, you got bruised. Yes, you had to put up with TV drones. I don't know all that? I've spent half my life cheering at football games and crying at football games—and praying you'd get back up. I know how much you love the game, and I know all the frustrations you feel about the game, and I know how useless you felt doing TV—doesn't that substantiate what I'm saying? But it was a game, wasn't it? It wasn't lifting heavy furniture. It wasn't air-traffic control in a blizzard."

"Thanks."

"I'm not saying I haven't been fortunate too."

"I'm glad you said that because I was just thinking about how tough it must have been for you down there in the mines. Trying to read the old stock portfolio by the little light on your hard hat. How well I remember the Bookman family, slaving away to make ends meet."

"Well, now that you mention it, you've never had to get up at four-thirty in the morning for days, weeks. Go through the grind of makeup. Stand on your feet all day. As I recall, you've mainly had to come *home* at four-thirty in the morning."

"Right, I was only playing a game. That's why Dreamer Tatum's got my medial collateral ligament on his trophy shelf."

"It was a terrible time for you, I know that. But have you ever stopped to think it may have been for the best? If you'd played another five or six years, who knows where we'd be now? You might be the real-life Boyd in this script. Coaching somewhere. For all your complaints about it, you didn't do badly with television. What, it was so tough continuing to be a celebrity, signing autographs?"

"I didn't choose television. It chose me. Was I supposed to turn down the opportunity, turn down the money?"

"No, you were supposed to turn down Kathy Montgomery."

That remark made me remember something: wives never forget. I wasn't sure about elephants.

Kathy Montgomery was the stage manager of our broadcast booth my first year with CBS. She was a homewrecker of young, shapely, blond, blue-eyed proportions. Shake said if she'd ever been in a Winter Olympics, she'd have won the Nordic combined. Okay, she took me hostage for a brief moment in my life. We had what my wife called an affair and I called a flirtation. It was a harmless thing. It was especially harmless—and downright hilarious—after Kathy decided she was a lesbian. And a few months later, after she decided she was no longer a lesbian, she found a network news president to take hostage. After him, she found the governor of Colorado to take hostage. The last I heard, a year or so

ago, she'd broken up the home of a United States senator from Florida. It would be a good guess that she ulti-
mately had the White House in her sights, although it
could be the Vatican.

"Kathy Montgomery?" I said. "I remember her. Pi
Phi."

Experience had taught me that it served no useful
purpose to bring up Jack Sullivan. He was the director,
writer, and producer of *Rita's Limo Stop*, a man who had
been a part of Barb's career much longer than Kathy
Montgomery had been a part of mine. Jack Sullivan had
been the genius behind the success of the series, the guy
who ate and slept with the show and rewrote the bad
scripts and introduced minor characters and plot twists
to keep it fresh. He was Barb's frequent dinner companion, close friend, and designated listener—and was accused of being a lot more—in those years when our
bicoastal marriage hit its share of bumps in the road. But
Jack Sullivan had been a totally different relationship
than the kind I'd had with Kathy Montgomery, or so I'd
been informed on those numerous occasions when I was
learning to go fuck myself.

Nicely, I said, "Babe, I apologize. I guess when I stop
to think about it, you have a right to think Kelly Sue
might be another Kathy."

The old peacemaker.

"You're damn right I do," she said. "You never mention her in all the time you've been back, then she calls
you over here!"

"Well, Kelly Sue Woodley is *not* another Kathy
Montgomery. Trust me, as they say in Hollywood. And I
didn't mention her to you because I wanted to avoid this
very conversation."

"Men," Barb said, almost spinning around in a circle.
"That is so stupid. If you'd mentioned her to me, we
wouldn't be *having* this conversation."

"We should have had a kid."

All that got was a glare.

I said, "Maybe if we'd had a kid or two we wouldn't be having this conversation."

"I don't believe you're saying that."

"I'm saying it."

"Don't."

"I already have."

"Then I'll have to remind you of something. *You* were the one who didn't want a kid."

"Wrong. *We* decided it wouldn't be a good thing."

"I don't remember it that way."

"You seldom remember anything the way anybody else remembers it."

"You didn't want a child. That's all I need to remember on *that* subject."

"*We* didn't. It's in my notes somewhere."

"Asshole."

"That's not in my notes. How many times did we talk about it? The nutty life we live. One of us always going off somewhere. You had the good line about it. We could be the Bicoastal Parents of the Year, produce the first terrorist toddler. We agreed it wouldn't be right to have a kid raised by baby-sitters."

"That was before we had Kelly Jean."

I slumped. "Look," I said, "not having a kid's never caused a problem before—let's don't let it cause one now."

"You brought it up."

I took a spin around the room. Emptied an ashtray. Freshened my drink. Gave Hume a gentle squeeze behind the ears.

Then I said to Barb, "I guess you don't count it as work that I've spent the best part of two years trying to get an NFL team. If you don't think it's hard work to smile at assholes and talk to them and entertain them, you've never been in the trenches."

She looked at me a moment, then said, "You don't even know why Daddy wants to buy a team, do you?"

"What do you mean?"

"I mean the real reason he wants a team."

"He knows it's a good investment, owning a team."

"He wants it for *you*, B.C. Not for him. Not for me. For *you*. So you'll have something to do."

"I have plenty to do," I said, trying to look self-assured.

I was trying to act "calm, cool, and collected"—the way Coach Honk Wooten wanted us to be going into a game against the Arlington Heights Yellow Jackets—but I frankly didn't know what the hell I was going to do with the rest of my life if we didn't get the expansion team.

Keep making speeches? Keep doing outings? Live off my wife?

I wouldn't be a good salesman. I couldn't sell a fried pie to a fat man. I couldn't fix anything. I could barely force a table lamp to take a 100-watt bulb without a fistfight.

I supposed I could go back into television—there were eight hundred cable channels now. Do color again, or sit in a studio and talk about the 3-4 defense, the Flex, the Nickel Package, the two-deep zone. But it wore me out to think about working with one of those pathetic Larry Hoages again—"If you ask me, Billy Clyde Puckett, I'd say that ball carrier's got some untapped daylight in him."

"Something more meaningful than playing in pro-ams, is what I think daddy has in mind," Barb was saying.

"I must have been somewhere else when Ed put his ego to bed."

"That remark is beneath you, even if Daddy deserves it."

"You're right," I said apologetically. "I'm sorry. I love Big Ed. You know that."

Barb ended our discussion the way she usually ended such discussions between us. She slipped out of her duds.

I met her halfway across the room.

Part Four

Taking It to the Shed

27

The next day a piece of good news got lobbed on us. Shake Tiller's book, *The Average Man's History of the World*, went on *The New York Times* best-seller list at number three. The news came by way of a call from Deborah Monahan, Shake's crackerjack literary agent in Manhattan.

Deborah Monahan was Shake's fourth crackerjack literary agent in the past eight years, but she was the first one that didn't wear peasant dresses, have a twitch in one eye, and dirt on her feet left over from the sixties.

She was a saucy, quick-witted brunette who wore tinted glasses and kept her hair pinned up—an alert woman who could carry on three conversations at once.

It was a quaint whim of Deborah's that she only represented male heterosexual clients, and she was known for her creative drive at helping a writer with a work in progress, and then helping promote the writer's work after it was finished. Shake said Deborah could wriggle out of a tailored suit and let her hair down quicker than any woman he'd ever met. In the world of publishing, she was known as "Desktop Deborah."

Deborah warned Shake not to expect his book to

climb any higher than number three. It was impossible to dislodge *Commit Adultery, Eat Fat, Be Happy,* the book that had been number one for 234 weeks, or knock off the book that had held number two for 179 weeks, *The Cat, the Dog, and the Rabbi.*

The agent promised to do everything in her power to see that Shake's book stayed on the list for as long as possible, but in the meantime, they ought to "cook." What about a sequel? Did Shake have any ideas?

He did. Another book with a goodly amount of white space in it. No reason to burden the reader with too much substance. The kind of book that would sell. Something he'd call *The Average Man's 100 Favorite People.*

"Oh, God, I just came," Deborah said. "Get back to you."

She called back in less than an hour and said she'd made the deal with the same publisher, Asterisk Books, six-figure advance. She added that it was the first thing she'd sold in two years without unzipping a fly.

We celebrated that night at Château d'Ouchy. Our usual table by the glass walls where we could see the lights of Évian across the lake, and down the lake in another direction to the lights of Montreux.

Human Dog joined me, Barb, Shake, and a young actress named Kitten Hollis for dinner. Kitten had a small part in the movie, but mainly she was Shake's Rack-Loaded Wool Driver of the Month. Hume's leash was attached to my chair. He lounged quietly under the table with his head resting on my loafer. Barb and Shake had the fresh trout, Kitten the small lobster. Hume and I had the steak Café de Paris.

One moment I promised myself I wouldn't forget was Kitten saying to her lobster when it arrived, "Wow. E.T., phone home." Another was Kitten saying, "Whoa, too much bread-ish."

During dinner Barb and Shake expressed an interest in going over to Montreux on a free day and trying to find the villa where Noel Coward had spent so much time, Noel Coward being one of their literary heroes.

Kitten Hollis remembered that she'd gone to high school in Huntington Beach with a boy named Rusty Coward. She wondered if he was related to that friend of Barbara Jane and Shake's. Noel, was it?

With a straight face Barb said it wasn't likely but you couldn't rule it out.

"Rusty was, like, a really good skateboarder," Kitten said.

Barb said, "Well, that makes it more of a possibility."

I confessed I was growing a little confident about our chances of getting a team, and I was giving serious thought to our uniforms.

Purple and khaki and white, I was thinking. But a brighter purple than the Vikings' purple. White jerseys with purple numerals for home, purple jerseys with white numerals on the road. Khaki pants with a purple stripe and white piping. Purple socks, black helmets.

White jerseys at home, I said, for the same reason the Cowboys wore white at home. If you wore the colors at home, every visiting team looked the same to your fans—guys in white shirts. Our uniforms would have geographic meaning. Purple for the color of a bad-ass twister, khaki for the sand-colored plains of West Texas.

"And men say women talk about clothes." Barb laughed.

Kitten said, "My younger sister never talks about anything *but* clothes. My older sister never talked about anything but drugs."

"Where's your older sister now?" I asked.

"She teaches modern language at Fresno State."

Now Shake laughed. "Way of the world, man. The hippie scum of the sixties and seventies are the thought police today. Their children are the health police today. Their children are junior golfers . . . and *their* children will be the aliens who keep trying to kill Ripley."

Kitten nodded as if she comprehended all that, then selected a corner of the ceiling to stare at.

Shake said, "Did we wear mesh jerseys at TCU?"

"They were perforated," I said. "You didn't save one?"

"I used to have one. I don't know what happened to it."

"I know what happened to it," Barb said. "You gave it to me. I wore it to a party out at the Boat Club and never got home with it. I think somebody smoked it."

I said, "I gave mine to Emily Kirkland, but I got it back."

"That's not all you got from Emily Kirkland," Barb said.

"She was a generous person."

"She had a thick waist."

I said, "You know, that's one of those ugly rumors girls liked to spread around about Emily. I was happy to put it to rest."

"Emily Kirkland," Shake said longingly. "She was on the all-star team. I'd have taken a run at that devil if I hadn't been bitterly opposed to promiscuity in those days."

"You'd have lost your kneecaps too," Barb said.

I said to Shake, "I offered to trade Emily to you for Barb. You wouldn't go for it."

"Wait a minute!" Kitten Hollis spoke up, looking at Shake. "You dated Barbara Jane?"

Shake smiled. "Just all the way through high school and college."

Kitten looked at Barb. "But . . . you married Billy Clyde?"

"He was taller," Barb said.

"We've all known each other since the first grade," I said, as if that was a good enough explanation.

Kitten turned to me. "Shake and Barbara Jane went together, but she married you?"

"She came to her senses."

"And you and Shake are still good friends?"

I shrugged.

Kitten looked back at Shake. "This has never caused any problems between the two of you?"

Shake said, "It might have if we'd ever grown up, but we haven't."

Kitten looked at all three of us, first one then the other, and back again. "And you people have always stayed close, like a good friends thing?"

We all nodded.

"Wow," said Kitten.

"I know," Barb said. "It's, like, really weird-ish."

28

That same evening Barbara Jane announced she was giving up her acting career. The rumor had been circulating through our hotel suite for days.

We were back from dinner and getting ready for bed when she confirmed the rumor. She would not seek, nor would she accept, her party's nomination for another movie role.

"You don't want to do that," I said casually.

"Don't tell me what I want to do."

"I'm not."

"You just said I didn't want to do that. Do I ever tell you what you want to do?"

"No."

"Then don't tell me what I want to do."

"I meant you don't want to decide something that important when you're angry."

"I'm not angry."

"I meant you don't want to decide something that important when you're happy."

No laugh.

I said, "Look, I know this film is bugging you. Are you sure it's not influencing your decision?"

"The problems on this picture have nothing to do with it. There are problems on every picture. I've been thinking about this for a year."

"Thanks for sharing it with me."

"You weren't around. I shared it with Shake. I got into this business by accident, if you'll remember. Burt Danby dropped me into a sitcom and it was a hit. Model becomes actress."

"You were a natural."

"Playing me, yeah. That's all I've ever done. You never heard me say I was going to be the next Meryl or Jodie. You never heard anybody else say it either. I've always known my limitations. It's time to hang up my jock."

"You really want to leave the business, huh?"

"I didn't say that. I love the business."

"I thought—"

"I'm going to produce."

"You're gonna be a producer?"

"I've decided it's a better life on the other side of the camera. Better hours. Make deals with the studios. Boss people around. Screw with the director, the editing. Walk away from a set when I get bored or tired. Let everybody else chug-a-lug the liquid Maalox."

"Who are you gonna produce for?"

"Me."

"You?"

"Us, I mean. Shake and I are forming our own company. You'll have a financial interest in it. End Zone Productions."

"I like the name. What will my duties be?"

"Criticizing. Shake will keep writing and directing. Our first project will be one of his scripts. It's time for me to do this, B.C."

"You almost sound excited about it."

"I am. I want to find us some office space on one of

the old studio lots. Paramount, Fox. In one of those old buildings, you know? Something from the thirties. Hollywood ghosts wandering around."

"You'll be in Hollywood, I may well be in Gully Creek, Texas."

"We'll fax."

"We can't fax Hume."

"Hume will be with his mother, where he belongs."

"What do we do with the New York apartment?"

"Keep it. We'll both be in and out."

"It seems like only yesterday we lived in New York. One of these days we could be living in New York, LA, and West Texas."

"*We* won't be living in West Texas, darling dearest. *You* might be living there part of the time."

"We keep putting distance between us."

"Maybe that's why we stay married."

"I thought love had something to do with it."

"Love means never having to live in the Texas Panhandle."

"Gully Creek's not in the Panhandle. It's halfway between the Panhandle and the South Plains."

"Love means never having to live halfway between the Panhandle and the South Plains."

"You used to like West Texas, babe."

"I did like West Texas. I liked the big-sky thing. I remember the times I was out there with Daddy when I was little. Sitting a well. At night it was like the stars might fall right on your head. But then I got older, and one day the price of oil dropped, and . . ."

And she roared laughing at that.

I said, "I don't know why we're even talking about this right now. I don't have a football team yet. I may never have a football team. I *do* have a production company."

That made her laugh again—and got me a hug.

29

The journey from Lausanne to Los Angeles with intermittent stops in Zurich and New York and Fort Worth was rigorous, to say the least. The highlight of the flight from Zurich to New York was the movie in which a handsome young man reminded me once again that kickboxers and laser-beam weapons were no match for a good old American right cross. The highlight of the other two flights was rejecting the cardboard filet.

Then came something else that ranked high on my list of silly-looking deals—the block-long white limo. You've seen them around. They come equipped with a bar, TV, fax, phone, sauna, kitchen, choir group, and symphony orchestra.

Embarrassing as it was, the block-long white limo was the only thing available for hire at D/FW during my stopover. So, thankful for the darkened windows, off I went to fool around for three or four hours before returning to the airport to board the flight to LA. I'd planned the stopover because I wanted to visit the wounded Tommy Earl.

As we were heading for Fort Worth, I said to my

driver I hoped our limo was outfitted with windows from Gang Resistant Systems, Inc.

"Yes, sir, all of our cars have it," he said. "The handguns hardly make a scratch on these windows."

My driver's name was Alex. He was a prematurely gray, distinguished man in his fifties. He said he'd lost his executive job at a bank in Fort Worth after working there twenty years because it was taken over by a bank in North Carolina. Scooter McGriff, the CEO of the Fort Worth bank, had secretly sought out the buyer and arranged the takeover. Scooter McGriff had sold the deal to the board and shareholders by saying they'd all make thirty percent on their holdings, him included, and nobody would be fired.

But as soon as the deal had gone through, it became public knowledge that Scooter McGriff had made considerably more than thirty percent on the takeover. For selling out his own bank and his own people, he received $142 million immediately and would be paid another $253 million in two years.

But that wasn't all. He was also getting 600,000 shares of stock in the new bank, and meanwhile, more than 25,000 employees in the Texas branches had lost their jobs.

I said, "An asshole like that doesn't deserve to live."

My driver said, "No, he doesn't. That's why I'm going to target practice three nights a week."

Sheila Bruner answered the door at the house on Pembroke.

She was still a trim, attractive blonde who always tried to look her best, even around the house. This day she was wearing twin pale green sweaters, a tweed skirt, and pearls. Barb would have called it a "uniform."

"Hello, Billy Clyde," she said evenly. "Please come

in. When I saw that stretch limousine pull up, I was afraid Imelda was back in town."

"I begged for a sedan," I said. "Big White out there was all they had. I'm between planes, if you're curious—on the way to LA."

I was surprised to see a cigarette in her hand.

"I don't remember you smoking, Sheila."

"I didn't for years. I do now. Small wonder."

She guided me to a chair in the living room.

"How *is* Wyatt Earp?" I asked.

She said, "He'll recover. I wish I could see as much humor in the situation as everyone else."

"You have to laugh at it, don't you? Come on. Nobody got seriously hurt—or do I have the wrong information?"

"No one was seriously hurt unless you want to count *me*. I am totally humiliated. It was all over the front page of the paper. The front page! You would think the *Fort Worth Light & Shopper*, one of only *two* major newspapers in the entire Metroplex, would have something better to print, but no, oh, no. They have to make us look like absolute trailer trash. My God in heaven, I don't know when I will be able to *face* anyone again!"

"I guess it's a little more serious than I thought. I wonder if I can speak to Tommy Earl? Is he upstairs?"

"He's not upstairs in *this* house. He no longer lives here."

I looked at her for a moment.

"I'm sorry to hear that."

"Don't be."

"Sounds like it was your decision."

"It most certainly was, and I can't think of another decision in my life that has given me more satisfaction."

"Was it all because of the publicity?"

"I think you know better than that."

"No, I really don't, Sheila. I did hear from somebody

there might have been a misunderstanding, uh . . .
something to do with Ody Bradshaw's wife . . . what's
her name?"

"Her name is Suzy, and she had nothing to do with it.
How does the name Tracy grab you?"

"I know a Tracy in New York. She's married to—"

"Billy Clyde, stop right there. I don't want you to
make a fool of yourself. Would you like to see photographs?"

"Photographs?"

"The kind a private detective takes. Tommy Earl and
Tracy Hopkins at Tuxedo Junction. Tommy Earl and
Tracy Hopkins in his car. Tommy Earl and Tracy Hop-
kins outside some sleaze bar on Camp Bowie. Tommy
Earl and Tracy Hopkins going in the Forest Park Apart-
ments to his sneaky little hideaway he didn't think I
knew about—two fucking blocks from here! Excuse me.
I seldom use that word."

Hopkins. I couldn't help thinking I'd finally learned
Tracy's last name. She was Tracy Hopkins.

I said, "I can only say I'm sorry about all of it. I hope
you all can work things out in the long run."

"My lawyer will be working things out, thank you."

"You know, Sheila, you guys have put a lot of years
into your marriage. You have the kids. I'm sure this
Tracy person doesn't mean a thing to Tommy Earl. One
Tracy in your life—"

"What about Michelle? Should I be upset about Angela? Or Jackie? How about Pam in Dallas? How far
back would you like for me to go?"

Around a sigh, I said, "Well, it sounds like the old
marriage counselor has his work cut out for him."

Sheila said, "We're miles beyond that point, I can
assure you. If you want to see Mr. Lower-Than-a-
Worm, he's recuperating in his 'secret apartment'

around the corner—Seven-B. I would imagine his rubber dolly is there with him."

I gave Sheila a little hug and wished her luck. She said she was very much looking forward to her new life.

"Okay, who the fuck is it now?" said the female voice that answered when I rang Tommy Earl's apartment on the house phone in his lobby.

I said, "Is this . . . ? Is Tommy Earl Bruner there?"

"If you're another one of Ody's shithook friends . . ."

"It's Billy Clyde Puckett."

"Right. You're in Switzerland, I'm in France. How's *your* weather?"

"I'm downstairs."

"You're really in the lobby?" Change of tone. "Come on up to Seven-B, the door will be open."

Tommy Earl was flopped down on a sofa in the living room, a Drew and soda on the end table. He wore jeans and a cotton sweatshirt with the left arm cut out to make room for his bandage. Tracy was in a bright blue skintight exercise ensemble under gray jogging shorts.

She greeted me by sticking her tongue in my throat and pressing the Guns of Navarone into my chest.

"Sorry to run off, Billy Clyde," she said. "I gotta go pump iron. Help yourself to a drink—and there's shit to eat in the fridge."

And she was gone.

"I won," Tommy Earl said. "He ruined my twelve-hundred-dollar cashmere coat. I only ruined his three-hundred-dollar loafer. He owes me nine hundred."

"What about his big toe?"

"Ody don't need a big toe to hit that duck hook. Claude, you remember what real bad jock itch felt like in high school? That's what my arm feels like, but it's getting better."

"Has she really gone to pump iron, or is she off to fuck a stockbroker?"

"There's a health club on the third floor."

"Nobody else lives in the building?"

"You shouldn't talk about her like that, Claude. You don't know her."

"I've known her all my life."

"Not this one—she's different. I'm in love, Claude."

"She'll be expensive, I know that much."

"I'm rich," he said. "Am I lyin' to anybody? I can't afford a divorce? Life ain't about nothin' but money and pussy anyhow. Why do you think a man wants to get rich in the first place? It's not about toys. A man wants to get rich so he don't have to take any shit. So he can fire any fucker in the world that pisses him off, especially a wife. You don't know that?"

"I was just with the lady on Pembroke. I was looking for you."

"Can you believe she put a private detective on my ass? I didn't know you could *find* a damn private detective in Fort Worth."

"Evidently she's had him awhile, and evidently you didn't make his job too hard. I heard about Michelle, Jackie, Angela . . ."

"Them scags didn't mean anything to me, Claude. They were just something to do. They weren't Tracy."

"I don't think I'd bet my stack on how different Tracy is."

"You'll see. You can book it. I guess you're on your way to LA, Claude. A columnist in the *Dallas Morning News* says the Tornadoes are a mortal lock—and he likes Hawaii's chances."

"That's not the same guy who said Joe Montana would never make it in the pros, is it?"

30

It was eight-thirty at night when I reached my room at the Beverly Hills Hotel, but nine hours later for me, body time. One of the messages waiting for me said Big Ed and Big Barb were in Bungalow 5A, please call. The other message, which had been left at 5:42 P.M., said Jim Tom Pinch was in the Polo Lounge with "April Dawn," and I was invited to join them for cocktails and stimulating conversation.

I figured Jim Tom was in town to cover the expansion announcement, so I called him first to see if he had any hot information. They paged him in the Polo Lounge.

When he picked up, I said, "I have a message here that says you're with a lady who either looks like Lana Turner when she was twenty or Lana Turner when she was fifty. Which is it?"

"It doesn't matter, she's gone," he said. "She's a real estate agent. She had to go show some property."

"At *night?*"

"That's what she said."

"You got dusted."

"Probably, but it's okay. She was a little bony for my taste."

"Was her name really April Dawn?"

"No. It was closer to Laura Rabinowitz. Want a drink?"

I said I was too beat up from the trip. I was on Swiss time. It was almost six o'clock in the morning for me.

"That didn't used to be late. You out here for rehab?"

"I'll be thirsty tomorrow night. Have you talked to anybody on the expansion committee? What have you heard?"

"Are they in town for something?"

"Funny."

But I was too tired to laugh.

Jim Tom said, "Yeah, I've talked to a couple of 'em. I hear there may be a realignment of some kind. But nobody will even drop a hint about the new teams they want. You'd think they were guarding their offshore bank accounts. It's fucking pro football, is all it is."

"Don't knock America," I said.

"America's the NBA now. You don't look at newspapers? They've bought every sports editor in the country. The space they get is criminal."

"The NBA. That's the Nike Basketball Association, right?"

"I thought it stood for Niggers Be Airborne."

"You better be careful," I said. "Say that word around certain Democrats, you can do jail time."

"Hell, you can't say *anything* anymore. Tell a joke to some PC jerk, you can get shot."

I said I needed to call Big Ed, let him know I was here.

"He and Big Barb were in here for a drink earlier. I waved at them. They came in with a couple that looked just like them. About the same age, only they were obviously West Coast. Deep tans, brighter clothes. Local socialites. The socialites looked around like they hadn't

been in the Polo Lounge since they used to drink side-
cars."

"Pasadena. Maybe Hancock Park."

Jim Tom said, "The joint was slam-dunk, but Big Ed
hit the maître d' in the palm, and the guy disappeared
for thirty seconds, came back with a hammer and nails
and some lumber."

I told Jim Tom I'd look for him at poolside tomorrow.
We'd have a McCarthy salad together, hold the beets.
He said he'd have a cabana. I said I'd expect no less.

I called the Beau-Rivage and left word for Barbara
Jane that I'd beaten the airlines again, then I rang the
Bookmans in their bungalow.

Big Ed answered. He said they'd had dinner in the
hotel dining room with Zeke and Sarah Baldridge. Old
friends from Pasadena. They were already in their robes,
relaxing, but I should come over for a nightcap, at least
to say hello.

I pictured them relaxing. Big Barb sitting at a dressing
table, studying herself in a mirror, wondering if she
ought to go to Buenos Aires and see Sarah Baldridge's
plastic surgeon. Big Ed in a chair by the fireplace, reading Herman Wouk again, *The Winds of War* or *War and
Remembrance*, his two favorite books because they were
about *his* war. Big Ed had tried to read other World War
II novels but he'd say they were lame compared with
Herman Wouk and pitch them in the nearest wastebasket after fifty or sixty pages, same as he did bidness docu-
ments that infuriated him or insulted his intelligence. He
had a sidearm delivery. Different from his daughter's
one-hand push with an unreadable script.

I brushed my teeth, washed my face, and threw on a
layer of Ban. I walked down from my room on the second floor and passed by the door of the Polo Lounge,
where I couldn't resist peeking in.

All I saw were silver-haired men and platinum-haired women, their heads lit up like a night game.

I smiled to myself and went out the side door and entered Bungalow World. I followed the dark stone walkways through the trees and shrubs and flowers and the scent of bimbo perfume until I came to 5A.

Big Ed met me at the door in a navy-blue cotton robe and leather slippers, and a skinny cigar in his mouth. We shook warmly, and Big Barb appeared out of the bedroom in a long gown and robe, smiling sweetly, having not removed her makeup, or having put some back on.

She truly was a handsome, slender woman for someone in her seventies. Money keeps you young and slim, I remembered somebody saying. We hugged, but only gently, and I kissed her on the cheek, but only lightly— Big Barb never wanted anything cracked, broken, or mussed.

I gave them a report on their daughter. She was beautiful and perfect, still my favorite smart aleck, even though the movie was having minor problems. I said I'd always be amazed at how many trucks, equipment, and people it took for one actor to look at another one and say, "You got a problem with that?"

Big Ed said, "I only know one thing about the movie bidness. I know the price of a ticket is always the same as the price of a drink at '21'."

"You've been saying that for years, dear, and I've never known if it was true," Big Barb said.

"It's absolutely true. When a movie was two dollars, a drink at '21' was two dollars. When a movie was four dollars, a drink at '21' was four dollars. When a movie was seven dollars, a drink at '21' was seven dollars."

I said, "Have you ever thought of going anywhere besides '21' when you're in New York, Ed?"

"What for?" He frowned.

Big Barb said she didn't see why so many movies

needed to have so much sex and violence in them these days.

I said, "It's interesting. Nobody ever thought it was too violent when James Cagney and Edward G. Robinson used to riddle guys and cars with machine guns. Of course, those movies were black and white. It was long before the special effects people figured out how to make blood spurt out of somebody's chest."

"Ooo, I hate that," Big Barb said with a shiver.

"I don't much care for some of it either," I said. "That's why I like Woody Allen movies. Everybody's witty, lives in a great New York apartment, and never has to go to work."

"It's the humping that gets me," Big Ed said.

We looked at him.

He said, "If you go by what they put on the screen nowadays, you'd think it was all people did."

"Hump?" I said, wanting to be clear on it.

"Any movie you go to. Sooner than not, some old boy and some old gal are gonna be ripping off each other's clothes, breaking out in a sweat, going at it. Humping, hunching, groaning—gnawing around like two goddamn anim—"

"Ed!"

That came from the missus.

Big Ed said, "I didn't do it. I'm talking about Hollywood."

"You've made your point," Big Barb said.

Big Ed turned to me. "My daughter's not doing one of those humping scenes in Shake Tiller's movie, is she?"

"*Our* daughter," Big Barb put in with a look.

"That's what I mean," Big Ed said.

I said, "There *is* a scene where her character does some humping, but Barbara Jane's a no-hump actress, you might say. She made Shake use a body double."

"Thank God for small favors," said Big Barb.

"Don't matter," Big Ed said. "All our friends are still gonna think it's Barbara Jane. They don't know about body doubles. Maybe they won't see the damn thing."

"Maybe they'll never finish it," I said.

No one even looked inquisitive.

"I need a drink," Big Ed said.

"I'm going to bed," said Big Barb. We squeezed hands, and she retired to the bedroom.

Big Ed fixed himself a Chivas-rocks, I had a Coke, and he filled me in on our schedule.

Tomorrow was a nothing day for us, but league-wise the commissioner would arrive and have a private meeting with the expansion committee.

Day after tomorrow, Thursday, the expansion committee would hear the grand final majestic presentations of the London Knights and Mexico City Bandits. Friday the committee would hear the grand final majestic presentations of the Hawaii Volcanoes and West Texas Tornadoes. We would be last.

The committee would assemble Saturday morning and try to reach a recommendation by noon. The other owners would then cast their votes in a conference call. The commissioner hoped he would be able to make the big announcement in time for the evening news.

Only one of the other prospective owners was on hand, I was surprised to learn. Tokyo Russ was in the hotel with his wife, Rachel, or "Mandy Rice-Davies," but no Neville Trill and no Bappy and Naomi Ramirez. I was disappointed. They were fun to look at.

Big Ed said, "They'll be well represented by their attorneys. Their attorneys will show a new video, make their cities look more wonderful than they were a year ago. They'll hand out new brochures, pass around the results of a new survey. Won't be much truth in any of it."

I said, "I'll tell you honestly, Ed, I think we ought to add more luxury boxes to our stadium plans, and tell the expansion committee about it. Go all the way around on the same level."

"Will people buy end-zone luxury boxes?"

"Absolutely. I kind of like the end-zone view if you're up high enough."

Big Ed chuckled. "The only thing I like about an end zone is when somebody from the team I'm rootin' for is standin' in it with a football under his arm."

I remembered that Jim Tom Pinch wasn't far wrong when he wrote once that no stadium would ever be good enough for an NFL owner until it was constructed entirely of luxury boxes and the owner could sell each leather swivel chair for $3 million every Sunday.

A luxury box was more elaborate than a sky box. A luxury box had carpet, sofas, chairs, bathrooms, air-conditioning, kitchen, bar, cooks, waiters, TV sets, and curtains you could draw to shut out the game when it got boring and you wanted to discuss stocks and bonds.

No NFL owner loved his city so much that he wouldn't move his team to nearby Nigeria if he could have a stadium with more luxury boxes. You could call it legal blackmail—Jim Tom often did, not that it mattered to the fans. Cities kept putting more luxury boxes in the stadiums, at the expense of taxpayers, to keep the owners from moving.

After all, luxury boxes were one of the four ways for the owner to earn money. The other ways were television, tickets, and souvenirs. As athletes became more expensive, luxury boxes helped pay for them.

Now I said, "Go with me on this, Ed. All the way around on the luxury boxes. You can mention it to the committee, or I will. I'm still worried about us being light on glamour. I'm talking about trying to compete with London and Mexico City and Honolulu for entertainment, charm, excitement. I remember the look on their faces six months ago when I said Ruidoso Downs was only a two-hour drive from where our stadium will be."

"I wouldn't worry too much about that. They know it's a growth area."

"You sure we're not under-brochured and under-easeled? Might be just as well, coming last. They'll be over-brochured and over-easeled by then. It may help that we'll be brief. You should have the last word. Any idea of what you're going to say?"

He said, "Aw, I'll just point out a bidness thing or two, and we'll take it to the shed."

31

Big Barb sailed off the next day in a limo to bring Rodeo Drive to its knees while Big Ed went to play golf at Wilshire Country Club, one of his favorite, old-fashioned courses, so I was free to lounge around the hotel pool with Jim Tom and engage in that time-honored sport of judging rack jobs.

The contest was largely between the second, third, or fourth wives of music company executives and the girlfriends of New Jersey gangsters.

The clear winner, however, didn't come from either group. It was the wife of Tokyo Russ, the hard-hitting Rachel, or "Mandy Rice-Davies."

She was as tan as most wives who lived in the Waialae section of Honolulu, where rich folks dwelled. She constantly walked around the pool in her white string bikini, not wanting anybody to miss the show. The sight of Rachel left burn marks on Jim Tom's soul. He said she made the girls on *Baywatch* look like a gymnastics team.

Tokyo Russ was at the pool in a black suit, white shirt, and black tie. He stayed in his cabana, which was three down from ours, and held meetings throughout the day. Swarms of lawyer-type people—men and women with briefcases—came and went. Some looked grim, some looked earnest, some looked like Japs.

In the interest of friendliness I decided to introduce myself to Tokyo Russ. I picked a moment when there were only two lawyer-type people with him and Rachel was sunbathing on her tummy.

In my khakis, a light blue short-sleeve button-down shirt with the tail out, and loafers with no socks I went over to him, hoping the fellow would-be NFL owner wouldn't take me for a pool cleaner.

He was a man with a kind face, a little gray at the temples.

I smiled and said, "Mr. Akagi, I'm sorry to disturb you, but I thought we should meet. I'm Billy Clyde Puckett . . . with the West Texas Tornadoes."

"Oh, yes," he said, rising. "You very famous man. Very great player."

"Well . . ." I said.

He offered a handshake. I took it.

"You Babe Ruth," he said.

I laughed.

He said to his two grim-faced lawyer-types, who struck me as aging yuppie slime, "This is Billy Clyde Puckett. Very great player."

"Benny Clyde," a yuppie slime said with a smile as we shook.

"I just wanted to say hello," I said to Tokyo Russ.

"Good to know you," Tokyo Russ said. "Maybe we play football games together someday, but, oh, I don't know, you Babe Ruth. Too good for Rushi."

"I doubt that." I smiled.

"This my wife," he said, nodding toward Rachel's outstretched body. "Rachel, this is very famous man, Billy Clyde Puckett."

I said hi to Rachel. She made a sleepy sound with her eyes closed.

I said, "Mr. Akagi, do you—"

"You call me Rushi," he said, cutting in. "Me Rushi, you Babe Ruth."

I laughed again. "Rushi, do you happen to know the other potential owners? Mr. Ramirez and Mr. Trill?"

"Oh, no," he said. "Not have pleasure."

"They're not here," the yuppie slime said. "But Mr. Ramirez is represented by Canton, Kinninger and Scrod, and Mr. Trill is represented by Cloyd, Gallagher and Roocher."

"I'm not familiar with those firms," I said, "but I assume Mr. Ramirez and Mr. Trill are well represented."

"You might say so," the yuppie slime said. "Canton, Kinninger handles NATO. Cloyd, Gallagher represents the Vatican."

"I won't worry about them, then," I said.

"You have very good luck," Tokyo Russ said, sitting back down, signaling that our chat was over.

"You, too," I said, and shuffled away.

Jim Tom and I ordered room service lunch to the cabana and had our McCarthy salads with bleu cheese dressing, hold the hated beets.

I asked if he'd heard of the high-powered law firms representing the Bandits and the Knights. All he knew about Canton, Kinninger & Scrod, he said, was that Ox Kinninger was doing two years in a soft-core federal joint in California for overbilling a computer client, and all he knew about Cloyd, Gallagher was that Ham Cloyd had just gotten out of a soft-core federal joint in Pennsylvania after serving eighteen months for overbilling the state of Missouri.

Jim Tom knew all this from reading a story in *The Wall Street Journal* in which Ham Cloyd said something that Jim Tom filed away as the Quote of the Year. What Ham Cloyd had said was "The thing that upsets me the most since I've been released from prison is how people question my integrity."

Jim Tom had enlisted the help of his magazine's international bureaus to find out why Bappy and Naomi Ramirez and Neville Trill weren't in LA for the big expansion decision. It wasn't that they didn't care about it, they'd just had more urgent things to do.

The Johannesburg bureau tracked down Bappy and Naomi in South Africa. They were in Bappy's hunting lodge in Mala Mala, up near the Mozambique border. The lodge was in a convenient location for him, very close to a game preserve. Bappy could shoot any animal that stepped across the boundary. Word had reached Bappy and Naomi, who were in Zurich at the time visiting some of their money, that a very nice-size Cape buffalo had been sighted in the vicinity. The call had come from Rolf, the caretaker of the lodge. Bappy and Naomi quickly hopped in Bappy's Citation 10, the world's fastest private jet, and flew to the lodge. It was an opportunity they couldn't pass up—a chance for Naomi to kill her own Cape buffalo, which could be stuffed and mounted next to Bappy's Cape buffalo on the wall of their living room in Cuernavaca.

Jim Tom said, "Aren't Cape buffaloes supposed to be dangerous? Like ill-tempered mothers? Want to come at you?"

"I have no idea," I said, "but I doubt if any of them have ever gone up against Naomi Sienkowicz."

The word from the London bureau of *The Sports Magazine* was that Neville Trill had intended to be in Los Angeles for sure, but he'd run into a problem at the last moment with Ron, Don, Denny, and Mitch, the four members of Throbbing Dicks, a hugely popular rock group Neville managed. Ron, Don, Denny, and Mitch had suddenly canceled a worldwide concert tour, preferring to stay home and light the crack pipe. It was Neville's job to get them to stop peering out the windows and convince them that it would be all right to leave their homes now—the giant clam with legs they'd been watching had gone away.

Jim Tom seldom dined without being surrounded by newspapers, and I always enjoyed hearing him comment on what he might be reading.

We ate in silence for a few moments, until Jim Tom shook his head sadly at something he read in *USA Today* and said, "Good Christ."

"What?" I begged.

"Here's a lucky son of a bitch. Guy out on Long Island kills a big rat that's been eating his tomato plants. He traps the rat and beats it to death with a broom. He calls the police to come get the rat and see if they find any more, but guess what?"

"No idea."

"He gets arrested for animal cruelty."

"Come on."

"I'm serious. Some humane society finds out about him, presses charges, wants him to do a year in jail, pay a five-thousand-dollar fine. Guy kills a rat but he's a criminal! Our country's in the hands of fucking lunatics."

I said, "I once heard Big Ed say you can add ten years to your life if you don't watch the evening news or read newspapers. It may be true."

"I don't like much of what's going on today," Jim Tom said, "but I can't think of a better time to live. I wouldn't want to go back too far. No air-conditioning."

"Or expense accounts."

"How far back does deodorant go?"

Jim Tom stretched, looked around. Then he said:

"If I could have picked my spot, I'd have been a Chicago newspaper guy in the twenties and a Hollywood screenwriter in the thirties. I'd have lived at the Garden of Allah and gotten drunk with Dorothy Parker and

Robert Benchley. Sunset Boulevard was a streetcar line then—and a bridle path. I'd have driven my Cord convertible to Bel Air to play golf with Howard Hughes and Clark Gable, or over to Lakeside to play golf with Bing Crosby. The courses weren't crowded then. In fact, nothing was crowded then except Calcutta. I'd have written *Casablanca* just as the war started. In the war I'd have been a correspondent for the *Herald Tribune* and raced Hemingway to the bar at the Ritz. After the war, I'd have written *All About Eve*. I guess I'd have been locked up during the McCarthy era. When I got out, I'd have written *Dr. Strangelove*. If I wasn't too tired by then, I'd have knocked out the memoir *Life Before the Electric Guitar*."

I said, "I guess while you were doing all that in the thirties, I'd have played halfback on the Davey O'Brien team at TCU, won a national championship. But . . ."

"But what?"

"But then I suppose Sam Baugh would have helped me get signed by the Washington Redskins and I'd have been in that game where the Chicago Bears beat us seventy-three to nothing."

"What would you have done in the war?"

I smiled. "After I raised the flag on Iwo Jima?"

Jim Tom suddenly clutched his heart and groaned. I was concerned for a second, but then I noticed it was only Rachel coming by again.

32

It's a law in California that if you rent a cabana at poolside of the Beverly Hills Hotel, you have to talk on the phone all day.

We ignored the law as long as we could, but I finally felt guilty about it and called T. J. Lambert. Aside from catching up on whatever was happening in Fort Worth, I wanted to make sure I still had a coach in case I happened to own an NFL team in the next forty-eight hours.

I reached T.J. at home and found him distressed about two bad deals.

Bad Deal Number One:

T.J. was sad to inform me that Dr. Glenn Dollarhyde had publicly embarrassed the university and might well be asked to resign as chancellor within the year. The board of trustees and the faculty were so outraged about what he'd done, it might not even be possible for Big Ed to save the chancellor's job.

I asked T.J. what Dr. Dollarhyde could have done that was more embarrassing than dancing in the hallways of campus buildings.

"He drank his nose black," T.J. said.

I said, "That's not a good enough reason to fire a chancellor who likes to win football games, is it?"

T.J. said, "There's more to it. I never knew this before, but the chancellor's obligated to deliver a sermon once a month at the University Christian Church. Did you know that?"

"No. What's the point?"

"Well, apparently the chancellor got hisself on the outside of a good bit of whiskey Saturday night. Nobody's sure he'd even been to bed, but he showed up for his sermon anyhow—still in a tuxedo from a society party he'd been to. He just stood up there for a while, holding on to the podium, trying not to fall off the stage. He finally started his sermon, but he didn't get too far along with his Jedediahs and Ezekiels before he threw up."

"He threw up on the podium?"

"On the podium. On his tux . . . on his shoes."

"Anybody down front get splashed?"

"Not that I know about. The idiot Rabbit Tyrance and his wife were in the congregation. Rabbit don't know shit about Jesus and them, Billy Clyde, but that's how he keeps his job—being in the right place all the time, like in church ever Sunday. He ran up to the podium. Him and two other men. Deacons or ushers, whatever they are. They helped the chancellor out. We have a cover story, me and his friends. We're saying Dr. Dollarhyde had a terrible attack of the flu. Maybe we can sell it."

"I'll support the story, if you need a character witness," I said. "The flu's always smelled like Jim Beam to me."

Bad Deal Number Two:

The burglary attempt. It was a bad deal that somebody would actually break into T.J.'s home. It was actually a good deal that T.J. and Donna Lou caught the burglar in the act. But it was a bad deal overall that the burglar turned out to be one of T.J.'s players.

"It's not an easy thing to do, having one of your own kids arrested," the coach said.

"You turned him into the police yourself?"

"Hell, yeah, he was a sorry damn thief."

"I gather he wasn't a starter," I said, allowing cynicism to rear its ugly head.

I was right. Corey Chad Hodges was a backup linebacker, a big blond shaggy-haired kid out of a Florida junior college.

"I knew I was taking a chance on him," T.J. said. "His eyes were too close together."

T.J. and Donna Lou had just returned home from dinner and a movie downtown. "A woman's movie," T.J. said. "Whole bunch of talkin' in it." Donna Lou was the one who actually caught the burglar, or rather realized the burglar was still in the house. She heard the noise that came from their bedroom closet.

That's where Corey Chad Hodges was hiding, having pocketed some cash and jewelry. The noise Donna Lou heard was Corey Chad Hodges letting go with a rapid succession of farts.

Donna Lou recognized a fart when she heard one, having lived with T.J. for so many years.

She motioned to T.J. that somebody was in the closet. T.J. tiptoed over, doubled up his fists, got ready for her to open the closet door. Donna Lou jerked open the door and T.J. dough-popped Corey Chad Hodges with an uppercut, not even waiting to see who it might be.

As the kid lay crumpled on the floor, dazed and moaning, T.J. could only shake his head in sadness and disgust when he saw who it was.

While Donna Lou called the police, T.J. helped Corey Chad Hodges to a chair and went through his pockets and retrieved the cash and Donna Lou's jewelry, saying to the kid, "What you got to say for yourself?"

"I learned somethin' tonight," Corey Chad Hodges said.

"What's that?" said T.J. "Don't get caught?"

"Hell, I knew *that*," the kid said. "Now I know not to eat no more navy bean soup before I go out on a job."

T.J. and Donna Lou gave the details of it all to the cops, and the cops gave the details to the police reporter for the *Light & Shopper*, and the paper had fun with the story. The headline said:

BURGLAR BREAKS IN, BREAKS WIND.

The story credited a "gas attack" with preventing the burglary, pointing out that the thief might have been successful if he hadn't been "betrayed by a bout of flatulence."

T.J. only had one question about the story. What did flatulence mean?

33

Jim Tom had brought an NFL press kit to the pool. All of the other sportswriters covering the expansion meeting were staying at the airport Marriott, but somebody in the NFL's publicity department had been aware of Jim Tom's habits, and had delivered his to the Beverly Hills Hotel.

There was only one thing in the press kit that I found of interest. It was the history of the "modern" NFL.

I knew pro football had started back in the twenties, the barnstorming days, when there were teams like the Canton Bulldogs, Pottsville Maroons, Frankford Yellowjackets, and Duluth Eskimos. And I suppose I was aware that the league as we knew it today wasn't actually formed until 1933.

What surprised me, however, as I studied the material, was how many changes there'd been involving the teams, even in the so-called modern era.

Here's how the league's press kit told it:

CHRONOLOGICAL HISTORY OF THE MODERN NFL
1933
National Football League formed with 10 teams:
New York Giants
Chicago Bears
Green Bay Packers
Pittsburgh Steelers
Chicago Cardinals
Philadelphia Eagles
Boston Redskins
Brooklyn Dodgers
Cincinnati Reds
Portsmouth (Ohio) Spartans
1934
Portsmouth Spartans move to Detroit, become
Detroit Lions.
Cincinnati Reds move to St Louis, become St. Louis
Gunners.
1935
St. Louis Gunners disband.
1937
Cleveland Rams join league.
Boston Redskins move to Washington, D.C.,
become Washington Redskins.
1944
Boston Yanks join league as expansion team.
1945
Brooklyn Dodgers disband.
1946
Cleveland Rams move to Los Angeles, become Los
Angeles Rams.
All-America Conference formed with 8 teams:
Cleveland Browns
San Francisco 49ers
Los Angeles Dons
Chicago Rockets

Buffalo Bisons
Miami Seahawks
New York Yankees
Brooklyn Dodgers
1947
Miami Seahawks move to Baltimore, become
Baltimore Colts in All-America Conference.
Buffalo Bisons change name to Buffalo Bills.
1949
Boston Yanks move to New York, become New
York Bulldogs.
Chicago Rockets change name to Chicago
Hornets.
New York Yankees and Brooklyn Dodgers merge,
become New York-Brooklyn Yankees.
1950
New York Bulldogs disband.
*All-America Conference disbands after four
seasons.*
Cleveland Browns join NFL as expansion team.
San Francisco 49ers join NFL as expansion team.
Baltimore Colts join NFL as expansion team.
New York Yanks join NFL as expansion team.
1951
Baltimore Colts disband.
New York Yanks disband.
1952
Dallas Texans join league as expansion team.
1953
Dallas Texans move to Baltimore, become
Baltimore Colts.
1960
Dallas Cowboys join league as expansion team.
Chicago Cardinals move to St. Louis, become St.
Louis Cardinals.
American Football League formed with 8 teams:

Dallas Texans
Los Angeles Chargers
Boston Patriots
New York Titans
Denver Broncos
Houston Oilers
Buffalo Bills
Oakland Raiders
1961
Minnesota Vikings join league as expansion team.
Los Angeles Chargers of AFL move to San Diego,
become San Diego Chargers.
1963
Dallas Texans of AFL move to Kansas City, become
Kansas City Chiefs.
New York Titans change name to New York Jets.
1966
Atlanta Falcons join NFL as expansion team.
Miami Dolphins join AFL as expansion team.
NFL and AFL merge. All 9 AFL teams join league.
National and American Conferences are formed.
Cleveland, Pittsburgh, and Baltimore volunteer to
join AFC. New lineup reads:
NFC:
New York Giants
Chicago Bears
Green Bay Packers
Detroit Lions
Dallas Cowboys
Washington Redskins
Los Angeles Rams
San Francisco 49ers
Minnesota Vikings
St. Louis Cardinals
Philadelphia Eagles
Atlanta Falcons

AFC:
Cleveland Browns
Pittsburgh Steelers
Baltimore Colts
Miami Dolphins
Kansas City Chiefs
New York Jets
Oakland Raiders
San Diego Chargers
Denver Broncos
Houston Oilers
Boston Patriots
Buffalo Bills
1967
New Orleans Saints join NFC as expansion team.
1968
Cincinnati Bengals join AFC as expansion team.
1971
Boston Patriots move to Foxboro, Massachusetts, change name to New England Patriots.
1976
Seattle Seahawks join AFC as expansion team.
Tampa Bay Buccaneers join NFC as expansion team.
1982
Oakland Raiders move to Los Angeles, become Los Angeles Raiders.
1984
Baltimore Colts move to Indianapolis, become Indianapolis Colts.
1988
St. Louis Cardinals move to Tempe, Arizona, become Arizona Cardinals.
1995
Jacksonville Jaguars join AFC as expansion team.
Carolina Panthers join NFC as expansion team.

Los Angeles Rams move to St. Louis, become St. Louis Rams.
Los Angeles Raiders move back to Oakland, become Oakland Raiders again.
1996
Cleveland Browns move to Baltimore, become Baltimore Ravens.
1997
Houston Oilers move to Nashville, Tennessee, become Tennessee Oilers.

The brochure failed to mention that all of the moving around and growing pains of the early days had to do with financial necessity whereas every move in the past quarter century could be traced directly to greed.

But Big Ed insisted he was in pro football for the love of the game, and I believed him. And I believed him when he said he'd be happy if all the pro teams went back to the old baseball parks, where they started out, and players went both ways, and nobody wore a face mask—the face mask took fear out of the game, by God.

I'm sure it did. I'm also sure it was a bad deal for dentists.

34

Still in the clutches of jet lag that night I begged my way out of two dinner invitations—one from Jim Tom, one from the Bookmans. Showered, shaved, dressed, started out the door to meet Big Ed and Big Barb, but glanced at the TV, glanced at the room service menu, glanced at the easy chair, surrendered.

The Bookmans had asked me to join them and another couple at Musso and Frank's in Hollywood. Big Ed had been going to Musso and Frank's for fifty years, ever since the days when you might see Clark Gable sitting in the next booth. Which was never why Big Ed went there. He went there because you might see Jimmy Demaret sitting in the next booth.

There had never been a question of me going out with Jim Tom. He had wanted me to accompany him to a new joint in Santa Monica called Le Hangout. A trendy place where savages in micro-minis roamed the bar and you could get abalone pizza.

I said, "Don't they break your legs if you try to get in and you're not with Mary Pickford and Doug Fairbanks?"

Jim Tom said, "I know the guy on the door. He collects hundred-dollar bills."

"Say hello for me."

My evening consisted of ordering club sandwiches, smoking, surfing TV channels, dozing, and reading.

I watched parts of three old black-and-white movies. All the characters wore hats, talked fast, and smoked two cigarettes at once. Every time they stopped talking or smoking, I switched to another movie.

Jim Tom called from Le Hangout to ask if I wanted to change my mind and come join him. He said the savages and shapelies were out in droves.

"What's the difference between a savage and a shapely?" I asked.

"Little things," he said. "A savage will fuck a Muslim. A shapely thinks a Serb is a mint."

Right now, he said, he was at the bar listening to two producers who knew everything about sports. A couple of loud dwarfs sharing a vial. One of them was betting the other one $1,000 he couldn't name the eight guys who've hit fifty or more home runs in a season.

"Even I know there are ten," I said.

"There are fifteen."

"I've got to stop leaving the country."

He said, "Anybody can get Ruth, Foxx, Greenberg, Mantle, Mays, and Maris. Then it's tough."

"Kiner."

"Good."

"Gehrig."

"Wrong. Forty-nine twice."

"I quit."

"Hack Wilson."

"I knew that when I was sixteen."

"Johnny Mize."

"I knew that, too. Oh! Junior Griffey."

"Now you're done."

"Ted Williams?"

"Nope."

"Hank Aaron?"

"Nope."

"DiMaggio?"

"Never."

"Harmon Killebrew?"

"No. George Foster."

"George who?"

"If you can't get George Foster, you've got no shot at Albert Belle, Mark McGwire, Cecil Fielder, and Brady Anderson."

"There should only be six. I'll never look at baseball the same again. Do those producers know you're a famous sportswriter?"

"I told 'em I was Ed Smedley, Prudential Insurance. I asked them if they knew a friend of mine in the movie business, Shake Tiller. They were babbling, but I think they said they'd never heard of him."

"Did you ask if they know me?"

"I did. They said Billy Clyde Puckett was a football announcer."

"They didn't know I played?"

"I brought it up. I said Billy Clyde Puckett was an all-pro running back with the Giants before he was a football announcer."

"What did they say?"

"They said for how much?"

35

Thursday morning six neatly groomed, bran-eating lawyers representing the London Knights marched into a hotel conference room and made their presentation to the NFL expansion committee.

Their presentation lasted three hours and twenty-three minutes. I had the clock on them, purely out of curiosity. I was in the banquet room down the hall that served as a combination media headquarters and hospitality suite.

There were comfortable tables and chairs and sofas in the media headquarters and hospitality suite, and food and drink were plentiful—a buffet and bar—but if you wanted to smoke, you were forced to go outdoors and poison the birds and flowers.

Not counting Jim Tom Pinch, I noticed only a half-dozen regular sportwriters on hand. Newspaper guys I knew from New York, LA, Dallas, Boston, Chicago. Hard-core pro football writers who covered every step the NFL took, like there was nothing else worthwhile in the cosmos.

I wondered why there wasn't bigger coverage, more writers. Jim Tom reminded me that the NBA play-offs were in progress. Nike was in the semifinals with Reebok, Adidas, and Converse.

Not that there wasn't a crowd. There must have been another fifty or sixty people swarming around the free buffet, jabbering, interviewing each other, sticking fruit in their pockets.

Jim Tom explained to me that these were local radio and TV types, reporters and freelancers from the Valley, Orange County, the suburbs—the roving bands of press rabble and paparazzi that went to everything in town, from sneak previews to the Golden Globes to supermarket openings to NFL expansion committee meetings.

The lawyers for the London Knights then came into the hospitality suite and spent an hour talking about finances and displaying an illustration of Neville Trill's new personally designed logo for the Knights. It looked like a silver and gold Darth Vader with a blue vaulting pole in his hand sitting on a red Shetland pony, but nobody in the media asked what I thought of it.

After lunch was when six neatly groomed, bran-eating lawyers representing the Mexico City Bandits marched into the conference room and made a three-hour-and-sixteen-minute presentation to the expansion committee.

Then they went into the hospitality suite and talked about finances, but I didn't hear any of it because Jim Tom and I had gone to the Polo Lounge by then to set up camp in a booth for the evening.

Sportswriters came and went, joining us for one or two drinks, wanting to "see how the better half lived," they joked. Guys from the NFL communications department dropped by for one or two drinks, neglecting to leave any hints about what the expansion committee was thinking.

We were visited by the normal quota of April Dawns, rebuilt ladies who said they were in the real estate business.

The April Dawns would order a vodka, eat a scoop of guacamole on a corn chip, get a phone call, and have to rush off to show property.

One of them hung around a little longer than the others. Long enough to put her hand on my thigh under the table.

"What room are you in?" she asked softly.

"I don't think you'd be interested in me," I said.

"Maybe you should let me be the judge of that." She smiled.

"I prefer the company of men," I said.

She gave me a look. "You're putting me on."

I said, "I love being in bed with a man."

"Uh-huh, sure."

"It's true," Jim Tom said. "He particularly likes fat guys with hairy legs. He doesn't even mind it when they fart and hog the TV clicker."

She wasn't sure whether to laugh.

"I hate all that myself," Jim Tom went on. "That's why I'm a lesbian."

They left together. I never saw Jim Tom the rest of the night.

Friday morning Tokyo Russ and his own group of neatly groomed, bran-eating lawyers marched into the conference room and stayed three hours. Later, Tokyo Russ revealed to the media that he had received the full assurance of Honolulu's city politicians and Hawaii's state politicians that funds were available to enlarge existing Aloha Stadium to accommodate 100,000 fans, and also that arrangements were in place with his limited partners to finance the $220 million entry fee.

That's what the buy-in price was up to now. Two-twenty big-large.

A nice little windfall for the thirty existing owners.

Admit two new teams, pocket roughly $14 million, according to my Paschal High arithmetic.

Since all of the potential owners were wealthy—Barb once estimated that her daddy was worth around $4 billion, counting oil in the ground—and all of the potential owners had access to acceptable stadiums, like London and Honolulu did, or plans to build modern stadiums, like Mexico City and us, and since all of the potential owners were considered to be located in good TV markets, you might wonder why the presentations of the Knights, Bandits, and Volcanoes took so long.

Lawyers like to talk. That was one reason. But the other reason was that not all rich guys liked to spend their own money. In fact, very few rich guys liked to spend their own money at all. What they liked was spending somebody else's money—and largely on themselves.

Much of the lawyer talk in the press conferences was all about the incredibly creative ways that the Knights, Bandits, and Volcanoes were going to finance their $220 million entry fees and massive operational costs.

In any case, it was after the lunch break that Big Ed and I went into the conference room to face the expansion committee, but without any lawyers, easels, graphs, brochures, or videotapes.

The expansion committee consisted of five owners. They were all relatively new to the game, having acquired the teams over the past five or six years. They were the owners of the Miami Dolphins, Denver Broncos, San Francisco 49ers, Philadelphia Eagles, and Washington Redskins.

None of them had been seen around the hotel. I figured it was because they didn't want to be subjected to any undue lobbying.

The Miami owner was Nat Recano. He'd made his

money in designer landfills. If you wanted your landfill to look like an uphill par five, Nat was your man.

The Denver owner was Andy Hardeman. He'd mainly married rich women twenty or thirty years older than him. It was a comfort to the league that Andy had never been charged with any of the mysterious deaths his wives had suffered in boating accidents.

The San Francisco owner was Jeremy Beal, the restaurant mogul. Jeremy had been in the forefront of helping develop "California cuisine." He was famous for revolutionizing the BLT. In Jeremy's restaurants you could only order a "PLT," which was pineapple, liverwurst, and turnips on Afghan bread. In the Bay Area it frequently outsold his okra burger.

The Philadelphia owner was Louis Pierpont, who was best known for inventing diet birdseed. Louis was credited around the resort areas of Florida for single-handedly keeping most blue jays from becoming so plump their colors faded.

The Washington owner was young Dusty Sutton, whose family had made a fortune in burial clothes. The business dated back to 1929. Their motto was: "Our customers love our clothes—they never take them off."

Big Ed wore his standard uniform to the meeting—gray sport coat, white pin-collar shirt, striped tie. I went with a brownish checkered cashmere sport coat, pressed jeans, dark blue denim shirt.

Big Ed and I were seated side by side at the conference table. We were offered coffee or ice water. We were told we could smoke. A couple of the owners were smoking cigars. Big Ed passed. I lit a Marlboro.

The members of the expansion committee delighted in making small talk for thirty minutes.

Andy Hardeman, the Denver guy, said, "Your stadium plans certainly seem adequate."

"With some minor adjustments," the Miami guy said. Nat Recano.

The league was already aware that if our stadium wasn't completed in time for our first season, we'd been assured we could play our home games at Texas Tech's Jones Stadium in Lubbock. Jones Stadium held 51,000 but the capacity could be increased to 60,000 with temporary bleachers.

Louis Pierpont, the Philadelphia guy, said, "I believe my father was stationed at an air base somewhere in West Texas during W. W. Two. I'm not sure which town it was near."

I tried to look fascinated by that information.

Jeremy Beal said he'd been in our part of West Texas once. He had catered a debutante party for a lawyer in Amarillo.

I fought off a laugh as I visualized a debutante in Amarillo.

Dusty Sutton, the Washington guy, asked some questions in regard to the climate in West Texas.

Somebody asked about the roads in West Texas.

Somebody asked about the population growth in West Texas.

It was in the middle of the chitchat about population growth that Big Ed's impatience got the best of him.

He reached in his pocket, pulled out a certified check for $220 million. It was the most zeroes that I, for one, had ever seen on a piece of paper of any kind. Big Ed sighed heavily, tossed the check on the table.

"Gentlemen," he said, "as we say in Texas, it's time to stop talking about the picture of the dog."

We got the team.

36

Word was leaked to us early Friday night that we were being selected. That's how we actually found out. The league did this so we would have time to invite people to the commissioner's press conference Saturday afternoon. Friends, relatives, bidness associates. Anybody we might care to have around to celebrate with us when the official announcement was made.

I was in Big Ed and Big Barb's bungalow, having room service dinner with them, when one of the commissioner's drones came around to give us the word.

The drone's name was Buddy Fry. He was a chubby little baldheaded guy in Sansabelt slacks who worked in the league's publicity office. A former sports information director at Vanderbilt, SMU, Arkansas, Oklahoma State, and the Gator Bowl.

The buzzer of the bungalow rang and when I opened the door, there was Buddy Fry. He flashed a big grin and said:

"Call your mama and tell her you're in the National Football League, hoss."

It was as good a way as any, I suppose, to hear the good news.

I don't mind admitting I was a happy guy. I didn't tap dance through puddles of water and swing on lampposts, but I did grin and reward myself with a sigh of relief that could be heard by my lungs and kidneys.

We invited Buddy Fry in for a drink. He took a beer and only stayed five minutes. Long enough to tell us they'd already done the conference call with the owners instead of waiting until tomorrow morning. We'd received twenty-nine votes. One owner abstained.

I said, "Who abstained? The prick who runs the Giants?"

"I'm not at liberty to say." Buddy Fry winked.

I asked what other team got in.

He honestly had no idea. His job was just to inform us. Everything was on a need-to-know basis.

I asked Buddy to join us for dinner in the bungalow. He said thanks, but he didn't get out of the office too often—he thought he might wander down to the Sunset Strip, see what that was all about.

I walked the drone outside.

I said, "Buddy, if you find yourself falling in love down there on the Sunset Strip, make sure she doesn't have a penis and balls."

"Dang, son, are you jokin'?"

"Just thought I'd pass along one of Jim Tom Pinch's travel tips."

"Hoss, I'll watch out for *that*," he said. "Appreciate it."

Big Ed was on the phone for the next hour, trying to do a wonderful public relations thing. He graciously volunteered to send his G-5 down to West Texas and bring all the mayors in our area out to LA as his guests for the press conference—the mayors of Lubbock, Amarillo, Plainview, Tulia, Floydada, Dimmitt, and Gully Creek.

It didn't work out.

The mayor of Lubbock had a golf game he couldn't get out of, the mayor of Amarillo was on a hunting trip, the mayor of Plainview didn't have anybody to run the cafe for him, the mayor of Tulia didn't have anybody to look after the feed store for him, the mayor of Floydada had gone to a bass-fishing tournament, the mayor of Dimmitt had just died, and the wife of the mayor of Gully Creek declined for him.

The mayor of Gully Creek was Coogle Boone, a man who was also the town's butcher and barber—he and his wife owned Boone's Grocery & Hair Styling. His wife said her husband wasn't available to come to the phone, and if that fresh meat hadn't been ordered, his ass was in a fuckin' sling.

My first call was to Jim Tom Pinch. It wasn't often I had an occasion to give *him* a scoop. I wisely had him paged in the Polo Lounge, which was where I found him.

He was enjoying cocktails with "April Dawn" and a girlfriend of hers, "Sunny Autumn," who was also in the real estate business.

I gave him the news.

"That's great," he said. "I'll see what kind of champagne the ladies prefer. We'll toast the Tornadoes."

"Which one of the debutantes is sleeping over tonight?"

"Both."

"*Both?*"

"Quickly in the forecourt, two on one."

An image instantly came to me of Jim Tom in his hotel room with April Dawn and Sunny Autumn. He was near death, being eaten alive.

"I didn't know you were a basketball fan," I said.

"I am tonight."

"This will be on the expense account, I assume?"

"Is that a serious question?"

"Dinner for Red Grange and Greasy Neale."

"More like Troy Aikman and Emmitt Smith. Wait a second, April wants to talk to you."

The real estate agent said, "Come join us, Billy Clyde. My friend Sunny is dying to meet you."

"I'd love to," I said, "but I'm fighting this darn staph infection, and it hasn't completely—"

She hung up.

I called T.J. at home to let him know he was going to be an NFL coach. Donna Lou answered. She said T.J. wasn't home but she'd bet I could reach him at He's Not Here.

"What's He's Not Here?" I asked in what I thought was a tone of pure innocence.

"Gimme a break, Billy Clyde," she said.

I said, "How do you know that place?"

She said, "Sheila Bruner told me about it."

"That was thoughtful of her."

Donna Lou reported that Sheila was so angry at Tommy Earl—at all men—she was calling every wife she knew and telling them where their husbands were hiding out to drink and chase women.

She was telling the wives about He's Not Here, the Cadaver, the It'll Do, Frederick's of Fort Worth, Cafe Society, the T&A, Tina's Paradise, Not Tonight I've Got the Blues, Mommie's Trust Fund, the Wander Inn, the Gimme Putt—every place she'd found out about.

I wondered if there'd ever been a man who'd made all those in one night and lived to tell it.

Donna Lou said Sheila had decided to get breast implants, have her eyes done, and dress sexier.

"That's how she plans to get Tommy Earl back?"

"She doesn't want Tommy Earl back. She's going to

become a new person. She's going after young meat. Men under forty."

"She didn't say 'young meat,' did she?"

"She said those very words. She said after she becomes the new her, she bets there'll be a lot of young meat around town that'll want to drop the hammer on her."

"She didn't say 'drop the hammer on her.' Tell me she didn't."

"She did."

"She's been hanging out with too many Junior Leaguers."

Donna Lou said, "You think so?"

I thanked her for the Sheila Bruner bulletins and said I'd call T.J. at He's Not Here.

She said to please tell him dinner was brisket, corn on the cob, butter beans, and mashed potatoes.

I said I'd be there myself if I could get a flight.

"Yeah, *what?*"

That was the cordial way Kelly Sue Woodley answered the phone at He's Not Here.

"You sound busy."

"Who is this?"

"Number twenty-three in your program, number one in your heart."

Ancient line, but people always liked hearing it.

"Billy Clyde!" Quick change to cheerful.

"Ready to move to West Texas?"

"Where *are* you?"

"I'm in Los Angeles. We're in the NFL, but don't tell Wayne and Ralph. It won't be announced till tomorrow night."

"Really? That's great. That's wonderful."

"I just wanted you to know I haven't forgotten I offered you a job."

"Well, I haven't forgotten I said I'd take it."

Kelly Sue informed me that she had put a big picture of me up on the wall of the joint. T.J. obtained the photo for her out of Wet Fart Lorants's publicity file, and she'd had it blown up to sixteen-by-twenty. It was a photo of me when I was playing for TCU. I appeared to be running for a touchdown against the Texas Longhorns.

"Or my life," I said.

She'd put a caption under it, in big letters. Something T.J. said about the kind of player I was. The caption read: I WON'T SAY BILLY CLYDE PUCKETT IS IN A CLASS BY HIMSELF, BUT IT DON'T TAKE LONG TO CALL THE ROLL.

"T.J. takes credit for that?" I said. "Bear Bryant said it. Bear Bryant said it about Joe Namath . . . or Lee Roy Jordan. He probably said it about several people. Is T.J. there? I need to talk to him."

"Oh, he's here. He's here twice."

"Put him on."

"When are you coming back to town?"

"I have no idea. When you're in a class by yourself, life's hectic. I miss the barbecue, though."

"And the barbecue misses you."

"Hug on yourself."

T.J. picked up the phone and I welcomed him to the NFL.

He said, "I'll be damned. That's just an upset, is all it is. It's just your big old upset."

He wanted to know what conference we'd be in, which division. I said I didn't know yet—it would surely be announced at the press conference.

"Don't matter," he said. "They all do the same shit. Off-tackle for two yards, draw play for no gain, go to the shotgun."

"Perhaps we can do something a little different," I suggested.

T.J. had some good news of his own. Good news for anybody who cared about the fate of the Horned Frogs football program. It looked as if Chancellor Dollarhyde was going to keep his job.

T.J. said, "The chancellor went before the board and made a very moving personal defense for himself. The board said he could remain as chancellor if he'd go to whiskey school for two weeks and accept Jesus in his heart."

"Hold it," I said. "I didn't think the board of trustees could hold a meeting without Big Ed."

T.J. said, "Those academic fruits and nuts took charge. They said it was an emergency meeting—too bad Ed Bookman couldn't be present. But it worked out all right. The chancellor whimpered and cried . . . went through a box of Kleenex. He explained that the reason he showed up drunk for his sermon was because he'd just found out his wife had leukemia, and she was probably going to need a rare bone-marrow transplant. Everybody on the board said this put things in a different light. They said they'd pray for her."

"Does the chancellor's wife have leukemia?" I asked.

"Fuck, no."

I waited till it was six o'clock in the morning in Lausanne to call Barbara Jane and tell her she owned a piece of an NFL team, but first I was obliged to speak to Shake Tiller. He answered the phone.

I said, "You know, a man who didn't go to Paschal High might think it was curious if another man answered the phone in his wife's hotel room at six in the morning, but I went to Paschal, so I don't think there's anything unusual about it at all."

"You calling from the Polo Lounge?" Shake wanted to know.

"No, I'm calling from the building across the street, and my camera's pointed at the bedroom window."

"Yeah, I'll have some more," Shake said.

"You'll what?"

"Barb warmed up my coffee. We're having a power breakfast."

"Fine."

"We're talking about our production company before we go off to make moving pictures. You want to talk to your wife or your dog first? Wait, I'll ask them."

Barbara Jane came on with, "Hi, you *are* calling from the Polo Lounge. Tell the truth."

"Why does everybody naturally assume I'm in the Polo Lounge?"

"I can't imagine."

"Honey," I said with sincerity, "allow me to be the first to tell you that you are now, as of this moment, an official owner of a National Football League team. We've been voted in. It'll be announced tomorrow."

"That's nice, what else is going on?"

After she finished laughing, she said, "Sweetheart, that's terrific. I know you're excited about it."

"Yeah, excited. Relieved would be in there somewhere."

"Are you and Daddy celebrating?"

"We've had an aperitif."

I heard her pass along the news to her partner in End Zone Productions, and I could hear Shake mumbling something.

She returned and said, "Shake says congratulations, he'll be happy to work with your wide receivers, teach 'em the famous fade route he invented."

"Tell him thanks, we'll need all the help we can get."

"What's a fade route?"

"It's a flat pass to the sideline, except Shake ran it in a

curve and Hose lobbed the ball. Shake would catch it falling out of bounds. It was impossible to defend if they timed it right. Sometimes Shake would stop short of the boundary and keep his balance. The defensive back would fly out of bounds. One day against Dallas—"

"*Thank you,*" she said, singing the words. Which I took to mean that I'd overestimated her curiosity on the subject.

I put her folks on long enough for Big Ed to ask her how many naked people he could look forward to seeing in the movie she was making. And long enough for Big Barb to ask what everybody in Europe was wearing now that the weather was warmer.

Back on the phone, I said, "Your daddy money-whipped 'em pretty good, babe. It was one of the great moments in sports. Talk about taking it to the shed. He took 'em."

Barb said, "I guess there's lots to do in a hurry now, huh?"

"You know, it's funny, babe. Now that we've got the team, I'm wondering if I can do the damn job."

"Of course, you can."

"The minute I heard the news, I'm all smiles, then the next minute I thought, great, all I've got to do now is get a stadium built, get an office complex built, hire a staff, assemble a team."

"You'll handle it."

"I hope you're excited too."

"I am, honey. I truly am. But mostly for you."

"I'll have to be spending a lot of time in Big Food . . . Gully Creek, I mean."

"I'll still be making this movie."

"What's the latest trauma?"

"Cubby Butler's in town. He wants a murder in it."

"Maybe Shake could kill Cubby Butler."

"You can't kill the money . . . unfortunately."

We didn't hang up till Barb put Human Dog on the phone and let him sing to me for a moment, after which I heard about the sudden fancy he'd taken to eggs Benedict.

37

It was what you'd call a major news day. The commissioner's press conference on Saturday was loaded with bombshells.

In a stunning, revolutionary, monumental move, the league voted to expand by six teams! Jim Tom labeled it Smote Forehead Day.

The NFL not only took in our West Texas Tornadoes, but it took in Tokyo Russ's Hawaii Volcanoes, Neville Trill's London Knights, and Bappy and Naomi's Mexico City Bandits. Moreover, the commissioner delighted in revealing that two other teams would be added—and not a moment too soon, he emphasized.

The other new teams would be located in Los Angeles and Cleveland.

"Venerable old NFL cities that were vacated for unavoidable reasons," the commissioner said, omitting the greed part.

This would be done as quickly as suitable owners could be found, and the commissioner said such individuals were right over there on the horizon, if he knew a thing or two.

So the NFL was a thirty-six-team "family" now, or

would be. Season after this one. Right around the corner, the commissioner said.

There would then be two conferences of eighteen teams each.

And no realignment. Bad rumor. Each one of the expansion teams was going into an existing division. Three of them into the American Conference, three of them into the National Conference.

The commissioner stressed that each expansion team would be placed in the division that made the most sense, geographically, and in two cases, historically.

It was for historic reasons, he said, that the new Cleveland Browns would enter the Central Division of the AFC. That's where the old Cleveland Browns were before they became the Baltimore Ravens. They would be in there with Pittsburgh, Cincinnati, Baltimore, Jacksonville, and Tennessee.

Same thing with the new Los Angeles team, the Stars. They would be entering the Western Division of the NFC, keeping company with San Francisco, Atlanta, Carolina, St. Louis, and New Orleans.

That's where the old Los Angeles Rams were before they became the St. Louis Rams.

Hawaii was placed in the NFC East, joining New York, Dallas, Washington, Philadelphia, and Arizona. This didn't make any more sense to some people—me, for instance—than Dallas and Arizona being in something called the East in the first place.

But I had to remember that the NFC East was a division made up of a group of owners who had the most clout in the league, the loudest voices, the strongest lobby, and I was sure of another thing: their wives wanted to be able to look forward to a road game in Honolulu every year, with side trips to Maui and Kauai.

Jim Tom took that thought for his article.

The London Knights went into the AFC East to

compete against the New York Jets, New England, Miami, Indianapolis, and Buffalo. The commissioner said he was delighted at the thought of New York-London becoming one of the great "oceanic" rivalries.

Jim Tom laughed out loud at this, but fortunately he was standing in the back of the room and only two or three people were disturbed by it.

The owners in the NFC Central had actually asked for the Mexico City Bandits to be in their division. They got them—with everybody's compliments, I might add.

This raised the mysterious question of what Green Bay, Detroit, Chicago, Minnesota, and Tampa Bay thought they had in common with Mexico City, but it was no more of a mystery to me than what Green Bay, Detroit, Chicago, and Minnesota had in common with Tampa Bay.

Although for different reasons, Big Ed and I were pleased that we went into the Western Division of the AFC, the division with Kansas City, San Diego, Denver, Seattle, and Oakland.

Big Ed saw it as the division with the best golf courses on road trips. I saw the AFC West as one of the weaker divisions, one in which we might do okay right away.

The commissioner acted excited about it. He predicted that a "natural geographic rivalry" would develop between us and Denver.

"One of those old wild west things," he said with a handsome, well-dressed smile.

In my memory, there wasn't much to see today in that part of the "old wild west" but highways, truck-stop diners, and gas stations. So as I understood it, the commissioner thought the Tornadoes and Broncos would be battling it out every season for bragging rights over all the unleaded pumps between Amarillo and Denver.

Jim Tom lifted that observation for his very own, too. "I steal without shame," he said.

Photo ops and handshaking and cocktailing followed the press conference.

Big Ed and I were asked to pose in assorted groups of people. With the beaming commissioner, with each member of the expansion committee, with the entire expansion committee, with the entire expansion committee and the commissioner, with various members of the media, and with numerous total strangers. Everybody grinned and shook hands enthusiastically in the photo ops, especially the total strangers.

Of course, it came as no surprise to any reporter that Rushi Akagi's wife, Rachel, or "Mandy Rice-Davies," was asked to pose in more shots than anyone else.

She was wearing a snug, skimpy dress that did justice to her outstanding rack.

There was one particular shot I definitely wanted to obtain a copy of. A treasure for the old den wall. It was the photo of Big Ed and me with Tokyo Russ and his lovely bride.

Rushi was calling me Babe Ruth again, I was glancing at the Guns of Navarone, Rachel was fucking the camera, and Big Ed was looking like a man who'd just said to Tokyo Russ, "I had friends on the *Arizona*."

Another rash of phone calls.

First I interrupted another power breakfast. I thought Barbara Jane and Shake might care to know that we were in the AFC West, and that everybody had been taken into the National Football League but the Paschal Panthers and Arlington Heights Yellow Jackets.

Big Ed was happy about the division, I said. On the road trip to Oakland, he could chopper down to play Pebble Beach and Cypress Point, or slide across the Bay to Olympic. When we went to Denver, he could play Cherry Hills and Castle Pines. San Diego would put him on La Costa. He could slip over to Prairie Dunes when

we traveled to Kansas City. And I didn't know what he'd
do in Seattle, other than complain about the rain.

The report from their end was that Cubby Butler was
still in town, and they were breaking camp soon. Heading for LA. They'd be shooting the last scenes out there.

"Hume's going to miss the Château d'Ouchy," I said.

Barb said he'd just have to make do with cheeseburg-
ers and fried chicken.

She said to come out soon as I could. I said I would.

I said I'd check in again in a few days, probably from
Gully Creek, Texas, from the cozy living room of our
double-wide.

"Our what?" Barb asked.

"You'll see," I said.

In the upset of the day, I found Tommy Earl Bruner
in his office at Gang Resistant Systems, Inc. He was usually out of there by noon, off to a tavern or a rendezvous
in his secret apartment, which was no longer a secret, of
course. It had become his home, things being how they
were in the old marital discord league.

I gave him the news about the Tornadoes getting in
the NFL and listened while he said something along the
lines of "hot damn shit."

Then he said it again when I told him Big Ed was
looking favorably on his plans for developing some of
the land within sight of where our stadium would be. I
said Big Ed had sounded willing to be his loan officer
and let him have the land for $1,000 an acre—if he could
help design the golf course.

Tommy Earl said, "If Big Ed's my banker, he can tell
me where to part my hair."

"What if he doesn't want a quarry on the course?"

"Fuck the quarry."

"Actually, he likes the idea of some quarry holes."

"I love the quarry."

"He'll want you to get started as soon as possible."

"We're there, Claude. Me and Ody."

Astounded, I said, "Ody Bradshaw? The man whose big toe you shot off? The man who tried to fuck your wife? The man who'll try to fuck your *next* wife? You want him in on the deal?"

"Business is business, Claude. You can't grasp business, can you? We're a good team. I conceive, he executes. Ody knows how to deal with them bureaucrats, get shit done. He's gonna be the best man when me and Tracy get married. He's not my best friend, but it'll make him feel good. He won't get so pissed off at me I'll have to shoot off another toe."

"This is a reality? You're marrying Tracy?"

"She's the love of my life, Claude."

"When's the wedding?"

"Soon as I get divorced."

"I hear from Donna Lou that Sheila's thinking about some self-improvements."

"Power to her. She'll like fuckin' them tennis pros. They all got wooden dicks."

"How do your kids feel about you getting divorced— or even getting married, as far as that goes?"

"Kids don't give a damn about anything, Claude— long as they've got cars to drive, money to spend, and brain-dead music to listen to."

"What are you doing in the office, anyhow? I thought I'd have to call five or six joints to find you."

"Man, we're snowed under. I can't get my glass out fast enough. We've had drive-bys out the ass, all over town. Seven dead, sixteen wounded. It's been great."

I said, well, it just seemed like there was good news everywhere.

T.J. was home when I called, but he couldn't talk long. He was busy watching the local news—a special

about three gang members who'd killed a man and
woman for no reason other than their car happened to
turn down the wrong Fort Worth street.

"They caught 'em," T.J. said. "Julio, Sedrick, and
Eddwerderum."

"Eddwerda . . . what?"

"I wrote it down. Eddwerderum. *E-d-d-w-e-r-d-e-*
r-u-m. His folks were taking a shot at Edward, you
reckon? But I don't know if he even had parents. Maybe
he just come up out of the cracks in the sidewalk like
them other two. Three lice with automatic weapons, and
nothin' better to do but kill innocent people. Wasn't
even a robbery. I say they don't even get a trial. Just stick
'em on a bamboo fence downtown. Leave 'em there for a
week. Let everybody see what can happen to you, then
burn 'em. And if any criminal lawyer tries to get 'em off,
stick him on the fence too."

I said, "You stick him on the fence just for *studying*
law."

On a happier subject, I told T.J. the league's expansion plans. He surprised me by being pleased that the
Tornadoes were in the AFC West.

"We'll be all over them pussies," he said. "We'll be
on them like fire ants on a hippie's leg."

Part Five

People Deals

38

I loved my double-wide in Gully Creek.

I needed something to make do as a temporary home, so the first thing I did was lease the best double-wide Mayor Coogle Boone could find for me, the mayor having said he could handle such things. The double-wide was provided by a company in Borger, Texas, called Stylish Homes by the Booger from Borger. It came in an off-white vinyl siding with a gray slate roof.

Jokingly, I'd asked the mayor if I could have beachfront. He wheezed that I could. Coogle was a rope-thin, partly bald fellow in his sixties with a memorable case of emphysema, which he doctored every fifteen minutes with a menthol cigarette.

Coogle arranged for the Booger from Borger to install the double-wide on Creek Street downtown, one block off Main. It was the only structure of any kind on the west side of Creek Street, the creek side. Thus, from my residence I was privileged to overlook the town's only body of water.

Gully Creek itself was about five yards wide and ten yards deep when it rambled past my temporary home. It was basically a bed of rocks, but it occasionally had water running through it, which were exciting days.

Creek fans probably knew that Gully Creek was actually a branch of the Prairie Dog River, which was actually a fork of the Red River. The Prairie Dog started over by Childress, near the Oklahoma line, and ambled up toward Amarillo but stopped way short and disappeared somewhat abruptly. My educated guess was that somewhere back in time a sandstorm ate it.

The creek slid out of the Prairie Dog River halfway between Mulberry Knot and Gasoline Hat. Some people observed that this was about as far away as you could get from an order of veal piccata and a side of fettuccine Alfredo. The creek then crawled back south through twenty miles of stumps and mesquite and finally met its own demise when it bumped into I-27. Before that, it passed through the town of Gully Creek.

From my redwood front deck I could enjoy the view across Creek Street. A panoramic view of Turner's Poultry & Eggs, a deserted concrete foundation with weeds around it, and Reece Gilliam's Office Products.

From my enchanting screened-in porch on the back I had what some would call a typical West Texas view. On clear days, you could see all the way to a Russian space station.

The double-wide came with a nice-size master bedroom and bath, a guest bedroom and bath, a large living room, a small but okay kitchen, and a wet bar. It had central air-conditioning and heating. Fortunately, there were enough stores in the region that I could tastefully furnish my temporary home in Early Pier 1 and Home Depot Provincial.

There was even a carport for my rented Cadillac-Buick. And thanks to Coogle's wife, Deana Merle, a husky woman with stringy brown hair who wore faded plaid shirts and high-top tennis shoes, my double-wide was landscaped handsomely. Deana Merle put in a small Bermuda lawn, some flower beds, and transplanted two big pecan trees from her own yard.

"I know you ain't no saint, but you're beautified anyhow," she said.

Coogle Boone did me one other favor. After the double-wide and the yard and the trees were in, I came home one day to find the mayor sprinkling a line of yellowish powder all around the property.

It was sulfur, I learned. Sprinkle sulfur around on a regular basis, Coogle said, you could keep the rattlers and copperheads away.

"Jesus, thanks," I said. "I hate those sumbitches."

Coogle said he'd never known anybody who liked them, and if he did, he wouldn't want to break bread with him.

"Make sure you use enough," I said.

A day later I was in Reece Gilliam's store buying fax paper and other office items, and I mentioned the nice thing Coogle had done for me, adding that I wasn't overly fond of reptiles, and I was glad to know about the sulfur.

"Coogle told you that?" Reece Gilliam said.

"Yes," I said.

He let out a big laugh.

"What's so funny?"

"Snakes love that shit," he said.

I swallowed hard.

"Get you a yard cat or a billy goat," Reece advised.

I slept with my eyes open and my shoes on for a week, and gave some serious consideration to going with two rings of sulfur, three yard cats, and four billy goats.

The sulfur seemed to do the trick, but I knew in my heart there'd always be those rattlers and copperheads out there who were crafty enough to break through any

line of defense if they decided they wanted to jack
around with me.

Nothing you could do about it. It was just something
you had to live with, like the possibility of a nuclear
holocaust.

Meanwhile, I leased three more double-wides from
the Booger from Borger, whose real name was Homer
Stebbins. They were to be used as the Tornadoes' temporary headquarters and were installed five miles from
town, over on the prairie where the construction company had already broken ground for our stadium, practice facility, and permanent offices.

Big hole in the ground for the stadium. Wide. Long.
Deep. A tourist attraction. Even people in the South
Plains and Panhandle who'd been to the Grand Canyon
drove over to see it.

A sightseer from Plainview, man in coveralls and a
painter's cap, said to me, "What you got right here,
that's a real big hole in the ground. I thought stadiums
was supposed to go up?"

"All football fields are sunken," I said.

His look told me he didn't accept that. Shaking his
head, he walked back to his truck and drove away as I
admired the bumper sticker on the back of his truck,
which said: KEEP HONKING, I'M RELOADING.

People from town came out to stare at the hole in the
ground.

Coogle Boone stood around with me one morning,
looking at the hole, smoking, wheezing.

"Anaconda Copper," he said.

"How's that?"

"Ever been to Butte, Montana?"

I said I'd been to Bozeman, Red Lodge, Bigfort, up to
Glacier, other places, but I'd missed Butte somehow.

"You ought to see Butte," he said. "Butte has this big
hole, right in the middle of town. Old copper mine. I'd

heard about Anaconda Copper since school. I remember a teacher saying somebody was richer than Anaconda Copper. I never forgot it. Me and Deana drove out to Butte on vacation one summer to see it. Butte's hole is a lot bigger than this one, I'll tell you that much."

"Well, we do our best," I said.

Big Ed had awarded the contract for the stadium to Benjamin & Snider, a high-powered construction company out of San Francisco. He money-whipped the company up front. He told the construction boss he wanted to see people working seven days a week, seven nights a week, he didn't want to hear about any goddamn weather delays, any parts having to be ordered, and the quicker they got the sumbitch built, the bigger the bonus would be for everybody.

Things were hopping in Gully Creek.

39

I didn't have to pin down Gully Creek geographically for Barbara Jane or Shake Tiller, but I did for almost everybody else I knew. I said to those who asked that it was only six miles west of I-27 at a point where you were exactly sixty miles south of Amarillo and sixty miles north of Lubbock, or, as the trucks flew, only forty minutes from either one.

Both Amarillo and Lubbock rise up out of the dusty flatlands. When you see their downtown buildings from a distance for the first time, you could be excused for thinking they looked like a practical joke God wanted to play on the Panhandle and South Plains.

Shake and I had played high school ball in a variety of West Texas towns, in nondistrict games and state play-offs. Who could forget the team bus running out of gas near Merkel when we were on our way out to play Odessa Permian in the semifinals? And how Coach Honk Wooten slugged the driver, breaking his jaw, and accused him of being a saboteur? Or, for that matter, how we lost the game because Snot Milburn, the Permian linebacker, not only put Shake out of the game by twisting his ankle but tried to gnaw his leg off?

Barbara Jane had been all over West Texas with her daddy, moseying around all his drilling rigs that were looking for money and all his pumps that were already making money. Big Ed had always bragged that he could find more oil with a goddamn Texaco road map than all of his geologists could with their college degrees and rock-sniffing devices.

Amarillo and Lubbock were first known to Indians and buffalo hunters, but after the discoveries of oil and natural gas in West Texas they began to sprout people, tree-lined streets, and office buildings.

These days Amarillo took pride in producing oil-field supplies, farm implements, and steaks the size of a spare tire. Lubbock sat on a branch of the Brazos River and took pride in being a distribution center for everything from toilet paper to auto parts. It also took pride in Texas Tech and the scholar-athletes on the football team who slaved through their rigid courses of Exercise Science and Sports Humanistics.

Big Ed and I were convinced from the beginning that halfway between Amarillo and Lubbock was the perfect spot for the stadium.

That's why I opened our first ticket offices and gift boutiques in Amarillo and Lubbock. It might have been a year before we fielded a team, but in my opinion it didn't hurt anything to have our logo on display everywhere.

There were problems with the design of our logo in the beginning, and some people might have thought I was being contrary about it, but I was a serious student of logos and proper football attire, as many people knew.

I'd hired Sims & Gingletter to design our Tornadoes logo. Sims & Gingletter was the most prestigious PR firm in the Dallas/Fort Worth area. They'd designed logos I'd seen for banks and other businesses. I'd even been impressed with their logo I'd seen on a billboard

for a successful Dallas restaurant called Thad and Car-
lotta's Mix-Mex Grill, not that I would have gone within
ten blocks of a place that boasted of sea bass enchiladas
and foie gras tamales. I had their "mix-Mex" right here.

Big Ed agreed with me that the Tornadoes' logo
ought to look like a tornado. A funnel. A dark badass
twister. The kind that dipped out of a low sky and picked
up an eighteen-wheeler in Tulia and dropped it on
Dookie.

I'd hoped I made myself clear about what I wanted in
the way of a logo when I met with the people at Sims &
Gingletter. Spivey Sims and Bart Gingletter weren't
around. I was told that "Spivo" was in San Francisco on
business and "Barto" was in New York on business, but
they certainly would be involved in the creative process,
I was assured, and nothing would be designed that Spivo
and Barto didn't "sign off" on.

Although the bosses were absent, a dozen people
gathered to meet with me that day in a large conference
room on a high floor of a glass bank tower in downtown
Dallas. Fresh-faced, vibrant, earnest, smiling young people who had names like Avery, Benji, Brett, Cole, Leif,
Colleen.

"Just give us all your thoughts," somebody said to
me, "and we'll take it from there."

"All of them?" I said, lighting a Marlboro.

Three people gasped and retreated to the far end of
the table.

"You aren't actually going to smoke, are you?" somebody said.

I said, "If I can't smoke, I'm afraid I'll have to find
another agency."

"We normally go to the roof," a young man said,
"but I'm sure we can make an exception. Colleen, will
you find Mr. Puckett an ashtray?"

Colleen brought me a paper cup of water for an ashtray. She put it down with a frown for me and a nasty look for the young man who'd asked her to handle the chore. Fetching an ashtray for somebody wasn't part of her job description.

I didn't particularly think Colleen looked fuckable unless your name was Ellen.

I made a long speech. Started off by saying a sports logo should be the kind that lasted a lifetime. Bad luck to have to change your logo. It should be easily recognizable. It should identify the team. You ought to be able to simply glance at the logo and know what team it was. The most prominent place for the logo would be on the side of the helmet. And ideally it ought to be something that gave the helmet a certain character. But the logo should be the kind that worked on gift items too—T-shirts, sweatshirts, warm-up jackets, replica jerseys, wristwatches, caps, towels, blankets, mugs, plates, paperweights, money clips, travel bags . . .

"Comforter!" a young man blurted out.

I looked at him. He looked at me.

But before I could say anything, a young woman said, "That comes under 'blanket,' Avery."

"Yes, it would, wouldn't it?" he said, and scribbled something on his yellow notepad.

Comforter in blanket family, I guessed.

The helmet, I said. Consider the helmet first and foremost when you are working on the design. The logo on the helmet, or the logo and helmet combined, that is the thing that constantly identifies a football team in every photograph in every newspaper and magazine as well as to the millions watching on TV.

"What's good for the helmet is good for the T-shirt," I said.

Four people jotted that down.

"Of course, the most famous football helmet is Michigan's," I said.

University of Michigan, I added quickly, before someone could ask me which NFL division the Wolverines were in.

"I'm sure you're all familiar with it," I said. "The yellow wings across the front, or I guess you can say they're wolverine ears, and three vertical yellow stripes running over the top. All of it on a field of dark blue. Maize, not yellow, I should say. Maize and blue. Michigan's official colors."

People whispered to each other. Asking how to spell *maize*, I assumed.

"The Michigan helmet has been around for more than sixty years," I continued. "Fritz Crisler designed it when he took the Michigan coaching job in 1938. Like a lot of teams in those days, Michigan had been wearing plain black leather helmets. All Crisler was trying to do was design a helmet that would make his pass receivers downfield easier for his passer to spot. I'm sure he wasn't trying to design the most distinctive football helmet in history, but that's what he did."

"Exactly!" one of the young men shrieked. "Style combined with function."

I said, "I guess you can say that, but it was accidental."

"Like the Meg!" a young woman spoke up.

"The what?" I said.

"Meg Ryan's haircut in that movie."

"Meg Ryan?"

She said, "I'll bet you anything when they made that movie they had no idea so many women would want to get a Meg."

Three people in the room stared at the young woman for a moment, but no more curiously than I did.

I said, "The thing about the Michigan helmet, it's not the logo but it may as well be. It's become synonymous with the university."

I opened a football magazine to a Michigan player. "What are the first two words that come to mind when you see this helmet?"

"Football helmet!" somebody shouted.

"I was thinking more like Ann Arbor," I said.

From the crowd: "Ann who?"

"Or Tom Harmon?" I said. "Old Ninety-eight?"

Blank faces.

"I'm just trying to give you some ideas," I said. "The main reason I brought up the Michigan helmet is because it obviously inspired the Ram helmet. I'm sure you're familiar with the Los Ange—I mean the St. Louis Rams' helmet. Blue with the gold horns coming out of the front, curling around the ears? I believe most people would agree that the three most recognizable helmets in pro football are the Rams, Cowboys, and Packers. The Rams with the horns, the Cowboys' lone star, Green Bay's white *G* on the green circle with the yellow background. There was a time when I would have put the New York Giants' helmet in the same category. The one I wore. The dark blue helmet with the red stripe over the middle and the white *NY* on the side. But when the team moved to New Jersey, they had to change the *NY* to *Giants*."

"Why?" Voice from the crowd.

"Why?" I laughed. "Because *NY* doesn't stand for New Jersey. The team moved, as I mentioned."

"Giants," a guy said, like he was trying on the word to see if it fit.

"Right," I said.

"Wordy," he concluded.

I laughed again. "That's one thing wrong with it."

Another earnest young man held up his hand. I acknowledged him.

"You're saying the star on the Dallas Cowboys helmet is, like, the lone star of Texas?"

I nodded.

"I've always thought it was a sheriff's badge, or, you know, like a Texas Ranger's shield or something."

I said, "I'm sure the Cowboys organization will tell you it represents the lone star of Texas."

He scribbled on his notepad. *Check Cowboys star.*

Another guy held up his hand.

He said, "I have a problem with the Green Bay logo."

"Oh?"

"It's a *G*, you said?"

"Yeah."

"But the team is in Green *Bay*, isn't it?"

He said the word *Bay* like he'd caught me in a lie.

"Uh-huh."

"I rest my case."

"You rest *what* case?"

"It ought to be *GB* in the little whatever circle on the whatever background. They obviously aren't interested in accuracy. If it's just *G*, they can be mistaken for, well, Greenland, Georgia, Grenada, Guam."

A young woman glanced at him and said, "I hardly think they could be mistaken for *Guam.*"

After that meeting, I guess I shouldn't have been surprised by the designs they came up with.

The first logo they submitted was a purple object sitting on top of a white bucking horse. If the purple object was supposed to be a funnel, it looked more like an ice cream cone, and I didn't know what the white bucking horse had to do with anything. That's what I told Benji and Brett, and that's what I thought they understood.

Then came the other logos. One with a white ice cream cone lifting up a purple bucking horse. One with the purple letters *WTT*, for West Texas Tornadoes, riding on the back of a cartoon football player. And one was a purple funnel that looked like an upside-down oil derrick dancing around in a white circle.

That was when Big Ed threatened to buy Sims & Gingletter so he could fire everybody and possibly even have Spivo and Barto killed. It was also when I took over the logo project myself.

First, I went back to Sims & Gingletter and told all the Bretts and Colleens they reminded me of the brilliant people who'd turned Kentucky Fried Chicken into KFC and turned the International House of Pancakes into IHOP—fixed it up so nobody could ever find a Kentucky Fried Chicken or an International House of Pancakes again.

Then I designed the purple tornado funnel that swirled around inside the sand-colored map of Texas.

Okay, it wasn't the Michigan helmet, but it wasn't Guam either.

40

Nobody would confuse Gully Creek with one of those little towns in Vermont where you go to watch leaves turn and comparative shop the maple syrup. But there had always been something about small towns I kind of liked, no matter where they were, and Gully Creek was no exception, light as it was on opera, ballet, and art galleries.

The population was only 6,700, scattered all around, but it was big enough to have a water tower, a main street, and a high school football team, the Gully Creek Fightin' Roosters. Their little stadium was behind the school, and the Fightin' Roosters could even play night games, Coogle Boone said, if everybody turned on the headlights in their cars and trucks.

Main Street was lined with red-brick buildings, two and three stories tall. You could go to Ben's Men's for your wrinkle-free twill pants and your polyester dress-ups. Ben Glenn was also the police chief. A sign on his wall said: THE LAW WEST OF THE SIX-PACK. You could go to Francine's More Than Jeans for your novelty embroidered shirts and blouses and a wool coat. To Ned's In-Home Furnishings for your dining sets and recliners. To

Theron's Paints for your interior wall and trim satin—
free computerized color matching. And of course to
Boone's Grocery & Hair Styling for your hamburger
meat, potato chips, and "let me lower them ears for
you."

Gully Creek's Times Square was the corner of Main
and Old Wolf Flat Road. Where the stoplight was.
Crawford's drugstore was on the southeast corner. Go
there for your Advil, toothpaste, Trac IIs, magazines,
smokes, paperbacks. Delbert's Video Rental and Computer Help was on the southwest corner. Popular
place—despite Delbert McConnell's breath, which
smelled like a rare combination of dead fish and pipe
smoke. The Tivoli theater, closed, occupied the north-
west corner, waiting for a tenant. It had once shown the
latest in John Waynes and Kung Fus, I imagined.

The northeast corner was a good place to look for me
around breakfast time, or noon, or dinner. Them Two
Women was the best restaurant in town. Storefront joint
with a long counter, booths, tables, and greasy grill. The
place specialized in country eggs and pattie sausage all
day long. Them Two Women were Dot and Freida. Dot
cooked and hollered. Freida served and bitched.

"You could call me a waitress if you want to," Freida
said, "but what I say I do is relocate pork."

Country eggs were the only kind you could get in
Them Two Women. The first time I was in there, I
asked Freida what "country eggs" were. She said Dot
cracked two eggs in a skillet but the yolk always broke on
one of them, sometimes both, so Dot would quickly stir
them around, maybe flip them up and over, and that was
your country eggs. An order looked like modern art in
yellow and white.

Over on Broadway Avenue was the train station,
which hadn't seen a train in years. It was an old stucco
building with a red tile roof, sitting there empty with the

glass broken out of the windows. It may have seemed huge at one time, but now it was about the size of the average 7-Eleven.

At one end of Main were two white wood-frame churches with steeples. Coogle Boone explained, "The little one's for Catholics and the big one's for Americans."

Down at the other end of Main were three blocks of large old houses on both sides of the street. Houses with wraparound porches and bay windows and a lot of latticework wandering about. The town's biggest trees were in those yards. This was the neighborhood where the rich people had once lived, the cotton farmers who'd built the houses with the wraparound porches and bay windows and crawling latticework.

Most of the old houses were vacant and needed considerable work, but Big Ed bought four on one of his whirlwind visits, and I bought one. Good future investment, Big Ed convinced me. He said when the Tornadoes turned Gully Creek into a "prime destination," they'd be worth considerably more than we paid for them, which was around $13,000 each.

One of the houses was already being restored and remodeled, turned into a bed and breakfast by Craig and Horace, two shirt-lifters from Lubbock.

I met them one day at the lunch counter in Them Two Women. Craig and Horace were sitting on the stools to my left, two little baldheaded guys, one in a turtleneck, the other in a Nehru jacket. The way Freida introduced me to them, she said in her loud voice, "You met the two queers yet?"

I looked at Craig and Horace with a faint smile, they looked at me with some uncertainty, then we all had a good laugh.

In my initial chat with Craig and Horace, they said they knew who I was, the man who was bringing the football team to the area. That was why they'd invested in the B and B. Visitors would be coming. I said I wasn't sure I was doing the town a favor; it would change, maybe even bring a Hardee's. Craig said he wouldn't mind a Target or a K mart.

Horace said, "What are your animals?"

"My what?" I said, caught off guard.

"Your animals? Your team animals? Doesn't every football team have its own animals?"

"We're the West Texas Tornadoes," I said. "No animal."

"Fabulous," said Craig.

Freida told Craig and Horace that I was married to a movie star, "Barbara Jean Booker."

"Oh, my God," Horace said, knowing who Freida meant. "That girl is fabulous. I watched that series— *Rita*—religiously. It's still in reruns."

"Here and there," I said.

Craig asked Freida for a cappuccino.

"Honey, that ain't got here yet," Freida said.

He settled for a mug of stewed dirt.

"Your wife is a wonderful actress," Horace said. "I imagine she'll be spending some time here. How exciting for us."

"I hope she'll be here more than she plans to right now," I said. "We'll have a permanent place here of some kind. Our main home is the New York apartment, but Barb has a production company in Hollywood now, and she's talking about another home on the Coast. We've been one of those 'bicoastal' couples, but with this NFL team I guess we're getting ready to be a *tri*coastal couple. We'll be living on the Atlantic Ocean, the Pacific Ocean, and Gully Creek."

Craig squealed, "I *love* that! Tricoastal. I can't wait to tell Eric and Burton in Houston."

"They're your friends, not mine." Horace sighed.

I said, "Thanks for the compliment about my wife."

Horace asked, "Who does she like in the business? I hope she likes Meryl. I adore Meryl."

"She likes Meryl. She likes Jodie."

"I'm *mad* about Jodie."

"Barb says Meryl and Jodie are the only American actors who thoroughly understand every role they play."

"Really?" said Horace, looking slightly confused.

I said, "Actors aren't too smart. They know how to *act* smart, but mostly they're just good mimics. Some of them can perform in a whole movie and be totally convincing and never know what the movie's about till they see it. They just go from speech to speech, doing what the director tells them to do, feeling what the director tells them to feel. It's still a talent."

"I don't think I like knowing that," Horace said.

Craig said, "I used to love Burt Reynolds, but he got old."

"More and more," I said, "you hear about that happening to people."

Freida warmed up our coffee—our stewed dirt—and said to Craig and Horace, "Let me ask you queers something. I got nothing against the way you live. Do what you want to, is what I say, long as you pay your check. But if there wasn't nobody in the world but men and women queers, there wouldn't be no more babies, and if there wasn't no more babies, it'd be the end of the human race, wouldn't it? What do you say to that?"

"Good," Craig smiled.

41

In late July I went out to the Coast to renew acquaintances with my wife and my dog.

I joined Barb and Hume in a guest room in Shake's house in the Hollywood hills. For years when Barb worked out there we'd stayed at the Westwood Terrace, but the place had decided it wouldn't take pets any longer—some rock star's German shepherd ruined it for everybody. He ate somebody's Sunday brunch.

Shake offered and Barb accepted. He promised it wouldn't interfere with his private life while she looked around for a place to buy.

His house was a rustic, ski-lodge-type thing in the old Hollywood hills. Surrounded by trees and shrubs, it had a little patch of lawn, four bedrooms, fireplace, small swimming pool. Not lavish, but cozy. It was up a narrow winding road where, on the way up, people pointed out to you that Joan Fontaine once lived here and Claudette Colbert once lived over there.

Shake and Kitten Hollis were still together. But Kitten was about to start looking for a filmmaker who'd give her a bigger part than the cameo she had in *Melancholy Baby*, and Shake would start holding auditions for his next rack-loaded wool driver. *Melancholy Baby* was now in post-production, which was a Hollywood term that meant editing and arguing.

I was sitting with Shake at a poolside table on this day. Barb had gone to look at houses with a legitimate real estate agent, and Kitten Hollis was floating on a little rubber raft in the pool.

I said, "I wonder what some of our old Paschal buddies would think if they saw us now? Sitting out here in Hollywood, not doing shit, looking at a bikini crawling up a starlet's ass."

"I'm working," Shake said.

"I doubt they'd accept that. I think it's more likely they'd hire a hit man to come visit us."

"Fort Worth people still come out here all the time."

"Paschal people?"

"And TCU people. L. C. Newman's here three times a year, always trying to sell me something. Gizzard Lip Stevens comes out on vacation, wants to tour a studio, see some tits. Emily and Norm always call, want me to take 'em to dinner someplace where they can see movie stars. They always want to go to one of those Spagos. I take 'em to Greaseburger. Tell 'em this is where Spielberg eats. They sit there looking for Spielberg for an hour. I get to eat something decent."

"If I'd ever thought Emily Kirkland would marry Norm Chappell, I'd have married her myself . . . saved her some agony."

"Norm got rich managing people's money in Austin."

"Yeah, but he's still Norm Chappell. How's your money?"

"It's doing all right. It hasn't gone to Argentina yet."

Shake met a money manager he liked in Charlotte some years back. Some guy named Jerome who'd gone to Duke, played a little ball. Shake thought the guy's wife was so pretty the guy would never run off from her,

taking everybody's money with him. Shake then hired a
tax man named Ira in New York, "for balance." Jerome
watched Ira and Ira watched Jerome. "You don't want to
go with wasp and wasp," he said. "Especially Kappa Sigs.
You might as well say, here, guys, steal my money and
tell me I made some bad investments."

Some of us envied the way Shake's life was set up so
neatly. He didn't even worry about paying his bills. He
had this tiny woman in granny glasses named Weata who
came in once a week to pay the lights, gas, and water,
type up shit, copy things, solve computer snags, buy
stamps, and balance the checkbook. Then he had Swoll
Up Inga to come in and clean, do the laundry, all the
housekeeping things. This freed him up to concentrate
on his art—as long as his money didn't run off to Argentina.

All of our investments, mine and Barb's, were in the
hands of Big Ed's people, so we didn't have to worry
about them being honest. They were honest or they
died. As for personal expenses, Barbara Jane had long
ago taken over the checkbook. I handled the checkbook
in the early years of our marriage, believing it was the
husband's job, but she didn't like me thinking that if I
came within $1,000 of having a balance every month—
our way or the bank's—everything was okay. So she took
over. It was a strange thing. Barb had never had to worry
about money her whole life, and yet she could spend two
days trying to find $37.50. But when I'd accuse her of
enjoying the game, like it was the *Times* crossword, I
never got much of a laugh.

End Zone Productions, the company Barb and Shake
started, was gearing up for its first movie, which Big Ed
was going to back, to get them off the ground, provided
there weren't too many naked people in it. The script
was an old one of Shake's, *Born, Married, Worked, Died.*

Barbara Jane was demanding a different title, insisting Shake's was too cynical.

"It's a good title," Shake was saying, and she shouldn't confuse cynicism with realistic humor—it was the perfect title for a film about an average guy who couldn't seem to get a lucky break. "It's the flip side of *Mary Poppins*. Average people will identify with it—see how it touches on all the shit they go through themselves."

"I'm not sure people think their shitty lives are all that amusing," Barb was saying.

"They will after they see the movie," Shake was saying.

"I know the title's meant to be humorous, but it's too complicated," Barb was saying.

"It's not too complicated when you put it up against *Midnight in the Garden of Good and Evil*," Shake was saying.

"Interesting idea—we make a comedy and the joke's on the audience," Barb was saying.

On and on like that.

I was staying out of it, but I had to confess I liked the title Barb was suggesting better. *Dead Beat*. If nothing else, it was six words shorter than *Midnight in the Garden of Good and Evil*.

The headquarters for End Zone Productions was at Paramount, inside the same famous gate on Melrose where Cecil B. De Mille used to enter and say "Hi, Joe" to the guard, and the guard would say, "Good morning, Mr. De Mille, *Reap the Wild Wind* is what I call a really great movie," and De Mille would say, "Thank you, Joe—when Paulette Goddard arrives, tell her to come straight to my office."

A minor Paramount mogul had allowed Barb and Shake to lease some office space with the understanding that the studio would have "first look" at the project they were working on.

Like Barb wanted, End Zone Productions was in one of the old office buildings that sat among other old office buildings, closer to the other old office buildings than it was to the airport hangars—"soundstages" to movie people—and the streets that looked like they were in a big city, except when the robots and pirates were milling around on their lunch break.

Shake was happy to be located in what used to be known on the lot as the Writers' Building, which went back to the days when it took only six weeks to get a movie done because the studio financed it. Which was unlike today, when it sometimes took six years just to find a rich Jap or a Cubby Butler. And if you wanted a piece of background music in the old days, you didn't have to hire somebody who wrote commercial jingles or themes for TV shows, you just stole something from some dead foreigner's concerto for piano and orchestra, and that covered Merle Oberon running up a hill.

I was taken on a tour of End Zone Productions. It was on the ground floor with a lawn in front and a parking lot in back. First, I walked into a crowded room with several desks and computers and phones and bulletin boards. Several young men along with Foxette and Fox-ine were trying to look busy when they weren't going to the coffee machines or the refrigerator.

The separate offices for Barb and Shake opened off this main room.

Barb's office walls were decorated with photos of us, Human Dog, her folks, sitcom pals, and blowups of me, Shake, and T.J. in that Super Bowl when we warped the dogass Jets—me juking a tackler, Shake snaring a lob on a fade route, T.J. looking down at a ball carrier he'd mangled, a photo that reminded me of that shot of Ali sneering down at Liston on the canvas.

A Super Bowl win stayed with you the rest of your life, but people sometimes asked me why I never wore my Super Bowl ring. It was because I'd had the top half of it carved off and put on a chunk of gold and made into a pendant for Barb, which she often wore around her neck. It was her favorite piece of jewelry. One of the great things about Barb, she'd be the last woman on the continent who'd try to impress anybody from *Vogue*.

Shake did wear his Super Bowl ring on occasion, mainly to impress Hollywood producers. They loved that macho shit. Shake also wished he'd taken up golf earlier. A lot of film deals were made on golf courses these days, he discovered, which was why he'd joined Riviera, had four sets of clubs, and was haunted by a 14 handicap.

I'd known how to play golf okay since I was a kid, good enough not to embarrass myself or suffer serious injury. I'd been taught by Uncle Kenneth. Shake used to call it a sport for geezers, but that was before he moved out to Hollywood and discovered it could help him get a movie made.

Mostly movie posters were on Shake's walls at End Zone Productions. Not just his own films, but classics he admired—*Casablanca, All About Eve, The Big Sleep, Dodsworth, The Americanization of Emily, Command Decision.* The great-dialogue movies, he called them.

The thing I liked best about their headquarters, it was only a short walk to the commissary. The commissary on a studio lot was merely a big cafeteria, but it had unspoken rules. Moguls and stars sat in a special section, writers in another, lesser producers and actors in another, nobodies in the main space. However, these rules never applied to Shake and me because of our football reputations. Sports was usually what moguls and stars wanted to talk about anyhow. So if I wanted to drift over to the commissary and sit down at a table with Cecil B. De

Mille, Paulette Goddard, and William Holden, it wouldn't be resented by the onlookers who knew anything about sports. Of course, Cecil B. De Mille, Paulette Goddard, and William Holden would have to be alive first.

The shooting of *Melancholy Baby* was finished before I got out to the Coast. Wrapped, as they liked to say.

The way the ending was resolved, Boyd suffered a mild heart attack at a game, brought on by three straight holding calls, and Enid rushed home from Switzerland to be on hand for his quadruple bypass.

The final scene read like this in the script:

INT. HOSPITAL ROOM—DAY
Boyd is awake, sitting up, recovering nicely from his surgery. Enid is with him.

Enid: They only did a triple. You were supposed to have a quadruple but evidently the back judge threw an erroneous flag.

Boyd: I love you, sugar. I'm gonna be a new man. We belong together. I've learned football don't mean as much as you do.

Enid: Did you learn that from me leaving you or you having a bypass?

Boyd: Don't matter. I've learned it. The biggest mistake a man can make is to keep practicing his mistakes.

Enid: Bobby Bowden.

Boyd: Right. There's lots of life lessons in football.

Never think the way you are today is the way you'll always be.

Enid: Vince Dooley.

Boyd: I mean it, sweetheart. It's how you show up at the showdown that counts.

Enid: Bear Bryant.

Boyd: I want to keep you, Enid. This is like a game day for me. I'm nervous as a pig in a packing plant.

Enid: Darrell Royal—will you stop it!

Boyd: I promise I'm gonna be a new man. You'll see. I'll tell you what. You could strike a match to my dick and I wouldn't be like I was.

Enid: (Laughs) What more can a girl ask?

She leans over, kisses him on the forehead, and we . . .

FADE OUT.

The End

That day by Shake's pool I kind of wanted to talk about my new challenge of being the general manager of an NFL team. I was wondering if I might be in over my head—to coin a phrase. You could say the only positive thing I'd done was hire Kelly Sue as my trusty sidekick-slash-Girl Friday.

When I didn't have lawyers for free agents calling me on the phone all day, I was dealing with Griff, the construction foreman for the stadium and office complex, reminding him of such things as the weight room shouldn't have windows in it, take them out, but the executive suites should, so put the sumbitches back in.

Griff kicked a bunch of workers' asses that day, then confessed to me that this was his last stadium job—he was going to become a sculptor. He said a house-builder friend of his had become a sculptor, and he was getting rich sculpting the heads of little kids for mamas and daddies.

"Near as I can tell," he said, "if you don't mind gettin' your hands dirty and you got two strong thumbs, there ain't much else to it."

But Shake was preoccupied, making movie notes on a yellow legal pad as he sipped coffee, and Human Dog was busy staring at Kitten's bronze body on the raft, so I was left to think of how the immortal Larry Hoage would have summed up my life in its current state. Larry would have said my future was definitely ahead of me.

42

It seemed as if Kelly Sue arrived in Gully Creek about thirty seconds after I offered her the job on the phone.

When I called her at He's Not Here I said her title would be assistant to the president, adding that she'd be in charge of doing everything I could think of, and everything I *couldn't* think of. Big things, little things, helping me run the operation. I needed help. Big Ed had thrown the whole deal in my lap and said he didn't want to be bothered till it was time to play the golf course he'd designed for Tommy Earl. I told Kelly Sue her starting salary would be $100,000 a year, plus a company car and expenses.

There was a pause, maybe even a gasp, when I mentioned the salary. Then she said, "Billy Clyde, you're not making a mistake. You can run me ragged and I'll do a good job for you, but I do have one question."

"What's that?"

"Are you *sure* you don't want to fuck?"

She arrived in her Accord with two large Samsonite suitcases, several hangers of clothes, and three canvas shopping bags.

Her stuff along with herself went into the guest bedroom of my double-wide on Creek Street. I made the decision that it would be all right for her to stay at my place while she looked around the vicinity—Lubbock, Amarillo, wherever—to find her an apartment.

All I asked was that she didn't leave a jar of moisturizing cream in the bathroom cabinet for Barbara Jane to find.

"I don't need *that* jackpot," I said.

"You certainly don't," she said in the voice of a good friend.

I introduced Kelly Sue to the wonders of Gully Creek. She met Dot and Freida along with their meatloaf, and most everybody else, including Coogle Boone, his wife, and his emphysema. She saw all the sights and was particularly impressed with the ring of sulfur around my double-wide.

She stayed with me a week before she found a nice apartment in Lubbock with a spare bedroom for when Susan, her daughter, came to visit. Her apartment was in one of those complexes that had a swimming pool for the tenants to share, all the young marrieds and young divorcées. The complex had a name that made it sound like it was in the Carribbean instead of West Texas.

"I won't mind the commute in my Lincoln," she said.

"Your Lincoln?"

"My company car. I thought I'd lease us a fleet of Lincoln Town Cars, what do you think? Get you an official Cadillac-Buick."

"Fine with me. Put logos on the side. White or black Lincolns?"

"Beige or gray. White's for weddings, black's for funerals."

"Good thinking. You just became head of our taste department."

"Hard to know I had any taste when I was slinging margaritas at the socialites on Camp Bowie, huh?"

"Not entirely."

Kelly Sue surprised me one morning at work by saying she was in love with Shake Tiller from afar. It wasn't from the jacket photo on his book *The Average Man's History of the World*—an old photo from his better-living-through-chemistry days.

Kelly Sue said she'd fallen in love with Shake from actually reading his book. "I'm taking some of his stuff for my own. Especially what he said about the sixties."

"What was that?"

"You haven't read his book?"

"I read it. I didn't memorize it."

"He said the sixties have been romanticized way too much. Flower children, Bob Dylan, make love, not war—all that bullshit. He said the sixties only amounted to one thing. Even ugly people could get laid."

After Kelly Sue told me about her going-away party at He's Not Here, I was sorry I'd missed it.

Sheila Bruner showed up uninvited with a male bimbo, some muscled-up guy in a ponytail. Sheila had overdosed on makeup and was sporting her new tits. They were bigger than Tracy's now.

Tommy Earl said, "Damn, Sheila, I've got to feel them things."

Sheila said, "You may not! They are no longer in your domain."

Tommy Earl said, "Well, they weren't in my domain when I had me a domain on Pembroke, were they? What do our kids think about what you've done to yourself?"

Sheila said, "Aubyn and Bryson are intelligent young

people. They completely understand their mother's desire for self-improvement and her effort to attain a greater self-esteem."

Tommy Earl said, "That's what them tits are for?"

Sheila said, "You are so crude. You really are."

Tommy Earl said, "Who's that hard-on carrier you brought with you? He gonna lead the clit search tonight?"

Sheila said, "Goddamn you, I hope I never lay eyes on you again!"

Tommy Earl said, "I'll squat down—you won't be able to see over them things."

Sheila said, "You go straight to hell—just keep the checks coming on time!"

Tommy Earl said, "It's a mere bagatelle, darlin'. Nice talkin' to you."

It didn't take Kelly Sue long to start looking like a lady executive. She'd turn up for work in dark gabardine blazers, pinstriped suits. I saw a light gray camel's hair jacket with black pants, a double-breasted navy blazer, an Oxford gray shirt dress, as she called it—slash up the skirt, showing leg when she sat around. All her skirts had slashes up the side. Legs a-plenty, I commented. Style, she said.

It crossed my mind that I might have created a monster.

But she obviously thought she ought to look as important and attractive as possible when she was representing the West Texas Tornadoes. Running the office. Moving around the territory dealing with this and that for me. Up to Amarillo, down to Lubbock, over to the stadium site. Her featherlight cell phone in the pocket of her blazer, her shoulder bag crammed with notes and paperwork and résumés of drones to hire.

She seemed to be everywhere at once, taking the job even more seriously than I'd imagined she would.

One day I got a memo from her. It said:

TO: Billy Clyde
FROM: Kelly Sue
Do you think there ought to be urinals in the men's rest rooms on the second level of our stadium? I sort of do. I tend to think that most men like to stand up when they piss, as opposed to squatting down.

If you agree, you may want to go point out to Griff that these urinals are presently missing, but there's a very nice concrete wall where they are supposed to be. You may also want to ask him why the subcontracting plumber likes to squat when he takes a leak.
Trusty Sidekick

Catching her at the coffee-maker between four-hundred-meter dashes one afternoon, I said, "Somebody we need to hire, and the sooner the better, is a salary-cap person."

She said, "I know what a captologist is."

"A *captologist?*"

"I heard somebody call it that on TV."

"Nobody really understands the salary cap in pro football. My pal Jim Tom Pinch knows more about pro football than any sportswriter in America, but when I asked him to explain the salary cap to me one time, he just laughed."

"I'll study it."

"No, you have other things to do. It'll take a full-time person. I want ours to understand the salary cap as good as anybody else in the league. It's crucial. It can make the difference in a winning and losing franchise."

The current salary cap in the NFL was $55 million.

That was how much a team could spend on player salaries each year. The salary cap was put in to keep the richest owners from buying up all the best players, or what he thought were the best players. The salary cap was designed to level the playing field, in other words.

How you divided the money up among your players was up to you. Some players naturally demanded more money than others. The top stars. You didn't meet their demands, they became free agents and went to another team. Your running back who could slip through a crack in a door, your quarterback with a dynasty for an arm, your linebacker who could de-jock a ball carrier.

But the salary cap had loopholes, just like tax returns, and a top-of-the-line "captologist" could find them.

That was about all I knew about it, I said, but I expected the smart person we'd hire to become a genius at finding ways to beat the cap.

"I know the perfect person," Kelly Sue said.

"Already?"

"Iris McKinney."

"What?"

While I rearranged my face, Kelly Sue said, "She's smart as a whip, Billy Clyde. She knows numbers. She's working as a temp now, but she needs a full-time job. I'm sure she'd move out here."

"She'll hit on the help."

"Yeah. Sometimes. So?"

"I don't believe this. You're saying you want me to hire a nymphomaniac for my salary-cap genius?"

"She's not a nymphomaniac. She sport-fucks occasionally, that's all."

"What does she know about football?"

"Why does the captologist have to know anything about football?"

"Kelly Sue, really. The woman I met—"

"Iris is bright as hell, Billy Clyde. You saw her right

after she'd been fired by an asshole. I wouldn't hire her if I didn't think she'd be terrific. Give her six months, she'll know more about the salary cap than the guy who *invented* the salary cap."

"I don't know," I said, still uncertain. "Men are from carpet, women are from hardwood floors."

"What does *that* mean?"

"I'm not sure, but I think it's deep."

"Billy Clyde, listen to me. Iris worked on the executive floor of a bank for ten years. I'll bet she knows every evil, deceitful, criminal, underhanded trick banks pull on people. It may not be legal or moral, but she'll get the job done for us."

That last part. That's what sold me.

43

The long distance conversation, as Kelly Sue remembered it, went something like this:

"Tornado office," Kelly Sue said, answering the phone while clacking the last sentence of a memo on her computer.

"Who's speaking?" Troubled voice.

"Kelly Sue Woodley. May I help you?"

"Kelly Jean the *bartender?*" Rude voice.

"Hi, Barbara Jane. We spoke once before—when you were over in Switzerland making a movie."

"What are you doing in Big Food, Kelly Jean?"

"What am I doing in Big Food? What's Big Food?"

"Gully Creek. Whatever."

"I work here."

"You *work* there?"

"I work here, yes."

"For the West Texas Tornadoes?"

"Of the National Football League, right."

"May I speak to Billy Clyde, please?"

"He's in a meeting."

"Tell him the meeting's over."

"He's not here, Barbara Jane. He's over at the stadium project. I can't believe Billy Clyde hasn't told you I work here. Is there something I can do for you?"

"Oh? You have duties other than fucking my husband?"

"*What?*"

"You heard me."

"Are you serious?"

"You know my husband two days and you call him in Switzerland? That's not supposed to make me think anything?"

"You flatter me too much, I'm afraid."

"Is that a fact? What *are* your duties, Kelly Jean?"

"Right now trying to remember my name's Kelly Sue."

"Excuse me. It's Kelly Sue in Big Food."

"What is this *Big Food* thing?"

"Nothing. B.C. can explain it someday."

"My title is assistant to the president of the club, Barbara Jane, but a little bit of everything is what I'm doing—and there's lots to do, believe me. I'm sorry about what you think of me. I guess it *is* a little weird, Billy Clyde and I becoming friends so fast. We just started laughing at some of the same things together, and, well . . . that was it. I'm doing a good job here, in case you're interested. You know, Barbara Jane, you'll like me when you get to know me. Most people think I'm an okay person."

"Let me just write that down real quick. *Plan . . . to like . . . Kelly Sue.* There. Got it."

Kelly Sue said she'd had to pause after that crack to make sure she wasn't bleeding. Then she responded, "Barbara Jane, would you like to leave a message for Billy Clyde?"

"When he comes back, tell him I need to talk to him about his father-in-law's health problem, and—"

"Mr. Bookman has a health problem?"

"I don't believe it's serious, but we need to talk about it."

"And there was something else?"

"Yes. Tell him it's finally sunk in. I married beneath me."

End of conversation.

When I called Barb back, she asked why I hadn't mentioned that I'd hired Kelly Sue. I reminded her that I'd said I was going to hire Kelly Sue way back when we were in Lausanne, and that she was going to like Kelly Sue a whole lot when she took the trouble to get to know her, and I would have told her I'd hired Kelly Sue when I was in LA if I hadn't been distracted by so much show biz chitchat, but more important, what was the deal with Big Ed?

Big Ed was as healthy and vigorous as any man I knew—you'd never have known he was in his seventies—so I wasn't all that concerned when I heard he'd fallen down twice at home and had seemed a little forgetful about one thing or another.

But Big Barb was distressed, a wreck. She was worried he might have latched on to a case of junior Alzheimer's, or might be suffering from a form of Parkinson's. That was why she insisted so strongly that he go to the headquarters Mayo Clinic in Rochester, Minnesota, and have a thorough checkup.

For three or four days Big Ed had rejected the idea there could be anything wrong with him—he didn't feel bad. But Big Barb finally talked him into the possibility of a brain tumor, so he went peacefully.

Barb joined her mother in Rochester, mainly to keep Big Barb calm. I felt I should be there, too, but Barb asked me not to come. She was afraid it might look to her daddy like we'd all showed up to give him a proper send-off to the Skipper—she'd let me know if they found anything life-threatening.

I called Big Ed just after he arrived in Rochester to wish him luck on the checkup. I said I hoped they didn't do anything more than recommend he switch putters.

In fact, he *had* brought his golf clubs along with him, he said, figuring he'd slip over to Minneapolis and play Interlachen after he got done at Mayo's. He said I probably didn't know it, but Interlachen was where Bobby Jones had won himself a U.S. Open the year he dusted off the Grand Slam. He'd never played Interlachen and was looking forward to it.

"I don't know what they're apt to find up here," he said, "but in case there's something going on I don't know about, I want everybody to know one damn thing. I'm Texas born, Texas bred, and when I die I wanna be Texas dead."

I said, "Ed, I'd never have known that if you hadn't told me."

Big Ed submitted to every test Mayo could think of. Hooking him up to contraptions, running him through X-ray tunnels, taking half his blood, asking him to swallow all kinds of shit, making him spend most of his time sitting in "the goddamn waiting room, looking at month-old magazines."

The result was, they couldn't find anything physically wrong with him, and that was a Lucille, as Big Ed put it.

But the most reassuring thing, Barb related, was how her daddy handled the psychological test they gave him, a memory thing. Trying to see if he was hanging out with junior Alzheimer's or Parkinson's. Barbara Jane and her mother sat in on it.

This doctor, a clinical psychologist, held a pamphlet in his hand, looked across the desk at Big Ed, and said, "Now, Mr. Bookman, I'm going to read you a story, and I want you to listen carefully."

According to Barb, the story went something like this:

"Annie went to town to do some shopping. Annie browsed through a department store. Annie found two items she liked and bought them. Annie met a friend for lunch. Annie had a nice lunch with her friend. Annie went back home to be there when the children arrived from school."

The clinical psychologist then gazed at Big Ed and said, "Now, Mr. Bookman, I want you to tell me everything you can remember about what Annie did."

And Big Ed said, "Who the fuck is Annie?"

That was when Barbara Jane knew her daddy was perfectly all right.

So it was just as I'd figured in the first place. Big Ed had only been preoccupied, not forgetful, and he'd only fallen down twice at home because he'd been working on his new golf swing.

44

All summer long Tommy Earl was in and out of Gully Creek, sometimes with Ody Bradshaw, but I didn't see that much of him, especially when he was with Ody—I was trying to avoid comas. I'd liked to have seen Ody's foot with the big toe missing, but I gathered it was a touchy subject, and I wouldn't have known how to bring it up without laughing.

Tommy Earl was busy anyhow, bribing state and county bureaucrats, getting his projects off the ground, or in the ground. His gated community, Tumbleweed Pointe—with the ominous *e* on the end. Getting the quarry dug for the championship golf course Big Ed had designed on seven napkins at River Crest Country Club.

Since Big Ed was his banker, Tommy Earl hadn't seen any reason to make any critical comments on Big Ed's unusual design. Big Ed had designed nine consecutive downhill par-four holes on the front nine, and a back side that consisted of back-to-back par-five holes twice and back-to-back par-threes twice, all of which was okay with Tommy Earl.

Six of the back nine holes would play around or over the quarry, which was developing a lake at the bottom.

Big Ed had decided he liked the idea of a quarry, now that he was getting more distance on his tee ball.

Big Ed flew out one day to check on the quarry lake. Tommy Earl happened to be in town, so the three of us went to Them Two Women for lunch.

It was the day Tommy Earl said he was putting in nature trails, bike paths, fly-fishing ponds, tennis courts, and a day-care center. I'd thought the golf course was all he'd wanted as a lure, and said so.

"Claude, you have to accommodate all the requirements of the modern-day second-home buyer. Tumbleweed Pointe will handle all their recreational needs. While we're sitting here, twenty more islands are being discovered off the coast of Georgia and South Carolina."

While I was wondering what that had to do with anything, Freida asked Big Ed if he wanted to try the catch of the day.

"What is it?" Big Ed inquired.

"Meatloaf," she announced.

I said to Tommy Earl that I'd thought Tumbleweed Pointe was going after retirement couples. Retirement couples didn't do "second homes," they did "homes," as I understood it.

"It's all covered," Tommy Earl said. "Tumbleweed Pointe will have something for everybody. I'm building a state-of-the-art retirement center. Just started on it. My geezers will have their own hangout—steam baths, pool tables, card rooms, cafeteria, pub, library, bingo parlor, putting green."

Like a clubhouse, he said. For the geezers who couldn't afford to join the country club where they could lose their golf balls in the quarry.

He said to Big Ed, "I haven't told you my latest deal, Ed. I've already made the arrangements. When I get my retirement center finished, all the funeral homes and probate lawyers in Amarillo and Lubbock are gonna come over on Friday nights and host free chili and fajita parties."

Tommy Earl and Big Ed had found a soulmate in each other when it came to city, state, and federal employees. They agreed that all bureaucrats were put on earth to do nothing but make pots of coffee, call in sick, and say no to anything anybody wanted from them.

"Ed, I've found out one thing," Tommy Earl said. "Rural bureaucrats are easier to deal with than city bureaucrats. The rural bureaucrats out here don't know about the wetlands regulations yet."

"That's a blessing," Big Ed said. "But I've still never met a bureaucrat I wouldn't like to see with his head on a curb and a bottle of cheap wine in his hand."

"Where are the wetlands?" I asked.

"Anywhere the gubmint says they are, right, Ed?" said Tommy Earl. "Buddy of mine was standing on a piece of land on the outskirts of Austin two years ago—have I told you this? He was explaining what he wanted to do to this guy from the Corps of Engineers. Kicking up dry dirt with his heel, dust blowing everywhere. He asked the gubmint guy where the wetlands were, and the asshole said, 'You're standing on it.' Motherfuckers are unbelievable."

Big Ed said he was acquainted with a home builder in Dallas who spent $150,000 and devoted three years to trying to get the twelve permits he needed to develop a piece of land, but by the time he obtained the last permit the first three had expired.

Tommy Earl said, "You know what the federal regulators do when they don't have any wetlands handy? They create 'em. God's honest truth. They buy some unplowed land from a farmer and *flood* the son of a bitch. Our tax dollars at work, Claude."

But Tommy Earl was thankful he only had to deal

with state and city regulators now. You had *some* chance with them, he said. You had *no* chance with the feds.

Big Ed chuckled and said to Tommy Earl, "Tell Billy Clyde how it works with the federal regulators."

Tommy Earl looked at me. "Let's say Senator Puckett writes a bill that'll make cigarette smoking mandatory on all airlines, okay?"

I smiled at the idea.

"The bill passes the Senate and House easily and gets signed into law by the president of the United States. So it's the law now, right?"

Big Ed said, "People can start smoking on airplanes again. That what you think?"

I shrugged.

Tommy Earl said, "Wrong. First, the mandatory new law has to be turned over to the gubmint agency in charge of enforcing it. A year goes by. Senator Puckett looks up one day and says, 'Hey, why ain't everybody smoking on airplanes yet?' He goes to see the bureaucrats. The bureaucrats say they're doing a study on it. Takes time."

With a grin, Big Ed said, "Another year goes by. Now Senator Puckett is hot. I mean hot. He's raging mad, frothing at the mouth. Here he's done something to serve the people but the bureaucrats are jacking around with him."

Picking it up, Tommy Earl said, "The senator goes back to the agency and says, 'I want this damn study completed, I want the law put to work, and I want it done now, by God!' The bureaucrats say they're doing the best they can, but it looks like they'll have to hire thirty thousand more smoking cops to ride airplanes and make people smoke. They say it could take five or ten more years to complete the study."

Big Ed chuckled a little harder.

Tommy Earl said, "The senator goes nuts. He cusses

and yells and says, 'I'm gonna fire all your asses!' He tries to fire everybody, but he finds out he can't. You can't fire a federal bureaucrat. The United States of America won't let you. What happens instead, the agency leaks to Evans & Novak that Senator Puckett once had an affair with a ten-year-old boy. So instead of the senator's bill becoming a reality, he's forced to resign, humiliated, ruined for life."

Now Big Ed laughed out loud. Bureaucrat humor.

Tommy Earl grinned and said, "So, Claude, you probably want to know how come so many stupid fucking laws get passed and put into effect so quick, don't you?"

"I was going to ask."

"The bureaucrats do it," he said. "They have a way of knowing which ones will piss us off the most."

45

There were worse things than bureaucrats in my little realm of the world, and they were called zebras. Therefore I didn't mind going to New York City in late August for an NFL meeting. I'd been appointed to the competition committee, and I was determined to use whatever influence I might have to stop the zebras from ruining the sport. They were throwing so many flags, the games looked like washrag sales.

Football got along just fine for one hundred years when blockers were forced to keep their hands or fists on their chests. Couldn't grab anybody. That was when defense ruled and games were won by sensible scores like 7–3 and 12–6. A high-scoring affair was 21–14.

Even when I came along, a blocker could reach out with only one arm. Now a monster could extend both arms, practically put a guy in a straitjacket, and it was up to the zebra to decide whether he was holding or not.

It was also true in my day that pass interference was when the receiver got mugged. A safety or cornerback broke the receiver's arm and said, "Now catch it, asshole," that was pass interference. Today the defensive back couldn't even breathe on a guy or a flag might drop. And this deal: two guys go flying down the field side by side, bumping and nudging each other all the way—it happened on every deep pass play—but a zebra all too often called "pushing off" on one of them. What was frustrating was how often the zebra called it when the receiver made a great catch or the defender made a great interception, a play that could turn the whole game around.

All this did when the call went against your team, even if the zebra was right on top of the play, was increase your suspicion that the striped-shirt asshole was behind on his child-support payments.

I was saying all this to Kelly Sue one morning in the office before I left for New York. We were drinking coffee, seeing who could smoke the most.

Television changed the rules, I said. The owners decided that fans wanted to see more scoring. They didn't trust the public's attention span. Jesus, if nobody was scoring touchdowns, they said, viewers would switch over to something else and their "quality" advertisers would complain.

This was why in the not-too-distant past they suddenly decided the ground couldn't cause a fumble. Let the offense keep the ball, maybe they'd score again, keep people from switching channels, going to an eight-car pileup on the first turn at Daytona.

Well, the ground used to cause more fumbles than anything for people like Red Grange and Tom Harmon and Doak Walker and Billy Clyde Puckett, just to pick some names at random.

Then about the time T. J. Lambert was winding down his career, the rule came in that you couldn't touch the quarterback. The flinger was too valuable, too essential to high scoring. Used to be, even after the quarterback had thrown the ball, a T.J. could chase him down and lay wood on his ass till the whistle blew.

But now it was a zebra's judgment call, like everything else. Did the linebacker hit the quarterback before, during, or after he released the ball?

T.J. was the original guy who said, "They don't even need the rule—just let the quarterback wear a dress."

There were seven zebras on the field and I said I'd risk the guess that most people had no idea what their jobs were, other than to trot around being blind or stupid or crooked.

"So educate me," she said.

"Okay," I said. "I'll start with the referee."

"He wears the white cap, right?"

"Right. He's the boss of the other zebras. He makes those signs with his arms, like he's directing traffic. Usually can't make his microphone work for TV. He can overrule the other calls. He stands behind the quarterback before the snap. The referee's responsible for backfield in motion and one or two other things, but he's mainly in charge of the quarterback's dress. Making sure the quarterback never gets a spot or a stain on his dress without some felon drawing a penalty."

"Where do referees come from?"

"T.J. says ready-to-wear."

Kelly Sue started to take notes. I asked why. She said for a white paper, for the staff. It was stuff they ought to know.

I said, "The umpire. He might be the most hated zebra of all. He stands in the middle of the defensive line, about five yards back. He makes the crowd-pleasing holding calls. Ever since linemen were allowed to use their arms and hands, there's been holding, in some form, on every single play. The league says umpires only call holding when it's flagrant, like a guy reaching his arm around somebody's back or pulling on a jersey, but any coach or player can tell you when the umpire most often calls holding. When it fucking kills you, that's when."

"Moving right along."

"Moving right along, there's your head linesman. He straddles the line of scrimmage on the sideline and watches for offsides. He watches where somebody steps out of bounds on his side of the field. Another thing he does is keep track of downs. Some head linesmen move a ring from their index finger to their little finger, keeping up with the downs. I've always thought it'd be helpful if they could count to four."

"You ask a lot of these people, don't you?"

"Line judge. I call him the head linesmen, part II. He looks for offsides on the other side of the field. One of his crucial duties is to keep time in case the official time-keeper's clock goes on the blink. His big moment comes when he gets to tell the referee it's the end of the quarter—like nobody else can see the scoreboard."

I frowned at my cold coffee. Kelly Sue warmed it up.

I said, "Okay, the back judge. He's back there about twenty-five yards deep in the secondary, favoring the same side of the field as the line judge. He's watching the wide receiver and the guy trying to cover him. The back judge is poised to call interference at all times, get himself on TV. He's one of the loose-ball guys, too—makes sure the ground didn't cause a fumble."

"That's right, the ground can't cause a fumble. TV doesn't like it."

"The side judge. He's another unindicted co-conspirator. He's back there twenty or twenty-five yards deep in the secondary, but over on the head linesman's side of the field. He's watching wide receivers and split ends on his side and more or less doing the same thing the back judge does, which means he's screwing up a nice afternoon, what was supposed to be a sports event."

"Last guy."

"The field judge. He's the deepest guy back there in the secondary, usually on the tight end's side of the field. He's in charge of the twenty-five-second clock. His other big job is to watch the tight end and the guys defending the tight end, see that nothing illegal happens. I say it might be kind of hard for the field judge to see any of that—way back where he is—but what the hell, he can make it up if he hasn't thrown a flag in the last two or three minutes."

"Thanks," Kelly Sue said. "You've made me really and truly, deep down, love the game more than ever."

The competition committee was an elite little club that exerted serious influence on the game. It practically ran pro football. When the committee recommended something in the way of rules, schedules, play-offs, trades, draft, salary limits, the owners generally approved it.

Aside from myself, it now consisted of two other general managers and four head coaches. Seven members were on the committee. An odd number was necessary to break a deadlock on an issue. Because I could "bring to the table" the experience of a former player, I'd replaced D. R. ("Dirty") Wandry on the committee. Dirty Wandry, a running back with the 49ers in his playing days, had been the GM of the Atlanta Falcons when he'd been shot and killed in an Atlanta shopping mall.

It wasn't unusual for people to be shot and killed in the parking lots of Atlanta shopping malls, but it hardly ever happened indoors. Dirty Wandry just happened to have strolled into a computer store when a gang war broke out around him. He caught two in the chest, fell instantly, and ironically died with his head resting on a lower shelf of video football games.

The other two general managers were gentlemen I hadn't met before—Jewell Slater of the Dolphins and

Ned Steakly of the Eagles. I'd heard of them. They'd been around for years and were respected as sharp operators.

Having been a TV person, I was acquainted with all four coaches. We'd had dinners together, gone over game plans before a telecast.

The Jets' coach, Gloomy Gus Norton, had been with the Broncos, Bills, Rams, and Saints. Moanin' Matty Burke, now with the Redskins, had been with the Chargers, Bucs, Raiders, and Seahawks. The Steelers' E. R. ("Ears") McBride had been fired from the Colts, Chiefs, and Giants. And Sleepy Jim Crowder, now spearheading the Colts, had been with the Patriots, Rams, Browns, and Cowboys.

We met in secret in a large suite at the Regency. It was elegantly furnished with antiques, a big living room, two bedrooms. The only explanation I was given for why the meeting was secret came in two words from Ears McBride. "Media shits," he said.

We were there for most of a day and night. It was cordial. The whiskey and food came promptly from room service, and often. It wouldn't be honest of me if I didn't confess that the poker game took up most of our time.

Gloomy Gus Norton liked to deal seven-card peek-and-turn high-low. Moanin' Matty Burke favored five-card high-low with two sluffs. Sleepy Jim Crowder used two decks to deal a game he called clusterfuck—you got thirteen cards and played your best five, high-low.

Everybody had long since adopted Ears McBride's language. Aces were anals, answers, spears, darts, and hard-ons. Numbered cards were dukes, tramps, forks, fevers, sexes, save-ins, ate-me's, nights, and tents. Kings were queers, queens were "whoors," pronounced that way, and jacks were pimps, but mostly they were just hair. Dealing, Ears would say, "There's some hair . . .

there's some more hair . . . there's too much hair for me."

I only lost about $600.

When we got around to discussing issues, I had just one suggestion to offer, but it was the zebra thing I felt strongly about. Make the zebras full-time employees of the NFL, men who could devote their brains and energies to the game. Today, it was just a hobby for most of them. A guy worked on a Sunday afternoon or Monday night, then went back to his door-frame business and the gin game with his bookie.

What they could do in the off-season, I said, was study their mistakes on film, think of ways to improve the rules and rid themselves of so many judgment calls, and take constant physicals and eye tests.

Everybody nodded thoughtfully. Ned Steakly, the Eagles' guy, said it was an idea that was probably worth bringing to the attention of the owners somewhere down the line.

I said we might even think about hiring private eyes to follow the zebras, but the other members thought I was joking and had a good laugh.

There was a long discussion I stayed out of—whether our halftimes should be longer than twelve minutes. I listened to how more than one important TV executive had complained lately that his network wasn't getting enough commercials in the halftime portion of the telecasts.

This caused some hand-wringing, some worried looks, and somebody said it was certainly something we ought to look at more closely.

The one decision that was made all day was on something the coaches were insistent about—that our next meeting should be over in Maui so we could squeeze in a little golf.

46

Barbara Jane called it our Manhattan co-op. I called it our $3,200-a-month maintenance. Sometimes we both called it the money funnel. But the main thing was, the apartment was in a reasonably secure building and once again nothing was missing.

Not that we owned too many things of value. All the electronic stuff, yeah, but no expensive paintings by dead guys. I looked to make sure Barb's antique jewelry that she never wore was still there. It was. She kept it hidden in a fake volume of Proust on the bookshelf in our library-den. The idea came from Shake Tiller, who'd said nobody in his right mind would pick up a copy of Proust, not even a literary burglar.

There was nothing else in the library-den anybody would want but us. A mess of memorabilia. Old game balls, trophies, framed magazine covers and photos from the days when I was a great American and a wonderful human being. All of my treasures were mixed in with Barb's. Framed print ads she found amusing from her modeling days, show-biz publicity stills, the first deck chair with her name on it, her Emmys for playacting in *Rita*.

Our building was in the East Seventies on Park Street, which most people called Park Avenue. We'd owned the co-op for ten years. The building was blessed with a helpful super and a good staff. One of the handymen even spoke English. We could go away for long periods of time and the doormen, hallmen, and handymen would look after our place like it was their own.

This was due to my admirable record of tipping the guys regularly for various chores when I was in town, and hitting them pretty hard during the holidays. Their Christmas bonuses were now up to a total of $3,000.

I'd never known what anybody else in the building gave them—the Broadway producer, the book author, the tooth dentist, the stockbroker, the four rich widows. Every co-op building in Manhattan had at least one Broadway producer, one book author, one tooth dentist, one stockbroker, and four rich widows living in it.

The staff must have been pleased with the way I treated their palms. If you didn't treat their palms, it was an open invitation for the staff to rent trucks and empty the joint. You would read about people in Gotham being ripped off all the time.

People came home from a trip and found nothing left but an ashtray full of cigarette butts, a dirty cup and saucer, and an open jar of instant coffee.

Jim Tom Pinch liked to tell about the time one of his editors at *The Sports Magazine* got knocked off. The editor returned from a two-week trip and not only found his TV sets, stereo system, and computer gone, but the thieves had exhibited a sense of humor. They'd drawn arms and legs on all of his Picassos.

I arranged a lunch date with Jim Tom while I was in town. Had him meet me at my favorite spot on Lexington, not far from my maintenance. The place offered good, simple luncheonette food, and the name of the place made it easy to find. It was called Luncheonette.

I'd been known to sit there for four or five hours on idle winter days. Grab a booth by the windows, eat two or three times, drink coffee, read papers, read a book, watch people slide around on the snow and sleet, trying to get to their optometrists and shrinks.

I was into the first of my baloney-and-American-cheese-on-rye sandwiches when Jim Tom arrived, ordered a cheeseburger, and said he wanted to apologize for roughing me up so badly.

He was talking about his story, the remember-when piece in the current issue of *SM*, the article he'd written about the Super Bowl champion Giants of twenty years ago.

I was fairly embarrassed about it. I'd practically been deified. Jim Tom had made it sound like I'd taken the team to the championship by myself, and won the Super Bowl with only marginal assistance from Shake Tiller, T.J. Lambert, Hose Manning, and Puddin Patterson, our great offensive guard, who'd let me cold-crawl his spine and do a Greg Louganis over the goal line to whip the dogass Jets—"in the waning moments," I was sure I'd read.

"That wasn't me," Jim Tom said. "I never wrote 'waning moments' in my life. An editor stuck it in. He'll die. I never wrote 'Navy won the toss and elected to receive,' either."

"You *did* write that Four Horsemen deal, though, didn't you? How'd it go? 'Outlined against a blue-gray October sky . . . ?' Wasn't that it?"

He said, "No, I wrote 'outlined against a blue-gray *April* sky.' Grantland Rice and I were covering Jack Nicklaus winning his fourteenth or fifteenth Masters."

"Granny must have been a hundred and twelve by then."

"True, but he could still see all the way to his carriage return."

As our repartee continued, I told Jim Tom I was sorry he'd left some important things out of his story—like me inventing the polio vaccine.

"Sorry. It was so long ago, I'd forgotten it. Like I forgot about those hit songs you wrote for *Guys and Dolls, My Fair Lady, Gypsy.* But I'm glad I got in the night you were with Simon Wiesenthal."

"The night I was with *Simon Wiesenthal?*" I grinned.

Jim Tom said, "Yeah, you must have skipped over it. It was a great moment when you said, 'Well, Simon, are you just gonna sit around Elaine's the rest of your life, or do you want to go find some Nazis?'"

I asked Jim Tom if he knew how the other expansion teams were getting along. Had he heard any delicious gossip in his travels? Uncovered any scandals I might soon be reading? All I knew, I said, was what I read in *USA Today,* which wasn't much, not to belittle what a big day it was in Gully Creek when the coin-operated *USA Today* machine was installed on the sidewalk outside Them Two Women.

No owners had been found for LA and Cleveland yet, Jim Tom said, although he'd heard some criminal lawyers were rumored to be interested in the LA franchise, and a group of tire workers in Akron were trying to arrange financing to own the new Cleveland Browns.

Jim Tom did hear that Bappy Ramirez had become bored with life in general and had turned complete control of the Mexico City Bandits over to his wife, Naomi. One of the first things Naomi had done at a cocktail party, which had unfortunately been leaked to the local press by a jealous person, was refer to their stadium under construction as "the Spickdome."

Nothing startling was going on with the rich Jap, according to Jim Tom's sources. Tokyo Russ was doing what he could to promote his wife's show-biz career, but the opportunities in Hawaii were limited. Which was why Rachel, or "Mandy Rice-Davies," was taking hula lessons and learning to play the ukulele and sing "Waikiki Moon."

The news was a little more exciting over in London, Jim Tom said, and I would be familiar with it if I didn't live in the musical past. Neville Trill had stolen a hugely successful rock group from another manager.

The group was called Bloody Hemorrhoids, and Neville had been widely quoted as saying, "I shouldn't be at all surprised if the Bloodys take heavy metal to heights Led Zeppelin never dreamed of."

I said to Jim Tom, "I'm happy to say I've lived a full life without ever hearing a Led Zeppelin record."

"Yeah, you have," he said. "Haven't you ever stopped at a red light next to a punk with a bad case of acne, the window down, and his tape deck turned up loud as it'll go? That's Led Zeppelin."

"Now that you mention it," I said.

Jim Tom had been traveling, as always. He'd followed a 100-meter sprinter around Europe, unable to keep from noticing the steroid rash on the athlete's shoulders; he'd traipsed after a golfer in Scotland and England, and he'd watched a Formula One driver try to kill himself in Spain—not in a race but by fucking everything on the Costa del Sol.

"Your expense account never gets much of a rest, does it?" I said.

"It's not all bluebirds and lemonade in the world of magazine journalism," he said. "I went to Provincetown. Ever been there?"

"Nope."

"Don't bother. This infantile feature editor talked me into doing a piece on 'The Sporting Cape.' Already had his headline. I could have fun with it, he said. See rich people on vacation, sailing, playing croquet, power jogging. Go to Hyannis, Nantucket, the Vineyard, Chatham, Truro, Provincetown. I wasn't familiar with the Cape, he said, like he was—spent his joyous boyhood days there—so I most likely didn't know the Pilgrims landed at Provincetown first, before they went to Plymouth Rock in . . . whenever. I thought okay, I can work with that. So I went. Didn't get a story, but I came back with a question for *him*. What year did the dykes land in Provincetown?"

"The Ellens were there?"

"Ellens, I could handle. I'm talking meece."

Jim Tom's plural of *moose*.

"It was brutal," he said. "They were everywhere. A straight person can't get a drink in a bar or eat in a restaurant till all the meece have been served. It's even hard to walk down the sidewalk. You can get decked by these maurading bands of big, husky, hairy-legged meece in their cutoff jeans, T-shirts, and hiking boots."

"Your Whitney Houstons didn't impress anybody?" I said.

"Not in the least. I might have picked a bad week. There was a local election coming up. I noticed placards, posters, messages on the T-shirts. The meece were trying to elect some multicultural, diversified, 'physically challenged' candidate—probably a one-legged black lesbian."

"Scratch two vacation spots," I said. "The shirt-lifters have Key West, the meece have Provincetown."

47

The radio voice was saying, "College football on a Saturday afternoon! The tapestry of the stadium—school colors splashed against the blue horizon! The scent of autumn in the air! The subtle russet of the trees! The bands are blarin', the cheerleaders are hoppin', and we've got a sheep-shearin' stemwinder of a spellin' bee comin' at you today! The Alabama Crimson Tide is here in Fort Worth, Texas, to meet undefeated TCU, and the Tide better have their hats on! The rip-roarin' Horned Frogs of Coach T. J. Lambert are led by a set of Touchdown Twins that have already wreaked havoc on three opponents. One of T.J.'s speed demons is slippery as an eel in a bucket of Jell-O, and the other's a rollin' bundle of butcher knives. Down here at TCU, they call 'em Budget and Avis Fowler!"

I was just turning into my reserved parking slot down by the north end zone and felt like I was listening to Larry Hoage, but even Larry couldn't have come up with "subtle russet," which almost caused me to bump into somebody's camper.

Heavy-duty annual donors to the athletic department, like me and a few hundred other loyalists, enjoyed reserved parking spaces right by the stadium portals, their names in white letters on a purple background. The signs looked something like license plates on fence posts. It was all along these rows of parking places, by the trees and concrete picnic tables, that the more elaborate tailgate parties occurred—elaborate if you wanted to use that word to describe Styrofoam ice chests filled with beer and sacks of barbecue ribs to go from Bust Out Jonah, Angelo's, and Railhead.

This was October. I'd driven from Gully Creek and arrived just before the kickoff. It was the first chance I'd had to see a TCU home game. I bought two hot dogs and a Coke and slipped into a section of the half-empty end zone I'd have all to myself.

I could have taken a better seat. As a season ticket holder, which I'd been for years, I owned four seats around the forty-yard line on the west side of the stadium, the press box side, but I wasn't in the mood to socialize with the old grads who'd be seated near me. Besides, I wasn't wearing anything purple. I was there in sunglasses, a pair of khakis, blue golf shirt, tan Hollywood windbreaker that said MELANCHOLY BABY on the back, and a black baseball cap that said FIGHTIN' ROOSTERS on the front.

The cap was in honor of the dead-game kids I'd watched lose to the Wolf Flat Geedahs 65–0—and nobody even knew what a Geedah was.

Gully Creek's quarterback, Hardy Gilliam, Reece Gilliam's kid, threw seven interceptions that night. Maybe if it hadn't been so dark. For his effort, anyhow, the kid got grounded and had his pickup taken away from him until further notice.

The Roosters' best running back, Chigger Payne, Deana Boone's baby brother, fumbled five times, and later received fifty licks on the bare ass from Coach Shug Armstrong's long wooden paddle. Ten for each fumble.

Deana Boone told me it didn't enter her head that the coach had dished out "excess punishment," not considering the crimes the little vagrant had committed. They still taught discipline in Gully Creek, she was proud to say.

T.J. seemed to have the Frogs ready. They came out for the opening kickoff looking like they'd raided a chemical company.

I thought the attitude might wear off, but Budget and Avis were everything T.J. had promised. They tore off huge chunks of yardage, first one, then the other. They were impressive indeed, even though they were playing an Alabama team that lacked two essentials: coaching and talent.

In my expert opinion, it didn't seem that big of a deal for the Frogs to beat this particular Alabama team 31–0. The Tide was in a down cycle, now being coached by a country gentleman named Pooty Ramsey. A former tackle under Bear Bryant, Pooty was the seventh coach Alabama had hired in an effort to find another Bear Bryant. But if the TCU game was any indication, Pooty would be gone in a month. His players did things that were so dumb, he might as well have suited up faculty members.

One of Pooty Ramsey's post-game statements in the *Light & Shopper* on Sunday morning summed up Alabama's performance.

He said, "Right now this minute, I think you'd have to say we're about twenty-two boxcars shy of bein' a train."

I went to the TCU dressing room after the game to say hidy to T.J. and congratulate his stallions, who were off to a 4–0 start, having wreaked havoc on down-cycle Iowa, down-cycle Miami, and down-cycle Tulsa before they trounced Alabama. In only four games Budget had gained 589 yards and scored eight touchdowns, and Avis had gained 532 yards and scored six touchdowns. They were already being compared with Tonsillitis Johnson and Artis Toothis, even Limejello and Orangejello Tucker.

First, I admired all the inspirational signs T.J. had posted on the walls. The most prominent sign was hung inside above the front door, a message every player was expected to glance at, maybe hop up and slap, as he left the room to enter the tunnel leading onto the field. The sign said:

PAIN IS TEMPORARY . . . .
PRIDE LASTS FOREVER.

I smiled and couldn't help thinking to myself that if you wanted to hear a really big laugh, you could try that on a pro team.

On another wall, over near the entrance to the showers and toilet stalls, I found one I knew to be original with T.J. This one said:

EXCUSES AIN'T FOR SHIT.
YOUR FRIENDS DON'T NEED
'EM AND YOUR ENEMIES
WON'T BELIEVE 'EM.

I found T.J. smoking a cigar, as were some of the players. I was shocked, but T.J. said it was a winner's reward. New ritual he'd started. Part of his treat-'em-like-grown-ups style of coaching. I'd never smoked in a locker room, and couldn't bring myself to do it now. Sacred place.

Rejoicing in the day's work, T.J. said, "Damn, I like to play them teams with big old fat linemen who can't move—their legs touch all the way to their knees." He looked up at the ceiling. "Send me as many of those as you can find, Lord."

"What'll you do for the Lord?" I asked.

"He don't need anything, does he? Don't he already have everything locked up?"

A lot of coaches liked to say it was God's will when they lost football games, but it built character. Pooty Ramsey was possibly saying something along those lines to his Alabama team at the moment.

As a player and coach, T.J. had always put defeats in a slightly different perspective. He'd say, "I wish to hell God would stop trying to make me a better person."

I was introduced to Budget and Avis, who were such great football players T.J. no longer saw them as Africranium-Americans. They were examples of the splendid youth our country could be proud of.

The coach said to his touchdown twins, "Boys, I want you to meet Billy Clyde Puckett, one of the all-time studs at TCU . . . *and* with the New York City Football Giants."

Budget and Avis had showered. They'd slipped into their jeans and were buttoning up their western shirts. Their faces were friendly, smiling. Each one stood about six-three, looked to weigh 225, had a remarkable physique, not an ounce of excess weight. We shook hands.

"I seen your picture on Coach's wall," Budget said with a grin. "You movin' out. You steppin' *high*, baby."

"I was just trying to keep from getting hurt." I smiled.

"You see that, Avis?" Budget said.

"See what?" Avis said.

"This man's picture on Coach's wall."

"What the man doin' on Coach's wall?"

"This man here? This man here was a runnin' dude, Avis. He tote the mail for TCU and the New York Giants."

"That right?" Avis said, studying me more closely. "You break some containments?"

"He broke his share of containment," T.J. replied for me.

"All right!" Avis said. And offered me a cult handshake that involved a routine I followed as best I could—fist, palm, fist, palm, fist, high, low, side, up, down, over. It wasn't easy without music.

"See, that's what we specialiss in, me and Avis," Budget said. "We go 'bout breakin' containments. Before a game Avis go see his sports psychologiss, I go see my hipmotiss."

I glanced at T.J. The coach shrugged.

"They get us ready to break the containments," Budget said. "Like we did today on the Cramson Tide."

"Yeah, baby!" Avis cried out. And they did that handshake thing.

I wished the Fowler twins luck for the rest of the season. Keep on breaking that containment, I said, walking away with the coach.

Alone with T.J., I asked him if Budget and Avis had asked for a sports psychologist and a hypnotist.

I was informed that the idea came from their daddy, Harold Fowler. He was a man who'd worked as a mechanic for Hertz most of his life, a fact that may have had something to do with the names he'd chosen for his sons. Harold Fowler acted as the agent and manager for Budget and Avis when they were jucos and T.J. was trying to recruit them out of Southeastern Institute of Assemblies of God & Plumbing in Clarabeth, Oklahoma.

The sports psychologist and hypnotist were part of the package Harold Fowler insisted on when the boys selected TCU to complete their higher education. The rest of the package included the usual items other successful college programs secretly offered—cars, clothes, money, blondes.

"They just think they have a sports psychologist and a hypnotist," the coach confessed.

"They just *think* they do?"

T.J. looked a little guilty. "The sports psychologist is on the English faculty. He's an associate professor. He meets with Avis on Friday and reads him some Zen shit—or tells it to him. Says stuff to him like, 'If you think you're lucky, you *are* lucky.' Things like that."

I said I wasn't altogether sure that came from Zen—it sounded more like Barry Switzer.

"Don't matter to me where it comes from long as it works," T.J. said. "I went over to the building where the actors and singers hang out, to what they call their Green Room . . . found me a girl drama student for a hypnotist. She dresses up like a gypsy, meets Budget in private, hypnotizes him after they talk awhile."

"How does she hypnotize him?"

"She reads to him."

"Reads him what?"

"Something on the front page of the paper. She says just about anything puts him right to sleep."

"It does me too—particularly if it's got the word *deficit* in it. But I've always thought you're supposed to go into a trance when you get hypnotized. Budget goes to sleep?"

"Budget don't know the difference. He takes a little nap, wakes up thinking he's a five hundred-pound bowling ball."

"A five hundred-pound bowling ball will break most of your containments."

"They're awesome, ain't they, my twins?"

"Outstanding."

T.J. said, "They're scholastic juniors, which means they'll be coming out next spring. I got to have one of 'em for the Tornadoes, Billy Clyde. I don't care how much Big Ed has to pay to get him—what you have to trade, whose dick you have to suck. Franchise A and Franchise B, is all they are."

I said I'd try to acquire one of the Fowler twins without having to turn into a shirt-lifter.

48

You had to write it off as a human-nature deal, was what I said about it. People sometimes acted crazy and there wasn't anything you could do about it—short of stuffing some Prozac down their neck. But that didn't always work either. I remembered this actress Barbara Jane knew who got off Prozac for six weeks and started crying at *Bonanza* reruns.

I was given to wonder if Prozac was what Rabbit Tyrance needed.

After the Frogs won four more games and their 8–0 record lifted them up to number five in the polls, Rabbit Tyrance began to visualize another national championship. He even began thinking about ways to celebrate TCU being number one in the football nation again, and one of his ideas was a ticker-tape parade in downtown Fort Worth, and he wanted me to serve as grand marshall.

I didn't hear that from Rabbit himself. He instructed W. F. ("Wet Fart") Lorants, the sports information director, to call me in Gully Creek and feel me out about it. Wet Fart did call—Weffert, I mean. I was first pleased to find out that at least Weffert hadn't lost his sanity.

Like me, he realized TCU had three games left to play, and anything could happen.

Weffert said, "Ackymeen, ahsay gee permatern."

If you ask me, I'd say we're being premature.

I said, "Weffert, I'm not gonna be a grand marshall in any parade, even if there *is* a parade, and Rabbit's a bigger idiot than ever."

"Angee nor harger bouty dee," Weffert said.

Ain't gonna get no argument outta me.

My own fear—and T.J.'s, too—revolved around a deficiency that developed in the quarterback department.

The trouble started in the other game I attended in person, the Air Force game in early November. That was the day T.J.'s regular quarterback, Jimmy Staples, a good little sleight-of-hand operator who could also throw the ball, suffered the injury that sidelined him for a month.

Jimmy scored on a twenty-two-yard option play and was so excited about making his first touchdown of the season, he kept on running through the end zone and bashed his head into the wall—on purpose. His way of celebrating. But this was unfortunate because Jimmy apparently forgot the wall was made out of concrete. They carried him off on a stretcher and took him to the hospital, where it was diagnosed he'd sustained a "jammed neck."

T.J.'s backup quarterback, Ryan Meek, played the rest of the Air Force game, where it was revealed that he didn't have an arm, couldn't throw a lick, but the Frogs were far enough ahead, they held on to win.

It wasn't a pretty sight when Ryan Meek attempted a pass, hoping to loosen up the defense. The ball either soared into the stands or punctured a hole into the turf. Hand the ball off to Budget and Avis was about all he was capable of, and even then there were some miscues.

I sat in one of my forty-yard-line seats that day.

There was the threat of rain and I wanted to be underneath the upperdeck, stay dry. This put me in a nest of old friends, old classmates, old acquaintances.

Tommy Earl and Tracy Hopkins were right in front of me. They'd been to all the home games together, so people had stopped asking Tommy Earl how Sheila was. Nearby, and quite vocal, were several ex-TCU gladiators. Humper Jones and his wife, the former Leta Joyce Culbertson, who'd been a Frog cheerleader, and Jack and Evelyn Snedeker, and C.P. and Celia Claunch, all of them wearing various shades of purple garments.

Poor Ryan Meek, the no-arm backup quarterback, didn't get much sympathy in our section.

"Get him outta there, T.J.!" Humper hollered. "The little turd couldn't hit the sky if you throwed him out of a airplane!"

"Don't try to pass, you ignernt shit!" Leta Joyce screamed each time Ryan Meek wobbled one into the ground.

Tommy Earl wheeled around to me at one point and said, "I like this kid—he's completed five out of his last seven handoffs."

Coincidence jumped up and grabbed me when I went down to the concession stand to get a Coke. I ran into Iris McKinney, my capologist.

Iris had eagerly accepted the job when Kelly Sue offered it to her on the phone, but she wasn't able to move to Gully Creek and start the job right away. She was working as a temp for a bank and had promised the man who hired her that she'd stay until after the first of the year. This spoke for Iris's loyalty and dedication, Kelly Sue said.

Iris looked about half-cute, I had to admit. She was wearing a pair of black pants, a beige cashmere turtleneck, a brown tweed blazer, and her shaded glasses were up in her hair. She was with Fake Doug Taggart, one of the He's Not Here regulars. He was red-eyed and looked a little overserved, in my humble opinion. They were buying cups of ice to put in their fruit jars of grape juice.

"Iris, is it you?" I said.

"Hi, boss," she said brightly. "Want a sip?"

"What is it?"

"Purple Jesus. Vodka and grape juice."

"No thanks."

"It was grape juice and gin when I was in school here," she said. "Gin was quicker."

"It would be, yeah."

She said, "That important fact was first uncovered by Nonie Clayton, my best friend in Chi Omega. She married an asshole named Theron Pratt and lives in Port Aransas now. All he does is fish. All she does is get stoned and look at oil tankers. They don't even have cable. I'm giving her a red nylon chair for Christmas."

"I didn't know you went to TCU, Iris," I said.

"I was long after you. I got here on the tail end of Tommy Earl's team. Tommy Earl, Hog Hailey, Skeeter Rowland, D. R. Cooles—that bunch of Cary Grants. My freshman year was Tommy Earl's senior year. But nobody knew I even existed for two years. I was scrawny, plain. I had to drink my way into their hearts."

"You awight now, baby," Fake Doug said, sliding his arm around her, a bit too close to her rack.

"You want to draw back a *nub?*" she said rudely, removing his arm.

To me, she said, "He thinks he's gonna get laid tonight."

"When I show you what I got, you're gonna want to," Fake Doug said.

Iris looked off, shook her head sadly. "The men I have to go out with."

Fake Doug said, "It's in my genes, don't you see? My daddy . . . hee, hee . . . when my daddy died, they had to jack him off before they could get the casket closed."

Iris said, "Jesus Christ, Doug. Do you ever say anything original? I heard that in *high school.*"

"Where'd you go to high school?" I asked her.

"Awrington Heights, your bitter rival."

I said I didn't know she was an Arlington Heights Yellow Jacket.

"Awrington Heights."

"*Awrington* Heights?"

"That's what our football players called it."

"Being funny?"

"No, just trying to say it."

I said it was too bad Iris wasn't already out in Gully Creek with us. There was a lot for her to learn about the salary cap.

"No sweat," she said. "I'm all over it."

I said let us know if there was anything we could do to help her find a place to live.

"Kelly Sue's on the case. She has a joint on hold for me where she's living—the Slippery Sands Apartments."

"Is that what she calls it now? Last week it was the Tally Me Banana."

"All I know is, it's in Downtown Lubbock City."

I said, well, I'd better get back to T.J.'s scholar-athletes.

"Go, Frogs," she said, and swatted Fake Doug's roving hand again.

49

I was on record as saying the only good thing about TCU losing a football game was the pleasure of getting to read Rick Lindsey's story about it in the *Light & Shopper*.

Rick Lindsey was the impressionable young sports-writer who'd been covering the Frogs for five years. He was a young man who worked hard and took pride in staying close to the team, but even Weffert Lorants found that embarrassing at times, like when Rick would shout encouragement to the Frogs from the press box. Rick had been known to holler at TCU's defensive unit, "Stop him, grab him, get him!"

It had earned Rick the nickname of "Hometown" in the sportswriting fraternity, but even this hadn't slowed him down on the laptop.

I considered Rick Lindsey's first paragraphs on the TCU losses to Brigham Young and Utah good enough to clip and mail to Jim Tom Pinch, who collected such things.

The lead on Rick's Brigham Young story read:

"Fate dropped a Krakatoa on gallant TCU's unbeaten season today, and the tidal wave that followed the Brig-

ham Young eruption drowned all Frog hopes of an undefeated season as the Frogs were without submarines
and swam for their lives before the flood of the surpris-
ing BYU Cougars, many of which are too old to be in
college, 27–24."

He took a different slant in his Utah story:

"The best team lost today as the never-say-die Frogs
got Tammy Wynetted from the end zone too many
times and Utah tabernacled its way to a 21–17 upset
mainly with the help of a referee and a head lineman
who didn't come from choir practice on the scoreboard.
The really sad part is, the Frogs would have had an undefeated season without their past two losses."

It would have been accurate to blame the two tragic
losses on the quarterback situation. Both BYU and Utah
threw strange nine-man defensive lines at T.J.'s
stalwarts, knowing Ryan Meek couldn't pass effectively,
and it was too much for Budget and Avis to overcome,
although they came close.

The Frogs did win their last game 34–7 over down-
cycle New Mexico to finish with a 9–2 record, but so
much for ticker-tape parades.

T.J. publicly accepted the blame for the two losses.
Said his team had been ill-prepared for unforeseen circumstances, and when this happened, you had to look at
the head man, where the buck stopped. And he pleaded
with the fans to stop ridiculing Ryan Meek, stop calling
for him to be dragged through the streets like Mussolini;
the boy did the best he could.

Privately, however, T.J. said to me, "That sorry little
rat. He couldn't hit a ten-yard pass if a terrorist had a
gun pointed at his mama's head."

The Frogs received feelers from two minor bowls.
They could play Stanford in Houston on December 30
in what used to be the Bluebonnet Bowl but was now the
Regal Crystaline Finish Auto Painting & Collision Re-

pair Celebration Bowl. Or they could play the University of Georgia in Atlanta in what used to be the Peach Bowl but was now the Donaldson's Year-Round 30 Percent Off on All Mattresses and Wicker Olympic Bowl.

T.J. opted to play Stanford and congratulated himself on being so shrewd in the decision. His shrewdness had to do with the fact that Stanford was a private school whereas Georgia was a state school.

"Stanford won't have all them ADS studs," he said.

ADS studs were something I hadn't heard about.

T.J. said, "Guys we used to call stupid, they're not stupid anymore. They're victims of Attention Deficit Syndrome. ADS. It started out with people recovering from a stroke. Doctors give stroke patients these tests to see what damage the stroke might have done to their thinking process. The athletic departments at the state universities now hire these test-givers to come in and examine their football players—see if the football players suffer from Attention Deficit Syndrome. If the test-givers decide they do, the studs get breaks on their grades and scholastic requirements. The state schools can even get a federal grant for each kid, for 'educating the handicapped.' Money comes rolling in on wheels from the federal gubmint, the blue-chip studs come rolling in from all over the country. You want to ask me again why I'd rather play Stanford than Georgia?"

50

We had all reached the point in our lives when we didn't want anything for Christmas, we didn't need anything for Christmas, and we swore nobody was going to *get* anything for Christmas. Everybody would always say that's fine, we'll just enjoy being together, doing peace on Earth, goodwill toward Americans. Then on the day before Christmas every year somebody would say, well, there ought to be a *few* packages under the tree, for God's sake, it *is* Christmas—so we'd all rush out to a mall and buy five or six presents for everybody.

Christmas was at the Bookmans' in Fort Worth again. It was a tradition. Big Ed sent his plane out to LA to fetch Barbara Jane, Human Dog, and Shake Tiller. They came in on December 21, the same day I drove down from Gully Creek.

Shake had been spending Christmas with us for the past few years. He was our orphan. He was oh for brothers or sisters, and his folks had crossed the river a long time ago.

He sometimes brought along a shapely, who was always made welcome, but this time he was empty. Kitten Hollis had moved in with Adolphe Menjou, or maybe it

was S. Z. Sakall—a Broadway producer, anyhow. Shake
had been holding tryouts for a replacement, but he
hadn't been able to make a selection.

All I wanted to do was cuddle up with my wife and
dog in front of the fire for four days, and eat so much
roast turkey and cornbread dressing I'd have to lie down
for a while every time I took three steps. All Barb wanted
to do was relax. And all Shake wanted to do was work on
a script and watch movies in his room, one of the seven
cable-ready guest rooms in the Bookman mansion.

Shake said cable was particularly valuable during the
holidays. If you had cable, there were enough channels
where you had a fighting chance to avoid *It's a Wonderful
Life*.

As it usually happened, we didn't get to do enough of
those things we all wanted to do. Big Ed made Shake
and I play cold-weather golf with him twice at River
Crest.

Meanwhile, Big Barb made Barbara Jane go to a
round of holiday parties her friends were giving—one of
Big Barb's chances every year to show off her movie-star
daughter. Big Barb also insisted on driving Barb around
their own neighborhood and other sections of town
where rich people nobody knew had built "embarrassing" houses.

Big Barb was simply amazed at how hideous all those
houses were—and the owners didn't realize it at all.
Houses with eight rooflines, she said, if you could believe it, some of them combining a severe suggestion of
Santa Fe with a strong hint of Palm Beach—in Fort
Worth, Texas, mind you—and all of them covered with
those ungodly imitation leaded windows.

"My word," she said, "it astounds me today how
money keeps falling into the hands of the wrong people."

When Barbara Jane was a teenager she used to be

infuriated by her mother's snobbishness, but she eventually realized Big Barb hadn't acquired it on purpose, gone out looking for it, and it wasn't really meant to be harmful, it was just . . . there. Built in. Something as much a part of Big Barb as her inherent good taste, as her generosity—and Big Barb was a truly generous person. She was quite well-known and respected around town for her fast-draw-on-the-checkbook support of the arts and her lavish gift-giving to the needy. So her mother's natural, unthinking snobbishness became a humorous thing to Barb, not to mention a source of material.

My wife picked up a line on this trip. While she and her mother were going to parties and running errands, they stopped in Jimmy Jack's Minute Mart on Camp Bowie to buy a few things for the house, but found themselves stuck in the checkout line. The Texas lottery was up to $44 million, and they were behind people buying heaps of lottery tickets.

Standing there, Big Barb remarked to Barb that it would be foolish not to buy a ticket. That in itself tickled Barb. Her mother needed money like . . . like what? Like Arizona needed cactus, like Florida needed alligators?

Barb said, "Right, Mom. Buy one ticket, go home and root for your thirty-two-billion-to-one shot."

It was then that Big Barb said, "I wonder, dear, do real people ever win, or is it always somebody from a trailer camp?"

Big Ed's good friend, Wildcat Burleson, was our fourth on the first day of golf, Tommy Earl on the second. Both days we played by Big Ed's rules. Hit till you're happy on number one, roll it over everywhere, especially in the rough and bunkers, one mulligan every three holes if you want it, one free throw per nine—pick it up and throw it from anywhere, no charge—and one ladies' tee per nine, meaning move up and tee off from up there.

"No point in playing golf if you can't enjoy yourself," Big Ed said. "I learned that the hard way. I played by USGA rules for forty years. All it did was make me lose sleep."

The fourteen-club limit didn't pertain to Big Ed either. I counted twenty-two clubs in his bag, including five drivers and four putters. He carried extra clubs so he could break the shaft on as many as he wished when they betrayed him and still have enough left to finish the round.

He never looked for a lost ball, which didn't count against your score anyhow. Another rule. "If a ball will hide from you once," he said, "it'll hide from you again. Let the son of a bitch rot in hell."

It was a wondrous thing, what Big Ed's rules could do for your score. It seldom required much skill to turn an 88 into 77.

Wildcat Burleson was around seventy years of age, a heavy-set fellow who wore a plantation hat and wall-to-wall cashmere and had a choppy golf swing. He didn't take the club back too far, and his follow-through was somewhat restricted. Both those moves were caused by the fact that he couldn't get the club around his nonbiodegradable stomach. But he designated himself as the humorist in our foursome.

After one of Big Ed's best drives: "Damn, Ed, I don't take *vacations* that long."

After Shake left a twenty-foot putt about ten feet short: "Does your husband play golf too?"

After I skied a three-wood off the tee: "Lordy, that's gonna come down with ice on it."

Shake rode in the cart with me and halfway through the round, he sighed. "Wildcat at the Improv."

The way Tommy Earl acted around Big Ed the next day was sickening.

Tommy Earl: "Great drive, Ed!" "Man, you killed that seven-iron!" "What a putt, right in throat!" "Oh, no, Ed, what a lousy break, you hit it perfect!" "Good shot, Ed, that's right on it!" "Here, let me get that out of the cup for you, Ed!"

On about the seventh hole, I strolled over to Tommy Earl on the green and said, "You're not even ashamed of yourself, are you?"

"Big Ed's my banker. Bankers like to have their ass kissed."

"You don't think you're overdoing it?"

"You can't overdo it, Claude. One of these days you're gonna learn something about business . . . 'oh, *great* putt, Ed!' "

We had drinks in the men's tavern after that round. Only a couple of young members were around. They were daytime drunk, slumped in chairs, snoozing. This was good. Nobody to come over and pat me on the back and say he was proud I'd finally made something of myself, or come over and ask what I was up to these days.

Shake glanced at them and said, "They're wishing they were as rich as their wives—so they could dump 'em."

When the talk got around to Gully Creek, Big Ed seemed more concerned about the golf course at Tumbleweed Pointe than he was about the stadium construction. He said to Tommy Earl that he thought the thirteenth ought to be a par-five instead of a par-four.

Tommy Earl agreed with him wholeheartedly, and said he'd get on it right away. Move the tee back, put the green closer to the quarry.

I didn't tell Big Ed everything that was going on in Gully Creek. He didn't want to hear it, he just wanted it taken care of. The team and the stadium were important to Big Ed, but they were only a small part of his commerce, which involved oil and gas production, and oil and gas exploration, banks and investment companies and real estate and only Big Ed could tell you what else. It was all a great big pile of bidness to me. He could have owned Malaysia, for all I knew, and he probably did own Saskatchewan.

"You ever made any business mistakes, Ed?" Tommy Earl asked.

"Oh, hell, yes," Big Ed said. "I didn't believe in television in the early days. I wish I'd gone into the airline bidness forty years ago—and gotten *out* of it ten years ago. I was too stubborn to get in the computer bidness."

"You haven't done too bad," Tommy Earl said.

"I've been very fortunate. I sure have. But if you want to ask me what I'm proudest of, aside from my wife and daughter, I'll tell you two things. One, that I had the opportunity—and privilege—to fight for my country in a war. And two, that I've been able to provide thousands of good jobs for people in this greatest country in the history of the world."

One of the holiday events for some of us was to spend an afternoon and evening in Big Ed's spacious, cushiony, leathery den watching pro football on his big digital screen.

This was the last weekend of the regular NFL season. I had to admit I hadn't been keeping up with the competition as closely as I should have, but then I didn't need to keep up with it all that closely to know that more than half of the thirty teams in the league could still make the play-offs, thanks to that disgusting thing called parity.

The regular NFL season was a long one, sixteen games, and I believed the only people who followed it closely until the play-offs were season ticket holders, owners, players, and gamblers. TV announcers were supposed to act like they did, of course.

Once again, thanks to parity, there was much at stake in this sixteenth week of the season.

The situation in the NFC East was typical of all the divisions. Dallas could secure the home-field advantage with a win over Washington, but Washington could earn a play-off berth with a win—if it was coupled with a loss by Philadelphia, a loss or tie by Carolina, or a loss or tie by Detroit. Or Philadelphia could earn a play-off berth if Washington lost, Carolina won, and Detroit tied. Or Tampa Bay could earn a play-off berth if Washington, Philadelphia, Carolina, and Detroit all lost while the Bucs defeated or tied Chicago.

Big Ed and Shake and I sprawled in Big Ed's den with snacks, beverages, and ashtrays, and watched the game between the Cowboys and Redskins, or, to put it another way, we tried to watch a football game while the zebras committed crimes and got away with it.

The referee in the Dallas-Washington game was Ernie ("The Spot") Kennerdine. He was said to grade higher every season than any other zebe, and for that reason he was usually the referee in the Super Bowl, but to most coaches and players he was known as John Dillinger. When he worked with an umpire named Bernie Gill, they were known as Bonnie and Clyde. And when Ernie worked with his whole regular crew, they were known as the St. Valentine's Day Massacre.

The thing about Ernie ("The Spot") Kennerdine, he was at least consistent. Almost any call he made would be in direct contrast to what you thought you saw on the replay.

Ernie loved to be on camera, loved his microphone, loved flags. He'd developed a distinctive way of signaling infractions. He'd move his arms in the fashion of a symphony conductor, and he'd say more words than were needed, drag it out, when he'd explain the call on TV.

Like this: "I have pass interference on number thirty-four, who has *not* heeded our warnings. I have an automatic first down for the offense, and we . . . are going . . . *that way!*"

I had an idea that one of the reasons I hadn't been all that popular with the network as an announcer was because of something I'd said on the air about Ernie ("The Spot") Kennerdine. I'd said it wouldn't surprise me some Sunday to hear Ernie say, "Offsides, defense. Five yards. Repeat second down. And here's a little something I wrote myself. That old black magic . . ." But I stopped there. It had been Larry Hoage who sang us into commercial with "Those icy fingers . . ."

All through the Dallas-Washington game the three of us kept talking to the TV screen as Ernie's flags kept Dallas from burying the Redskins.

I was saying things like "Way to go, Ernie. That was holding if I ever saw it. What are the Redskins giving you for Christmas?"

After a highly debatable roughing-the-passer call, Big Ed said, "It's a good thing I'm not the Dallas coach. I'd be out on the field with my hands around that bastard's throat."

I said, "All I wish for Ernie Kennerdine is a dramatic public nervous breakdown."

"This is funny shit," Shake said. "I didn't know what I'd been missing. This revives my interest in pro football."

Ernie and his crew became total criminals in the last minute of the Dallas-Washington game.

The Cowboys were ahead by three and were on the Washington four-yard line, third down and two inches for a first, poised to put it out of reach. A Cowboy runner went off-tackle and gained two yards, but Ernie spotted the ball short of a first down.

This reminded us of how he'd gained his nickname—"The Spot." Dallas had to settle for a field goal, and although the kick looked good both live and on the replay, it was ruled wide. Redskins ball on their own twenty-yard line, forty-eight seconds to go.

Washington had no time-outs left, so the odds weren't too good the Redskins could drive far enough to kick a tying field goal, much less score a touchdown. But that didn't take into consideration the two roughing-the-passer calls and the two pass-interference calls against Dallas. Suddenly, the Redskins were on the Dallas fourteen, eight seconds left.

Figuring they had time for two plays—if a pass into the end zone didn't work, they'd take the field goal—they first went for the win. The replay showed the receiver not only never had possession of the ball, he didn't have both feet in bounds. But the back judge—good friend of Ernie's—called it a touchdown. The Redskins kicked the extra point and won by four, 28–24, and only a cynic would bother to bring up the fact that Dallas had been a three-and-a-half-point favorite.

Since the game was played in Dallas, I thought it was a minor miracle that Ernie and the crew were able to get out of the stadium alive, even under a heavy police escort.

One of these days, I remarked to Big Ed and Shake, it wouldn't surprise me if a zebra got assassinated, picked off by a fan who'd smuggled a gun into the stadium. And a good defense lawyer, I said, wouldn't have a bit of trouble getting the assassin off.

Plead self-defense, that was all. Zebras were ruining the man's life, destroying his health, wrecking his marriage, driving him crazy. Any jury in America would buy that.

51

The Bookmans always held what Barbara Jane called "the dreaded open house" on Christmas afternoon and evening, after the family feast. Friends, neighbors, bidness associates, they were all accustomed to dropping by and having cocktails, in case they weren't drunk yet, and eating a lot, in case they hadn't eaten yet, and glazing you over by talking about things that were of no interest to anyone whatsoever. Maybe Big Barb.

A lavish help-yourself buffet of turkey, ham, roast beef, and all the trimmings, was set up in the dining room. Pour-your-own bars were set up in the living room and den, every beverage on hand except eggnog.

Big Ed's position on eggnog was that people hadn't drunk eggnog since 1947, and he'd never understood why anybody ever drank it in the first place, seeing as how it tasted like something you took only if you were severely constipated.

Maydee and Garnett Richardson were responsible for the Christmas dinner and the dreaded open-house preparations and just about everything else that went on around the place.

They were the black couple that lived in the eight-room cottage out back in the middle of the gardens. Garnett and Maydee had been with the Bookmans for thirty-seven years, and while all of us thought of them as personal friends, even part of the family, they still acted like all they wanted to do was please you.

Garnett was the most cheerful person I'd ever known. He wore a constant grin, he could fix anything that needed fixing, and if he was anywhere close by, he didn't want you to lift anything heavier than a fork or a drinking glass.

Maydee sang in her church choir, could pop her chewing gum loud as a gunshot, was one of the great cooks, and may have been the last woman in the United States who ironed.

Their cottage was complete with fireplace, central air, satellite dish, and every so often it would be exquisitely refurnished and redecorated by Big Barb. Their home would have been the envy of any middle-class couple in the country, as would their dueling Toyotas, their salary, their insurance, their medical plan.

Their son, Ben, was ten years younger than us, someone we'd only known as the little kid we used to chase, hide from, toss around in the air, and terrify with ghost stories. It was after we'd gone off to try to conquer New York that Ben grew up to be a model youngster, a guy who earned an appointment to Annapolis—and without any help from Big Ed that we knew of. Captain Ben Richardson was now the skipper of a guided-missile cruiser, the USS *Shiloh*, the kind of warship that could sit out in the ocean and fire a rocket that would mess up a whole pile of A-rab Muslim Arafats. Maydee and Garnett were extremely proud of their son, but no more than Big Ed was.

Big Ed liked to say that Maydee and Garnett and Ben made you think there was still some hope for America.

Maydee and Garnett had put up the tall tree and decorated it in the living room near the live-in fireplace, and they joined us to open packages before they served us the feast at the large round mahogany table in the dining room.

I successfully defended my title as the worst gift wrapper in the English-speaking world. The way to identify a gift of mine for someone was to look for the present with no ribbons around it but plenty of Scotch tape, a package that looked like mice might have been nibbling on the corners.

I didn't give anyone a single present that didn't have a West Texas Tornadoes logo on it, including my wife's oversize T-shirt nightie and Human Dog's squeaky funnel, one of the pet items Kelly Sue had thought to stock in our boutiques. In exchange, I mostly received things that were associated with socks, pajamas, and cartons of Marlboros, although Barb found something I'd treasure as a desk ornament—an old New York Giants helmet like the one I'd worn when I was a great American.

The door chimes started sounding around four in the afternoon.

Garnett was right on it. In his black trousers, white shirt, black bow tie, and big grin, he welcomed the guests. The first three waves were all rich friends of Big Ed and Big Barb.

This sent Shake Tiller scurrying to his room to hide and watch two movies at once, nimble on the clicker. Men were from two channels at once, women were from Oprah.

Barb and I moved around the house separately, helping out as hosts, me dealing as best I could with the inane talk. "Isn't that a new Oriental rug?" I'll have to ask. "Aren't Maydee and Garnett wonderful?" They still are. "Don't you love that Chinese tapestry?" More than my own life.

I was even lucky enough to get in on the end of Wildcat Burleson's hilarious joke about the blind golfers: ". . . and then the rabbi said, why can't they play at night?"

Big Ed and Big Barb both tipped me off to be on the lookout for the Middletons, Sonya and Taylor.

I was told to notice how much the couple had changed in a year. I didn't see how they could have changed too much. They'd still be in their sixties, still be rich and thin, still be violently opposed to smiling.

Big Ed now called them "the silly couple." The reason, Big Barb explained, was that Sonya and Taylor had decided to become liberal Democrats, believing it would make them more unique in Fort Worth social circles. Big Barb said to prove how liberal they were, Sonya and Taylor now included dozens of "tiny little brown and yellow people" among the guests when they entertained at home.

I couldn't very well have missed Sonya and Taylor. They floated into the party looking like Russian ice dancers, him in a tight black jumpsuit and a Lenin cap, her in a flowing chiffon thing and a pained expression.

In my brief moment with them I learned they were building a new, modern home and were designing it themselves. Every wall would be concrete and this immensely talented Mexican artist they'd discovered would re-create all of the most interesting multicultural graffiti they'd admired and photographed on the underpasses and along the tolls road around Detroit, Philadelphia, Cleveland, and New York.

"I don't see any Negroes among the guests," Sonya said, looking around with disapproval.

Taylor said, "Hmmm, no. Nor any Latinos. Perhaps we should leave, darling, if it's making you uncomfortable."

"A drink first?" I offered.

"Perhaps one," Sonya said.

Relief eventually began to arrive in the form of the friends I'd invited. T.J. and Donna Lou came in, as did Tommy Earl and Tracy. I'd also invited Kelly Sue, who was spending Christmas in Dallas with her daughter, Susan.

Although I'd cleared Kelly Sue's invitation with Barbara Jane, I still thought it was a risky thing to do. Barb and I hadn't discussed the congenial phone conversation she'd had with Kelly Sue.

But I figured there couldn't possibly be a better time and place for the two of them to finally meet in person.

Lot of people around, holiday spirit in the air. It probably wouldn't result in too much broken furniture.

52

The minute T.J. came in he got on the outside of a turkey leg while Donna Lou drifted into the crowd to look for a conversation about the Middle East, being into issues and answers now instead of cakes and cookies.

"Sumbitch Ernie Kennerdine," T.J. said, spending a moment to talk about the "stickup" he'd seen, the Dallas-Washington game. "I've never known a zebra to have a more dire effect on my sphincter, and I was only watching on TV."

"He'll never let you down," I said.

"Flag-happy old sap. I'm not looking forward to having him work any of our games."

"We'll just have to beat everybody so bad Ernie can't make a difference," I said.

T.J. and his Frogs were leaving tomorrow for the Stanford game. They'd have three days of workouts in Houston before the Regal Crystaline Finish Auto Painting & Collision Repair Celebration Bowl. He invited me to stand on the sideline with him, "look like one of them phony celebrities who suck up to their alma mater when they're winning."

I said as much as I'd like to be there in person for the

clash of the titans, I only went to bowl games that were named after fruit, flowers, and plants, but my heart would be with the Purple.

I asked if he had any idea who the school might hire as his successor. He said he'd recommended his defensive coordinator, Bobby Stokes, but Bobby wouldn't get the job. The idiot athletic director would pick the man. Act like he was conducting some kind of national search.

"Well, as they say, Rabbit's always had delusions of adequacy. But if he doesn't come up with somebody decent, I'm sure Big Ed will get involved . . . and money-whip a good man out of the Pac-Ten or the Southeastern Conference."

"I'm leaving a good program behind. Man can keep winning here."

"You're not leaving Budget and Avis behind."

"Fuck no. Black Jesus is goin' with *me*."

"Which one's Black Jesus?"

"Budget. He's a lttle bigger, little faster, little more dedicated. We got to have him with the Tornadoes— whatever it takes, Billy Clyde."

"What do you call Avis?"

"Black Moses."

"You want Black Moses, too, don't you?"

"Not as much as I did. He's become about half-difficult. Between you and me, he's taken too much of a liking to whiskey and women."

"That doesn't make him any different than how we were."

"He can't handle it, though."

T.J. pulled me into a quiet corner and said they'd managed to keep it out of the papers a month ago, but this coed had accused Avis of dragging her down a flight of stairs in her dorm and attempting to rape her. Chancellor Glenn Dollarhyde handled the situation. He offered the girl a full academic scholarship and guaranteed her a 3.5 grade average if she'd "rethink" the incident. She rethought it and came to the conclusion that Avis had gotten his hand caught in her hair and it was *him* who'd been dragged down the stairs, after which they'd been rolling around on the lawn, acting out a scene from drama class, and Avis's dick had accidentally fallen inside of her for a couple of moments, but no harm done.

I said, "I don't believe there's ever been a chancellor who likes football as much as Glenn Dollarhyde."

That wasn't all, T.J. said. It had been kept out of the papers again, but Avis had been arrested for drunk driving last week. He was stopped at 3:00 A.M. with another girl in the Porsche with him. Avis called T.J. and T.J. called the junk-yard dog, Sidney Marvin Rosenberg, to get Avis out of jail.

The lawyer showed up promptly and took charge of things. After discussing it with all parties involved, Sid Rosenberg concluded that the girl had actually been driving the car, regardless of what the arresting officer thought he saw, which was the car weaving all over the street, only one head behind the wheel.

And if it came to trial, Sid Rosenberg's defense would be that Avis couldn't possibly have been driving the car—he was eating pussy at the time. Avis would have been too busy to be driving. But the lawyer was certain the case would never even come to trial, telling T.J. that the DA wouldn't dare enter a courtroom if he knew he had to go up against "the savage Jew."

It all reminded me of something I'd always known—that it took more than good athletes to build a successful football program.

When T.J. asked Avis what the fuck had gotten into him, all he'd said was "Coach, I'm sorry, but that vodka and snatch just keeps callin' to me."

* * *

Tommy Earl was a proud-looking gentleman when he waltzed in with Tracy, her hair in a new cut—the Meg—and clad in a terrifying low-cut red dress, the skirt at mid-thigh, her body trying to explode out of it.

We didn't see the dress until she slipped out of the full-length sable coat Tommy Earl had bought her, having made bells on bobtails ring.

Getting her first glimpse of Tracy from across the room, Barbara Jane whispered to me, "Too tight and too cheap."

We walked over to greet them and Tommy Earl said to Barb, "Come here, girl. I don't get many chances to hug a movie star."

As they hugged, Barb said, "It looks to me like you brought one with you, T.E."

"Don't touch her, you might burn your hand," Tommy Earl said.

Tracy elbowed him, then turned to Barb. "Hi, I'm Tracy Hopkins. I've never met anybody in the movies before. This is, like, a real honor."

Barb said, "Thanks, but it's not a very honorable business. Please make yourselves at home." And slid away, pretending she had a chore to do.

She may have seen Wildcat Burleson coming.

"Good God-a-mighty shit, darlin'," Wildcat said as he rushed up, staring at Tracy. "You remind me of my first three wives!"

Tommy Earl, always impressed with rich guys, stuck out his hand, saying, "Good to see you, Mr. Burleson. Did you know Ed Bookman and I are in business together. Yep, out in West Texas? I didn't know whether you knew that or not."

As Wildcat shook Tommy Earl's hand he kept gaping at Tracy.

"This is somethin' else right here. How much you want for it, son?"

Tracy indignantly said, "How much does he want for *it?* Did you just call me an *it?*"

Wildcat said, "Darlin', why don't you go get yourself a glass of Chablis . . . whatever women drink."

Back to Tommy Earl. "I'm serious, son. How much you want? Hell, let's cut to the chase. I'll give you two million for it right now, right here on the spot. Offer's good for five minutes."

Tracy said, "Christ. I've never seen a drunk before, have I?"

Wildcat said, "Darlin', this here's man talk. Go on over there and sit down, give them Brenda Gazangas a rest."

Tracy said, "Give my *what* a rest?"

"Them love jugs," Wildcat said, causing Tracy to glare at Tommy Earl and say, "Are you gonna stand here and let him talk about me like that?"

Tommy Earl said, "Aw, heck, he's only paying you a compliment." A glance at me. "Am I lyin' to anybody?"

I couldn't avoid grinning at Tommy Earl's diplomacy.

"Fine, I'll handle it," Tracy said, wheeling on Wildcat. "You think you're so rich you can say anything you feel like to people, but you know what? Your turds don't float no better than anybody else's!"

"You're a pistol, ain't you?" Wildcat Burleson grinned. "Darlin', you'll grow to love me when I dip you in so much jewelry, you'll look like moon over Miami."

Tommy Earl smiled at Wildcat. "I can't say I blame you for being taken with my lady, Mr. Burleson. She's something else. But the deal is, we're gonna be married."

"Gonna marry it, are you?" Wildcat said.

"I sure am."

"Shit," Wildcat said. "Guess I'll have to catch it on the rebound."

Tracy said, "Tommy Earl, I believe I've been entertained enough by Fat Santa Asshole here. I'm thirsty."

We watched her swivel-hip to the nearest bar.

53

In the upset of the day—maybe the year—Barbara Jane greeted Kelly Sue Woodley like the sister she'd never had.

We both saw her enter the foyer, looking snappy—pants, sweater, blazer—and went over to meet her, Barb smiling as she said, "Come in this house; you're too attractive to be anybody but Kelly Sue."

Barb clutched her tenderly by the arm. This while Kelly Sue and I traded hello smiles and nods.

Kelly Sue said, "Barbara Jane, I'm so happy to meet you at last, but I have a confession. I was starting to like Kelly Jean."

Barb laughed—genuine, no fake—and said, "Merry everything, all that holiday stuff. What would you like to drink?"

"A glass with any kind of wine in it would do," Kelly Sue said, as Human Dog bounded up to yap at her heels.

Kelly Sue picked up Hume and loved on him. "I know who this handsome guy is." Hume responded by trying to lick her nose off.

Kelly Sue came alone. She'd driven over from Dallas.

Her daughter had passed on coming with her, opting to go out on a date.

"Did you have any trouble finding us?" I asked.

"No, I just followed the money."

Barb smiled and took out a cigarette.

"Thank you, Lord," said Kelly Sue. "A smoking house." She put Human Dog down and took out her own cigarette. I lit Barb's Merit Ultra Light, then Kelly Sue's Merit Ultra Light, then my Marlboro.

A glass of white wine turned up in Kelly Sue's hand, courtesy of Garnett, as we stood in the living room, Kelly Sue looking around, waving at the people she knew across the way—T.J., Tommy Earl, Tracy.

I said in a low voice, "Barb has a name for the future Mrs. Bruner. Too Tight and Too Cheap."

"That wasn't nice of me," Barb said.

"No, it's perfect," Kelly Sue said, glancing around. "Isn't Shake Tiller here? I want to meet him."

"You will," I said. "He's hiding upstairs."

"Who's he hiding from?"

"He says you only have to do so many parties in one lifetime and he's already over the limit."

Barb said, "Want to see the rest of the hotel?"

"I'd love to."

First, Big Ed came over to us, saying, "Here's the young lady who does all of Billy Clyde's work." A little humor there.

Big Ed took her hand and patted it.

In all the trips Big Ed had made to Gully Creek to check on the progress of the golf course, or go over a few things with me, he hadn't been around Kelly Sue more than two or three times—she'd always been off doing other things on behalf of the Tornadoes.

She might have been in Amarillo replacing the woman who'd been hired to run our gift shop and ticket office because the woman couldn't remember to keep paper in the fax machine.

Or she might have been at the stadium site, yelling at Griff, the construction foreman, because his workers had cut the underground TV cable again, and every set in town had gone dark, and it better be fixed within the hour or he was dead meat.

Or she might have been over at the landscaper's hut asking him why he thought a practice field of artificial turf needed a sprinkler system.

Kelly Sue said to Big Ed, "Great. 'Young lady.' I'll take it."

Big Ed said, "That's what you look like to me. I won't ask your age."

"Please, *don't*," Barb said with a look for her daddy.

Kelly Sue grinned. "Thanks, Barbara Jane, but I'd lie anyhow."

"I just heard the other day you're from Alabama," Big Ed said.

"I am, yes, originally. I was born in Tuscaloosa—and I went to the University of Alabama."

"I knew Bear Bryant quite well. He was a great coach. He was a greater man. Were you in school when Bear was there?"

"I sure was. I remember the year we lost a football game. Everybody took to their bed."

Barb and I laughed. Big Ed smiled. Then he said, "Well, you're doing a damn fine job for us. What do you think of West Texas so far?"

Barbara Jane answered for her. "She thinks it's pretty far west and very much Texas. We're going to show her around now, Daddy. Go talk to rich people."

The tour of the house eventually led us to Shake's guest room.

We didn't bother to knock before entering, old pals like the three of us. We found him stretched out in an easy chair. He was wearing jeans and a corduroy shirt and bedroom slippers, and his feet were propped on an ottoman, and he was flipping around with the TV clicker.

I said, "Shake Tiller, man dedicated to his art, this right here is Kelly Sue Woodley."

Shake looked at Kelly Sue and struggled to his feet. I'd never seen him look at a woman the way he did at Kelly Sue.

He wasn't sizing up another shapely adorable, Foxette or Foxine, roommate savage, rack-loaded wool driver. This was a guy looking at an extremely attractive *mature* woman—something new for him. It was an instant intrigue deal.

And he was looking at Kelly Sue like that even before she said, "Oh, my, it's really you. Shake Tiller, you're my favorite author. I've adopted your book . . . and I have to tell you right off, the line I'm claiming for my very own is what you said about the sixties—even ugly people could get laid. I love that. It's mine now."

Still looking at her, Shake said, "Want to form the perfect race?"

Part Six

Your Basic Teammates

54

Having never much enjoyed being on a busy eighteen-lane freeway that was in a holy war with a busy twenty-four-lane freeway, it comforted me to know that when the end of the world came, it would take all of the striving, sprawling, bustling, burgeoning, vibrant southern cities with it.

A lot of those cities used to have charm and were manageable before progress hit them with a shitload of concrete.

The way we handled Houston, we cut it down to size. We never strayed too far from our hotel in River Oaks, except to go to the Astrodome.

I said *we*. It was all of us who'd had our minds changed, after all, about going to the Regal Crystaline Finish Auto Painting & Collision Repair Celebration Bowl.

Our minds had been changed by Big Ed and his private jet. He suggested, he offered, we went. All of us included Barb and I, Big Ed and Big Barb, and the loving couple, Shake and Kelly Sue.

Big Ed's people made all the arrangements concerning hotel rooms, game tickets, limos. We flew down the day before the game, stayed in one of those high-rise galleria hotels—the Medical Oaks, Barb called it—and only left the hotel long enough to go to the game, although Big Barb squeezed in a few hours at Neiman's.

Shake and Kelly Sue were registered in separate hotel rooms, but they were never in one of them, and the only time we saw them was at the game, where they talked constantly about one thing or another, even while TCU was making us proud.

The Frogs gave T.J. the going-away present of a 29–7 victory over Stanford in what quickly became a drab bowl game, Stanford being without any Attention Deficit Syndrome studs or any other kind of hired help to make it a contest.

T.J.'s lads jumped on Stanford early, Avis Fowler doing most of the damage. Launching his effort to win next season's "Hikesman Trophy," as he referred to it, he rushed for 206 yards from scrimmage and even returned a punt sixty-eight yards for a touchdown. Budget was content to let Avis hog the glory. Budget reeled off some nice gains, but mainly let himself be chased out of bounds when he carried the ball, obviously trying to avoid injury, protect his NFL future.

I was semi-sentimental enough to want to go to the dressing room and congratulate T.J. on the win, on a good final season, on the excellent job he'd done for TCU football, bringing us up to the level of other winning major college programs in the country, and if that meant nobody had outcheated us, so what?

I asked Shake if he wanted to go with me, but I wasn't sure if he heard me—he and Kelly Sue were still busy talking. They'd talked through three TCU touchdowns.

Off and on, I'd overheard such words as *bile, loathsome, plague, contemptible,* and such phrases as "breed them with wart hogs," "spread them on the floor of a bird cage," "they're two steps below highway litter."

Without asking, I'd gathered their conversation had something to do with film critics.

I'd commented to Barbara Jane that this was the first time Shake had been with a good-looking woman he could converse with since . . . well, since the old days with her, Barb.

I stood in a corner of the dressing room with Chancellor Dollarhyde, Rabbit Tyrance, and Weffert Lorants and listened to T.J.'s farewell address to his scholar-athletes. T.J. embraced the game ball they'd given him and spoke from the heart.

He said, "The thing I'll miss most is working with you kids. I've always liked to think of myself as a teacher more than a coach. A big slice of my heart will always be with the Purple.

"There comes a time when a man needs a new challenge in his life, and that's what I'm doing. I don't know if I'm up to the challenge, but I'll give it my best, just like you will here with your new head coach. They're gonna get you the best man available."

Rabbit quietly said, "You better believe it. I'll know who to hire. I've known 'em all—Bear, Darrell, Frank, Joe, Bobby, Steve."

Weffert said, "Om spar."

I'm inspired.

"Amen," said Chancellor Dollarhyde, a little wobbly.

I turned back to T.J. He was now saying:

"Self-discipline is your greatest asset. As you've heard me say before, don't be bitter about a disappointment—the world ain't listening anyhow. When the going gets tough, always remember how the little pissant David was a forty-point dog when he went up against Goliath. Luck don't pick sides. The man who complains loudest about the way the ball bounces is usually the sumbitch who dropped it.

"Let me remind you who your winner is. Your winner

is the man who, when he starts thinking he don't have the best of everything in life, he decides to make the best of everything he *has*.

"Now, I expect you people to work hard . . . keep on winnin'. You got the talent, you got the character. But if you *don't* work hard, you're gonna find out all the fame and glory and attention you've attained, it'll goddamn run off quicker than a spotted-ass ape. Good luck to you."

There were shouts and applause. Weffert Lorants, I think, may have shed a tear.

55

We celebrated New Year's Eve at Them Two Women. Gala.

The morning after the game, Big Ed's jet flung us back to Fort Worth in less time than it took to read *USA Today*. That's where we retrieved our Cadillac-Buicks. Mine and Kelly Sue's. Then we did the motorcade to Gully Creek, Shake riding with Kelly Sue to discuss the murky shiftiness of meaning, Human Dog riding with me and Barb.

We made the three hundred miles in about six hours, stopping for chicken and dumplings at a Cracker Barrel, and twice for Hume to wet down the mesquite. We got there in the late afternoon.

Shake and Kelly Sue peeled off at Lubbock and went to the Tally Me Banana apartments. We pledged on our cell phones to meet around eight for cocktails and dinner.

Barb finally got a tour of Gully Creek. I showed her the stadium going up—guys working through the holidays, money-whipped by her daddy. She saw the golf course and quarry taking shape, all of the enchanting storefronts, and the white-frame Victorian house I'd bought at the good end of town by Horace and Craig's chic B and B.

Looking at the house from the outside, Barb said, "Gee, it looks like we can really do something with this for only—what—six hundred thousand?"

She was more impressed when she saw the inside. Big rooms, high ceilings, fireplaces, pegged floors like you could find in Connecticut farms, she said.

I said, "I thought, you know, we'd fix it up, and after the Tornadoes are in business, it'll be better to live here than in one of Tommy Earl's tract mansions at Tumbleweed Pointe."

"Live here *part-time*, you mean."

"Fall here, winter LA. Spring New York, summer . . . Hume's choice."

"You know what?" said Barb excitedly. "This is a perfect job for my mother. She'll love doing it. She'll find the architect, the builder, the decorator. She'll turn it into something quite wonderful."

"I'll get her a double-wide all her own. Would she stay in it?"

"Are you *sick?* She'll commandeer the G-5. Wing in, wing out."

Barb was amazed at my double-wide, how nice it was. "People could actually live in these."

"People do," I said.

"Beachfront," she laughed, standing out on the screened-in porch, looking down at the rocks and weeds in the creek.

"That's what I asked for."

"What's that yellow-looking powder around the house outside?"

"My life-support system. Sulfur. It keeps the *s*'s out."

"Oh, shit. Does it work, I hope?"

"So far. But I don't know when their next convention is."

"Why couldn't we have gotten the football team in Honolulu? There are no *s*'s in Hawaii, boy. The missionaries scored high marks with me on that deal."

"Hukilau." I grinned.

"You love Hawaii. Don't pretend you don't."

"Hey, bro, we catch fish, smoke him up plenty good, you betcha."

"You've loved it every time we've been there."

"Hali hocky tiki."

"What do we wear to this restaurant tonight?"

"Got anything that needs to go to the cleaners?"

Shake and I did Banana Republic, Barb and Kelly Sue did Gap.

We took a table by the wall in Them Two Women, under the Tornado poster. An artist's sketch of a nameless ball carrier, stiff-arming the air, face mask obscuring whether he was black, white, orange, damask—my idea. Why run the risk of pissing off some activist assholes before we'd even played a game? His lower body was a funnel, the funnel lifting him up out of the stadium, and the large block purple type above him was shouting, TORNADO FEVER—CATCH IT!

Kelly Sue framed the poster and hung it in the joint. She'd hung one in every establishment in town—and all over Lubbock and Amarillo and as many places in between that would let her in the door.

Dot and Freida had mopped the linoleum floor, put on clean aprons, and arranged for the balloons that bumped around on the ceiling.

We were the only people in there at first, aside from the two brooding, slow-moving high school girls who'd been hired as waitresses for the night.

"This here's Nita and that there's Jennelle," Freida said. "They don't live in no library, but they can get you whatever you want."

To Barbara Jane, Freida said, "I seen you on the TV. You look just like you do."

Barb said, "Thank you. *Rita* is still in reruns, I'm happy to say . . . here and there."

"Who's Rita?" Freida asked.

"Uh . . . my character."

"Oh. Well, I must have saw you lots of times. You sure are pretty for a growed-up a-dult."

We asked Nita and Jennelle for ice and water and soda setups for the bottles of Junior and Count Smirn that made the trip. The girls brought all of it, each of them holding a lighted cigarette in one hand as they plopped the stuff down, moved it around.

Nita took a drag, blew out the smoke in an amateurish way, and said, "Anything else? When y'all want to eat?"

"A little later," I said.

Shake said to the girls, "I guess you ladies would rather be almost anywhere else but in here tonight, huh?"

Jennelle said, "Wouldn't you?"

Shake said, "Well, here . . . maybe this will help cheer you up." And gave them each a $20 bill. "Happy New Year."

Nita and Jennelle were bug-eyed, staring at the money, neither one sure if it would be all right to take it. They looked at Freida, who was behind the counter. They held up the bills and Nita said, "He just gave us this, Freida. Is it okay if we . . . are we supposed to keep it?"

Freida said, "You girls might as well learn something they ain't gonna teach you at Gully Creek High School. If a man offers you money and don't want nothin' in return but his dinner, *take the fuckin' money*."

"Good advice," Barb said, smiling at the girls.

"Are we the only people coming in tonight?" I called over to Freida.

"They'll be along," Freida said. "Some are at church, some are still workin'. We're full up with reservations."

"Reservations?" I said. "I didn't make a reservation."

"I did," Kelly Sue said.

A loud oath suddenly came from the kitchen, Dot yelling, "Goddamn son-of-a-bitchin', motherfuckin' bag of cocksuckin' shit!"

"Burned her hand again," Freida explained to us, then hollered back at the kitchen, "Want to sing it a little louder, Dot?"

Nita and Jennelle giggled, over in a corner, smoking.

Dot came out and held her hand under cold water at the sink. Didn't look at anybody, didn't speak to anybody, went back to the kitchen.

We heard from Freida there was a set menu tonight. She said the entrée was a special Dot thought up, chicken-fried chateaubriand with cream gravy.

The idea of chicken-fried chateaubriand was entertaining enough to all of us, even if Freida hadn't called it "chateau briggan."

We were also informed that the "chateau briggan" with cream gravy would be served family style with a lettuce and tomato salad, hash browns, French fries, mashed potatoes and brown gravy, pinto beans, green beans, black-eyed peas, cream peas, turnip greens, fresh corn cut off the cob, cornbread, biscuits, and bread pudding for dessert.

"I may move here," Shake said. "Fuck Hollywood."

Kelly Sue got a laugh out of my wife when she said, "Barbara Jane, if we don't want to go to the trouble to eat all that, we can just buy a tub of lard and pour it over us."

The locals began coming in around nine, the men in

their best coats and neckties, carrying brown paper bags, the women in dresses and do-it-yourself permanent waves.

Kelly Sue and I smiled and nodded at the ones we knew as they walked past us to their own tables. They all stared at Barbara Jane and Shake Tiller. Two more strangers in their midst.

When Coogle Boone and Deana came in, I motioned them over and introduced them to Barb and Shake.

"Won't you join us?" Barb asked. "I'm sure we can make room." No, they'd sit at the counter like they always did, Coogle wheezed, putting out his menthol in our ashtray.

Freida raised her voice. "Deana, you've seen Billy Clyde's wife on TV. She's a movie star! Barber Jane Booker. She's in that show about them ladies who run the funny restaurant in New York City . . . they're all pretty and they don't never get dirty? You've seen it, I know you have."

Deana said, "If it comes on after nine o'clock at night I haven't never seen it, I can tell you that much. I'm the only person in Amurka who ever said 'Who's that?' when they ast me about Johnny Carson."

"I'd surely like to wish everybody a happy and prosperous new year," Coogle Boone wheezed.

Deana said, "If anybody thinks I'm gonna be awake at midnight, they got two more thinks comin'."

"You just gonna eat and go home?" Coogle asked his wife.

"If I don't get glaucoma and lose my way," Deana said.

While we ate ourselves into a stupor and drank ourselves sober, I talked about the life of an NFL general manager who didn't have a team yet, and Kelly Sue talked about the life of the general manager's assistant.

I said, "My day starts at six A.M. here at the counter, where I can get a decent breakfast before I go to the Rotary Club breakfast in Plainview. Then I go to the office in the double-wide at the stadium site. That's where a guy's waiting to see me—he wants to sell me an outdated exercise machine for the weight room."

Kelly Sue said, "This is after he's sent me over to the construction site to kill a painter and a Sheetrocker."

I said, "When I get rid of the exercise guy, Kelly Sue says I better go ask the construction foreman why his roofer's putting cheap asbestos shingles on the offices instead of wood shingles like the plans call for."

"They'd done half the roof of the weight room before we caught it." Kelly Sue said.

I said, "I do that, then I go back to the office to see another guy who's waiting for me—he wants to sell me purple game shoes. I tell him we're gonna wear white. He says white's out. I tell him I'm bringing white back—go sell colored game shoes to the Gully Creek Fightin' Roosters."

Shake asked, "What are their colors, the Roosters?"

"Red and rooster," I said.

He said, "I was gonna guess that."

Kelly Sue said, "Maybe this is the day he reminds me I have to go to Amarillo and make one more try at selling a luxury box to Lenore, this bitch who runs the bank. I've sold eight luxury boxes to other asshole bankers and six to asshole car dealers. I've even sold one to the owner of an Italian restaurant in Amarillo, which I'm sure is a dope front because nobody ever eats there, but one more luxury box down is how I see it."

I said, "Maybe this is the day she reminds me that I have to speak to the Lions Club in Hereford . . . or maybe it's the day she tells me I'd better get over to the stadium because none of the concession booths on the ground level have doors in the back. So how the fuck are the concession people supposed to get in there? Crawl over the counter? For that matter, how are the hot dogs and cold drinks supposed to get in there?"

"That really happened?" Barbara Jane said.

"Oh, yeah," said Kelly Sue. "It's all part of the Gully Creek Follies."

I said, "I get a minimum of six phone calls a day from free agents or their lawyers. I tell 'em I won't know what we'll need till after the expansion draft, but stay in touch, send videos. Then of course I've got uniform manufacturers hustling me—and none of them have come up with the shade of purple I want for our jerseys and helmets. It's either too light or too dark. I've told all of 'em what I want is somewhere between TCU and the Minnesota Vikings. . . . Anyhow, all things considered, I don't have a lot of time to worry about air pollution."

The next thing we knew, it was time to ring out the old and ring in the new. I was aware that Kelly Sue had slowly been doctoring Dot and Freida's jukebox. She'd said that if she was going to be dining in there often, she wanted to listen to something better than what was available.

Like she'd never understood the popularity of Garth Brooks. And she'd rather be deaf than have to endure that power-hitting lineup of current pop artists, all of them screeching words you couldn't really hear to songs that had different titles but the same melody. Well, so-called melody. Forgettable crap was what it all was.

Now, however, thanks to Kelly Sue's ingenuity, the jukebox was stocked with anthems. The best of Willie, Merle, Kris, and Patsy, plus some of Kelly Sue's other old favorites. Reba's version of "Only You," B.J.'s "Somebody Done Somebody Wrong Song," LeAnn's "Blue."

Such was our musical fare throughout the night. Barb and Shake each complimented Kelly Sue on her tuneful jukebox.

"I'm a melody person," Kelly Sue said. "If you can't hum a song, why is it a song? That's my question."

Shake said, "We'll be discussing that up at Harvard next month."

There was no rendition of "Auld Lang Syne" on the jukebox, so what happened when midnight rolled around, we settled for the old Merle anthem, "Today I Started Loving You Again."

Barb and I gave each other a long, heartfelt kiss while Shake and Kelly Sue indulged in a longer and juicier heartfelt kiss. Then I gave Kelly Sue a little smack on the lips and a squeeze, and Shake gave Barb the same thing.

For a while, we all laughed and talked about the New Year's Eves of our basic youth.

We tried to remember the names of clubs that no longer existed, recalled saying nicely to a bartender, "Gimme a bourbon and ginger or I'll kill you!" Did we really ever drink a rum Collins, a stinger, an old-fashioned?

"I give you Chianti," Kelly Sue said, and everybody roared.

"I give you Lancers," said Barb, and we roared again.

We remembered what happened when the clock struck midnight. You and your date suddenly turned into Burt Lancaster and Deborah Kerr in the sand, or Julie Christie and Omar Sharif in the snow, only you were standing on a dance floor, soon headed for the backseat of a car.

Shake and Kelly Sue wisely accepted our invitation to spend the night with us, stay in the guest bedroom of the double-wide, rather than try to drive back to Lubbock. I said there'd be too many morons on the road, all of them trying to become a holiday highway statistic, and it would take only one to ruin your entire evening.

When we got home Barb and I took Human Dog out on a leash to do his job and investigate grass and leaves. It was an unseasonably warm night, which was why we stayed inside the sulfur.

56

In the middle of January the T. J. Lamberts moved into what Tommy Earl called his "masonry dream house" at Tumbleweed Pointe. Tommy Earl had built the house on spec and was asking $515,000 for it, but he gave T.J. his "ministerial discount." Only $508,500.

The house was in a prime location, right above the quarry behind the fifteenth green. Concrete-block construction. Four bedrooms, four baths, entertainment center, swimming pool, tile flooring, granite countertops, Thermador appliances—the ultimate in "high-end living."

Concrete block was the only way to go in the region, Tommy Earl told the Lamberts. "Keep them reptiles out from underneath you."

T.J. bought a shotgun.

My coach arrived just in time to go to New Orleans with me for Super Bowl Week, but we didn't stay for the game. Nobody ever stayed for the game if they weren't obligated to stay for the game. All we missed was being there in person when Ernie ("The Spot") Kennerdine and his zebras led the Kansas City Chiefs to their 34–27 win over Dallas, a ten-point favorite.

Super Bowl Week was always one long party, especially when it was held in New Orleans. If you went early in the week, you needed medical attention by Thursday, the French Quarter taking its toll.

We went to two network cocktail parties and skillfully avoided most of the network people. We attended the commissioner's annual "State of the Game" press conference, which Jim Tom Pinch had long ago named "Deep Zebra," the press conference always turning into a defense of all the rotten calls during the season.

In the Q & A part of the commissioner's press conference, sportswriters would ask about the worst penalties during the season—each one an utter atrocity—and the commissioner would claim that the league's cameras, with different angles, had shown that every zebra call was an accurate one, and the sportswriters would roar laughing.

We ran into Dreamer Tatum. He was a sports agent now in the business of robbing people like me, a general manager. We had a New Orleans doughnut and coffee together at an open-air cafe on the river.

Dreamer said he was happy being a Republican now. He'd been the director of the Players Association for eight years, fighting for the rights of man. But when white linebackers started making $20 million over five years, he thought he'd better get in on it.

I said I hoped Dreamer would deal with me honorably if I tried to sign any of his clients in the future. Compete fairly, as we had on the field.

"I'm bringin' fairness back to the profession, Clyde. I won't be droppin' no fine print on you, baby."

T.J. asked Dreamer if he represented any free agents we might be interested in—any that didn't need immediate bone surgery or suffer from mysterious illnesses.

"I just signed two everybody's gonna want," Dreamer

said. "A wide receiver and a free safety. You can't afford 'em."

"Maybe we can try," I said. "Who's the receiver?"

"Todd Mitchell. Kid with the Rams. Big-time talent. Hands. Speed. Kind of a free spirit . . . good for the media."

T. J. said, "Free spirit says dopehead to me."

"No, no, no." Dreamer laughed. "He's a health nut. Vegetarian."

"That's worse," I joked.

Dreamer said, "Todd's a six-million-dollar player."

"Over three years," I said.

"Over *one* year," said Dreamer.

"His spirit's too free for me," I said. "Who's the safety?"

"The one and only Hepatitis Diggs."

"That troublemakin' shitass?" T.J. said. "He's a stud, but I wouldn't want him around. He'll poison your whole team."

Dreamer said, "That's a bullshit rumor the Cowboys started."

"I read it in the paper," T.J. said.

"That's what they wanted you to do."

"Well, I did it."

Dreamer said, "Listen to me. The Cowboys drafted him number two. He went to three pro bowls. Then he asked for more money and they fucked him around. That's why he laid out all last season. Contract dispute. That's why I've got him now. His other agent didn't know how to deal."

T.J. said, "What were his mama and daddy tryin' to spell when they wrote *Hepatitis* on his birth certificate?"

"*Harry*," said Dreamer—and busted up.

I said, "Dream Street, you're telling me he's okay? He's not all earrings, tattoos, and headlines?"

"He's a good person, Clyde. I wouldn't handle him

otherwise. I want to sell you this guy. He's quick, he's a hitter. Reminds me of me."

I looked at T.J. He shrugged.

"We'll talk some more," I said to Dreamer.

Socially speaking, we let Jim Tom get us drunk one night in the Quarter, going from joint to joint. We left him at 2:00 A.M. on Bourbon Street making a financial arrangement with two rack-loaded wool drivers who said they were a mother-daughter combo.

57

Iris McKinney, my captologist, arrived in February and got settled in her apartment next door to Kelly Sue in the Tally Me Banana complex, but after looking around at all the young marrieds and middle-aged divorcées who lived there she gave it a new name that stuck—the Velveeta Arms.

I soon discovered Iris was one of those people who didn't have a private life—she shared hers with everybody. If you had the time, she'd let you in on everything she'd ever done, and everything everyone in her family had ever done, including all the intimate details.

Having a cup of coffee in the office with Iris, or having an after-work drink with her, was to invite a description of her ex-husband's dick.

Iris couldn't run an errand without coming back to tell you about overhearing this woman in Crawford's drugstore who'd said, "I went to Amarillo last week and it did my ego so much good."

Or coming back to tell you about this woman ahead of her at the register in Francine's More Than Jeans who'd bought a pair of fisherman shoes and two cello-

phane bags of Romantic Hours stretch satin panties in
assorted colors, three for $7.66.

Every day seemed to have at least one laugh riot in it
for Iris—an enviable trait, if you stopped to think about
it.

The first thing I did with Iris was sit her down and ask
her to tell me what she thought she knew about the
salary cap.

"I know backs make more money than linemen," she
said. "That's why they get more pussy."

I said that was a start.

She asked if I could get my hands on some standard
NFL contracts she could study. I said I could probably
get some examples from an agent friend named Dreamer
Tatum. She asked if he fooled around. I said I'd appreciate it if she would get serious.

She said it didn't take a genius to know one thing
about the salary cap. The bonus was the key ingredient.
"Say you have to give a guy a ten-million-dollar bonus.
You spread it out over five years. Only two million a year
counts against your salary cap. It's a good deal for us,
capwise, and it's a good deal for the player, taxwise. I'm a
quick study. This is not a complicated thing, Billy
Clyde."

I said it would get more complicated when we had
forty-five players. One way or another, our annual payroll would have to stay under $55 million.

She said, "When you start dealing with the agents
and lawyers, I'll sharpen my pencil. There are all kinds
of games we can play with bonuses and benefits. How
about we cut a guy, then resign him and put most of his
new salary in a bonus? Neat, huh? And there's always the
good old reliable numbered account in Switzerland."

I smiled appreciatively.

She said, "My girlfriend Julie called me last night
from Fort Worth. She says she's curing her headaches

now with aromatherapy. She rubs peppermint and joy essential oils on her neck and forehead. She found out about aromatherapy from a truckdriver who was hauling fifty crates of Crown Royal to Tennessee. Julie says she only watches two things on TV now—ice skating and the shopping channel."

Iris howled at all that.

I had to confess I was glad to have Iris around to take up the laugh slack after Kelly Sue started taking so many days off and long weekends to visit Shake in LA.

It was after Kelly Sue's fourth trip to the Coast that I said something to her in the office one morning about her "relationship" with Shake. I said I hoped she realized it wasn't going anywhere.

She said, "Jesus, I'm perilously close to having a social life and I've got to take shit about it."

I said I just wanted her to keep in mind that Shake was a no-heat kind of guy. Understand that the first time she ever gave him any heat about anything, or asked him to do something he didn't want to do, or disagreed with him on a subject he felt strongly about, she'd be in the history books.

She thanked me for my concern and reminded me she was a grown-up.

I said I didn't mean to pry, but had she thought about what was going to happen after the fucking?

She said it was her impression the fucking wasn't going to stop any time soon.

I said when it became irregular.

She said irregular fucking was better than no fucking, wasn't it?

I said when the fucking stopped.

She said like altogether?

I said yeah, for her. Not for him. Six months from now he'd be fucking some shapely adorable who'd taken him hostage. He wouldn't be able to help himself—it was called Hollywood.

She said she knew I'd always been a romantic. My romanticism had a way of getting out of control, didn't it?

I said that was an answer?

She said what was my problem?

I said I had two problems. One, I obviously didn't want to lose a good assistant to the president for the wrong reason, and two, I didn't want her to suffer any heartbreak.

She said I wasn't in danger of losing my assistant to the president, and heartbreak was an old familiar fellow—she knew how to handle him. And she quoted from Reba, saying whose heartbreak was it anyway?

I said life wasn't a country song.

She said since when?

I said, well, in that case she wasn't grounded.

She laughed and said, "You know what, Billy Clyde? I don't care what happens . . . or *when* it happens. I'm having fun. I don't just go out there and jump in bed and stay till it's time to come home. We've had a great time. I've seen Hollywood, Beverly Hills, Bel Air, restaurants, movie stars. Fun stuff. Ask Barbara Jane—she's been with us a lot."

"I have."

"What does she say?"

"She says it's none of my business."

"I saw your house over the weekend."

"What house?"

"The house Barbara Jane's buying. She made an offer and I believe they've accepted it."

Phone call. Same day. Moments later. Barbara Jane and Billy Clyde. To put it in script-writing terms.

"What's this about a house?"

"I've been meaning to tell you. It was sitting there empty. I saw the sign in the yard. I called. The agent came. I saw it. I made an offer. The owners accepted. He lost his job at some bank here and they've already moved back to Michigan—they were anxious to get rid of it."

"Where is it?"

"In the flats. Your favorite neighborhood."

Barb was right about that. What was known as the Beverly Hills flats was that area between the Beverly Hills Hotel on Sunset Boulevard and the township of Beverly Hills, only a matter of blocks between them. On Beverly Drive and Rodeo Drive, the two main streets between the hotel and the town, were where many of the Monticellos had been built during the silent-film days. A bunch of Theda Baras had once lived in most of them.

"You bought a house in the Beverly Hills flats? What'd it cost, ten million dollars?"

"I stole it. Seven-fifty."

"Does it have a roof?"

"A year ago he was asking three million. Six months ago he was asking two million. He was desperate. I felt bad about paying him so little, but Shake said, 'He's a banker, what did he ever do for anybody? Fuck him.' That made me feel better. So we've made a good deal, Lucille. But it's small . . . really rundown. It needs a lot of work. It'll be months before we can live in it, but Shake says we can keep staying at his place. He kind of likes having Hume around."

I asked if the seven-fifty had come out of my bank account, her bank account, or our bank account. End Zone Productions bought it, she said. The company would think up some ways to use it and write it off.

I asked where it was, exactly, in the flats.

Well, that was why it was so cheap, she said. It was a block down from Sunset, and three blocks east of Beverly. Three or four. It was a corner lot on one of the cross streets nobody ever knew the name of, and . . . actually it had all happened so fast, she wasn't sure what street it was on.

Redford, Rockford, Brandon, Briggan—one of those.

I said I hoped it was Briggan. I'd love to live on Chateau Briggan.

58

Like everybody else, I was shocked when TCU hired John Smith as the new head football coach. All I could do was make the comment that for a total unknown, he at least had a flamboyant name.

The first word I got that somebody named John Smith was going to be hired came from W. F. ("Wet Fart") Lorants. He called three hours before the official announcement to ask for a job in our sports information department. He didn't know if we had an SID yet, but he'd take anything.

The second word I got came from Bobby Stokes, the defensive coordinator, who called two hours before the official announcement to ask for a job on our coaching staff.

The third word I got came from Paula Cox, "Payday Paula," who called one hour before the official announcement to ask for a job as a secretary or anything else we might have available.

I hired all three.

Weffert became our SID, and T.J. was delighted to get Bobby Stokes for his defensive genius and Paula for his "Haldeman" again.

Weffert said the idiot Rabbit Tyrance had found John Smith at Flick State, a Division II school in Flick, Kansas. The AD had hired him based on one brief conversation with the man. Rabbit reported to the chancellor that he'd known 'em all—Bear, Darrell, Bobby, Steve, Joe, Barry—and John Smith had what it took.

Dr. Glenn Dollarhyde had hiccuped his approval.

Bobby Stokes was particularly perturbed at not getting the job himself. He'd acted as the interim coach after T.J. left. He'd been in charge of recruiting and had brought in an impressive group on signing day, February 8, including the most-wanted offensive lineman in the state, Daydrion Hunt, who was six-seven, 322, out of Houston Jordan, and the most-wanted linebacker, Sheweeta Curry, out of San Antonio Jackson.

Paula Cox said, "I don't know how smart John Smith is, but he looks like a goober."

Weffert said, "Ooks tooby akky spars toomy asbin."
Looks to me like he aspires to be a has-been.

Tommy Earl was among the ex-lettermen and boosters and rabid alumni who attended Rabbit Tyrance's Meet the New Coach party at Mira Vista Country Club.

He said John Smith didn't look like a goober. He looked like a man who wanted to sell you an appliance but couldn't tell you how it worked, what it cost, or when it could be delivered.

Big Ed had tried to hire a "name" coach to replace T.J. Money-whip a proven winner out of the Big 10, Big 12, Pac-10, or Southeastern Conference. But they'd all turned it down for the same reason.

You didn't follow a successful coach, they said, and T.J. had been extremely successful. Even if you won, the credit would go to the guy who'd left you a solid program. You waited for one or two coaches to fail, fall on their asses, *then* you took the job.

I understood their logic. Great coaches rarely replaced great coaches—in college or the pros. It was another one of nature's laws.

When Big Ed couldn't hire a brand-name coach, and when he also heard from the faculty members on the board of trustees that this was a good opportunity to hire a man who'd be interested in improving the academic standards of the football program, he lost interest in the selection process.

In a private moment, Big Ed said, "It never ceases to amaze me, Billy Clyde. We pay professors to *teach* people things in this country, but they never seem to learn shit about real life themselves."

I said it was definitely an amazing thing.

Big Ed said, "It occurs to me that college might be the biggest joke ever played on parents."

Weffert Lorants was responsible for a new development inside the gates of Tumbleweed Pointe.

Weffert and Sick Norma, his wife, and their four small kids were eager to leave Fort Worth and move to West Texas—or anywhere. Stunted Oaks, their neighborhood in Fort Worth, had become a playground for the mindless, soulless, scum-sucking teenage terrorists. Drive-by shootings in Stunted Oaks outnumbered drive-bys in any other Fort Worth neighborhood by 20 percent. That was according to the most recent survey.

The teenage terrorists were one reason his wife, Sick Norma, was sick so much, and the other reason was because she'd just always seemed to come down with things.

Tommy Earl asked Weffert how much he could afford for a home. Weffert said if he could unload his house in Stunted Oaks to some fool who liked gunfire, he could probably buy something in the eighty-thousand range.

Weffert got it across to Tommy Earl that he sure did want to live in a gated community, but he didn't play golf, he didn't understand people who didn't talk about anything but golf, and he didn't see why you had to be a golf nut to live in a gated community.

"I acky bo. Veppers arter oo sumpin fur boars," Weffert said.

Tommy Earl understood that.

I like to bowl. Developers ought to do something for bowlers.

It was the beginning of what Tommy Earl called his two-bedroom "big-looking houses that ain't." Fake upstairs, eight-foot ceilings, kitchen opening onto "the great room," which opened onto the laundry room.

Weffert bought the first house in Bowling Forest.

It was on Bowlanes Drive, near Alley Bowl Court, a block off Strike Cove, two blocks from Split Lane, and around the corner from Spare Circle.

Bowling Forest sold out in no time, and Tommy Earl congratulated himself again on being a man of vision.

59

The little guys with beards and Rita Hayworth's hair were movie stars, I said. So were the women with their heads shaved. They were working in movies themselves at the moment, and Kelly Sue just had to forgive me for not knowing their names.

Kelly Sue did a good job of hiding her disappointment when no recognizable movie stars showed up for the world premiere of *Melancholy Baby*. Most of the invited guests on hand at the theater in Century City were family members and friends of people who'd worked on the film.

Cubby Butler, in a leisure suit, a Brutus haircut, and a six-inch-long earring, introduced Barbara Jane and Shake and spoke to the audience before the showing.

He said it was the most enjoyable experience he'd ever had on a film—lasting friendships had been made among the entire cast and crew—and he was proud that *Melancholy Baby* represented his swan song as head of Mitsutani Pictures.

He said he only hoped his new production company, which would have offices on Rodeo Drive, and was now hiring, could make a "dramady" as penetrating as this one.

Jim Tom Pinch, trustworthy scribe, and Deborah Monahan, Shake's crackerjack literary agent, had both wanted to attend the premiere, but circumstances beyond their control had kept them away.

Jim Tom sent a fax that said:

"In the glamorous, helter-skelter, whirlwind lives you folks lead, I'm sure you may not realize it's the middle of March. Which means I'm covering the NCAA hoops tournament. Good luck with your epic, but like most Americans right now, I'm preoccupied with tall black people."

Deborah Monahan explained in a phone call to Shake that she was sure he, of all people, would understand why she couldn't leave New York—couldn't even leave the phone. She was caught up in an "auction" involving another client, Niam Semaster, a nice man who deserved a break. He'd had all six "literary" novels rejected, so he'd turned to serial killers and four publishers wanted this one.

Shake shared the title of Niam Semaster's thin but exciting novel with us: *Count the Intestines*.

Audiences at world premieres were always kind, generous, receptive, and gracious, and the same could be said of the people who saw *Melancholy Baby* that night, although I thought they laughed in several of the wrong places.

Next day came the reviews.

One critic said of *Melancholy Baby* that it was a laudable effort but it fell short of being a fully satisfying film.

Another critic said the film was vaguely humorous but failed to address or even echo the serious issues facing women today.

And another critic said the occasional flares of originality, the cynical and satirical humor, and the thought-provoking theme hardly constituted a sufficient explanation for why the film had been made in the first place.

Shake loathed film critics, and all the reviews did was change Shake's idea of how they should die. He no longer wanted them to suffer long, painful, crippling, disfiguring diseases. He wanted them to sink to their knees and beg for mercy before he gleefully shoved them into the boiling lava.

But Shake knew critics didn't keep people out of the theaters. People went to see a movie because they liked who was in it, or they liked what it was supposed to be about, or somebody said kill yourself if you missed it.

I believed all that was true. I personally had a list of ten things that had kept me out of movie theaters for years. Not necessarily in order, they were:

1. COMIC STRIP CHARACTERS.
2. MIME.
3. KABUKI.
4. CZECHOSLOVAKIAN TRAINS.
5. ROCK MUSICALS.
6. INTERPLANETARY WARS.
7. FANTASY.
8. KIDS.
9. BLAME ME FOR SLAVERY.
10. DON KNOTTS.

60

While I was out in LA for the premiere, my wife and my dog gave me a tour of the house in the flats. Hume seemed to like his fenced-in backyard better than anything else. I liked the street name. It was close enough to Chateau Briggan that I could get away with calling it that.

Barb promised the house would be adorable when her mother got through with it.

I wondered if it wasn't too much for Big Barb. She now had the Beverly Hills house to do over and decorate, the Gully Creek house to do over and decorate, and the luxury box in our stadium to decorate.

Not in the least, Barb said. Big Barb was buzzing about, full of ideas—it was the happiest her mother had been since Big Ed brought in the Scurry County field.

One of the things I learned about End Zone Productions on that trip was that casting was about to begin for *Stud-Lovable*, a not-too-old script of Shake's that had been passed on by baby moguls at major studios.

Barb had talked Shake out of doing *Born, Married, Worked, Died*, or *Dead Beat*, as she called it. The audiences were never going to get it, she'd finally convinced him, and if they *did* get it, they'd all commit suicide. Besides, *Stud-Lovable* was more now-ish.

And I didn't need to concern myself for a moment that Barb had used that word seriously. She swore she didn't.

The way Shake described it, *Stud-Lovable* was the antidote for a football movie like *Brian's Song*—not that any professional athlete had ever sat through that old tearjerker without doubling over in laughter.

I was given a peek at the script so I would know how Shake was depicting the modern NFL hero. The opening was revealing.

FADE IN:
INT. SUPERMARKET—DAY

Three NFL stars sit at a table signing autographs for crippled children, senior citizens, and paraplegics. The players are CHUCK, WILEY, and CEPHUS. Their salaries are in the millions.

A sign says each player is charging $50 for an autograph. The line of autograph seekers is long. The athletes are testy.

A little kid in a wheelchair confronts Chuck.

Little Kid: Wow, Chuck Stewart. You're my favorite running back in the whole world.

Chuck: Cash. No checks, no credit cards.

Kid in wheelchair hands over the $50.

Little Kid: Can you put "To Bobby—hope to see you walking next time?"

Chuck gives the little kid a dirty look.

Chuck: I sign my name. You want a novel, go to a fucking bookstore.

I flipped over several pages to see if "Chuck" was going to remain a great American and a wonderful human being.

INT. HOTEL BAR—NIGHT

Chuck is having a drink. He is approached by MISTY, a killer blonde, who carries a manila envelope. Misty looks angry.

Misty: You think you can just make it with me and never call again? What do you have to say for yourself?

Chuck: I love you.

Misty: You smartass! I'm selling these to the *Globe* and *Enquirer*. We'll see what your wife thinks of them!

She slams a handful of photos on the bar. Chuck looks at them.

Chuck: (unconcerned) For one thing, she'll think it's trick photography. She's never seen me with a bone like this one.

                                                    CUT TO:

61

As much fun as I was having on the Coast, events dictated that I slide on back to Gully Creek and help T.J. prepare for the expansion draft and the regular college draft. It was April and the expansion draft was coming up in two weeks. We had a franchise, now we needed a team.

The thirty existing owners agreed to put ten players each on the block—a total of three hundred players to choose from—so that we four expansion teams could stock our rosters with as many as forty men.

Helping us stock our teams was a generous thing for the other owners to do. Without being able to obtain some veterans, all of us would have had to go into our first season with nothing but the few free agents we would sign, along with the rookies we'd get in the regular NFL draft. If that were the case, the Tornadoes, Knights, Bandits, and Volcanoes wouldn't be competitive at all—and TV executives would pout.

I came home to the list of players available in the expansion draft. It was provided by the league office along with their bios and résumés and present salaries.

T.J. and I studied the athletes on paper and film and

made lists of the players we wanted first, second, and third. There weren't that many immortals among them, but this was expected. The other owners weren't *that* generous.

Big Ed zoomed out one day for a discussion about which players we'd go after and how much we ought to spend. Big Ed didn't care how much we'd spend if we got value—and Iris could keep a sharp eye on the cap.

The three of us were at one end of a conference table in our new executive office building. It was next door to our stadium, which was still under construction, and adjacent to the practice fields—one natural grass, one artificial turf—and the weight room.

Weight room, by the way, was hardly a suitable name for something that could pass for a spa in an expensive resort. It featured every modern exercise contraption, whirlpools, saunas, rub-down tables, and a cafeteria.

The expansion draft would be conducted on a telephone hookup with Commissioner Val Emery in New York, Coach Elmer Slack of the Knights in London, Coach Bingo Huffman of the Bandits in Mexico City, and Coach Peanut Griffin of the Volcanoes in Honolulu.

T.J. wasn't overly impressed with his rival expansion coaches. He'd known all of them in the past as ordinary players and even more ordinary assistant coaches.

"They lighter than Kleenex" was how T.J. had assessed the abilities of Elmer Slack, Bingo Huffman, and Peanut Griffin.

But now in the conference room T.J. was saying he wanted Sheep Dog McWorter for his middle linebacker, and I was saying Sheep Dog McWorter was older than Pop Warner—he'd been with the Bears for twelve fucking years.

I said, "How can a guy play middle linebacker if he's on a walker?"

"He's a tough sumbitch," T.J. said, "And I need some

savvy at middle linebacker. I think we can get two more years out of him. He was All-America at Nebraska and he's been to five pro bowls."

"In his youth," I said. "I'll tell you the most interesting thing about him. Sheep Dog is his real name—how his folks christened him. His nickname is Psycho."

Big Ed asked where he was from, what he looked like.

I said he was from Red Ant, Nebraska, and he looked pretty much like a Sheep Dog. Then I said, "Okay, T.J., you want him, you can have him. Nobody else is gonna draft him. But I'm taking a rookie linebacker in a high round of the regular draft. Preferably a guy who doesn't already have a dozen steel plates in his legs."

T.J. said, "I'll get one season out of him."

"We're down to one season now?"

"You're gonna apologize to me, Billy Clyde, after Sheep Dog starts steppin' on dicks for us."

I said I wanted to go after Shea Luckett for our quarterback. T.J. said he wasn't sure about that—Shea Luckett looked like a clothes model. I said it didn't bother me that Shea Luckett was a handsome kid with a suntan and used to be a surfer.

"He's ready to run a team," I said. "He's been a backup at Green Bay for four years, but I think he could have started for half the teams in the league. He's mobile, he's smart, he has a hell of an arm."

Big Ed looked troubled. "How's he spell his name?"

"Shea Luckett?" I said. "*S-h-e-a.*"

"Thank God," Big Ed said. "I was gonna say if he's named after that Cuban guerrilla shitass, he's not playing on *my* goddamn football team."

"Che *Guevara?*" I laughed. "I haven't thought of him in a while."

Not in years. Not since half the guys I knew dressed like Che Guevara, only with more epaulets, and half the girls I knew dressed like Pocahontas.

T.J. said, "Shea Luckett's gonna be expensive, Ed, but I've got to have me an experienced milker. I can't go with a rookie."

I said, "He's not the only quarterback we're looking at, but he's the one I'd want to play for."

"Get him," Big Ed said.

I said, "Ed, while I'm on the subject of spending your money, Dreamer Tatum's shopping two free agents around. We've looked at their highlight videos. We'd like to have both of them. They won't be cheap either. Todd Mitchell is a wide receiver. He's leaving the Rams. I know you've heard of Hepatitis Diggs, the free safety."

Big Ed smiled. "I remember when the Cowboys got him. Four years ago, was it? Somebody said his name alone was worth seven interceptions."

"He's got a good nickname too," I said.

"What's that?" Big Ed asked.

"Blood Test."

62

Freida was relocating pork from Dot's kitchen to my plate, and I was saying all the rumors were making me sad. Rumors about all the places that were supposed to be headed for Gully Creek—K mart, Eckerd's, Blockbuster, Radio Shack, and Hardee's to the west, and Target, Ace Hardware, McDonald's, Home Depot, Circuit City, Winn Dixie, and Holiday Inn to the east. What had we wrought?

Freida said, "That's I-27 Eye Care goin' in down by the little church for Catholic people. The owner was in the other day. We can use that, is what I say. Most people around here don't know whether to shit or go blind."

"You don't mind the threat of all those Home Depots and K marts coming in here?" I said.

She said, "I been in them places in Amarillo. You can't find what you want, and if you do, you can't find nobody to sell it to you."

I said, "I just hate to see our quiet little village get ruined."

"I wish we had a roller rink again," Freida said. "We used to have one. I thought it was fun. You want some fresh coffee?"

Tommy Earl joined me for breakfast. He glanced at my plate, at the country eggs that looked like something on a painter's palette and my combination of pattie sausages and strips of crispy-chewy bacon.

"I want that exact same thing," he said to Freida.

"Biscuits and gravy?" she asked.

"Only as much as you can carry," he said.

He turned to me then. "Well, it's done. Me and Ody Bradshaw did it. We went to Downtown Split City."

I lifted my coffee mug in a toast.

He said, "I went to Fort Worth yesterday and told him I didn't need his ass for a partner—he hadn't done shit out here anyhow. I know how to do everything on my own now. Jack with a bureaucrat, get a house built, pave a road, landscape the deal. Ody didn't have shit to do with the golf course."

"You've done good," I said.

He said, "I've created everything in Tumbleweed Pointe, including my own mansion in The Pointe. Quarry Lane, Quarry Lane II, Quarry Knob, Sunset Terrace, Moonrise Ridge, Clubhouse Road Cove, The Coves, Bowling Forest. You know I've done it all."

"There goes the best man in your wedding—which is when?"

"June. Tracy wants to be a June bride."

"She thinks it's more legal, I guess."

"You're my best man now. Will you do it?"

"Of course."

"Hell, the only reason I asked Ody was because he was my business partner, but now he's not, so fuck him."

He explained how he and Ody divided up their commerce. It sounded to me like T.E. got the best of it.

Ody took He's Not Here, Tommy Earl took Tuxedo Junction.

Ody took the three Pasta Capones in Dallas, Tommy

Earl got Bust Out Jonah, the all-conference barbecue joint.

Ody took the Weatherford residential development, Tommy Earl kept Gang Resistant Systems, Inc.

Ody took the property where the Zanzibar Charismatic Evangelical Baptist Prayer Church & Late Night Supper Club was located, Tommy Earl got the warehouse where the Harley-Davidson Buttfucking Spookhunter Avengers were located.

Ody took the Gay Hindus Temple, Tommy Earl got the vacant lease space on both sides of it.

"I've released him as a friend, too," Tommy Earl said. "For good."

"Great," I said. "I'm buying breakfast."

"He's fucking Sheila."

"That's not possible," I said. "But even if it is, why do you care? She's your ex-wife."

"It's a matter of honor."

"If you think Sheila's fucking Ody just to hurt you, I can think of worse people she could fuck."

"Like who?"

"Like one of the Buttfucking Spookhunter Avengers."

"Naw, in her mind, Ody's worse. The reason I know they're fucking, people have seen 'em playing golf together at Mira Vista."

"Sheila plays golf now?"

"It's all part of the new her."

"Well, just because they've been seen playing golf together doesn't mean they're fucking."

"Yeah, it does."

"It does?"

"You've played enough golf to know why, Claude. Would you play golf with a woman if you weren't fucking her, or tryin' to?"

I said his logic, among other things, was devastating.

Then I asked if he knew whether Ody's wife had any suspicions about something going on between her husband and the former Mrs. Bruner?

"Suzy?" Tommy Earl shrugged. "No way to tell what she thinks about anything—she's a fucking Shih Tzu."

63

The day of the expansion draft our telephone hookup in my office made it seem like we were sending up Big Ed's P-38 squadron and several others to intercept flocks of Zeroes.

Everybody had at least four phone lines—me, T.J., Kelly Sue, Iris—and there was much jabbering, dialing, keeping people on hold.

Having worked it out ahead of time, Kelly Sue and Iris had arranged to make available by phone all of the players we might be tempted to draft, along with their agents or lawyers.

We'd naturally been in contact with some of the bigger names earlier in the month. The honeymoon period. No serious money talk yet.

A little panic set in on me just as we started. That was because Commissioner Val Emery informed us that we'd be drafting in alphabetical order, which meant that we'd be fourth in the first round, which also meant that Honolulu, London, and Mexico City would each have a shot at Shea Luckett before it was our turn.

You were given fifteen minutes to make each choice. Time enough to reach a player and his agent on the phone, see if they were still interested in your organization, get a sense of how difficult they'd be to deal with now.

I held my breath—and left nut—for forty-five minutes while the other three teams all selected players other than Shea Luckett. Mexico City even took a quarterback ahead of him, Robbie Buster, a left-handed passer who'd been throwing interceptions for the Jets for five years.

"I've got Shea Luckett on line two!" Kelly Sue hollered.

"Where'd you find him?" Iris asked.

"At home—in Half Moon Bay, California."

"At *home?*" Iris said. "Good thinking."

I pushed a button and picked up. "Shea, this is Billy Clyde Puckett, the GM of the Tornadoes. Coach Lambert and I want to make you our first-round choice. How would you like to be a starting quarterback in the NFL?"

I was gratified by Shea's quick response.

"Surf's up, dude," he said.

I allowed T.J. to waste our second-round choice on Sheep Dog McWorter, and listened in when T.J. spoke to him on the phone in Red Ant, Nebraska.

"Dog, how you doin'?" T.J. said.

Sheep Dog moaned, "Aw, I'm just sittin' here tryin' to find a part of me that don't hurt."

"I took you in the second round, Dog. I'm countin' on you to be my defensive leader."

"I don't know, T.J. I think I'm about done."

"You can get your ass undone—for one or two more years. We'll make it worth your while."

"Money does pep me up some. What's it like down there?"

"It's about like Red Ant, I expect. Wide open spaces. You'll like it."

"Y'all got a grocery store?"

"Why, hell, yes."

"Well, we don't."

T.J. and I argued briefly over the third-round pick. He wanted to take Dunlap Gross, the defensive end with the Cardinals, who had a bad knee, and I wanted to take Royce Harper, the offensive lineman with the Redskins, who had a werewolf for an agent.

Knee or werewolf? It was a toss-up, actually. But I pulled rank and we took Royce Harper. I knew he could start for us, and the werewolf, Slugger Iverson, wouldn't be the only killable agent I'd have to deal with.

When I spoke to Slugger on the phone, he said, "My guy does it for the Redskins five years, no injuries. My guy suits up, he plays. My guy holds, he double-teams, he pulls, he does it all. Nobody beats my guy off the ball. My guy goes for top coin. You offer, I listen, we talk, we fax."

I wanted to tell Slugger he'd earned the wrong nickname in life. It ought to be Present Tense.

We thought we came out of the expansion draft better off than the other clubs. Of the thirty guys we selected, T.J. figured we'd taken maybe six offensive starters and maybe seven defensive starters. It almost felt like we were assembling a football team.

It was the worst-kept secret in pro football. That we wanted to build our team around Budget Fowler, the TCU locomotive, ace of running backs. Code name: Franchise.

To do this, we needed to start by having the number-one choice in the college draft so we could obtain the rights to him. All four expansion teams wanted the first pick, naturally. Whether any of them wanted Budget Fowler, I didn't know, but one of them might have been smart enough to take him, given the chance, knowing we'd pay any grotesque amount for him.

So that situation had to be avoided in some way.

When Commissioner Val Emery put out the press release announcing that we would indeed have the number-one draft choice over the Volcanoes, Bandits, and Knights, you could have said I was euphoric, if you used such a word, but I was also inquisitive as to how it came about.

The only thing the commissioner stated publicly was that the selections had been decided in a fair, mathematical formula he'd personally devised, the intricacies of which were too complicated to explain.

I had a good laugh when I learned later on that Val Emery didn't devise the mathematical formula until after Big Ed loaned him his private jet to take his family on a vacation to Paris.

"I hear old Tokyo Russ thought about putting the fix in himself a week later," Big Ed said. "Well, that's how smart your Japs are. They come up short again. When I get to know Tokyo Russ better I'll have to ask him if any of his relatives were in the air over the Leyte Gulf in October of '44. They might have been some of the sons of bitches I shot down."

When Iris learned that Budget Fowler was going to be our property for sure, she suggested an idea to Big Ed that made him say, "By golly, you just earned your keep, little lady."

Iris suggested that Big Ed sign Budget to a "personal service" contract and put him on the payroll of Bookman Oil & Gas. That way, many of the millions we'd be paying him wouldn't count against our salary cap.

What a dame was all I could say about it.

"Told you so," said Kelly Sue, wallowing in the glory of having talked me into hiring Iris in the first place.

* * *

"Budget, Budget, Budget!"

That was the cry of the draftniks in Madison Square Garden as the commissioner walked to the microphone to announce our number-one choice.

Once upon a time the draft wasn't such a big thing. Coaches and scouts casually convened in New York, had some drinks, thumbed through the *Street & Smith College Football Annual*, and made their selections.

It was different now. The two-day NFL draft had become such a big deal it had been moved from a hotel ballroom to the Garden in order to accommodate all the team personnel and agents and lawyers and press and sporting-goods reps and families and players and draftniks.

Draftniks were hard-core football fans who studied every team's needs and the college talent pool every year and were certain they knew which player would be selected by each team in all twenty rounds.

They were frequently right, but when a team would make a surprise selection, the draftniks would hiss and boo and let the owner and coach and general manager know they'd made a ghastly blunder.

In another life, draftniks would be members of terrorist groups.

I'd invited Kelly Sue and Iris to go to New York with T.J. and me and Budget and his daddy—sort of a reward. But Kelly Sue said she'd rather use the time to go back out to LA, and Iris said she had a chance to get lucky with a good-looking gentleman who lived at the Velveeta Arms.

"How'd you meet him?" I asked Iris. "Sitting around the pool?"

She said, "I found him wrapped in swaddling clothes, lying in a manger."

"A married gentleman?" I said.

"Not on Thursdays."

While we posed for pictures with Budget in the Tornadoes jersey I'd brought along for the occasion, we could hear the draftniks telling the Volcanoes, Bandits, and Knights who to pick.

"Ervis, Ervis, Ervis!" they chanted just before the commissioner announced that the Hawaii Volcanoes selected Ervis Bree, the running back from North Carolina.

"Sidweed, Sidweed, Sidweed!" they hollered just before the commissioner announced that the Mexico City Bandits selected Sidweed Jones, the big fullback from Wisconsin.

"Larry, Larry, Larry!" they yelled just before the commissioner announced that the London Knights selected Larry Frazier, the strong-armed quarterback from Central Military Catholic.

We were surprised so many prime prospects were overlooked in the early rounds. T.J. chalked it up to idiocy on the part of our competition.

We took Pluribus Uram, the wide receiver from Minnesota, in the second round. All-Big 10, heart, hands, 6-1, 185, 4.4.

Pluribus attended the draft and was on hand to do photo ops with us. Pluribus showed up with dyed-green hair. It represented the color of money. Money was his hobby, he explained. "The kind of money I like best," he said, "it comes in paper and it's got that picture of Ben Franklin on it, you know?"

ReRun Moses was our third-round pick. Tough ball carrier from Ohio State—6-3, 234, 4.8. He could rest Budget Fowler, or tandem with him, or block for him.

T.J. was shocked when Fryer Pye was still available in the fourth round. All-America defensive back at UCLA. Hitter, smart—6-2, 200, 4.5.

As deep as the sixth round we got B. L. ("Big Load") Alfred, the All-America offensive tackle from the University of Texas—6-6, 325. "Hell, just squat and shake hands, is all he has to do," T.J. said.

There were others down the line we thought might pan out.

I liked LaDaminion Walls, the tight end from Louisiana Tech, even though his first name was tougher to pronounce than his hometown of Natchoosish, Mississippi.

We both liked Andre Humphrey, the All-America defensive tackle from Florida State, although T.J. was bothered that Andre was still available as late as the seventh round. He wondered if Andre might have a more serious police record in another state. In Florida, his rap sheet only listed shoplifting and credit card theft.

We celebrated by going upstate to Elaine's at Eighty-eighth and Second, a place I often referred to as Eileen's and T.J. often referred to as everything from Earlene's to Nadine's.

Back when we were great Americans and wonderful human beings with the Giants, we used to go up there with Shake. Sit around for hours, eat, drink, terrorize the serious book authors who hung out in the joint, ask Elaine which one of the four Jacqueline Bissets was the real one.

Elaine sat with us for half an hour. She asked about Barb and Shake and said Jim Tom had been in last week. Then she went off to another table to stroke some show-biz and literary celebs.

We put some whiskey and pasta down our necks and enjoyed the scenery. I wasn't sure whether I saw four Marlene Dietrichs or three, but I know I saw two Mark Twains.

It was a good draft.

64

Budget Fowler told Tommy Earl he wouldn't be needing fourteen bedrooms but he did want a ten-car garage.

Tommy Earl said whatever Budget wanted, he could have—Budget was going to be the most prominent resident of Tumbleweed Pointe. T.E., master builder, would just take that $1.8 million spec home he'd started behind the third green and expand it, include all of Budget's requirements.

"Ain't nothin' prominent about it," Budget protested. "I'll be livin' here full time, you know?"

Tommy Earl said he understood everything Budget wanted in a home. All the comforts and conveniences. But a design that would be faithful to the land around the house.

"Piss on the land," Budget said when the two met in my office. "I want a place that's faithful to *me.*"

"Exactly right," Tommy Earl said. "I was talking about the panoramas, bringing the outside in."

"That's dirt outside there, man," said Budget. "Don't be bringin' that shit inside my house."

The amount of money we paid Budget Fowler to carry a football could never have been made public. Rumors, you couldn't do anything about. But to verify that a number-one draft choice was being paid enough to buy his own B-one bomber would serve only to destroy the morale of his teammates.

It was a tiresome thing, but sportswriters loved to write about money today. Except for Jim Tom Pinch, every sportswriter I read in this Age of Greed seemed to be enamored of money matters—players' salaries mostly.

Any day I expected to pick up a paper and read something like: "Sam Gump, a $32.7 million quarterback with one year left on his three-year contract, tossed a screen pass to Bubba Zapp, the $24.3 million running back, who will soon become a free agent, and after getting a block from Tim Hulk, the $5.8 million tight end, who only recently invested in a Ford dealership with his lawyer-agent, Bitsy Fink, the runner gained thirty-seven yards down the west sideline in front of the luxury boxes that sold for $2 million each in our $280 million stadium that was built at taxpayers' expense."

Nobody was happier for us to have Budget Fowler on the Tornadoes than Tommy Earl. Budget would only add to the aura of Tumbleweed Pointe, be another lure, a super celeb inside the gates.

Tommy Earl went after every player we signed, rookie or vet, and he got most of them because Tumbleweed Pointe offered a neighborhood in every price range— from Budget's mansion in The Pointe, where Tommy Earl himself lived, to Weffert Lorants's home in Bowling Forest.

Tommy Earl's first two residents in Tumbleweed Pointe were Todd Mitchell and Hepatitis Diggs, those free agents in Dreamer Tatum's stable. I signed both of them to three-year contracts in the $6 million range.

Todd Mitchell and Hepatitis Diggs were looking around the property when they took a fancy to the three-bedroom condos that went for $250,000. They were the most expensive condos because they were "water-golf," as Tommy Earl described them, meaning they offered a view of a pond and part of a golf hole. The pond was stocked with fish. Throw a hook right outside your door.

Todd Mitchell asked what the less expensive condos looked at.

"Condos, mostly," Tommy Earl said.

I wound up buying the condos from Tommy Earl, thanks to Iris McKinney. She suggested we throw the condos in on the players' contracts, get to knock a half-million off our cap.

That was the same day Iris told me about a young woman named Carol she'd met at the Velveeta Arms. Carol only drank purified water with eggplant cut up in it. The gallon of eggplant water was covered and placed in the refrigerator overnight and strained the next morning.

"She drinks it to keep her balanced," said Iris, who then screamed with laughter as she added, "Carol says she doesn't trip over the ottoman in her living room near as much as she used to."

65

As long as Tracy Hopkins could be a June bride, she didn't care what kind of church she was married in. Tommy Earl could pick the church. The Gay Hindus Temple, for all she cared. She said the only religion she belonged to was "the Church of Bankology."

I thought I had an idea of what that was even before Tracy explained it to me at the rehearsal dinner.

She said, "We who are members of the Church of Bankology devoutly believe that all physical and mental stress can be processed out of your body and mind if you have a sizable bank account."

"And I suppose," I said, "the larger the bank account, the less likely it is for a person to suffer physical or mental stress?"

"Buddy, you can tap dance to *that* tune," Tracy said.

The rehearsal dinner was at Bust Out Jonah, which, to my way of thinking, made the barbecue ribs at the rehearsal dinner the best thing about the whole wedding deal.

There was a cluster of rack-loaded wool drivers at the rehearsal dinner as well as the wedding. Other members of the Church of Bankology, I squandered a guess.

They were friends of Tracy's from Naughty Girls Lingerie and Members Only Lingerie. Some of their dry-wall and roofer husbands showed up for the barbecue but skipped the wedding.

Tracy had been gone from that life—modeling lingerie—for months. With Tommy Earl having to spend so much time in Gully Creek, he'd put her in charge of Gang Resistant Systems, Inc., the "flagship" of his empire. She'd apparently done a good job—the business was still growing.

Tracy couldn't very well take personal credit for the increasing number of gangs in the major cities of Texas, no matter how many times she stuck her head out her office window and hollered, "Go get 'em, teenage scum," but she'd stayed on top of quality, orders, deliveries, installations. Watched the money real close, going out, coming in.

T.J., Kelly Sue, and Iris had all been invited to the wedding, but each one had an excuse for not going.

The coach was too busy getting all the things fixed that kept going wrong with the half-million-dollar house Tommy Earl had sold him.

T.J. gave me a message to take to Tommy Earl: "Ask him how come my smoke detectors start chirpin' every time my lawn sprinklers go off?"

Kelly Sue said she'd rather use the time to go out to LA. We'd made the trip together three times but her trips greatly outnumbered mine, not that I didn't love my wife and my dog as much as she thought she loved Shake Tiller and my dog.

Say hello to Tyrone Power and Rhonda Fleming, I told her. She said she would if she saw them, but she'd probably be with Fredric March and Janet Gaynor. It was a running joke between us, and although I was about to run out of names, I did have Cornel Wilde and Gene Tierney rat-holed.

Iris McKinney couldn't go to Fort Worth because an opportunity presented itself for her to bag another married chap from the Velveeta Arms.

I said, "Iris, do you know anything about any of the wives of these guys you're knocking off?"

She said, "I know they have to do all the homemaking shit and I get to have all the fun—ain't it great?"

The wedding went smoothly enough, if you wanted to compare it to a hockey game.

It was a 3:00 P.M. ceremony in the small chapel of the University Christian Church, Dr. Glenn Dollarhyde, the chancellor, presiding.

No family present for either the bride or groom. Tommy Earl's mother had died of a heart attack two years earlier while watching a daytime talk show. Tommy Earl's elderly dad had passed away while staring at the color photograph of an enchilada dinner in a magazine. T.E. had invited his kids but his son, Bryson, wouldn't leave the porn on his computer, and his daughter, Aubyn, was taking a tour of poverty-stricken areas of Mexico on a non-air-conditioned bus with three other commies from the University of Texas.

Tracy's parents had been expected to attend, but they'd been forced to cancel at the last minute. Nobody to look after the discount cigarette store and gas pumps in Waycross, Georgia, her old hometown.

There were about twenty guests, mostly employees of Gang Resistant Systems, Inc.

While I stood up with Tommy Earl as his best man, Tracy's maid of honor was Penny, from Members Only.

The bride wore a too tight and too cheap white cocktail dress.

Penny and the four bridesmaids wore pale blue too tight and too cheap cocktail dresses. The bridesmaids were Vikki and Nugget from Members Only and Carmen and Niki from Naughty's.

Tommy Earl's groomsmen in their assortment of Chevy-blue suits were four of his old TCU teammates, Hog Hailey, Skeeter Rowland, D. R. Cooles, and Quinton Casterfuller. Hog, Skeeter, and D.R. could all provide me with worry-free health care, I found out, and Quinton and his wife owned and ran Marveline's Bath & Linen over on Berry.

"Dearly beloved, friends and Frogs," Dr. Dollarhyde said at the beginning, around a couple of hiccups, "we are gathered here in the holy stage of macaroni—"

"Do what?" Tracy said.

The minister mumbled to himself for a moment, Bible in hand.

I heard, ". . . sacred bonds . . . buya books . . . who give him . . ."

Dr. Dollarhyde then gazed at Tommy Earl and said, "I, Tracy . . ."

Tommy Earl said, "I, Tracy . . . fuck, I ain't Tracy."

"I, *who?*" said Tracy.

Bridesmaids snickered, groomsmen coughed.

"Over this way," Tommy Earl said, tugging on the chancellor's sleeve.

"Where 'bouts?" Dr. Dollarhyde said.

"I, *Tracy*," Tracy said, getting his attention. "Let's take it from there—and how much vod did you step in today, old-timer?"

"Is it time?" the chancellor said.

"Is it time for *what?*" Tracy said irritably.

"Amen," the chancellor said.

"You got that right," Tommy Earl said.

I said to the chancellor, "Glenn, you want to take a little breather, maybe grab some black coffee?"

"In sickness stand your health," he said. "For better or for soup. Love, honor, and furnish your babies."

Dr. Dollarhyde then went into another mumbling mode. Two minutes. His head bowed, eyes closed. We could only watch.

Suddenly, his eyes flashed open and he raised his finger to the ceiling.

"What man has put asunder, let the numbers join together!"

Tommy Earl looked at Tracy. "Does that sound right?"

"What do *you* think?" said Tracy.

Dr. Dollarhyde smiled. "With the power vested in me, I now pronounce you dead and wife. You may kick the bride."

We heard the woman's voice seconds later.

"You left out something!"

We turned around to see Sheila at the back of the chapel.

Sheila called out, "You didn't ask if anybody could show cause why this couple should not be married."

"*My God!*" said Dr. Dollarhyde, crouching down, shielding his head with his arms. "The voice is coming out of the sky!"

Tracy called back to Sheila, "I don't recall your name on our invitation list, honey."

The bridesmaids sat down on benches, crossed their legs, assumed they could smoke.

Sheila said, "I just happened to be in the foyer. It's my volunteer day to sell our Junior League cookbook. This is one of our locations."

"Jesus Christ," Tracy said, looking away.

"He's here, Billy Clyde!" Dr. Dollarhyde said, still cringing. "He's up on the roof!"

I said to Tommy Earl that I'd try to take care of the ex-wife if he'd take care of the chancellor. Tommy Earl, with his groomsmen helping, started trying to transport

Dr. Dollarhyde to a sink. Tracy joined her bridesmaids for a cigarette.

"I think you're really married, Tracy," said Vikki from Members Only. "I mean . . . I think it counts."

Penny, the maid of honor, said it definitely counted. She said she'd been to weddings where the bride and groom made up their own vows, like where they talked about drugs and freedom and illegal search and seizure and things like that, and when the preacher got around to saying the couple was man and wife, that was all it took to make it official.

"So I guess I'm married," Tracy said.

I filed out with the guests and now stood alone with Sheila in the foyer by the table of Junior League cookbooks. That was when Suzy Bradshaw barged in, babbling hysterically.

She was in tears as she screeched at Sheila, "How dare you sleep with my husband! You're a terrible woman!"

Sheila calmly said, "Suzy, you must control yourself."

Suzy yelled something in Japanese that might have amounted to the same thing as "Die, Yankee dog!"

It was in the next instant that Ody Bradshaw bolted into the foyer, a bit out of breath.

"I'm sorry," he gasped. "I tried to catch her, but she was in the Jag and I was in the Rover."

"I certainly hope you can do something with her," Sheila said.

"I can," Ody puffed. Then he grappled with Suzy and picked her up and carried her off under one arm, her little feet kicking, her still screeching in Japanese.

Looking back, Ody said, "She ain't really dangerous. I'll get her home and calm her down with some yard work."

Sheila and I walked outside and watched Ody toss Suzy into the Range Rover and drive away.

Remarkably composed, Sheila turned to me and said, "What are you doing tonight, Billy Clyde? Any plans?"

"What?"

"I thought we might have dinner . . . or something."

Her Brenda Gazangas hadn't lost their shape or any weight, most normal men might have noticed.

"Thanks, but I better hit the road," I said.

"You must feel quite alone these days . . . Barbara Jane always off somewhere else. I had a dream about the two of us the other night."

"You did?"

"I dreamed we were together in an earlier life."

"No kidding?"

"We were *very* happy."

"I'll bet we were."

I started walking away.

She said, "Call me next time you're in town—seriously."

"Sure thing," I said, and I picked up a little speed as I headed for my Cadillac-Buick.

66

The accidental death of Bappy Ramirez in July stunned everyone around the league. I may have been less stunned than most, however. As I mentioned to Barb, the biggest surprise to me was that Bappy didn't drown in a bathtub, like Naomi's two previous husbands did—he died in a bungee jump.

In his continuing effort to avoid the boredom of life in general, Bappy had adopted bungee jumping as his new favorite sport. But he went about it a little differently than other bungee jumpers.

He liked to do it from the 250-foot platform he'd had constructed on his property in the South Africa bush, about a mile from his hunting lodge, and preferably when wild animals were milling around beneath him.

Bappy had lured a colony of leopards and a pride of lions to the spot with lamb shanks, London broils, and veal chops. He'd been fattening them up so they'd become docile and friendly, making it easier for him to shoot them later on.

Danger was Bappy's hobby. He was quoted in the obits saying, "Life without danger is like—yes, I think—escargots without garlic butter."

It was a new bungee that did him in, the one Naomi had brought him from a shopping spree in Cape Town. Evidently, he forgot to measure the length of it before leaping off the platform.

A search party had gone out looking for Bappy when he didn't show up for high tea. The search party had consisted of Naomi and Rolf, the caretaker of the lodge, Soupy Eggleston, the pilot of their Citation 10, Chef Timothy, who traveled with them everywhere, and six faithful Zulus.

They'd found him crumpled in the grass, wearing only his red bikini briefs—it had been a hot day.

Naomi was questioned by two police officers but was cleared of any part in the incident. The rumor around the league was that Naomi had cleared herself by giving each of the officers $50,000 and his own Zulu to take home.

Bappy's body was flown to Mexico City in the C-10 and he was buried among his ancestors in the tomb he'd already designed and had built. The tomb overall wasn't quite as large as the Lincoln Memorial, but the sculpture of Bappy aiming his rifle equaled the size of Abe sitting in the chair.

There were three wills. The sister, Olga, produced a will from five years earlier leaving her everything. Carlos ("The Leaf") Garcia, who ran the family business, produced a will from three years earlier leaving him everything. But Naomi produced a will that was written only one year earlier, and it left her everything. The will had been witnessed by Rolf, Soupy, and Chef Timothy. Naomi said she would see that Olga continued to live in the style to which she'd become accustomed, and Carlos ("The Leaf") Garcia would stay in charge of the family's agricultural endeavors.

The Mexico City Bandits were another matter.

Bappy was hardly in his tomb before Naomi applied

to the NFL to move the franchise to Houston. If not Houston, then Los Angeles. If not Los Angeles, then Cleveland. Those cities all needed teams, didn't they?

Commissioner Val Emery denied the request, so Naomi started a telephone campaign with every owner in the league, begging them to let her move out of Mexico City.

She even got me on the phone one day.

"Billy Clyde, you cute man, this is Naomi Ramirez," she said, "You're a Texan, so you may know me better as Naomi Lauranette Foster of Dallas."

"I certainly know who you are," I said.

"I know you must be familiar with my problem. I'm calling to enlist your help. Wouldn't you rather see the Bandits in Houston, or Los Angeles, or even Cleveland?"

"I don't know about Cleveland." I chuckled.

"Believe me, Billy Clyde, *anywhere* would be better than Mexico."

"There are a lot of problems involved, Naomi, if I may call you that."

"You certainly may. What problems?"

"Well, for one thing, you have a big stadium being built."

"If you knew the Mexican people as well as I do, you would know the stadium is no problem. They'll tear it down and take it home."

"Take it home?"

"Precisely. They'll take the benches home for living room furniture and take the Astroturf home for bedroom carpet. Billy Clyde, if the other owners in the National Football League think I'm going to continue living in this filthy, poisonous, disease-ridden country, they are very much mistaken."

I said she had my support—Mexico had always tried to kill me—but I doubted it was going to do her any good. The owners had voted to expand to Mexico City and London in the first place because they wanted to explore foreign markets.

She sighed and said if every city could just be Dallas, there'd be fewer problems in the world. She wasn't giving up, she said.

Then she thanked me for listening, and we hung up.

The training camps had barely opened when the other two expansion teams faced problems that also captured the public's fancy.

The one that got the most attention involved Larry Frazier, the strong-armed quarterback from Central Military Catholic who'd been drafted by the London Knights. He'd quietly undergone a sex-change operation and had become known as Laura Frazier.

The quarterback said he didn't see what difference a name made if you could hit the receiver on 584 Q-Post Swing.

But if the league insisted, he said, he would agree to be listed as Larry Frazier on TV and in newspapers and in the game programs. In his private life, however, he said he would continue to be known as Laura, especially to his husband, Frank.

Not surprisingly, the quarterback received the full support of Neville Trill, who said, "I cannot understand why the league is in such an abominable dither over this. For years there have been rumors of sex-change operations in World Cup soccer, but it hasn't lessened anyone's ability. If anything, it has brought certain teams closer together. And while the league says it has a rule that no woman can compete in the NFL, we know Larry is not really a woman, don't we? Except to Frank, of course."

T. J. Lambert was among those who couldn't understand the quarterback's decision at all.

"Why does a shirt-lifter want to be a woman?" he said. "Don't he know he's just gonna have more competition suckin' dicks?"

When the Tiki Torch Palms made the network news I called Barbara Jane to make sure she knew about it. We laughed and relived some fond memories. We'd once stayed at the Tiki Torch Palms when *Haul Cane Road* was being shot on Kauai.

Hawaiians were quick to inform you that Kauai was the oldest of their isles, the first one burped up by the undersea volcano that created the chain. All the hocky-licky-lau aside, I knew it as the most beautiful place I ever hoped to see, if beauty could be judged by lush tropical trees and flowers, rippling brooks, mountains, canyons, waterfalls, natural swimming pools among lava rocks, hidden white beaches—and all of it within view of the bright blue Pacific.

Haul Cane Road, in case you don't remember, was the movie of the best-selling novel that told the story of a missionary family that made itself enormously wealthy off the land and Hawaiian labor, then one by one turned into drunks and crazies. Barb played Claudia, the sane sister, the one who refused to eat poi or learn the hula or throw herself off a cliff. It was her first big-screen role.

We'd stayed at the Tiki Torch Palms for six weeks during the shooting, and that was where the Volcanoes were headquartered at their training camp. Tokyo Russ had taken the Volcanoes to Kauai to get them away from the hubbub of Honolulu. He'd rented half the hotel for the team and coaches.

The Volcanoes made the network news when it was revealed that Tokyo Russ had ordered surveillance cameras installed in all of the rooms and hallways of the resort hotel. This was his way of making sure his players didn't break training rules.

The NFL Players Association jumped right on it and started yelling about "right to privacy," and the Volcanoes themselves boycotted workouts for two days.

It was their own business, they said—in fact, it was the "American way"—if they wanted to idle away their free time smoking Hanalei Gold or Waimea Dread. Not that they did, but if they wanted to.

The officers of the Players Association then fought a little dirty. They publicly accused Tokyo Russ of choosing Kauai as a training camp for nostalgic reasons. The route of the planes that bombed Pearl Harbor, they pointed out, had been directly over Kauai.

Buckling under to that charge, Tokyo Russ removed the surveillance cameras and apologized to the players for his "thoughtless" act.

Of course, it didn't take long around the league to hear a different explanation for the surveillance cameras. It was said to be Tokyo Russ's way of trying to keep up with the late-hour activities of his wife, Rachel, or "Mandy Rice-Davies," who was currently appearing nightly in the piano bar of the Tiki Torch Palms.

Her and her ukulele.

67

If you'd never been to a pro football training camp or major league baseball's spring training, you could be excused for thinking they were similar, but the two were drastically different. Pro football camp was drudgery compared with the fun and frolic of baseball's spring training.

I'd lived through many a pro football camp and I'd observed some baseball spring training when I'd done outings in Florida. What I'd basically observed about baseball spring training was the players getting drunk and laid and suntanned when they weren't playing catch. Meanwhile, the managers worked on their golf games and sat around telling stories about Koufax and Drysdale to attentive groups of suntanned sportswriters.

The Tornadoes trained at home at our excellent practice facility next door to our almost-completed stadium. The players lived in the condos and townhouses Tommy Earl had built on spec at Tumbleweed Pointe.

Here again it was different in my day. When I was with the Giants we trained on the enchanting campus of Mohican Tech in upstate New York. We lived in the barren rooms of a dormitory. Concrete floors, prison

beds, no TV, no phone, an electric fan for air-conditioning. Nothing but you and your playbook. In some cases,
a boom box, which forced you to limp down the hall
often and tell somebody to turn that shit down or suffer
the consequences, which might involve dealing with
T. J. Lambert on the subject.

My memories of training camp were all wrapped up
in calisthenics, laps, drills, blackboards, aches, pains,
film, and monumental boredom.

My big treat of the day would come on a free break
between drills. Going across the street from the practice
field to the little grocery store and buying a pretzel and a
root beer. The rest of the time I was caught up in making sure I knew the difference between 32 Up-Ride
Slant and 29 Flex Crack-Read Sweep.

But most of our plays were simple. Even Booger Sanders, the Gulf Coast redneck, easily learned Fullback
Angle, Off-Tackle Isolate, and Counter Trey, where
Puddin Patterson and Sam Perkins would pull and lead
the blocking for me.

T.J. was incorporating some of that old stuff—and
the simplicity—into his ground attack, which would feature the one and only Budget Fowler.

I looked in on our training camp at least once a day,
but usually in the afternoon. The mornings were mostly
conditioning and agility drills—coaches hollering at guys
to run-run-run, dig-dig-dig, move their fat asses.

There was football in the afternoons—the offense
working on timing, the defense on recognition. It took
hours and days of repetitious practice for the players on
a team to learn each other's mannerisms and idiosyncra-
cies so they could function under game conditions.

One afternoon I watched Shea Luckett, ReRun
Moses, and Budget Fowler work on 23 Fake-Dive
Sweep—one of my old plays—still T.J. was confident
they could do it in their sleep. Over and over, Shea took

the snap, faked a handoff to ReRun, and flipped a pitch to Budget.

But eventually they started fucking it up on purpose. Shea and ReRun bumped into each other twice, and Budget dropped the pitch three times.

"You fuckers tryin' to see if I'm awake?" T.J. hollered.

ReRun was a talkative sort. He hollered back, "No, man, we knew you was awake 'cause we heard you fay-rit."

Fay-rit was ReRun's pronunciation of *fart*, just as *two-rid* was his pronunciation of *turd*, and *few-check* was his pronunciation of *fuck*.

His pronunciations kept you on your toes.

On another afternoon I watched Todd Mitchell run a down-and-in and Shea try to hit him on a rollout.

Todd was a good-looking young man whose laid-back attitude and general behavior brought to mind the word *mellow*. On the day I signed him, he'd said, "I like to lie in bed for a while after I wake up in the morning to assemble my surroundings. I ponder my place in the universe, then I turn into my psyche, check my karma, and get my balance for the day. I can then go into the universe with a positive attitude and a protective shield of love."

Four out of five completions on the rollout weren't good enough for T. J. Lambert.

"Let's go, do it again," the coach yelled.

Todd yelled back, "That's six out of six, Coach!"

"That right, Overdose?" T.J. roared. "Well, six out of six ain't nothin' but adequate!"

After ten out of ten, they went on to something else.

Royce Harper, who was looking like our best offensive lineman, was the guy who actually came up with Overdose as the nickname for Todd Mitchell.

Royce was an intense player who made the coaches

smile with his hustle, and kept everybody alert with his nicknames for those teammates who arrived in camp without one.

Shea Luckett immediately became known to Royce as Sunset Beach, Sunset for short, and Budget Fowler became known as Luxury Size, or Size for short, and all of the reserves were called Hope-I-Do, or Hope for short.

Although the other offensive tackle we were counting on, B. L. ("Big Load") Alfred, already had a nickname, Royce gave him another one—Brain. This was because Royce had overheard Big Load say to T.J. that what he liked to do before a game was "rest my brain for competition."

In my opinion, it was to T.J.'s credit that he put together a smaller staff than the other teams in the league. Today it seemed like every NFL team had a coach for each position—a linebacker coach, a tight end coach, a strong safety coach, to say nothing of a "strength" coach and a psychologist.

"I don't want to hear that many voices," T.J. had said. "All they do is argue, try to prove they're smarter than one another."

T.J.'s staff consisted of Bobby Stokes, defensive coordinator, Richard Yates, offensive coordinator, Hoppy Ingram, special teams, Mickey Boggs, offensive line, Rudy Nichols, defensive line, and Jerry Monk, scout.

Harold Fowler, Budget's daddy, who was on the payroll and always hanging around, decided he needed a title.

As a joke, T.J. came up with "special contributist," but Harold liked it and had business cards printed.

HAROLD FOWLER
SPECIAL CONTRIBUTIST
WEST TEXAS TORNADOES

All but two of T.J.'s coaches came from other NFL teams. His two coordinators came from college football—Bobby Stokes from TCU, of course, and Richard Yates from Arizona State.

Offensive and defensive coordinators on pro football staffs ranked above assistant coaches in salary, prestige, and command. Most assistants hoped to become coordinators someday, and most coordinators hoped to become head coaches.

T.J. hired Hoppy Ingram away from the Packers. Hoppy was known for a voice that could carry to the next county. He was a special teams taskmaster who didn't believe opponents should be able to return punts or kickoffs more than two yards upfield. At the same time, he believed his team should be able to return punts and kickoffs a minimum of thirty yards.

Mickey Boggs, who was in charge of weight gain and weight loss and yelling at the offensive line, came from the 49ers but said he wasn't sorry to leave San Francisco—"I was gettin' sick of all that fuckin' wine talk."

Rudy Nichols, who was in charge of weight gain and weight loss and hollering at the defensive line, was plucked from the Falcons' staff. He liked Atlanta, he said, but he'd never gotten used to the two hours it took him every morning to get from his house in the suburbs to the vicinity of downtown. If he didn't leave home by 4:30 A.M., he said, it could take four hours.

Jerry Monk, our scout, came from the Bears. He'd been a familiar figure around the league for years. He spoke in a whisper, he was a serious snoop, he virtually lived on the road. He never saw fewer than two college games on a weekend during the season, and most often he'd find a way to see four games—Thursday night, Friday night, Saturday afternoon, Saturday night. He constantly networked with sportswriters, SIDs, assistant coaches, and acted like he knew everything that was going on in the sports world whether he did or not.

Merely to greet Jerry with a nod was to hear him whisper, "Al's leaving the Vikes. Giants put him in charge of the D. Trojans just signed Seminoles for ten-year home-and-home . . . hear about Pepper in Boston? *Miami Herald*. Column . . ."

Richard Yates, the offensive coordinator, was an energetic young guy who brought a lot of ideas with him from Arizona State. He was next in line for the head job with the Sun Devils, but he was tired of the recruiting wars in college football, figured he'd aim at a head pro job.

One thing T.J. made clear to Richard Yates was that Richard wasn't going to call the plays during a game. Richard could sit up in the booth in the press box and make the occasional suggestion on T.J.'s headset, but T.J. didn't want a guy upstairs talking to the radio in the helmet of his quarterback, a setup like most NFL teams had.

Shea Luckett wasn't going to have a radio in his helmet where he couldn't hear anything but static half the time—or some tricky shit Richard Yates might want to try in order to prove he was smarter than the defensive coordinator on the other team.

T.J. made this clear to Richard Yates when he hired him.

"I want your passing offense and I want you to formulate the game plans and I'll take your occasional suggestion during a game," T.J. had said to him, "but that's where it stops."

Richard Yates had said he wouldn't respect any head coach who didn't think the same way. Bright guy. Diplomat.

"I swear I don't understand how a head coach can stand around and let somebody else call the plays for him," T.J. said at one of his regular 5:00 P.M. press conferences during camp.

He was in his office in his sweats, passing out cans of beer and talking to the five sportswriters who were living with us and would be covering us throughout the season.

T.J. had a way of making good copy. He added to his statement:

"I'd rather see a church burn than let an offensive coordinator call plays for me."

The five sportswriters, part of what Weffert Lorants called our "family," were Ted Deekins of the *Fort Worth Light & Shopper*, Crew Slammer of the *Dallas Daily Herald*, Herbert Strum of the *Lubbock Avalanche Standard*, Scoop Beal of the *Amarillo Express-Sandstorm*, and Jimmy Stutts of the *Abilene Times-Bugle*. There were radio and TV reporters who dropped in on us from time to time, but you could sound bite their asses and be rid of them in no time. In pro football it was the regular newspaper guys you needed to cultivate, become pals with if possible, share a mutual trust with. They'd be sneaking around, getting close to some of the players and assistant coaches, probably finding out things you didn't know, or more likely finding out things you didn't *want* to know, much less see in print.

The last thing you wanted to do was make an enemy of those guys—they were to be used. They were your print messengers to the players, your leakers, your apologists, your alibi artists, your trial balloonists.

It was chiefly Weffert Lorants's job to look after our newspaper guys, keep them informed, comfortable, entertained, well fed, and as far away from thirsty as possible. I gave him an unlimited budget to do all that with because I'd found out right away he needed it.

I invited all five writers, one by one, into my office for a drink and a get-acquainted session when they arrived in Gully Creek. I'd asked Kelly Sue to be present, figuring they might be dealing with her much of the time.

In the course of conversation Kelly Sue mentioned to each writer that she'd looked into the way other NFL teams handled it, and it seemed the league suggested two ways to lighten the financial burden on the newspaper and the writer himself.

She said, "For each day you're covering us, here or on the road, we can give you a per diem of $250—the current cost-of-living fee proposed by the league—or we can simply pick up your room and food and entertainment expenses. Which do you prefer?"

Each sportswriter answered firmly with the same word:

"Both."

Weffert did a good job of taking care of our journalistic "friends." He took the writers to Them Two Women almost every night for dinner. He arranged honorary memberships for them at Tumbleweed Pointe Country Club—no dues and no monthly tab. The writers could sign for whatever they wanted. Food, drink, full set of golf clubs. Tommy Earl would send their bills straight to us. Weffert drove the scribes up to Cloudcroft, New Mexico, one weekend to beat the heat, relax in the mountains.

Iris McKinney even helped out on the entertainment front with two of the writers, the guy from Fort Worth and the guy from Dallas—once she found out they were happily married.

I thanked her for choosing the papers with the largest circulation.

"Loyalty is my middle name," she said.

68

One reason Barbara Jane came to visit in early August was to have a say in what our Funnelettes were going to wear. She was afraid if she stayed out of it, they'd wind up in purple-sequined bathing suits.

Tryouts had already been held for our Funnelettes, our pep girls, or our "Dallas Cowboy Cheerleaders," as T.J. called them, and they'd been selected before Barbara Jane came to town.

T.J. had said, "I just want our Dallas Cowboy Cheerleaders to be better-looking than anybody else's Dallas Cowboy Cheerleaders, including the Dolphins'. Miami's got some damn good-looking Dallas Cowboy Cheerleaders, in case nobody's noticed."

Unlike some of the other NFL teams, our cheerleaders were going to be salaried and would make road trips, so more than three hundred girls from all over West Texas showed up for the day and went through their dancing and tumbling routines in our almost-completed stadium.

I appointed Kelly Sue the head selector, but asked that she strongly consider the opinions of myself, T.J.

and Iris. What I'd basically said was "Fuck the tumbling, we want rack-loaded wool drivers."

"I guess that means you don't want them to know algebra either." Kelly Sue grinned.

We carefully ruled out all the teenagers, the mothers of school-age children, the grandmothers, the plumpos, the anorexias, and those we figured for closet meece.

T.J. thought we struck a good racial balance for our area of the state, twenty-one white babes, three black chicks. Ideally, he said, we'd probably like to have a couple of Hispanials and even an Oriental chink, but finding Hispanials and Oriental chinks with good enough racks wasn't easy in any part of the country—at least that's what he'd observed in his travels.

The committee thanked him for his input.

I took the heat from the unhappy stage mothers whose daughters didn't get chosen.

The mother of the girl with the heftiest thighs said, "Who's the person in charge here?"

I said that was me.

She said, "You ain't takin' no baton twirlers?"

I said, "No, ma'am, we're not."

"We done drove all the way from Dumas."

"I'm sorry for your trouble," I said. "I thought we made it clear in our ad and on the radio that we were only interested in dancers."

"My Oleta Lynn over there," the woman said, "she could twirl that goalpost if you dug it up, but no baton twirlers, you say? That's a lot of shit, is all that is. And you call yourself a football team."

I was generally pleased with our group. We'd wound up with what I thought were numerous look-alikes for Vikki, Nugget, Carmen, and Niki, the lingerie models. In fact, you could say there were a couple of look-alikes for Tracy Hopkins Bruner.

Now we were in the dining room at Tumbleweed
Pointe at a large round table, assembled for lunch and
the costume discussion—Barb, Kelly Sue, Iris, Donna
Lou Lambert, T.J., me, and Hume, the only pet that
would ever be permitted in the clubhouse.

Tommy Earl had hired a big-time chef from a four-
star restaurant, so we all had things for lunch that were
either tall or wide or looked like model airplanes. After a
brief debate over exactly how the chef should die, we
settled down to discuss the costumes for our cheerleaders.

"No white boots," Barb said. "No shiny white plastic
boots and no purple-sequined bathing suits. That's to
start."

"Well, there goes my one idea," said Iris, who then
squealed with laughter.

"You don't think so, really?" Kelly Sue said to Barb
with a grin. "White patent-leather cowboy boots and
purple-sequined bathing suits with this big hair? I think
it has West Texas written all over it."

"Sounds good to me," T.J. said.

"It would," said Donna Lou.

"Maybe for a car date," Barb said, "but not in a stadium in front of . . . what does our stadium hold?"

I said, "It's coming in at around seventy-two thousand five hundred."

"In front of seventy-two thousand five hundred people who've just come from church," Barb said. "I would
also like to see us avoid those little shortie shorts and
halter tops of the Dallas Cowboy cheerleader ilk."

"Now, I don't know about *that*." T.J. frowned.

"Yeah, let's think about that for a minute," I said.

"There's nothing to think about," Barb said. "Our
girls are not wearing skimpy little pants that barely cover
the crack and the clump."

"The Crack and the Clump," I said. "I saw that. It was with Val Kilmer and . . . who was the girl?"

Iris squeaked.

I said, "All I'm saying about the Dallas cheerleaders . . . the way they look, the way they dress, they've probably had a lot to do with the success of that organization."

"That's absurd," said Barb.

"No, it's true. I have friends who've known some of those girls personally. Rosie Staubach, Tonya Dorsett, Emma Smith."

"When you're through being funny," Barb said.

"Tonya Dorsett?" Iris said with a glint.

Barb said, "Kelly Sue and I have already discussed it and we agree. We're going to wear one-piece playsuits."

"Aw, shit," T.J. said.

"T.J.!" Donna Lou glared.

"I meant curried chicken salad, or whatever it was I had for lunch."

Barb went on, "I'm talking about a little sleeveless top with a short pleated skirt and white panties underneath. White playsuit with purple trim."

"With white sneakers and athletic socks," Kelly Sue added.

Barb said, "Turtleneck sweaters with the short pleated skirts in cold weather. I think our girls will look classy, very collegiate."

"Is that what we want?" I said.

"Yes." Barbara Jane and Kelly Sue said it simultaneously.

"I guess that does it," I said. "Kelly Sue, you're in charge of the playsuits."

Pushing away from the table, T.J. said, "I'm just sorry we lost out on that clump deal."

* * *

Another reason Barbara Jane was in town was to check out 10 Main Street. As much as I hated to leave my double-wide, my beachfront property, the old Victorian house at the south end of town became ready and I moved in. It was a terrific place, right down to the last brass fixture—the furniture, the carpet, the colors, the wood, the modern kitchen, everything. But why wouldn't I like it? Big Barb had dipped it in money.

All the time Big Barb had been whipping the place into shape, I'd hardly seen her. My mother-in-law would zip in on the old G-5, stay around for two or three hours to do something with a painter, plasterer, carpenter, electrician, or decorator, then zip out again. She'd done the same thing working on the house in LA.

Barb and Hume had moved into 3219 Chateau Briggan a few weeks earlier. I'd gone out there to admire my home in the Beverly Hills flats, so it had only been proper for Barb to come take a look at her home in the Gully Creek flats.

I was sure Barb and Hume's departure from Shake's house was a happy day for Swoll Up Inga and Tiny Weata, his caretakers. They didn't mind Kelly Sue being in and out because if it wasn't Kelly Sue, it would be another attractive lady. Swoll Up Inga and Tiny Weata had grown used to working around some shapely adorable who'd become the honored recipient of a Shake Tiller scholarship.

As a joke, Shake had once placed a personal ad in the *Los Angeles Times* that said:

ALL PAMS ON DECK!

Wealthy, sensitive, generous gentleman seeks 6 starlets who ideally resemble the killer babes on *One Life to Live* to join him on luxurious yacht and help him squander rest of

HIS LIFE ON SEX, DRUGS, AND ROUND-THE-WORLD
CRUISES. NO NAUTICAL EXPERIENCE REQUIRED.

He received sixty-three applicants, including some
keepers.

House on house, I pointed out to Barb, I had a better
deal. From the front door of 10 Main Street, it was only
a short walk to Them Two Women, but from the front
door of the house in the Beverly Hills flats, it must have
been over a mile to Armani.

69

It was in Budget Fowler's contract that he didn't play
exhibition games, or "pre-season" games, as the league
preferred to call them. I didn't blame him for wanting to
skip the moronic exhibitions, but I acted disappointed in
his attitude, which was how I got $1 million lopped off
his annual salary, but what was another million to a guy
who was making enough to buy his own B-1 bomber?

I wouldn't have played in exhibition games either if I
could have gotten out of them. Neither would Shake or
T.J. or Hose Manning. Any guy who'd proved his worth
to the team, whose job was secure, would rather have
eaten okra than play an exhibition game. But in our case
back then, we were trying to sell tickets. Remind old-
time Giants fans of Ken Strong, Harry Newman, Mel
Hein, and Ray Flaharty, or semi-old-time Giants fans of
Gifford, Rote, Conerly, and Huff.

Exhibitions today were idiotic and meaningless unless
you were a rookie trying to make the squad, in which
case they were opportunities to commit robbery and
mayhem and get away with it.

Today in the NFL almost every ticket was already
sold for every home game before the regular season

started, and it was no different for the beloved Tornadoes in our first season—we were sold out, flush.

So we were like everybody else. We put absolutely no emphasis or importance on winning the exhibition games. I couldn't imagine why any fan would even buy a ticket to an exhibition game unless he had a cousin trying to make one of the teams, or unless he wanted to get out of the house for two or three hours. He wasn't going to see anything resembling an NFL team.

T.J. didn't let his studs go more than one series of downs in our three exhibition games, all on the road, against the Saints, Falcons, and Eagles. I attended the games even though I knew they couldn't possibly be as thrilling or entertaining as Tommy Earl's wedding.

I didn't know anyone who held it against T.J., or our team, when the Saints beat us 35–17, when the Falcons beat us 28–10, and when the Eagles beat us 31–7.

We saw some good things. We liked the way Pluribus Uram and LaDaminion Walls ran their routes, the way ReRun Moses lugged the ball without much blocking, and the way B. L. ("Big Load") Alfred was trying to grab and hold. Showed want-to, T.J. commented.

Only a couple of guys on defense were impressive. Andre Humphrey, the shoplifter from Florida State, didn't look bad rushing the passer, and Fryer Pye called attention to himself with his three-game total of six pass-interference penalties.

There was also an indication that we'd taken a fairly good placekicker and punter in the expansion draft, Joachim Schnaufer, the foreign guy who'd been with the Jets. He kicked a forty-eight-yard field goal against the Saints, and a forty-six-yard field goal against the Falcons.

We all liked the way the team was coming together, and we liked our schedule even better. All four expansion teams had been given a break for their inaugural season. The expansion teams would all play home-and-home with each other. That meant that in our case we had two games each with the Hawaii Volcanoes, the London Knights, and the Mexico City Bandits.

In other words, six games where we wouldn't be tragic underdogs.

You couldn't call it much of a break that our first four games were on the road, but it was done that way in order for our stadium to be completed before our home opener, which would be draped in ceremony.

In every establishment of Gully Creek you could have found a copy of our AFC West schedule on the wall. Big poster. Kelly Sue deal.

WEST TEXAS TORNADOES

A 31	—at Kansas City Chiefs
S 7	—at Oakland Raiders
S 14	—OPEN
S 21	—at Seattle Seahawks
S 28	—at San Diego Chargers
O 5	—KANSAS CITY CHIEFS (home)
O 12	—OAKLAND RAIDERS (home)
O 19	—LONDON KNIGHTS (home)
O 26	—at Mexico City Bandits
N 2	—HAWAII VOLCANOES (home)
N 9	—DENVER BRONCOS (home)
N 16	—at London Knights
N 23	—MEXICO CITY BANDITS (home)
N 30	—at Denver Broncos
D 7	—at Hawaii Volcanoes
D 14	—SAN DIEGO CHARGERS (home)
D 21	—SEATTLE SEAHAWKS (home)

It took some doing, some last-minute shuffling, but Big Ed worked it out with the league where we'd be playing Hawaii in Honolulu on December 7, Pearl Harbor Day. It was a personal thing.

Utilizing all of his skills as a wordsmith, Weffert Lorants put together a handsome little document, a mini-brochure, on the Tornadoes after T.J. had settled on his starting lineups. We mailed them out to all of our season ticket holders and to every news outlet in the region, and also in the name of PR we distributed them to every bidness concern we could get an address on from Abilene to Clovis, New Mexico.

MEET THE WEST TEXAS TORNADOES was what it said on the cover, and that was over the top of a posed action shot of Budget Fowler in game togs doing a high-knee, cross-over, stiff-arm deal.

I might have exercised my editorial powers on some of Weffert's thumbnails if we hadn't been in a hurry. As it was, I didn't get a chance to read it until it was already back from the printer and I was sitting with it at breakfast one morning in Them Two Women.

Weffert started with the offense first.

SHEA LUCKETT—No. 8
Quarterback 6-2 220
Half Moon Bay, California
This cool engineer, once an international surfing star, is ready to lead his own NFL team after serving as the Green Bay backup signal caller for four seasons. An All-American at Southern Cal, he's known for his gritty, competitive nature, not to mention his versatility and whippet-type arm. Comes from a prominent dental family.

BUDGET FOWLER—No. 32
Running Back 6-3 237
Deep Sandy, Oklahoma
Physically impressive, this monstrously talented

runner figures to unturn no stones in setting NFL records before he's done. No. 1 draft choice of Tornadoes. Coach Lambert predicts nothing but distinctive marks from this fleet and rugged leather-lugger. Unanimous All-America last season at TCU. Nation's leading rusher. No on-job learner he.

RERUN MOSES—No. 20
Fullback 6-3 234
Atchergethia, Georgia
Sound on fundamentals, this rock-ribbed ball-toter also excels as a blocker. Expected to provide one-two punch with Budget Fowler. Ran for average of 3.4 yards per carry at Ohio State. Talkative competitor and listed by coaches as "most natural" football player in training camp. Lacks speed but heart as big as his meals.

PLURIBUS URAM—No. 82
Wide Receiver 6-1 185
Beaudine, Texas
A multitalented player who may be the most athletically-gifted member of the team. All Big 10 at Minnesota. Second-round draft pick. Noted for his speed, good hands. Likes to joke that he chose Minnesota over Texas schools because he thought it was in Canada and wanted to live in a foreign country. Interesting note: His mother once won national contest and $20,000 first prize for house with the most cockroaches in it.

TODD MITCHELL—No. 87
Wide Receiver 6-1 194
Squaw Valley, California
A bona fide steal as a free agent. Three-year starter for the Rams, this well-rounded athlete is known as

a pure, classic receiver. Runs routes with the moves of the ski racer he one-time was. Has unique attitude about life. Says his karma has allowed him to enjoy life everywhere he has looked for it. "With my protective shield of love," Todd says, "I can get high on fresh air."

B. L. ("Big Load") ALFRED—No. 78
Offensive Lineman 6-6 325
Houston, Texas
Projected as an immediate helper in the offensive line the minute he was drafted. This University of Texas star wasn't too active in the sprints during camp, but he's shown excellent progress in his mobility. Coach Lambert says Big Load exhibits a sound work ethic and is predicted to be a steady performer. Aside from eating, Big Load says his favorite pastime is watching the Weather Channel.

R. B. ("Real Butter") SIMMONS—No. 71
Offensive Lineman 6-7 319
Far River, Kansas
This veteran of many NFL wars with the Giants, 49ers, and Chiefs brings a stabilizing influence to the Tornadoes' offensive line. He is prominently penciled into Coach Lambert's plans. He appears to be unbothered by recent groin and hamstring injuries and completely recovered from asthma attack in training camp. 14th year in league.

BUDDHA PORCH—No. 51
Center 6-5 298
Hoover, Illinois
Another "steal" in the expansion draft, according to Coach Lambert. A sterling performer for 8 seasons with the Patriots, Buddha joined the Tornadoes with a renewed sense of dedication. Needs no

replacement for the deep snap. His storybook journey to the NFL once led him throughout the Far East on tramp steamers. Named by his father, Dr. Henry Porch, who still teaches a course in Comparative Religion at the University of Illinois.

ROYCE HARPER—No. 64
Offensive Lineman 6-5 299
Bitter Wind, Colorado
Shy of none when it comes to intangibles, this former all-pro that the Tornadoes plucked from the Redskins figures to open sizable holes for Budget Fowler et al. A sound individual in every way, this broad-shouldered top-notcher had all the coaches smiling throughout camp with his intensity. Most "vocal" player on team. Entertaining type who thinks up nicknames for teammates. Unfortunately, many of them can't be printed in family matter.

MARCUS TARVUS—No. 73
Offensive Lineman 6-4 311
Slinkard, Tennessee
An All-Southeastern Conference stalwart at Kentucky, he literally bloomed in camp and won the job over more seasoned men. Champion powerlifter in high school. Hopes not to cloud his career with injury, as it has sometimes been. Solidly constructed lineman who anxiously awaits the birth of his fourth child.

LaDAMINION WALLS—No. 89
Tight End 6-5 253
Natchoosish, Mississippi
A rapidly developing rookie, "Laddy" has ideal size and range for an NFL tight end. The Tornado braintrust expects him to use his physical tools to

become an outstanding terminal post. Dazzled teammates in weight room with his 470-pound bench press. Curtailed by upper-body muscle injuries during his first two college seasons at Louisiana Tech, but bestowed much credit on himself as a senior.

JOACHIM SCHNAUFER—No. 17
Placekicker/Punter 6-0 180
Hamburg, Germany
A former soccer star in Europe, he was brought to the Jets five years ago and transformed into one of the league's top field goal and extra-point men. Booms punts as well. Coach Lambert was pleasantly surprised to find him available in the expansion draft. Known for his stern attitude and fanatical nature, he was given many nicknames during camp but the one that seems to have stuck is "Swasty."

Weffert then devoted his prose to the defense.

DUNLAP GROSS—No. 55
Defensive End 6-5 263
Long Creek, Iowa
This talented giant came late in the expansion draft, but the coaching staff expects him to lead the team in sacks. He was a top rusher for the Cardinals for 7 seasons. Four Pro Bowls. A former All Big-10er at Michigan, the only concern is if his knee holds up.

ANDRE HUMPHREY—No. 66
Defensive Tackle 6-3 280
Sugar Beach, Florida
Nobody is more enthusiastic about this All-America rookie from Florida State than T. J. Lambert.

Astoundingly, he was still available in the seventh round of the draft. "I see in his eyes my kind of football player," says Coach Lambert. "There ain't a ounce of give-up in him."

MOSTIS CHARLES—No. 99
Defensive Tackle 6-6 296
Birmingham, Alabama
A real hole-plugger, this expansion draftee comes from a notable career with the Bills. An All-America at Auburn, his aggressive nature and quickness make him a tough fellow to block, as his two Pro Bowl appearances testify to. Mostis played both ways in college, but now says, "I believe you can derive the most satisfaction from releasing your football instincts on the ball carrier."

LAVAR TATE—No. 91
Defensive End 6-4 289
Goldsboro, North Carolina
Here's another gem that was found in the lower rounds of the NFL draft. Indicative of his gridiron skills is his 4.6 speed, which can spell doom for opposing quarterbacks. Lavar was second-team All-Southeastern Conference at the University of Georgia, and led team in strips and stumbles. Coach Lambert flatly predicts Lavar will be a force to be reckoned with.

JERMAINE ADAMS—No. 37
Outside Linebacker 6-1 260
Lake Mountain, Missouri
Another top draft choice. Agile and strong, Jermaine proved his worth at Iowa State where he led the team in tackles against the rugged competition of the Big 12. Lists Bible as favorite book and God as favorite person. Says "staying focused" is key to

good football, or driving a nail. Appears to be completely recovered from tears to anterior cruciate
and medial collateral ligaments.

SHEEP DOG McWORTER—No. 54
Middle Linebacker 6-3 245
Red Ant, Nebraska
Primed for plenty of action is this 12-year limp-off
causer from the Bears, one of the league's most
respected battle-scarred veterans. Coach Lambert's first defensive choice in the expansion draft.
Experienced to the point of no return. All-America
at University of Nebraska where he played on
three national championship teams. About going
to a warm-weather team, Sheep Dog says, "It are
the fulfillment of a dream." Sheep Dog is his real
name, by the way. His friends call him "Psycho."

YOHANCE REED—No. 50
Outside Linebacker 6-1 239
Toopagamma, Mississippi
Here is a rookie from East Louisiana AT&N who
step by step made it to the starting lineup. He did
it with consistent physical tackling and a tenacious
spirit. Obvious nickname: "Yo-Yo." Has 4.5 speed
and a 32-inch vertical jump. Track star in college.
Specialized in what he called the "hop it, step it,
and jump it." Coach Lambert says, "Yo-Yo's apt to
make me out a genius for taking him."

EDGEMON HILL—No. 13
Cornerback 6-1 208
Chicago, Illinois
A five-year standout for the Eagles, this expansion
vet is known for his one-on-one stoppage ability as
well as his recognition factors. Known to teammates as "Domer" because he played at Notre

Dame, Edgemon exemplifies what you want in a cornerback, not including a rash of injuries that have sometimes hampered his performance.

FRYER PYE—No. 31
Cornerback 6-2 200
Dallas, Texas
Intimidator is the key word to describe this consensus All-American from UCLA, a valuable fourth-round draft pick. More praise was authored on him in training camp than any other player. A bright-eyed and intense competitor, a meritorious career seems ahead of him as a mainstay. Keeps team laughing with his colorful use of the language, as in, "Don't be wastin' no worriation about me lookin' for people to hit. I be hittin' any man wants the footsball."

JEFF DAVIDSON—No. 21
Strong Safety 6-0 190
Brookline, Massachusetts
Steady and reliable best described Jeff's career with the Oilers, although he has been less blessed from the physical well-being standpoint. Nagging shoulder injuries caused him to miss most of last season, which was why he was placed in the expansion pool. Endured some contact work and scampered well in camp, however. A Harvard grad, Jeff is one of a scant few Ivy Leaguers in NFL. Known to use big words, read thick books, worry about downtrodden.

HEPATITIS DIGGS—No. 43
Free Safety 6-1 185
Beaufort, South Carolina
Best speed (4.4) and vertical leap (36 inches) on squad. All-everything as high school tailback, but

switched to defense and won glory as authoritative hitter at Clemson. Drafted No. 2 by Cowboys. Three spectacular Pro Bowl seasons in Dallas before contract dispute kept him idle last year. An eager free agent signee by Coach Lambert. Impact player deluxe. Nickname: "Blood Test."

I handed the brochure to Freida in Them Two Women, saying these were our heroes.

"I hear they're all rich," she said.

"They are."

"Even the nigs?"

"Yeah, but I wish you wouldn't call them that."

"What am I supposed to call 'em?"

"People." I smiled. "People works."

She looked like she'd have to take that under advisement.

70

If I had to pick the thing that surprised me the most in that fastest year of my life, it would be the afternoon in August when Kelly Sue dropped it on me that Shake Tiller wanted to get married.

"To who?" was all I could think of to say, stunned as I was, shocked, and otherwise dumbfounded.

"To *me*—who do you think?" she said.

We were sitting in a corner of the grill at Tumbleweed Pointe Country Club. Through the big glass windows we could see the stadium in the distance and a part of the golf course in another direction.

She'd stuck her head in my office and invited me to come have a drink at the club—there was something important she wanted to talk about. I'd thought she was going to ask me for a raise, and I was more than prepared to give her one.

I said, "Shake Tiller asked you to marry him in a voice you thought was serious?"

"He certainly did."

"He said, 'I love you, Kelly Sue—I want us to get married.' It was that kind of thing?"

"More or less."

"Did he say when? Like did he suggest a particular decade?"

"Sometime soon. Sometime in the next few months."

"Is he into some new product I don't know about?"

"He wasn't *into* anything."

"He wasn't drinking?"

"We hardly ever drink."

"What's he been reading lately?"

"We've been seeing each other for seven months. Why don't you think it's possible for him to ask me to marry him?"

"Because it's not possible."

"What's not possible? That he asked me or that we should do it? You think he's only asked me once? We've been talking about it for three weeks. I'm not sure I want to. I mean, I love him—I'm in love with him, but . . . I don't want to ruin what we have. I'd move out there and live with him, I know that much. But marriage . . . marriage ruins things. Marriage has ruined things for everybody I've ever known—except for you and Barbara Jane. And if you guys didn't lead such harrowing lives, I'm sure your marriage would be in the shit, too."

"Secret to a successful marriage. Lead a harrowing life."

"You know what I mean. You both have interesting careers. You travel. Absence makes the heart do stuff . . . I'm telling you something you don't know, right?"

"Secret to a successful marriage. Live apart."

"You haven't done badly by it. You've tricked life, is all I know."

"We've had our problems. It hasn't all been strawberry shortcake."

"I know about one of them. Kathy Montgomery. But you got past it."

"Did Shake tell you about Kathy Montgomery?"

"Barbara Jane did."

"Really?"

"Yes. I was telling her what a great marriage you two have, and she said the same thing you did—that you'd had some problems."

"Did she mention Jack Sullivan?"

"Who's Jack Sullivan?"

I laughed. "Never mind."

"Barb had a thing with somebody named Jack Sullivan?"

"I never got to paint it on the fuselage but it was a confirmed kill in my mind. Doesn't matter now."

"I can't see Barbara Jane having an affair."

"But you can see *me* having an affair."

"You're a man."

"Jack Sullivan was an attractive guy. A director. Smart, clever. They worked close together for five or six years in TV. It's ancient history."

"Well, people can fall off. Circumstances . . ."

"You and I could have fallen off."

"No, *you* could have. I had nothing to lose . . . but we didn't."

"But we could have."

"But we didn't."

We lit up.

"God, when I think what's happened, Billy Clyde. Here you are my best friend now, and Barb's my second-best friend, and I'm in love with *your* best friend. Speaking of falling off, are you fucking Iris?"

"*What?*"

"You heard me."

"No."

"That wasn't very convincing."

"No, goddamn it!"

"You better not be."

"Why, you'll girl-talk it with your second-best friend?"

"I'd never rat on you, Billy Clyde. You must know that. Jesus, you've given me a life. A year and a half ago I'm tending bar in a joint next door to Ewell Dwell, chiropractor, but you come in and . . . it's like thanks for the exposure, I've got my own show now. All I'm just saying is, I've noticed you and Iris getting a little chummy, and . . . it's there, you know. Anytime."

"I know it's there. I don't know Iris? I probably know Iris better than you do now. But she's never even hinted at a sport-fuck, and if she ever does, we'll laugh and forget it. She makes me laugh. She's also smart as hell, as you promised, and the reason we've gotten so chummy is because *you're* not around as much. And as long as we're having this intimate talk, I'll tell you something you may not want to hear."

"I know what you're going to tell me."

"No, you don't."

"Yes, I do."

"What am I going to tell you?"

"You're going to tell me about the conspiracy."

I held my empty glass up to a waiter. She held her empty glass up to the waiter.

"Are we talking about the same thing?" I said.

"If we're talking about Barbara Jane and Shake's sly little plot to keep something from happening between you and me—just in case something *was* happening between you and me. You three are so damn close, so protective of each other. Shake takes a swipe at me, dolls me up with Hollywood, I forget about you."

I glanced over to see if the waiter was speeding it up with the drinks.

She said, "Maybe they felt they had some cause to think I was a homewrecker. I suppose I should take it as flattery. I don't know if anything serious would have ever come of it between you and me. I guess it might have on my part, if I'd never gotten to know Barbara Jane. Hey, you were number twenty-three in my program and number one in my heart, right? I'll tell you this. If you'd been single, I'd have stepped over dead children to get to you."

"It's my sensitivity and interest in the arts. It does that to women."

"That and your knowledge of the two-man rotation zone. I've always been a sucker for it."

As my fresh Junior and her fresh vod came, I said, "I knew about the preemptive strike from the first minute. I saw it coming on Christmas Day—when Barb greeted you like the sister she never had. I was born in Fort Worth, but not yesterday. I thought it was great, though. You and Shake would have some laughs. I didn't want you to get hurt in the deal, but I thought it would do him good to hang out with a dynamite lady for a change, a woman with some intelligence, instead of a rack-loaded wool driver."

"I hate that description."

"Blame him. What I *don't* know is whether *they* knew that I knew . . . or know. Am I speaking English?"

"They don't. At least they haven't told me if they do. Shake told me about the 'plot' four months ago. He asked me if I was interested in you. I said I could have been, but my God-fearing Christian upbringing saved me from making a fool of myself. He confessed. He said his assignment in the beginning was to distract me from you in case there was some heat between us. He said it wasn't bad duty, after all. I'm glad he added that part, or I would have had to slug him. But he says that's not what it's become now. He says he's never felt this way about any woman before, and he thinks it must be the same thing as love because he feels about me like Bogart felt about Bergman. I believe him, and I love him too, and we really are talking seriously about getting married, or living together, me moving to LA."

"Have you talked to Barb about the plot?"

"No. And I'd never be the one to bring it up."

"Does she know about this marriage talk?"

"She's all for it."

"You're the sister she never had."

"It's more like we've become really good friends. I adore her."

"This is amazing. Shake and I have known each other since we were ten. We've been best friends our whole lives. We played high school ball together, college ball together, pro ball together. Aside from my uncle, his folks were the only parents I ever had. I was with him in the hospital when his mother died after the car wreck. I was with him when his dad died after a stroke. He helped me find a good nursing home for Uncle Kenneth and helped me convince my uncle to turn himself in, and helped me get him there. We know everything about each other. Neither one of us has ever made a move, a decision, had a problem, needed help, or wanted to do something the other one didn't know about. This is the first thing he's never told me."

"I think he's waiting for me to say yes, then spring it on you."

"How close are you to saying yes?"

"I'm close. Close to moving out there, anyhow."

"Pretty tough choice, having to decide whether you want to live in Hollywood or Gully Creek."

"I live in Lubbock. That makes it easier. We've talked about me working for End Zone Productions—like running the office. They have a lot of things going on. *Stud-Lovable* is getting ready to shoot, finally. They've inherited a project from Paramount. They have a TV series going to pilot. They both want me to work there."

"You can handle that with ease. I'm sure you'd be a big help to them. It sounds like I'm losing a trusty assistant but gaining the sister-in-law I never had. What'll I do around here?"

"Iris. She can do everything I can do, and do it better. Pay her a lot of money and keep her busy—for your own safety."

"I'll buy you dinner," I said, standing up.

She stood up. "Where?"

"Where else? I think it's meatloaf night."

"I'll meet you there. I have to make some calls."

We strolled out of the club together.

"I'm glad we've had this talk." I grinned.

"Me too. It was important."

"These things needed to be said."

"Yes, they did. *Now* can we fuck?"

Walking away to her car, she looked back, still laughing at her own exit line.

Part Seven

All in the Game

71

In many ways my life from September through December wasn't worth donating to the homeless.

I rarely saw my busy wife and Beverly Hills dog, Kelly Sue had resigned and moved out to the Coast, which left me with one less pal to hang out with, the weather in West Texas was either too hot or too cold—and sometimes a norther—and when the Fightin' Roosters got off to a 4–1 start on their season, more than one sportswriter wrote that the Tornadoes were the second-best team in Gully Creek.

You could have blamed our four losses to start the season on the fact that Budget Fowler pretended his ankle was pinching and didn't play. Or you could have blamed it on our defense being slower than humidity, which was T. J.'s profound description.

The loss in the opener to Kansas City 24–14 wasn't so disheartening. Shea Luckett threw a couple of touchdown passes. Even the performance in Oakland wasn't totally embarrassing. We could blame the 28–17 defeat on three phony zebra calls that kept Oakland drives going. Some kind of Ukranian asshole kicked a fifty-seven-yard field goal to beat us in Seattle 17–14. What depressed us the most was that we could have beaten San Diego so easily, except that ReRun Moses fumbled right at the Chargers' goal, and Laddy Walls later dropped a fifteen-yard touchdown pass that hit him in the chest, and yet we only lost 28–24.

T.J. somehow controlled his temper in the locker room after the San Diego loss. He told LaDaminion Walls not to worry about dropping that easy touchdown pass, it wouldn't happen again. It mainly wouldn't happen again, T.J. said, because he never intended to *call* the fucking play again.

When he went over to Rerun Moses, the coach said, "Moses, have you ever heard of Mr. John Heisman?"

ReRun said, "Sure. The old co-atch. They named the trophy after him I should have won."

"You finished third in the Heisman vote. Budget Fowler came closer than you did—and Budget would have won it if it hadn't been for another shithead Notre Dame quarterback, but that ain't my point. Did you ever hear what Mr. John Heisman said about fumbling?"

ReRun shook his head no.

T.J. said, "Mr. John Heisman said it's better to die a baby than fumble the football. You want to think about that for a while?"

ReRun said, "I played like a two-rid, Co-atch. I few-checked up."

T.J. said, "If you're telling me you played like a turd and you fucked up, I'm not gonna argue with you."

The failures of those first four games moved T.J. to put up a big sign on the wall of the home dressing room that said:

**BAD TEAMS ARE CREATIVE.
THEY CAN ALWAYS FIND A
FUCKING WAY TO LOSE.**

As if that would fix things.

Our only consolation was that the other expansion teams also lost all four games, and by worse scores, and without looking as good. There were some encouraging signs. Shea Luckett for one. Dandy arm. Pluribus Uram for another. Good hands, didn't mind traffic. ReRun Moses was doing his best to give us a running attack. And we dressed well.

Jim Tom Pinch called to make me feel better.

"I was coming down to do a piece on the Tornadoes," he said, "but I think I'll wait till you start playing football."

Before our all-important home opener against the Chiefs I called Budget Fowler into my office to see what I could do to stop his ankle from pinching. Here I was, the guy who'd paid for the B-1 bomber, but I couldn't get it off the runway. His daddy came with him.

I said, "Budge, have we got a problem I don't know about?"

He said, "I haven't been treated right."

I said, "Are you joking? I'm paying you enough to feed your whole state of Oklahoma for a year. You want the million back I knocked off your contract? If that'll get you in a football suit, fine. We need you."

"You'll have to talk to our agent," Harold said.

"I thought *you* were his agent," I said.

"I was, but Budget got a chance to be bigger than he is. Budget can be big like a city, you know what I'm sayin'? We needed help to do that with."

"Who's your agent now?"

"He'll be here in a minute. He's talkin' to T.J."

"He's in town?"

Budget said, "Yeah, he flew in last night. He recognized the importance of my situation as it pertains to my predicament and come on down here."

About then was when Dreamer Tatum came in the door.

"Clyde, my man. How you be?"

I could only chuckle as I stood and shook hands. Dreamer was prosperously dressed in a dark three-piece suit. Carried a briefcase.

"I might have known," I said.

We visited for a while, told some war stories, replayed some games that held Budget's interest. Budget found it hard to believe the ground used to cause fumbles.

Dreamer eventually said, "Clyde, let's you and me go drink some whiskey in private, see if we can get my hoss here back in the rodeo."

We went over to the club and took the same table where I'd heard that Shake Tiller was Humphrey Bogart and Kelly Sue Woodley was Ingrid Bergman.

Boy, I was a sloppy GM, I learned from Dreamer. I'd left bonus clauses out of Budget's contract, but Dreamer was sure it was an oversight.

Dreamer said, "Clyde, you and me know football talent when we see it. I've never seen a franchise like him. This kid's got the physique of a heavyweight fighter and the speed of a sprinter—with moves in between."

"Not when his ankle's pinching."

"We're gonna get that done right now, baby." He took a legal pad and a pen out of his briefcase. "See, one thing is, Budget's been bothered by Avis having a bad year at TCU. Kid comes back to try to win the Heisman and he's got no team with him and a dunce cap for a coach. No help at all. I don't have to tell you how bad the Frogs are, Clyde."

No, he didn't. The Frogs had lost their first six games by a combined score of 259–0, and the toughest part of their schedule was still ahead. Average attendance for home games was down to fifteen thousand, and Avis's ankle was pinching badly. Coach John Smith was saying it called for more Bible study. Rabbit Tyrance was saying he'd known them all and he believed in the things John Smith was trying to put in place. Chancellor Dollarhyde was out of detox and devoting his attention to academic matters. I'd written him a note suggesting some things he could do with his annual fund drive if he didn't get rid of John Smith and Rabbit Tyrance by the end of the season. I seriously doubted if mine was the only letter he'd received on the subject.

I asked Dreamer if he was going to represent Avis Fowler.

"I've got him," he said. "He'll go high but he's no Budget."

We got it done for Budget by me giving in on every demand. Dreamer could brag that he got my other knee.

Budget would receive $100,000 for every game in which he gained over one hundred yards from scrimmage, $200,000 for every game in which he gained over two hundred yards from scrimmage, $200,000 for every game-winning touchdown he scored, $300,000 if he went to the pro bowl, $300,000 if he was selected on the Associated Press's All-Pro first team, $500,000 if the Tornadoes made the playoffs, $1 million if we won the AFC title, and $2 million if we won the Super Bowl. I laughed out loud when Dreamer divulged that he was getting 30 percent of it all.

Finally, Dreamer wanted one more thing. It wasn't a deal breaker, he said, just a thought. He was familiar with End Zone Productions and wondered if Shake Tiller could use Budget in any small parts during the off-season—Budget really liked movies and wanted acting to be his next career. I said I'd inquire.

"He's real good at the limp," I commented.

I asked Dreamer where he was headed from here. He said he was off to negotiate with Nike.

72

Everybody came to Gully Creek for the home opener in early October. The G-5 brought Big Ed and Big Barb, then went out to LA and brought Barb and Hume and Shake and Kelly Sue. The Bookmans and Shake and Kelly Sue all stayed in guest rooms at 10 Main Street. It was a house party, but with Barb and her mother and Kelly Sue to do the chores instead of Maydee and Garnett. I doubted if Big Barb had made a bed in forty years, but I got the idea that she enjoyed the quaintness of it, and I could tell she was intrigued by the dishwasher and disposal.

Jim Tom Pinch, big-time sportswriter, even came for the occasion. I put him up in one of Tommy Earl's town houses with a fully stocked bar and fridge and his own Cadillac-Buick and blank receipts for lodging and car rental. He arrived early enough to be further entertained by Iris McKinney for two days.

He said, "I think the Tornadoes may already be my favorite team, but it's too bad football has to fuck up a perfectly good weekend."

There was no question that the disturbance in front

of the stadium detracted from the festive atmosphere of our home opener.

We'd named it West Texas Stadium and I was extremely proud of it. Seating all the way around made it a perfect bowl. Natural turf. No advertising anywhere. A soft drink or bank didn't give us the scoreboard or the two huge outdoor TV screens at both ends. Big Ed's pocket did it all.

The call came when we were already up in Big Ed's luxury box, eating and drinking and complimenting Big Barb on her carpet and furniture and the tasteful way she'd had it decorated. I'd invited Tommy Earl and Tracy to join us. I hadn't seen Tracy in a while. She still looked too tight and too cheap, but Tommy Earl was still proud of his trophy.

Ben Glenn, the police chief, was calling to tell me there were all these nitwits down on the street who were angry about our name. Over a hundred protesters, he estimated. Yelling, chanting, waving placards.

"They say tornadoes kill people," he said. "They're sayin' you better announce you're changing the name of the team or they'll starve theyselves to death."

"What do they look like?" I asked.

"There's nobody I've ever seen before. They look like all them hippies used to look. But some look older— might have had their houses blowed away at one time or another."

"Do they have a spokesman?"

"A what?"

"A leader. Organizer."

"Yeah, there's a scruffy old boy seems to be in charge, hair down to his belt. He's the one wants 'Armadillos.' Got him a sign. Others want 'Hogs,' 'Chaparrals,' 'Mesquite' . . ."

"*Mesquite?* The West Texas Mesquite, great."

" 'Mules' . . ."

"Christ."

" 'Quail,' 'Geese' . . . What you want me to do? I can't shoot 'em."

"I'll think of something. Just leave 'em alone."

I informed everyone of what was going on downstairs.

Big Ed said, "A *protest?* We're a football team, we're not gonna blow anybody's house away! Who stirred 'em up? We got some kind of goddamn guru in town I don't know about?"

Barbara Jane said, "The Fighting Gurus—that's not a bad name for a team. Why didn't we think of it?"

Shake said, "I like it. What are our colors?"

Barb said, "Cumulus."

Kelly Sue said, "Cumulus and blue sky."

Big Ed said, "I don't think this is all that funny, frankly."

Big Barb said, "People just don't have enough to do these days."

Big Ed said, "College students, I'll bet. Pissing away Daddy's money. One of these days there's not gonna be anybody in our universities but American football players and Korean SAT's! I hope I live to see it."

Tommy Earl said, "Somebody ought to go down there and tell the fuckers this is a football stadium, not an abortion clinic."

The way it was handled, I reached Iris in our lavish press box. She was with Jim Tom. They were having a pre-game snack of barbecue ribs. It had been Kelly Sue's idea to hire Bust Out Jonah to cater our home games.

On my instructions, Iris rounded up one of the high school bands and a group of our Funnelettes in their playsuits. Together they serenaded and entertained down on the street until all the protesters were stoned and taking naps on the concrete.

* * *

Budget Fowler's running and Shea Luckett's passes kept us in the game the whole first half. Our defense would give up a touchdown, but we'd drive and tie it up. The half ended 21–21.

We fell behind 24–21 halfway through the third quarter after the Chiefs' placekicker booted an ungodly fifty-five-yard field goal.

But we got lucky in the last quarter. Andre Humphrey, our Florida State felon, who'd been nicknamed "Felon" by Royce Harper, stripped the ball away from a Chief runner, and recovered it inside their thirty-five. Budget immediately tore off a thirty-two-yard touchdown run, and we went ahead.

Then Fryer Pye made a leaping interception that gave us the ball on the Kansas City forty-two, and Budget ripped off a forty-two-yard touchdown run. For the day, Budget gained 209 yards from scrimmage and we won the game 35–24.

I went down on the sideline for the last four minutes and congratulated all our coaches and players. Hugs and cult handshakes abounded.

Budget reminded me that he'd earned $200,000 by gaining over two hundred yards from scrimmage.

T.J. said, "We were luckier than a three-dick coyote, but I'll take it."

Hungover and pussy-whipped, Jim Tom nevertheless managed to bat out a deadline story for *SM*. His lead read:

By Jim Tom Pinch

Outlined against a blue-gray October sky, the Four Horsemen rode again last Sunday, but this time it was across a desolate West Texas prairie. While their names are still Pestilence, Famine, Death, and Destruction in dramatic lore, they were all rolled into one when a hoss named Budget Fowler burst on the football scene and galloped around in such stupendous fashion, an urgent plea was sent from the press box up to Grantland Rice to come back down here and help out with the adjectives.

Desolate prairie? Jim Tom heard about it four days later after I'd read his story in the magazine. I called him in New York and said, "What is this shit? I give you Iris and you give me *desolate?*"

73

The note I received from my wife, which she wrote after she got back to the Coast, went a long way toward making me feel better about things in general. Not that I was preparing to write a letter of my own to the human race and apologize for taking up space in it.

Barb's note said:

Dear One:
I feel so ashamed. Selfish, dumb, embarrassed—and anything else you want to add to the list. Try thoughtless, that's a good one.

Why do I feel all these things?

Because I did not completely realize until I came down there last week what all you have been up to, what an incredible undertaking it has been, and what it all means to you.

It was so much fun to see you so involved in everything, and to watch you trying to hide your enthusiasm and pride in what you have accomplished.

How could I have not known all that? Why

did I have to be in a football stadium again to realize it?

I will tell you why. It is because I have been so frivolously self-absorbed in my own shit, like I'm fucking Joan Crawford or somebody.

Well, I'm not Joan Crawford. She didn't go to Paschal.

B.C., I am so proud of what you have done— and are doing. I am so very sorry I have not been more supportive or sympathetic or whatever a good wife should have been. Please blame most of it on Hollywood and let me off with a suspended sentence.

I love you, and Hume says, "Stomp the Seahawks, Daddy."

My note back to Barb read:

Dear Vivien:

Thanks for fighting so hard for me to get the part. I feel sure I can handle it as well as Clark could have. I only hope they put in more love scenes for the two of us.

I do have a problem with the title, however, and would like to speak to Cubby about it. My main question is: gone with WHAT wind?

Like, why should we care if a wind is gone if we don't know where it came from in the first place, or who it belongs to?

I would like to suggest *Melancholy Wind*. What do you think?

One more question. How long have you been British?

See you at Tara,
Beely Claude

74

Parity in the National Football League was something I detested when I was a broadcaster, and often said so on the air, which was another reason the network executives didn't shower me with begging and whimpering to keep me from leaving the business.

The thing called parity didn't exist when I played the game, when I was a great American with the Giants. The teams that worked the hardest, spent some money, and used their heads were the teams that won consistently. Good coaches, smart systems, and competitive athletes were the keys to success. If the franchise didn't go the pocket to have all that, it didn't win, and didn't deserve to win. It was Atlanta.

Then along came this idea to legislate equality. I don't know where it came from. I'd like to think it came from a bunch of cloud-brained counter-culture idealogues out of the sixties getting control of the league, except that every football person I ever knew missed the sixties completely—they thought Vince Lombardi ran the country and Ohio State–Michigan was a better way to spend an afternoon than wondering if the answer was blowing in the wind.

It's more likely that parity somehow became a good friend of the owners—maybe they met at a yacht race—and the owners decided they could all make more money from television if there were more good teams around, which meant that the good teams should slip to the level of the bad teams.

Whatever the reason, I came to the conclusion in our first season that I didn't just like parity now, I loved parity. My next new car would be a parity. When my broker wanted to churn the account again, I'd tell him to sell Akagi Tissue and buy NFL parity. If Barbara Jane and I ever got divorced, I'd marry parity. And why not? It was parity, more than anything else, that got us to the Super Bowl.

By other names you could have called it the expansion draft, that wonderfully benevolent gesture which helped us stock the team with just enough experience, and then our pushover schedule, which essentially guaranteed us six wins over the other expansionistas, a word Barbara Jane coined in broad daylight.

It would be hard to estimate how much fun I would have had as a broadcaster talking about the Tornadoes winning the AFC West with our foolish-looking 8–8 record, and then winning the two play-off games on a combination of sheer luck and what was either the ineptness or the financial interest of the zebras.

"Break up the Tornadoes," I might have said.

T.J. liked to think that his coaching expertise and inspirational leadership had made the difference in our season. And Budget liked to think he and Nike carried us all by themselves without any help from their blockers. But it had to be said that we couldn't have made it to Jacksonville for the Super Bowl without our opponents sinking to the level of guttersnipes.

We realized shortly after the middle of the season how critical that first win over Kansas City had been.

Almost every team in the league was playing no better than .500 ball. Parity was in control. So what that meant was this: given the fact that we were thrashing—and would continue to thrash—the other expansionistas, we might need to beat only one more credible team to win the division, or at least make the play-offs as a wild card.

Our record was 4–6 at that moment. We'd lost to Oakland and Denver, but we'd easily beaten London and Hawaii at home—Shea Luckett and Pluribus Uram becoming a nifty passing combination to complement Budget's running, and we'd trounced Mexico City on the road, Budget gaining 267 yards and another $200,000, me narrowly evading Naomi Lauranette Foster, avoiding all scorpions—the state bird—and coming away without what Weffert called "Monty Zoomer's revenge."

A zebra had cost us that Oakland game. We had the Raiders down 17–14 on a rainy day. They launched a late drive that carried to our twenty, but we held for three plays. Then on fourth down Hepatitis blazed in on a safety blitz and hit their quarterback just as he was throwing a pass. The pass fell incomplete. It should have been our ball to run out the clock, except a late flag turned up on the field. Hepatitis was called for roughing the passer.

T.J. went nutso-wacko and I do believe he would have shot the referee if he'd had a gun. Didn't help. Oakland scored two plays later and we bitched all the way home about the 21–17 loss.

The Denver loss was a different story. One of those games where all of our guys took the same day off. It looked as if the Broncos had put in our game plan instead of Richard Yates. Their defense seemed to know everything we tried to do—and we were embarrassed 38–10.

Even Budget hadn't looked like himself, and in a

home game. He was held to under one hundred yards and suffered two instances of self-tackleization.

When a team has a bad day like that, the best thing a coach can do is write it off as if it never happened. That was how T.J. handled it in the locker room. He never mentioned the result. He just sought out a few players and calmly discussed fundamentals.

The people of Gully Creek had wanted to "do something" to entertain the "foreigners"—the Brits and Hawaiians—when they came to town. I had to explain to the locals that pro teams didn't have time to be entertained on the road. Pro teams went to a destination on Saturday, held a light workout, ate dinner, went to bed, played the game the next day, and hauled ass immediately thereafter. I further felt the need to point out that the players on the Knights and Volcanoes were Americans.

Neville Trill didn't make the trip with the Knights. He was on a world tour with Bloody Hemorrhoids. I was disappointed. I'd have enjoyed taking him shopping in town and then to dinner at Them Two Women.

I did run into Horace and Craig in Them Two Women the week of the game, and I couldn't resist sharing the information with them that the star of the Knights was a quarterback named Laura or Larry Frazier.

"You don't mean it?" Craig said alertly.

"I do mean it."

We discussed what Laura or Larry Frazier had undergone in the way of surgery.

"He is so brave," Horace said. "He truly is. We would love to have him stay in our B and B, you know."

I said he would be obligated to stay with the team at the Westerner in Lubbock. All of our visiting teams stayed at the Westerner in Lubbock.

"Perhaps he can stop by for a drink," Craig said. "We'll call the hotel Saturday evening."

"I can't wait for the game!" said Horace.

"Do you go to the games?" I couldn't help asking.

Horace said, "Oh, dear boy, we have season tickets. Our seats are terrific. We're right on the thirty-five-goal yard."

Laura-Larry Frazier, or the "transmorferdite," as T.J. called him, had a good day against us, even as his team lost handily 41–21. He hit three long touchdown passes on our nickel defense, for which Hepatitis Diggs caught a whole cradle of shit.

But back to our dilemma. Of the six remaining games, three were against expansionistas, which we figured to bag, and the other three were against Denver on the road and San Diego and Seattle at home. Somehow or other, we needed to bag one of those.

T.J. seized the moment as an opportune time for his cheating lecture to the squad. I happened to walk into the dressing room in the middle of it, having been on the way there in the first place to tell three of our players that Tommy Earl was complaining about rent payments being long overdue.

"That white Ivy League turd who can't cover deep is one of 'em," Tommy Earl had said. "I guess Harvard don't teach months of the year."

I said Jeff Davidson was from a wealthy Eastern family, and wealthy Eastern families traditionally didn't believe in paying for things unless threatened with a lawsuit.

T.J. was saying, ". . . and I want to see more late hits. There ain't nothin' wrong with a late hit when you're winning the game—but not on third down. If it's not third down and we're up by a good margin, treat yourself. Let some sissy know when we put on our hats we play Tornado football.

"I want to see more holding. Big Load, you ain't holding often enough to suit me. And you ain't either, Real Butter. You people need to study Royce in the films. Royce holds on ever damn play, and his get-caught percentage is lowest in the league. Why do you think we run Budget over Royce so many times? Work on your holding skills, men.

"You cornerbacks, I'll swear. How many times I gotta tell you that most chucks don't get called? If you can't chuck the receiver inside the five-yard rule, chuck the sumbitch *after* that! I don't care if you undress him—I'll take a penalty over a touchdown, and you take the fryer pye, Fried Pie. And you safeties. Our pass rush is savin' your butts. Everybody knows you're slow and you ain't got no bicycles to hop on, so you just gotta rely on your savvy. But aside from that, you can put your hands in a man's face and push off, can't you? You forget that? Again, I'll take the penalty over a touchdown all eight days of the week.

"Our safety blitz ain't doin' us much good. It especially don't do us much good when we got it called and it don't happen. Bobby's gonna work harder with you on that. But I'll tell you what I'm not in the mood to hear from any of you again, all of you. 'I come unfocused, Coach.' That's bullshit, is all that is. You don't come unfocused in a football game. You want to come unfocused, you find another line of work. Schoolteacher or some fuckin' thing.

"I've only got one minor complaint with you defensive linemen. I don't think some of you are usin' enough grease on your jerseys. Vaseline's cheap, men, and it ain't goin' out of style. Other than your ability, it's the only other thing you've got to counteract them sumbitches who can hold an elephant.

"Offense, you're clickin' real good. All I'm gonna add is more picks. Pluribus and Todd, you're both good at it, so I don't think we'll get caught too many times when we need to block some fucker out of his man coverage.

"I don't need to tell you we're in this dogfight. We got us a chance to write sports history. We can be the first expansion team ever to make the play-offs in our first season. If we could do that, I'd cut off my left arm up to here. I'm right-handed, of course."

T.J. always thought it helped to leave 'em laughing.

75

To explain the poor performance of the Tornadoes in Honolulu, where we barely got away with a win, you first had to take into account that our American Airlines charter required fourteen hours to make the journey. This was because we were delayed getting out of San Francisco by a fog that reached all the way down to every Bay Area resident's plate of eggplant milanese with basil chutney on the green gnocchi.

Next you had to consider that most of the staff were on strike at the old nostalgia-cloaked Royal Hawaiian Hotel, where Big Ed insisted we stay. He wanted to re-live memories of what may have been the happiest days of his life—that time when he was a devilish young man who dined and danced in the tropical breezes of the out-door pavilion with Mamie Stover's girls before taking them to bed and telling them how many Japs he'd killed lately.

Then you had to take into consideration that our team, after being released on Saturday night to see the sights, got hopelessly trapped in an awesome mai tai front that blew in out of nowhere on Waikiki Beach. Rumor also had it that Shea Luckett, our handsome quarterback, ran into Rachel Akagi, or "Mandy Rice-Davies," that night and she drove him out to look at the moonlit waves on Pipeline. When the statute of limitations was over, I'd ask him about it.

Finally, you had to give some thought to the fact that Hawaii Coach Peanut Griffin had spent days and nights watering down the natural turf in Aloha Stadium and converting it into ankle-deep mud in an effort to slow down Budget Fowler.

Those four things combined to hold us to a 6–0 victory, which we wouldn't have accomplished if it hadn't been for two fumble recoveries that set up field goals by Joachim ("Swasty") Schnaufer. One fumble was caused by Yohance Reed's hard lick. The other time, the ball just happened to roll under Sheep Dog McWorter while he was lying down.

The ironic side of it all wasn't lost on Big Ed. As he said over his first Chivas-rocks on the flight home:

"Hell of a thing. A German beat the Jap on Pearl Harbor Day."

In between the wins over Mexico City and Hawaii, the Denver Broncos beat us again, but we made them work for it this time. The final score was only 27–20. They at least saw the real Budget Fowler. He gained 173 yards from scrimmage and it was his tough ball carrying that kept us in it till the middle of the last quarter.

There was a chance that our second Denver game might best be remembered for Sheep Dog McWorter getting thrown out for intentional biting. After being penalized twice for the infraction in the first half, a Denver runner's hand wound up in Sheep Dog's mouth again in the third quarter, and the aging "Psycho" was sent to the sideline to stay.

T.J. took it well. He said he'd never fault one of his players for trying.

The coach even held in his anger after the San Diego loss, although nobody had ever pissed away a game like we did. We'd played well the whole day, every part of our offense clicking, and we were leading the Chargers 35–31 and the Chargers were back on their own thirty-five-yard line with only two seconds left to play.

Up in the luxury box, Big Ed had lit a cigar and we were congratulating ourselves on being in the play-offs as San Diego's last play unfolded. A long pass toward a Chargers receiver who was waiting for the ball on our forty-yard line near the sideline.

So what? Our cornerback Edgemon Hill was right there with the receiver, right behind him. All Edgemon Hill had to do was let the receiver catch the ball, then tackle him or push him out of bounds—game over.

But that wasn't what Edgemon Hill did. He suddenly darted in front of the receiver and jumped up to make the interception. And the ball sailed over him and landed in the arms of the receiver, who then pranced untouched down the sideline for the winning touchdown.

"What the hell was *that?*" Big Ed said.

I said, "It was basically the dumbest fucking thing I've ever seen."

Big Ed said, "Would you mind telling me what god-damn good an interception was gonna do us?"

I said, "I think that might be a question T.J. will ask Edgemon Hill."

"Good God a-mighty," Big Ed said. "The son of a bitch went to Notre Dame too. I guess that's supposed to make me feel better."

I looked down on the field and watched Edgemon Hill on his knees beating his fist on the ground at his stupidity. That was while T.J. was stomping on his head-set and kicking any loose object he could find.

However, T.J. was calm in the locker room. I stood nearby as he sat down next to the tearful cornerback and said, "That play was my fault. I lost the game. I thought I'd covered every eventuality that could happen in a football game, but I missed this one. I just flat forgot to tell all you people that when it comes down to one last play, it's more important to win a game than it is to make an interception. I don't know how I could have overlooked it, but I sure did."

Later, when I was alone with T.J. in his office, he said, "Conventional wisdom's not on our side, Billy Clyde. The conventional wisdom is, our defense sucks."

What was worse than losing a football game was that I almost lost a good friend later that day when Coogle Boone blew up his home with him in it. Thank goodness—or the Skipper—for one thing. Deana Merle had been out in the backyard when it happened or she'd have gone up with it.

The unlucky mayor did it to himself by accident. He was sitting on his glass-enclosed front porch in the house on Old Wolf Flat Road smoking a menthol cigarette while breathing from an oxygen tank to treat his emphysema.

Yeah, you could say it was dumb, I guess, if you were a nonsmoker.

Fortunately, Coogle didn't suffer any serious injury, other than being without a home, and he was released from the hospital in Plainview that night. In fact, the minor burns he sustained weren't as bad as the bruises he got from Deana Merle slapping him around.

I'd rushed over to see him while he was still in the hospital, and he tried to explain how it happened.

He said, "Aw, Billy, like I usually do when she ain't around, I was just having a smoke while I was breathin' through my respirator, and somehow the cigarette did something it ought not to have did."

Dean Merle said, "Name of God, if he ain't a bigger

idiot than any of them Three Stooges we watch on TV—not that we've got a TV no more."

According to the Lubbock paper, witnesses said the explosion sent flames spiraling over one hundred feet in the air and could be seen as far away as Wolf Flat.

Assistant Fire Chief H. M. ("Hook") Louis of Plainview was quoted saying, "It went off like a bomb and sent flames right up through the front of the house. When we got there the house was pretty near d-o-stroyed, and a tree in the yard was ablaze, and power lines was on fire in the street. It's a miracle nobody got kilt."

I moved Coogle and Deana Merle into one of Tommy Earl's condos in Tumbleweed Pointe that evening. The condo was fully furnished and cable-ready, and Iris loaded it up with all kinds of food and drink.

I told them they could live there rent free for as long as they wished, not to worry about a thing. I told them if they liked the condo and decided they wanted to buy it, or buy something else on the property, I'd loan them the money and they could take their own sweet time paying it back. I said they'd both done me a lot of favors in the past and it was my privilege to help them out. Deana Merle cried and gave me a bear hug.

It was the least I could have done for a smoker. And it was also the night I quit.

76

For our last regular season home game against the Seahawks—it merely meant the division title to us—T. J. Lambert was all over the media, pleading with our fans to "open up a can of thunder."

In the newspapers and on TV and radio, T.J. said, "On Sunday I want to hear 72,500 nonstop screamin', thunderin' lunatics makin' them Seattle visitors think they're in a real tornado."

As it turned out, Budget Fowler had a little more to do with it than the screaming, thundering lunatics, who did scream and thunder as well as crash and burn from the contents in their thermos bottles and fruit jars.

When it counted the most, when we needed to drive eighty yards for a winning touchdown in the last four minutes, Budget carried the ball fourteen straight times and rammed into the end zone from three yards out with only fourteen seconds left on the clock. That gave us the 24–21 victory and gave him $700,000—two hundred large for scoring the winning touchdown and five hundred large for us winning the division.

I hadn't thought about the money in the midst of the

drama, but Budget spoke of it in our jubilant dressing room.

"Way to go, Budge," I said, giving him an embrace. "You were something else today. Took it to the shed. Did you get tired out there?"

"Ball ain't that heavy, baby." He grinned. "I took it to the *bank* too—you know what I'm sayin'?"

My guess was, a team of experts from NASA and MIT were called in to help the NFL figure out who won the other divisions and who the wild cards were. The formulas were too confusing for normal human beings to understand or even play like they did.

In our conference Pittsburgh won the Central with an 8–8 record over Cincinnati and Baltimore, which also had 8–8 records, and the East was won by Buffalo's 9–7 record over Miami's 9–7. The three wild cards were Miami, Baltimore, and Cincinnati.

Over in the NFC, it was the same story. Washington won the East with 9–7 over Dallas's 9–7. San Francisco won the West with 9–7 over Carolina's 9–7, but Detroit clearly took the Central with its 9–7 over Atlanta's 7–9. The wild cards were Dallas, Carolina, and New Orleans.

Any fans who were enthusiastic followers of the other expansionistas would have to wait till next year.

The Mexico City Bandits finished 0–16 and Naomi Lauranette Foster vowed to continue her fight to have the franchise moved. She said she would agree to move to almost any city "where one might accidentally, if no other way, trip over an interesting conversation." And what was wrong with Berlin, where she'd been spending some time lately? Wouldn't Berlin, if you stopped to think about it, be a natural rival for London?

The London Knights, behind the leadership of Laura-Larry Frazier, finished 4–12, and Neville Trill said, "It's been a rather diabolical year, all things considered, but I'm quite pleased." It was safe to say that Neville was even more pleased when Bloody Hemorrhoids went platinum.

The Hawaii Volcanoes finished 1–11, having carved out a tough win over Mexico City, but Tokyo Russ said he'd found the experience enjoyable, he'd seen signs of encouragement, and promised to become more involved in the team as soon as he'd exhausted every effort to find his wife.

Through a mathematical error in the play-off formula that wasn't discovered until months later by a professor at MIT, Pittsburgh was forced to go into the wild card round instead of us. It definitely should have been us, but "sir la veeb," to quote Weffert Lorants.

So the Tornadoes got the week off while the Steelers and the three wild cards duked it out in the first round of the play-offs. That was our first stroke of luck.

I took part of the time to go out to the Coast for a few days and lay around the pool at Chateau Briggan with my wife and my dog.

It worked out that I spent some time around the pool, but mostly with Hume. *Stud-Lovable* was in production—an interior scene being shot at Paramount—and Barbara Jane, producer, was in a show-biz mode. That wasn't exactly the same as a French army captain leading an infantry charge at Verdun, but it did keep her preoccupied. She slept with her eyes open and got up two or three times in the middle of each night to make notes.

So many things were going on with End Zone Productions by then, Barb and Shake said it was a good thing they'd hired Kelly Sue to help them keep up with it all. Kelly Sue was doing a fantastic job, Barb said. Very organized, unrattled, good instincts.

"All-star deal. I knew it first. I saw it with my own eyes. I see very well as far as my eyes are concerned," I said, borrowing from America's most-loved sports announcer, the Emmy-winning Larry Hoage.

Shake and Kelly Sue were still living in sin, happy as high school lovers, and as yet there were no plans to fuck it up with marriage.

End Zone Productions now had two TV shows going to pilot, one of which, incredibly enough, was *Melancholy Baby*. They were in partnership with Cubby Butler on that one.

Cubby wanted the actress to be much younger than Barbara Jane was in the feature. That was so the series would "skew with the Gen X's and echo boomers." Barb was saying it wouldn't work if the actress was young—a bimbette teaches English lit in college, oh, sure—and would Cubby mind squirming around on this?

I went over to Paramount one day to have lunch in the commissary with Barb, Shake, and Kelly Sue. While I was there I got the feeling I was being stared at. Then several Tom Cruises and Brad Pitts came over and shook my hand and said congratulations on the season.

The four of us watched the first-round play-off games on Shake's big screen—Pittsburgh against Miami, and Baltimore against Cincinnati. If Pittsburgh won, we'd play Buffalo next week. If Miami won, we'd play the winner of the Baltimore-Cincinnati game.

Barb put show business aside that day to root for Pittsburgh because I told her we'd have a better chance against Buffalo than either Baltimore or Cincinnati.

She asked why I thought so.

I said, "We might run into a blizzard up in Buffalo. In football, weather is the great equalizer."

Shake said, "You don't want bad weather in Buffalo. You can beat Buffalo straight up."

"You keep up with pro ball now, do you?" I said.

Shake said, "Enough to know the AFC East never

sees a ground game. They're all pass-happy in that division. Budget Fowler can run on Buffalo."

Kelly Sue said, "If it was just a matter of cities, wouldn't you have to pull for Miami over Pittsburgh?"

"No," said Shake. "It's the other way around. Miami has too much going for it already. Miami Beach, South Beach, Coconut Grove, Key Biscayne. Miami doesn't deserve to have a winning football team, too."

"Well, just *fuck* Miami, then," Kelly Sue said.

When Pittsburgh won the game, thereby sending us to Buffalo next Sunday, I asked Barb if she wanted to go.

"Do you mind if I skip it, honey?" she said. "I'm up to my neck in problems here."

I said, "No, it's okay. But you're gonna miss out on some good chicken wings—and I know a chic bar where you can get a shot and a beer."

"That's the part that hurts the most."

"You know, if we somehow beat Buffalo, we'll probably play Pittsburgh. Want to go to Pittsburgh?"

"It's the same deal. I've got these problems here in Tinsel Town."

"Tinsel Town," I said. "It's all alabaster and sham."

"Right." She grinned. "With a popcorn machine for a heart. But if you make it to the Super Bowl, count me in, sport."

77

The game of football has always been populated with smart coaches and dumb coaches. If you wondered how dumb coaches ever found employment in the college ranks, all you had to do was look to the athletic director or the chancellor, and if you wondered how dumb coaches ever found employment in the pro ranks, all you had to do was look to the general manager or the owner. And if you looked deep enough, it invariably came down to money.

I had no idea how much Buffalo had been paying Clipper Hudley—until our game got him fired, I mean—but it must not have equaled the salary of a convenience store clerk.

Clipper Hudley was one of those football people who'd made a career out of having a nickname. Edgar Hudley couldn't have gone anywhere in life, except to a job at Prudential, maybe, but Clipper Hudley made All-America tackle at Boston College, and strictly on his nickname. Then he got into coaching and because other coaches could beat him regularly, they helped him stay in coaching. He slowly became lovable old Clipper Hudley, "the kind of man you want your son to play for." He became a part of the Good Old Boy Coaches' Network. Half of the coaches in the NFL had recommended him for the Buffalo job.

So it was that Clipper Hudley made a decision on the opening kickoff of our game that was as far removed from intelligence as Gully Creek was from the Beverly Hills flats.

We kicked off to the Bills and their returner, a little guy named Zippy Jackson, picked up the ball in his own end zone. He brought it out, darting here and there, making our guys miss him, and suddenly he broke free down the sideline. It looked like he might go all the way, but he cut back to the middle of the field, and Hepatitis Diggs mercifully made a dive and tripped him up at the fifty-yard line. Close call.

And then we saw a flag. Swell. Always fun to see a flag on the first play of a game. I instantly figured face mask—and the Bills would get fifteen more yards, be on our thirty-five. They already had great field position on a subfreezing day with snow in the forecast.

But the flag was for offsides on the kickoff against us. That was where Clipper Hudley's colossal brain cells did us the favor. He took the penalty—we would kick off again.

The thing that happened next was what Clipper Hudley deserved for being so stupid. We kicked off to Zippy Jackson again, but this time he lost his footing at his own ten-yard line, staggered, juggled the ball, lost it, and Hepatitis recovered the fumble on the Bills' eight-yard line.

In two plays Budget was in the end zone and Swasty kicked the point and we took a 7–0 lead that Buffalo could never overcome. We scored another touchdown on a pass from Shea Luckett to Todd Mitchell, a twenty-two-yard fade route, and the Bills got a touchdown in the second quarter after they recovered a ReRun Moses fumble, which I thought the ground caused, on our four-yard line.

Nobody even threatened to score in the whole second half. That was because the snowstorm made the game look like Norway. A cross-country ski racer couldn't have made a first down. We took it 14–7.

It was T.J.'s idea to do a funny thing, and I went with him. We went over to the Buffalo locker room and T.J. presented Clipper Hudley with the game ball. For taking that offsides penalty on the opening kickoff.

"We have confidence in our return game," Clipper said, not thinking the gesture was as funny as T.J. did. "We thought the kid could break one."

We?

The snowstorm let up enough for our American charter to get out of town that night, but it didn't keep Clipper Hudley from getting fired.

The Steelers had beaten Miami 35–17 in the other AFC play-off game, so we couldn't devote much time to reveling in our conquest on the flight home. We had to think about going to Pittsburgh on Sunday for the championship game of the American Conference.

Remembering that Budget Fowler would have $1 million riding on it, less Dreamer Tatum's 30 percent, distracted me momentarily from the game plan T.J. was trying to discuss.

You could argue that the coach of the Steelers, Ears McBride, was dumber than Clipper Hudley and find thousands to agree with you—surely every football fan in Pittsburgh to start with. It was something that would be debated around the league for years to come.

Ears McBride was another coach who'd failed upward. The coaching fraternity liked him because he could tell jokes and they liked his poker slang, which I'd heard my share of in two expansion committee meetings.

I hadn't been able to forget that a full house was a "cramped cottage," and a hand with three queens in it was a "beauty parlor."

Our battle with the Steelers came later in the day after the Detroit Lions had upset the Washington Redskins to win the NFC, and it was what you'd call your basic thriller, nothing heart patients needed to observe too often. It was a three-pack Juicy Fruit game for me.

The Steelers scored first, but we tied it 7–7 on a thirty-four-yard run by Budget. They scored again, but we tied it 14–14 on a long pass from Shea to Pluribus Uram. They scored again in the fourth quarter to go ahead 21–14, but then we scored, remarkably, with only forty-five seconds left in the game, when they tried a pass to keep a drive going, run the clock. Fryer Pye made a one-handed interception and zigzagged sixty-two glorious yards for a touchdown.

His celebration dance in the end zone, before he was mauled by teammates, drew a horrendous chorus of boos from the home crowd, but I thought Fred Astaire and Gene Kelly would have been impressed with it.

Then Fryer encouraged another wave of boos and hisses when he responded to the crowd by giving them several gestures that more or less said: "May all of your cocks fall in the Susquehanna River and wind up on fishing boats in Chesapeake Bay."

What then happened on the conversion try became a prime candidate for any video of NFL bloopers.

We lined up in a "swinging gate," as if we were going to try for two points, sending Shea, the quarterback, Buddha, the center, Laddy, the tight end, and Royce and Real Butter, the guards, way over to the right.

Our other six players took their usual positions in front of the goalpost.

Teams often did this to give the defense something extra to worry about, but the "swinging gate" would quickly shift back to normal positions at the scrimmage line, and the routine extra point would be kicked.

Figuring we were obviously going to kick the point and send the game into overtime, Ears McBride nonchalantly ignored our "swinging gate"—and so did the Pittsburgh defense.

Whereupon, Shea called for the snap from center, as calmly as he could, being stupefied, and walked into the end zone for the two points.

That was how we won the game 22–21.

The crowd was stunned to silence. Up in our visiting owner's booth, Big Ed was stunned to silence. I was stunned to silence.

All I could do was stand there and look down on the field where four things were taking place at once.

T.J. was being hoisted on the shoulders of some of our players.

The rest of our players were racing onto the field and piling on top of each other and rolling around clutching their sides in laughter.

Ears McBride was being shoved and cussed and swung at by some of his assistant coaches. Police were trying to intervene.

And it had occurred to the offensive unit of the Steelers that they should rush onto the field and try to pound the shit out of the defensive unit of the Steelers.

I turned up the sound on the TV in our booth in time to hear Larry Hoage saying, "Oh, brother. What we have down on the field right now is something this old baritone has never seen before, and I see pretty well as far as my eyes are concerned."

It was a few moments before I realized we were in the Super Bowl.

78

For the first Super Bowl ever held in Jacksonville, Florida, the city rolled out its Atlantic Ocean, its St. Johns River, its Intracoastal Canal, its fishing streams, its far-flung shaded neighborhoods of old and new wealth, its famous golf courses bulkheaded in swamps, its aircraft carriers from the naval base, and probably injected all of its alligators with Valium in an effort to provide hospitality and impress the visitors who came to the place that took pride in calling itself the First Coast.

You learned things from the locals. For one thing, Jacksonville called itself the First Coast because Ponce de León once glanced at it as his ship sailed by, and because Jacksonville was north, almost in Georgia, whereas Miami was south, part of Cuba.

It was a six-hour drive to Miami, but it was only an hour-and-a-half drive to Sea Island, Georgia, where you could see even more golf courses and more far-flung shaded neighborhoods of old and new wealth.

If you liked, it was only a forty-five-minute drive to St. Augustine, which was older than Jerusalem—where you could see the Fountain of Youth—and only a two-

and-a-half-hour drive to Disney World, where you could see Europe.

We got the beaches and Detroit got the river. That meant we were headquartered all week at the Ponte Vedra Colony Resort, right on the ocean, and near the best golf courses, thanks to Big Ed's influence with the commissioner, while the Lions were headquartered at the Gator Summit Convention Hotel downtown, right on the river, and near the stadium.

Which wasn't called the Gator Bowl anymore, as it had been for fifty years—except by football people and local residents. When the Jaguars entered the league and the Gator Bowl got itself revamped, fashionably modernized, luxury-boxed, and private-clubbed, it began to be auctioned off to a series of corporate sponsors.

For our Super Bowl, the huge block-lettered signs on both the west and east facades proudly presented the current name:

FIDUCIARY TRUST 30-YR. TREAS.
MUNICIPALS & 3-MO. T-BILLS
INVESTMENT GROUP STADIUM

Somebody said the company had outbid an organization called http://wwwcschlep/EatScienceN.) by $10 million for the rights.

Detroit's fans outnumbered ours three to one. According to ticket sales, there were forty thousand of them in town, and they were everywhere you looked, gobbling up all the shrimp, even trying out the gator tail.

Most of our fans had driven from West Texas, a three-day and two-night journey, depending on how long they'd been detained by the Gulf Coast casinos that blazed a winding trail from Shreveport to Biloxi.

If any of them had found Git After It, the joint that was making Booger Sanders rich, I wagered they didn't make the game at all—they were still licking honey off the nude dancers and waitresses.

It made sense that the Lions had more people on hand. Detroit came in a fourteen-point favorite, after all. Even our own "family" of sportswriters had been writing that we hadn't played anybody.

Ted Deekins of the *Fort Worth Light & Shopper* took delight in reminding his readers that while Detroit's record of 11–7 didn't appear to be that much better than our 10–8, the Lions had plowed through a much tougher schedule. The Lions had beaten teams like Dallas, Chicago, and Minnesota, in contrast to us beating teams that crawled out of the clown car in a circus.

Herb Strum of the *Lubbock Avalanche Standard* wrote that before the final whistle, we'd stand a good chance of being arrested for masquerading as a football team.

Scoop Beal of the *Amarillo Express-Sandstorm* told his readers that if they wanted to see how to make their own sausage, they should pay attention to what Detroit was going to do to us.

Jimmy Stutts of the *Abilene Times-Bugle* expected the game to be interrupted several times to sweep our blood off the field.

Crew Slammer of the *Dallas Daily Herald* wrote: "The prospects aren't that dismal for the Tornadoes. After they join all the Spanish galleons that went down off the coast of Florida, maybe they'll find a defense among the gold coins."

It was all bulletin-board stuff for T.J.

Privately, I wondered if Weffert had orchestrated it— doing his part for our team's motivation.

Big Ed and Big Barb and Big Ed's big bag of twenty-six golf clubs went to Jacksonville with us on the team charter. Big Ed thought it would look like he was more concerned if he traveled with the team. Big Barb was amazed at the size of the commercial airliner—she hadn't been on one in years.

The G-5 was sent to the Coast and brought back Barb and Hume and Shake and Kelly Sue.

It was beautiful weather in that last week of January, temps in the high seventies mostly, so Barb and Kelly Sue did the beach in front of our hotel every day, soaking up sun while they talked on their cells to End Zone Productions. Hume didn't have a cell but enjoyed barking at the birds and sniffing shells and wondering what a sea turtle was.

Big Ed played at least six golf courses, from Amelia Island to Ponte Vedra and back again. He said that damn TPC course, that thing with the little greens sitting in the middle of all that sand and water, he'd send some F-18s off one of the carriers to napalm that silly son of a bitch.

Big Barb limoed to Sea Island and spent three days with two of her old sorority sisters, one of whom had divorced and remarried and moved there from La Jolla.

There were numerous parties all week, thrown by networks, Nikes, realtors, Ducks Unlimiteds—some on gambling boats—but we felt obligated to attend only one. That was Commissioner Val Emery's intimate little get-together for 3,500 people in the old train station downtown.

Big Ed and I said hello to the Detroit owner, Tyler Watson, and met his new wife, Mopsy. Tyler Watson had made a fortune on Wall Street without going to prison and always wore an orange-and-black-striped Princeton tie. He was so devoted to Princeton, in fact, that he was trying to have the Detroit colors changed from royal blue and silver to orange and black.

Tyler said, "By all means, the very best of luck, but the important thing is just to be here, isn't it?"

"Like shit." I smiled, but Tyler Watson didn't laugh, and Mopsy was admiring a muscular young waiter.

There were the six of us—the Bookmans, Pucketts, and Shake and Kelly Sue. We were supposed to be ten, but Tracy Bruner made Tommy Earl go out on a gambling boat, and Iris and Jim Tom were just a couple of old shut-ins.

We all grabbed one drink in a plastic glass from a bar exclusively serving brands of unheard-of whiskey, plucked one fried shrimp off a passing tray, noticed that a calypso band was threatening to entertain the crowd, and beat it out of there.

We went to The Landing, a shopping mall on the waterfront downtown. We found an expensive restaurant half-empty. We dined on an upstairs outdoor terrace where we could look down on the hordes of fans milling around or squatting in groups, all of them wearing replica jerseys of both teams—our purple, Detroit blue. It was fun to watch them throwing their Kentucky Fried Chicken bones in the St. Johns River.

Shake and Jim Tom went with me three times to sit in on some of the player interviews during the week. They were held in the ballroom of the Seminole Tower Hotel downtown, which was NFL and CBS headquarters. Except for Jim Tom, who was staying with us, the other seven hundred sportswriters that the interviews were held for had to come from Holiday Inns as far away as the Jacksonville airport, or Daytona, or Brunswick, Georgia.

Players had learned not to say much about their opponents at Super Bowl interviews—they didn't want to make a bulletin board.

The Lions' accomplished quarterback, Riley Ferguson, an eight-year veteran, mostly talked about his Domino's Pizza franchises and his collection of antique sports cars, but said he'd studied the films and he had tremendous respect for the Tornadoes' defense.

The Lions' Jamal Booker, their flashy running back, mostly talked about his Nissan dealerships and what he thought were the best long-term buys on the big board, but said he'd studied the films and he had as much tremendous respect for the Tornadoes' defense as anybody else.

The Lions' O. F. ("Oklahoma Face") Wilhite, their all-pro middle linebacker, said he'd studied the films and he had as much tremendous respect for the Tornadoes' offense as any of the Detroit offense did for the Tornadoes' defense, if not more so.

Oklahoma Face Wilhite talked briefly about being a rodeo bull rider during the off season. He said he was working on a country song about it called "Eight Seconds of Thunder," but so far he'd only written one line, which was "eight seconds of thunder, and you."

It was the general view of the sportswriters that our Shea Luckett provided the best copy when he was up on the stage at the microphone.

Our handsome quarterback enthralled the listeners with his detailed description of Hanalei Bay's left curl, and hinted at more than a dozen famous Hollywood actresses he'd nailed when they were teenagers.

Budget Fowler didn't choose to speak at all. He said he'd do his speaking on the field Sunday. But Dreamer Tatum invited himself up on the stage to answer as many questions in regard to Budget's finances as he thought were appropriate. Not many were.

Shake and Jim Tom went with me to the NFL hospitality terrace for a cup of coffee while our Harvard man, Jeff Davidson, was being interviewed.

We left the moment Jeff said he was embarrassed to see the media paying this much attention to a sports event when there were so many more important issues in the country—the need for government to socialize medicine, pay for free insurance, free housing, free transportation, provide jobs for the criminally insane, and keep big business from strangling every . . .

We returned thirty minutes later to find the audience taken with Pluribus Uram trying to describe what it was like at home while his mother was winning the national contest for the house with the most cockroaches in it.

Pluribus was saying, "We did some side-steppin' around there for a few weeks, but when the man brought the check for twenty thousand scoots, we had us a killin' spree, I *mean.*"

The two head coaches appeared on Friday afternoon for the last of their mass interviews before the game.

The Detroit coach, Art ("Double Dutch") Dowdy, went first.

He explained the origin of his nickname for those who weren't all that familiar with his history. He said he'd been called Double Dutch since high school, and he couldn't recall exactly who'd given him the nickname, but he guessed it had something to do with his square head and the fact that he'd always liked cheese.

He said his Lions were ignoring that fourteen-point-favorite thing—they knew anything could happen on a given Sunday. He'd seen a lot of given Sundays in his day, and each one was a different given. He said he hoped the zebras would stay out of it and let the boys play ball.

The one laugh he got was when he stole a line from Lou Holtz and said, "On this team, we're all united in a common goal—to keep my job."

T.J. covered up the Lions with praise. He said he just hoped his team could make a game of it.

"We're just a pack of poor little orphans from a little town in West Texas," he said. "We haven't beaten anybody."

I sort of wished T.J. had thought of a better response than the one he gave the writer who said, "Coach, would you comment on some of the games your team won this season? I believe you've said that some of them turned your stomach."

T.J. said, "I was misquoted on that deal, son. Don't nothin' turn my stomach but two warm titties on my back."

I looked around and to my discomfort counted eight female sportswriters in the audience. I found Weffert in the hotel press room and sent him on a mercy mission. To apologize to the ladies and tell them T.J.'s mind was so much on the game, he'd forgotten he wasn't in a locker room.

Weffert reported back later that the ladies weren't insulted in the least. As a matter of fact, they'd all agreed it was about time a football coach struck a blow for feminism.

79

The hot-air balloon race between the north and south cavalry hats didn't quite come off as planned.

That was during the pregame show. The fellows in the gondola of the southern cavalry hat inflated it too rapidly and too often, and it was last seen heading out toward the Atlantic, or Saturn.

In the meantime, the handlers of the northern balloon let go of the ropes that were holding it, and it flew across the field, bumping the gondola along the ground, two people spilling out, before it bounced off the goalposts, deflated, and fell into an end zone section. It was announced that only two fans had been taken to the hospital, but they weren't seriously injured.

"They'll be bad hurt after they talk to their lawyers," Big Ed said.

After a woman and man in costumes, who were identified as Scarlett O'Hara and Rhett Butler, made show dogs wearing blue and gray sweaters take turns chasing each other, it was time for the national anthem.

"The Star-Spangled Banner" was performed by five bare-chested young men in gray swim trunks with gold bandannas tied around their heads. They constituted a popular southern rock group called Sweaty Little Confederates.

Uniquely, they managed to change the tune of our national anthem into something resembling Hurricane Camille, with intermittent strains of two eighteen-wheelers colliding head on. If anyone in the stadium heard the sound of the Blue Angels doing their fly-by on what you could only guess was rockets' red glare, they didn't bother to look up.

Due to Big Ed's influence with the commissioner—or I should say the commissioner's fondness for Big Ed's private jet—we were assigned the Jaguar's owner's box in the Gator Bowl. It was spacious, comfortable, and well appointed, although Big Barb felt the walls would have been more attractive if they'd been antiqued.

Our cheering or moaning section in the box consisted of the Bookmans, the Pucketts, Shake and Kelly Sue, the Bruners, Iris, and Human Dog. Confronted with a brutal deadline, Jim Tom Pinch needed to be in the press box with his laptop and pharmaceutical aids.

My moaning started the minute I realized the zebras who were going to work the game were referee Ernie ("The Spot") Kennerdine and his loyal crew—Dopey, Sneezy, Bonnie, Clyde, Pretty Boy, and Scarface.

In the first half alone they called us for holding four times—nullifying a sixty-five-yard touchdown burst by Budget—and for pass interference three times, and defensive holding twice, all of which made it possible for Riley Ferguson and Jamal Booker to carry the Lions down the field for the three easy scores that put us behind 21–0.

After the third holding call, Barb yelled down at the field, "Nice call, *thief*—how long have you lived in Detroit?"

And it was after the fourth holding call that she yelled at the zebras, "You miserable motherfuckers!"

"My dear!" said Big Barb.

Shake said, "It's Hollywood, Miz Bookman. I know two or three nuns out there who talk the same way."

"Shake Tiller, you've never been serious in your life," Big Barb said.

Barbara Jane said, "That fucking zebra is obviously two house payments behind."

Her mother said, "He is?"

"Asshole!" Barb yelled again at the field.

On the big TV screen in the Gator Bowl, and on our TV screens in the box, the slow-motion replays suggested that only half of those calls even remotely made sense.

What the flags mainly did, of course, was convince me that Ernie and his loyal crew had bet the Lions—they could relax, get some sun, tell jokes in the last two quarters.

"The important thing is just to be here," Shake said hilariously.

"I'm going down to the dressing room for a minute," I said as the clock ticked away the end of the second quarter.

Shake said, "Tell T.J. to work on their weak-side cornerback. He must have made all-pro with his mouth. I don't think he's gonna hurt too many people with his arm tackle."

"Fay-rits! That's all we look like! A bunch of fuckin' fay-rits!"

ReRun Moses was summing it up in our dressing room at halftime.

Budget Fowler and Pluribus Uram both had Richard Yates, the offensive coordinator, shoved into a corner and were jabbering at him at once. Each one thought he could still win the game for us.

"I want the football," Budget said. "Get me the fuckin' ball!"

"You want to beat these cockroaches," Pluribus said. "Get the fuckin' ball to me, baby!"

"I want the fuckin' football!" Budget reiterated.

ReRun got in on it, and said, "Detroit's a bunch of pew-sees. We can run it up their cue-nits."

I found T.J. in a corner with Bobby Stokes, the defensive coordinator.

T.J. was saying, "Bobby, Detroit ain't worth a shit, and here they've got us down by three touchdowns. We can catch these people. We can *beat* these people! But not unless we shut 'em down in the second half. We can't let 'em piss another drop! Now, you and me gotta find some fuckin' schemes that'll shut their asses down, all right?"

They started scribbling on a blackboard. I interrupted long enough to pass along to T.J. what Shake had said about Detroit's weak-side cornerback.

"Tell Shea," T.J. snapped. "Ain't nothin' gonna do us any good if we can't stop these fuckers."

I delivered the cornerback information to Shea Luckett.

"I'll take his ass to the shed and see what happens," Shea said.

I said, "You're moving the ball on 'em, Shea. All we need's a break or two . . . things can turn around. We're not out of this."

I wished him luck and went back upstairs.

80

While people at home were watching commercials and replays of the first half on TV, those of us lucky enough to be in the stadium were seeing about ten thousand soldiers move into position down on the field. Half of them wore Confederate gray and half wore Union blue. Officers on horses from both armies were waving swords and trotting around while cannons were being shoved into place.

The Florida State and University of Florida bands had finished marching and it was time for the Super Bowl's anxiously awaited halftime extravaganza.

Each year the producers of the Super Bowl halftime extravaganza tried to outdo all previous Super Bowl halftime extravaganzas. I think it was agreed among our group, at least, that this one succeeded.

I missed part of what the PA announcer opened with, but eventually I heard him saying, ". . . and the heroic battle of Gettysburg was the turning point of the war. Some call it a Union victory. Others here in the old south say it was a stalemate. But we all know one thing for sure—the brave sons and fathers and uncles on both sides fought furiously for the causes they believed in.

Here now we see the Union lads assembling their defenses on Cemetery Ridge as the Rebels fall in line for General George Pickett's famous charge. That's the dapper General Pickett down there on his white steed."

Having another cocktail upstairs in our box, Tommy Earl said, "Pickett wasn't even in the fuckin' charge. He'd gone to a snack bar."

"Decisions like that often help a person live longer," I said.

Tommy Earl said, "The Civil War wasn't about slavery—that's all a pile of shit. Lincoln had a bunch of slaves. The Civil War was about machinery. Thirty years later there couldn't have been a Civil War. Everybody would have had reapers and cotton gins. The north had more plows and wouldn't sell 'em to the south. That's what pissed off Robert E. Lee and them so bad. Our slaves kept telling their plantation owners to calm down. They all said, 'Master Beauregard, you need to have another mint julep and put your feet up. Ain't no need to get your butt shot off. They're fixin' to invent the tractor any day now—you can set my ass free to play basketball.' It was a shame the south didn't have more patience. It put us back a few years. My daddy said it was 1937 before the double-dip ice cream cone came to Texas."

"Is that all true?" Tracy asked.

"Yeah, it's true," said Tommy Earl. "You just didn't read about it in your history books at school. That's because all the fuckin' history books are written by northerners, just like your newspapers. Am I lyin' to anybody?"

I noticed the long lines of Confederate foot soldiers starting to move slowly out of the end zone and march down the field. They were pointing their muskets at the Union troops, who were dug in on the set-decorated mound that was supposed to be Cemetery Ridge.

The PA announcer was then saying, ". . . and so on

that fateful day of July the third, 1863, the great desperate charge began . . . in all its clangor, drums tapping, the Confederate battle flags fluttering proudly, the Stars and Stripes planted firmly on Cemetery Ridge, a nation's existence trembling in the balance, an individual's honor at stake . . ."

Tracy said with a frown, "*Eighteen sixty-three?* What year did Columbus discover America?"

Nobody answered. We were too caught up in the cannons suddenly terrifying most of the horses, which were turning into bucking broncs and tossing their cavalry officers onto the ground.

But not General Pickett's white steed. The white steed reared up twice, wheeled in retreat, scattered two Confederate brigades, and as General Pickett held on dearly, found an exit ramp and galloped out of sight.

". . . but undaunted by the return fire, the gallant Rebs sprucely marched ahead into the very valley of the Shadow of Death," the PA announcer said.

Which was when the gallant Rebs took it upon themselves to break into a run toward Cemetery Ridge. Those Confederate officers who'd stayed on their steeds went with them and rode up onto the set decoration and began slashing at the Union troops with their swords, wounding several and enticing others to slam their caps to the ground and cuss at the Rebs.

By that time, TV was covering the action.

Some hand-to-hand combat began as more and more Confederate infantry poured over Cemetery Ridge. It soon became evident that most of the Union troops hadn't signed on for actual fighting—they located their own exit ramp and went sprinting through it.

As the largest Confederate battle flag was raised over Cemetery Ridge, and the last Union soldier was limping out of the stadium, the PA announcer was saying, "Well, sir . . . heh, heh . . . it looks as if our Confederate boys were determined to win this one . . . heh, heh . . . right the wrongs of history, so to speak. What about a big round of applause for all of our fine volunteer reenacters and all of the many . . ."

81

Maybe it was true that we'd lulled the Lions to sleep in the first half, as Jim Tom mentioned in his story, but you had to give some credit to Ernie ("The Spot") Kennerdine and the other zebras. They made contributions that you couldn't very well call insignificant.

Whatever the case, we got semi-back in the game on our first offensive series of the second half. Shea called an audible from our own twenty-two-yard line—a simple play we knew as Send Budge. Our tight end went in motion to the right and our right tackle and right guard blocked straight away, and Budget followed all three of them while Pluribus Uram took their sissy cornerback on a deep post.

Their linebackers must have been discussing what their Super Bowl rings should look like because nobody touched Budget on the seventy-eight-yard run. He walked the last fifteen yards, nodding in the affirmative, then flipped the ball to Plury to spike for him. After that, they did side-straddle hops and push-ups.

Swasty kicked the point and that made it 21–7, Detroit.

The Lions roared back with a drive that seemed to

have six points stamped on it. In rapid succession they moved from their twenty to our forty, most of our defenders looking like they'd flopped down, spread their legs, and said, "Oh, yeah, baby—bring it."

But then something wonderful happened. Something that gave me the distinct impression that Ernie the Spot had made a second half bet.

Riley Ferguson hurled a long third-down pass and the Lions' receiver clearly caught the ball on our five-yard line. He'd beaten Fryer Pye by three steps. Fryer stripped the ball away from him after they were a full yard out of bounds. That shouldn't have mattered, but the zebra ruled the pass incomplete.

I didn't know what the zebra could have been looking at, but right then I didn't give a shit. I'd take the call.

"I've always said the officials do a great job," I said to everybody in our box.

When the replay flickered on the big TV screen in the stadium, the boos from the Detroit fans might have been heard in St. Augustine.

Nothing much happened after that until late in the third quarter when Shea got a drive going for us, although not without the help of the zebras.

Ernie the Spot gave us the three consecutive first-down measurements that belonged in the Museum of Modern Art. Taking advantage of our good fortune, Shea Luckett decided it was time to try his favorite pass play.

He sent Todd Mitchell on a left-side drag route underneath. He dispatched LaDaminion Walls, our tight end, on a curl-in over the middle to occupy the linebackers. Over on the far right, Pluribus started out on a deep post, but cut sharply across the middle. Our name for it was Play-Pass-Post.

After faking handoffs to Budget and ReRun Moses,

Shea hit the wide-open Pluribus with a thirty-five-yard bullet, and Pluribus sped into the end zone.

"Yes!" Barb shouted like a groupie.

Swasty's foot was true again, and we were only behind 21–14, and the anger of Detroit's fans at Ernie the Spot was growing louder.

"I wonder how long old Ernie's gonna stay with us?" Shake said.

"There's no way to tell." I shrugged. "Right now, I'm trying to decide whether I'd rather lose big or lose close."

The fourth quarter arrived while Detroit coach Art ("Double Dutch") Dowdy was screaming at Ernie the Spot near the sideline, right in his face, almost giving him clavicle shots. The referee took it calmly.

It could have been the two consecutive offsides penalties in the middle of the last quarter that did it. They rubbed out big gainers for the Lions. Or it could have been the holding call that rubbed out a Detroit touchdown pass. Or it could have been all that, plus the earlier calls that went against the Lions, everything combined.

Barbara Jane saw the rowdies first. "What are they doing?" she said, nudging me, pointing.

There were about twenty Detroit fans, some not wearing shirts, their chests and faces painted blue and white. They came down out of the stands and ran onto the field and attacked Ernie the Spot as he was flipping on his mike and starting to explain another infraction against the Lions.

The network director didn't show it, naturally— staunch news journalist that he was—but Big Ed had his field glasses on the scene and gave us a play-by-play.

"They've got him down," Big Ed said. "They're hitting him. One of 'em's got him by the throat! One of 'em's got something—could be a knife! Damn, that was a hell of a punch right there. They're spitting on him

and clawing at his arms! Where are the goddamn police?"

"They're coming," I said, noticing they were coming.
Then some of the players and coaches on both teams
were running out on the field. I wasn't entirely sure
whether the Detroit players were going to try to help
rescue Ernie the Spot or help kill him.

"Christ, it *is* a knife!" Big Ed shouted.

Keep in mind that I had mixed emotions. For the first
time in my life, a zebra had been doing me some favors.
On the other hand, who could argue that one less
crooked or incompetent zebra in the world wouldn't
make it a better place?

Shake said, "This is great, man. I've been waiting my
whole fucking life to see this."

"You're actually grinning at this," Kelly Sue said to
him accusingly.

"Yeah," he said, grinning even more.

Ernie the Spot's attackers were finally subdued and
seven of them were apprehended, the others escaping
through exit ramps. Ernie the Spot was plopped on a
stretcher and wheeled to a tunnel where an ambulance
appeared. There was a smattering of applause for him,
but I doubted if he heard it. In the stunned silence of the
stadium, you could hear the siren of the ambulance
belching in the distance.

It was the next day before anybody learned how seriously Ernie the Spot had been hurt. He survived the
attack, but he'd encountered multiple stab wounds to his
chest and abdomen, a broken neck, two broken arms, the
loss of his upper dentures, and was said to be in a severe
mental state.

There were always relief zebras on hand in case one
of the working crew sustained a freak injury, like turning
his ankle, or throwing his shoulder out while reaching
for a flag too quickly, or being accidentally trampled by

players, or suffering a concussion by bumping into the tits of a cheerleader.

Russell ("Rat") McCullough donned the white cap and came on the field to work the last eight minutes of the game. He was another referee familiar to all NFL players and coaches—actually the man who was given credit for inventing the "encroachment" and "taunting" penalties that hadn't improved the game as much as they'd been responsible for increasing the number of commercials on the telecasts.

Rat McCullough and the other zebras worked a flag-free game in the last eight minutes, as might have been expected after what had happened to Ernie the Spot. Outsmarting Double Dutch Dowdy, T.J. figured as much and told our offensive linemen to hold like they were grabbing a Funnelette, and told our guys on defense to intimidate physically like the Lions were A-rabs.

We tied the game 21–21 with four minutes to go.

From our own forty-five-yard line, Shea spotted Detroit in man coverage and in T.J.'s words "audiobulled" a rollout play he'd only used once all season—he was basically a dropback passer. The play was called Roll-Action-Fly. Shea faked a handoff to Budget and rolled out to the right while Pluribus, who'd split wide to the left, streaked down the sideline, blazing past the coverage.

Shake saw it first. "Aw, baby. Good-bye."

Then Shake hollered, "Pull the trigger, Shea!"

Pluribus was shockingly open at the Detroit ten-yard line and Shea's perfect spiral hit him right in stride.

"Textbook," Shake said.

Pluribus stopped abruptly at the one-yard line, then playfully tiptoed in for the touchdown. Instead of spiking the ball, he placed it gently on the ground and stood at attention and saluted it—until he was gang-raped by teammates. Swasty's kick hit the crossbar but made it over.

Up in our luxury box, we at last permitted ourselves to get excited. Even Human Dog was yapping.

"I hesitate to mention it," I said to one and all, "but I think we can win this sumbitch now."

Barb said with a grin, "So do I. We've got too much character to lose this game now—right, Daddy?"

Big Ed said, "You can say that again out loud. It's character, by God, that counts. Always did, always will."

Big Barb said, "All things considered, it's quite an attractive stadium, except I would have used a darker green in places."

Tommy Earl said, "All I know is, these fuckers are sellin' houses for me. I'm gonna give 'em all free memberships in the club."

Tracy said, "You will not! Why give 'em anything? I wouldn't give shit to anybody who makes more money than I do."

Iris said, "This is pissing off Jim Tom. It's going to take him longer than he thought to write his story. I'll have to give him a love offering."

The Lions made a couple of first downs after our kickoff but then stalled and were forced to punt. Now there was only one minute left in regulation play, score tied, and we were on our own twenty-four-yard line, third down and six yards to go for a first.

I was hoping we wouldn't try a pass, risk an interception. Just run some more clock, get off a good punt, and have something saved for overtime.

It was timeout on the field and T.J. was talking things over with Shea Luckett. But when I saw ReRun Moses come out and Fryer Pye go in as a fourth receiver, I said, "Oh, shit, we're gonna throw."

Barb said, "Isn't that what you would do when you're trying to win?"

I said, "Not in this situation. If it was a movie, I guess you would, but I hope to God we don't have Jimmy Stewart at quarterback and Jack Oakie for a coach."

The play was the only one in T.J.'s repertoire that had a complicated name—Switch Right Flex-Quick Zap-23 Crack-Read Toss.

As I recalled, it had taken our guys a month to even be able to say it.

Pluribus Uram and Todd Mitchell split wide on both sides of the field. Fryer Pye was in the flanker slot between Pluribus and Laddy, the tight end. Budget was the lone running back.

Shea took the snap and turned to his left as Budget started loping to his right. Shea then flipped a little pitch to Budget, who gathered in the ball and suddenly exploded, heading through the gap between Plury and Fryer.

Pluribus had darted inside to help double-team the defensive end. Fryer had faked a pass route, then screened the outside linebacker, then went after the free safety. Laddy Walls, meanwhile, had taken off downfield to occupy the strong safety.

As complex as all that might have sounded later when Shake and I described it for our ladies in the box, it was just a simple running play.

And it did what T.J. hoped it would. When we lined up with four receivers and only one running back, it made the Lions' defense read *pass*. Their backers played loose and their secondary drifted backward—and that was all Budget needed.

Our B-1 bomber was at full speed when he spurted past the line of scrimmage. He broke a tackle on the outside linebacker that Plury had only gotten a piece of. He broke a tackle on the sissy cornerback we'd left alone. He broke a tackle on the strong safety that Laddy had only irritated. And he literally ran over the free safety that Plury had been unable to reach.

Budget was all alone with his foot on the peddle from Detroit's thirty-five-yard line to the end zone. The nearest people to him were our Funnelettes. I didn't get to see him cross the goal and start doing an old-fashioned twist with three of the Funnelettes—I was too busy, furiously looking back upfield for a flag. Force of habit.

I think I was still looking for a flag when Swasty kicked the point that made it 28–21, West Texas Tornadoes.

We kicked off with a squib and the ball scooted crazily down to their fifteen-yard line, where two Lions couldn't decide which one wanted it. One of them took it just in time to get dough-popped by Hepatitis Diggs. We recovered the fumble on Detroit's five-yard line, but Shea knelt and used up the clock—Coach Lambert wanted to hold the score down.

Down below, amid the hysteria around our bench, my favorite sight was that of Big Load and Real Butter trying to lift each other up.

Upstairs, Barb and I hugged and kissed. Around us, everybody else was hugging and kissing. Kelly Sue was even hugging Tracy. Tommy Earl was even hugging Big Barb.

"What just happened here?" I said to my wife as I held her. "Did we win a Super Bowl or something?"

"I'm so proud of you, B.C.," Barb said. "Of what you've accomplished. You put it all together, sweetie. Don't tell me *you* don't feel proud right now."

Kelly Sue heard that as she stepped in to give me her own hug of congratulations.

"Well, if he doesn't, I do," she said. "I'm pretty sure we couldn't have done it today if I hadn't hung all those Tornado posters in every joint from Lubbock to Amarillo."

I laughed and said, "Hell, I guess I must have accomplished *something*. I'm more exhausted than I was when I played and we won it."

"There could be a film in this," Kelly Sue said seriously, "although I don't know—football doesn't do foreign."

I could only look at her with amusement.

82

That sly little doll, Iris McKinney, had slipped around behind my back—just in case—and ordered five dozen baseball caps and T-shirts to be manufactured and shipped to Jacksonville. They haughtily said:

SUPER BOWL CHAMPIONS
WEST TEXAS TORNADOES
(WE STILL HAVEN'T PLAYED ANYBODY!)

Bumper stickers would come later.

The players and coaches were all wearing the caps and T-shirts by the time Big Ed and I reached the dressing room. Big Ed wore one of the caps when he accepted the Vince Lombardi Trophy from Commissioner Val Emery on television. A totally unknown CBS interviewer held the mike. His dark hair was thick and parted in the middle, giving him wings.

I put on a cap and pulled it down low to protect my eyes from the champagne that kept spewing from all directions.

Big Ed said to America, "This was a victory for our whole organization and for the people of West Texas. I want to congratulate every player and coach for getting the job done. I particularly want to congratulate my son-in-law, Billy Clyde Puckett, our general manager, for putting the organization together. It just goes to show what people with character can do. Character, by God, counts—it always did, it always will. That's something our hypocritical politicians in this country can learn. One of these days if we're not careful, we're gonna look up and see . . . where you going with that microphone, son?"

He was coming to me, as a matter of fact.

I'd been thinking of what I might say. I was feeling those things Barb mentioned—pride, sense of accomplishment—but I didn't intend to say that to America. Talk about myself. Not unless I could add that it was the finest cast and crew I'd ever worked with, and the movie would soon be opening at a neighborhood theater near you.

What I said was: "I want to thank Ed Bookman for his confidence in all of us. Big Ed never meddled. He let us run the show. He wanted to own a team in the National Football League because he loves the game . . . loves his country. Of course, we're a happy bunch right now, but I want to take this opportunity to remind everybody that a dedicated official was injured today in an ugly and unfortunate incident. Ernie Kennerdine was calling 'em as he saw 'em—and I think you have to say the breaks balanced out. Speaking for all of us, Ernie, I just want to say you have our prayers, and words can't describe what we really think of you."

The mike then went to T.J., who looked solemn in victory. Soaking wet with champagne and sweat, but solemn.

He said, "I hear Budget Fowler's the MVP. That's as it should be. But I want to say this was a team win. We got it because we're winners in life. You've got to be a winner in life before you can be a winner on the field. Some are gonna say we were lucky, but luck is what happens when preparation meets opportunity. We proved today that football's not a contact sport—it's a *collision* sport. Dancin' is a contact sport. And I want to say one more thing. We ain't gonna get cocky. Like I'm gonna tell these men here, you never know a ladder's got splinters till you slide down it."

Then a grin as he yelled, "How 'bout them Tornadoes?"

I pumped the hand of every player in the room. To Budget, I said, "You saved your best for last, stud."

"Yeah, well, you see, I do my speakin' on the field of battle, like I said, you know what I'm sayin'?"

Dreamer Tatum found me in the next moment.

"Clyde, my man."

I shook his hand and said, "Let me guess. You want to renegotiate?"

"You readin' my mind, baby."

When things had quieted down somewhat, T.J. and I drank a champagne toast to each other.

He said, "You know, Billy Clyde, there's one bad thing about a coach doin' this, what we done this season."

"What's that?"

"If you don't do it all again, they hang your ass in effergy."

Iris stayed in Florida with Jim Tom for a couple of days to try out some new positions. Tommy Earl and Tracy stayed over for more than a couple of days—he wanted to investigate a swamp between Jacksonville and St. Augustine he thought he could upholster. Alligator Pointe.

The Pucketts, Bookmans, Shake and Kelly Sue, and Human Dog boarded the G-5 on Monday and headed for West Texas, where we'd all ride in the victory parades in Lubbock, Amarillo, and Gully Creek.

We were on board the plane, somewhere over America, when I noticed Big Ed and Big Barb had dozed off, her head on his shoulder.

Shake and Kelly Sue were sipping drinks as they each read a script and made hasty notes in the margins. I might have chuckled quietly.

Next to me, Human Dog was curled up in Barbara Jane's lap. I rubbed him softly behind the ears and wondered if he was dreaming about barbecue ribs or eggs Benedict.

I leaned back and sighed and said to Barb that my game plan after the parades was to take some time off and hang around the house on Chateau Briggan a good while—see what it was like to be married again.

"I'd like that a lot," my wife said, snuggling closer. "What do you think our Super Bowl rings ought to look like? Smaller than an Oscar, I guess—but hubcaps and flashlights all the way?"

"No," I smiled. "I was thinking more like a birthday cake on steroids."